The HAPPINESS PROJECT

BOOKS BY PIPPA JAMES

I Will Survive

PIPPA JAMES

The HAPPINESS PROJECT

bookouture

Published by Bookouture in 2019

An imprint of StoryFire Ltd.

Carmelite House
50 Victoria Embankment
London EC4Y 0DZ

www.bookouture.com

ISBN: 978-1-78681-691-7
eBook ISBN: 978-1-78681-690-0

For Jonathan and Emily, who bring smiles, silliness and laughter into my life, and for my husband, who survives living with three book-lovers.

NEW YEAR'S EVE

CHAPTER ONE

Having crunched her way up the snow-covered driveway, Frankie Wood knocked on the front door with more confidence than she felt, while Kate Lambert shivered next to her.

'Hey, Alison, it's us, let us in,' Frankie shouted through the letterbox, when there was no immediate answer. 'We've brought wine and I'm not leaving until the bottle's empty. Don't make me down it on your doorstep.'

'Are you sure she won't mind us just turning up like this?' Kate asked hesitantly, tucking her fringe up into her hat.

Frankie wasn't at all sure. She had been completely certain when they'd cooked up this plan at Kate's house, but that confidence – brought on by those first two glasses of wine – was now ebbing away. She flicked her hair, trying not to let her uncertainty show.

It had seemed like a great idea: Frankie's son Liam was staying over with his nana and Kate's husband Matthew was home to babysit her kids, so the pair of them were free to go and look after Alison in person. Because, after all, New Year's Eve was far too significant a date for someone to spend alone, especially when that someone had only lost her mother-in-law three days ago and even more especially when that she was closer to her mother-in-law than her own mother. And while Frankie stood firm on that, she was still a little too scared of Alison to turn up alone, or, in fact, completely sober.

Not that Frankie was going to back out now. 'It'll be *fine*,' she said.

'Maybe we should have sent a text to let her know we were coming?' Kate muttered into the scarf she had pulled up over her face to keep out the cold wind.

'We know she's in… we've brought wine and, well, she wouldn't have *mentioned* being on her own on New Year's Eve if she didn't want company, would she?' Frankie said, as she stamped the snow from her heels. Although, she thought, she was definitely no expert in what Alison was thinking.

A light in the hallway came on and a petite figure was silhouetted walking towards the front door. There was the clink of a chain being put across before the door opened a crack, to show part of Alison's frowning face.

'Hi, can we come in?' Frankie held her breath and tried to remember why she'd thought this was such a good idea. A couple of months ago she would have run a mile rather than spend time with Scary Alison, but then… a lot had happened in the last few months and now she couldn't really imagine life without the terrifyingly organised school mum.

Something about Alison's actions tonight seemed strange to Frankie: why had she left it so late to cancel their dinner plans once she had known Simon wouldn't be around to babysit?

Finally, without opening the door further, Alison said, 'I'm not really dressed for company, I didn't expect…'

'It's just me and Kate,' said Frankie, 'We don't count as company – as long as you're not naked, we don't care. And if you *are* naked, we'll just close our eyes.'

'Please, Alison. I don't think Frankie's going to give up, and I don't want to have to stand out here all night. It's freezing.' Kate's voice pleaded behind her.

Alison nodded, closing the door a little to remove the chain before opening it fully to let them in.

Frankie looked at Alison's 'not dressed for company' outfit as she passed her. Skinny jeans and an oversized roll-neck poncho jumper which swamped her, making her look all the more tiny and frail. Frankie shook her head in disapproval. 'I was hoping to catch you in a leopard-print onesie,' she said and was rewarded by a look of outrage on Alison's face and the sound of Kate giggling.

'Is it very cold out there?' Alison asked, taking their layers to hang up in the cupboard.

'It's brass monkeys,' Frankie said. 'But at least it keeps the wine cool. Where do you keep your glasses?' She brandished the bottle in front of her as she pushed open the door to the kitchen.

'Oh, let me.' Alison darted ahead of her. 'You'll have to excuse the mess – I really wasn't expecting anyone.'

The kitchen was, of course, immaculate except for a sink of washing-up water, a plate, glass and cutlery on the draining board. Frankie rolled her eyes in Kate's direction, who shook her head while she tried to stifle a laugh.

'Well, I must say, Mrs Lund, I judge you harshly on your house-keeping skills,' Frankie said, kicking off her heels and readjusting the woollen dress that had ridden up indecently on the walk over. 'And just as soon as I've finished this bottle of wine – and possibly one other – I'll be storming out of here in disgust. Ah, thank you.' She accepted the glasses and poured the wine into two of them while Kate produced a bottle of elderflower fizz. 'Is that your fake wine for preggos?' she asked.

Kate nodded as she poured her special bubbles into a wine glass, and wrapped her enormous cardigan tightly around herself. Frankie wasn't sure there were many things more depressing than pretending to drink in order to forget you were three months into an entirely unplanned pregnancy. Although, Kate *seemed* to have recovered from the initial shock and gave the impression that she was now happy to be having a third child. But then, Frankie thought, it was probably possible to hide quite a lot under that cardigan.

Once they were all sitting comfortably, shoes kicked off, Alison curled up in the armchair and Frankie stretched out on the sofa, while Kate settled herself on the huge footstool, Frankie raised her glass. 'Right, can I be the first to say good riddance to this year and I bloody hope the next one's better!'

The other two nodded and held up their glasses in agreement.

Despite being 'entirely unprepared for visitors', Alison managed to produce breadsticks complete with a herb dip, some cheese twirls – which definitely looked homemade – and, once those had disappeared, a box of chocolates with a dark red lid.

'These look very fancy,' said Frankie, leaning forward from her corner on the sofa and choosing one at random. She turned towards Kate and whispered, 'I think she might have forgiven us for turning up without warning.'

Kate smiled, taking the box and holding it up to read the descriptions of the chocolates on the bottom. 'These *are* posh.' She passed the box back to Alison, who put it down without taking one.

'I take it back,' said Frankie. 'She's not forgiven us – they're poisoned.'

A smile broke across Alison's face for the first time all evening. 'No, no.' She shook her head. 'These were a Christmas present, but…' She stopped talking and her eyes began to well up. 'Maggie bought them for me just before, well…'

She paused and Frankie could see the strain on her face as she spoke about her late mother-in-law. Frankie had only met Maggie a couple of times, but been greeted both times like a long-lost friend, and she had immediately fallen in love with her slightly anarchic tendencies and her infectious smile.

'And,' Alison continued, 'she gave them to me the first time I visited her for Christmas, back when I was trying to make a good impression. I said I really liked them, even though I didn't, and she went on buying them for me every year.'

'You never told her?' Frankie said, confused. She would never have pegged Alison as someone who couldn't tell her mother-in-law she didn't like some chocolates.

Alison shook her head.

Frankie watched as Alison began to crumble into tears. She let Kate rush over to give her a hug, still a little too wary of Scary Alison to get that close. *No*, she thought, *not so scary these days*. Picking up the tissues from the bookshelf next to her, she moved across to try and provide some sort of comfort, moving Maggie's chocolates in Kate's direction from the coffee table as she went.

'Sorry,' Alison was saying, wiping her eyes and sniffing.

'No, don't be, it's okay,' Kate said.

'It's fine. Totally normal to cry over chocolate.' Frankie put the tissues on Alison's lap before retreating to a safe distance. Frankie was rewarded by the smallest laugh from Alison, as the corners of her mouth tweaked up.

Obviously, Maggie's death – even though they knew it was coming – had been awful. Two days after Christmas, while the rest of the world was trying to work out what to do with all the leftover turkey, Frankie had received a text from Alison to say Maggie had passed away. Frankie had phoned Kate immediately to try and work out what to do, but they had reached the conclusion that the only thing they could offer Alison was a shoulder to cry on while Simon was snowed in, down in Eastbourne, having gone to visit an elderly uncle, to break the news of Maggie's death in person.

Alison blew her nose and sat upright in the chair. 'Anyway, Kate, how was your Christmas?'

Kate had just picked a chocolate, and stopped with it half-raised to her mouth before she garbled, 'Oh, er, fine. Y'know, presents and a big meal.'

'Well, at least one of us managed to have a good Christmas,' Frankie said as Kate tailed off. 'Although next year I think it should be my turn.'

'Oh no, why was yours so bad?' Alison asked.

Frankie sighed and flicked her ponytail. 'It was just the whole being around Mum with her "Isn't it lovely to have Liam home?"

hints and then being around Laura and her Mr Perfect Boyfriend all Christmas.' Frankie was used to being upstaged by her sister, but now she and her son Liam had finally moved out of her mother's house, his return (albeit just for Christmas) was all her mum could talk about. 'And I don't have a job any more and might lose my house.' She took a large swig of wine, draining her glass. 'I just hate that they're going to be right about the whole *Frankie can't cope as a functioning adult* thing. It's the worst when my mother's right.'

Alison leant forwards to refill Frankie's glass, emptying the bottle. 'Wait, let me get another,' she muttered as she headed back to the kitchen.

'Here,' she said, a few seconds later when she reappeared with a new bottle of white and set about opening it with a corkscrew. 'So, what happened to that delivery job you had, Frankie? You've only been doing it a few weeks.'

'I quit – I know, I know.' She put her hands up defensively. 'I shouldn't have left a job that was paying me actual money that I could use to pay the rent, but I just couldn't take it any more.' She noticed Kate's head lean over on one side in an understanding gesture. Frankie closed her eyes to avoid the sympathy. 'You remember how icy it was on Christmas Eve? Well, my parcels didn't arrive until gone eleven and then I was rushing so much to get the damn things delivered that I managed to slightly crash Mum's car in the process.'

'What happened?' Alison asked, with a disappointed look that reminded Frankie of her mum's reaction.

'Are you alright?' Kate looked worried.

'No, nothing, I'm fine, it's just that I scratched the side of Mum's car. I'd done six sodding hours of deliveries and most of that money would end up paying to get the scratch – I say scratch, I mean dent – fixed. By the time I got back home, Liam was already in bed and I'd missed him putting out his stocking and drinks for Santa and everything. Then Mum kept pointing out how much nicer it would have been if we hadn't moved out, so we ended up arguing… And it's a shitty job and I couldn't keep it anyway, not really, not once Mum starts using her car again and the hours are too unpredictable… So, anyway, I quit and now I don't have a job.' She fell silent and waited for their judgement.

Alison raised her newly filled glass. 'Then let me be the first to say good riddance to bad jobs and let's hope next year brings a happier one.'

'I'll drink to that.' Frankie raised her glass.

'That could be your New Year's resolution,' Kate said, helpfully.

Frankie sighed. 'Yeah, right, like anyone ever really does those.'

'I do,' Alison said. 'Every year.'

Frankie rolled her eyes. Of course *Alison* would.

'I think that's a really good idea of yours, Kate,' Alison carried on, getting up from her seat to open the drawer of the console table. 'Here,' she said, turning back with a notebook and pen. 'Let's write down our New Year's resolutions now, and then maybe later we can start off the "To Do" lists. We're so much more likely to achieve them if we say them out loud – like a little pact. So, Frankie, what's yours?'

'Oh, I don't do resolutions.'

'Get a new job?' Kate suggested.

'Yes,' said Alison, nodding at Kate as though Frankie hadn't spoken. 'Although, maybe something more long-term, with career progression too.'

They both looked at Frankie.

'Fine,' she said, realising she was not going to be able to get out of this. She wasn't sure building her career was top of her life improvement list right now, although it was a depressingly long list. Obviously, she needed to stay solvent and remain in her own house. Right behind that would be working out how to do this whole 'parenting' thing, looking after Liam herself and not relying on her own mum. Then there was Ben. She needed to try and not stuff up her new relationship. There was also the small matter of Liam's birth father, Jeremy. She couldn't ignore his requests to meet his son for too much longer. This was why Frankie didn't make lists – once you started, they became long and overwhelming and made you want to hide until they went away (which they never did).

'Now,' continued Alison, 'with your experience in hospitality, I'd have thought you'd be looking at those jobs at the hotel.'

'What jobs?' Frankie asked.

Alison leaned forward to refill the wine glasses. 'You know, Heppleton Hall? I was reading last week that it's going to reopen under new ownership. I'm sure they'll be recruiting.'

'I don't have any experience in hospitality,' Frankie pointed out, gesturing with her wine glass, the liquid swirling dangerously close to the rim. 'I have experience working in a pub and qualifications for bugger all.'

'Oh, I'm sure that's not true…' Kate said, reaching an arm towards her.

'Don't be ridiculous.' Alison shook her head. 'Dealing with customers – pub regulars and new clientele – is valuable experience. Not to mention being able to handle difficult customers. You'll have picked up some understanding of how a business runs, you know about orders and money. It all counts.' Alison smiled. 'Email me your CV and I'll take a look at it for you. You should definitely apply to the hotel.'

'Thanks,' Frankie said, finding herself surprised again at Alison's kindness, as well as her optimism that Frankie would have a CV at all, let alone one worth looking at. Keen to move on before it became too much, she pointed at Kate. 'And Kate's New Year's resolution should be to have another baby.'

'That's not so much a *resolution* as an *already decided*,' Alison laughed, handing round the chocolates again.

'I've never gone in for New Year's resolutions either,' Kate said, in a slightly apologetic tone. 'Would I be allowed a new pregnancy resolution instead?'

'Like what?' Frankie asked, wondering what the difference was.

'Well, I suppose I've been thinking about what I might like to try and do differently this time around.' She put down her glass and began rubbing an invisible piece of dirt from her finger. 'I mean, with Amelia, everything was so new, and I was so nervous of making a mistake, I just kept trying to second-guess everything, then with Reuben, coming along so soon after, I was just trying to keep going. I think with this one,' she paused to look down at her slight pregnancy bump, 'I want to be a bit less worried about everything.'

'Chill out,' said Frankie. 'Have a Zen pregnancy.'

'Yes. I want to enjoy it all a bit more. Y'know, like my friend Natalie says, you need to glory in the wonder of it all.'

'Sorry, who is Natalie?' asked Alison.

'Oh – I remember who she is,' Frankie said, smiling as she recalled the whole ridiculous situation. 'This is your husband Matthew's best friend's ex-girlfriend. You used to be friends, until she ran off with another man and fell pregnant and now none of you speak to her. Is that the one?'

'Well, yes, but… actually, I've spoken to her a few times over Christmas. With us both being pregnant… And we *were* friends. She's very positive about pregnancy.'

'Oh God, Kate's going to turn into an earth mother!' Frankie exclaimed, inhaling dramatically. 'She'll be all slings and organic crap and "*no, don't give the baby a kebab!*" '

'You didn't!' Alison stared at her, shocked.

'Is that what you think of me?' Frankie stared right back. Just because she was ten years younger than Alison and a single parent didn't mean she… well, okay, maybe she wasn't the *most* responsible parent.

'No, of course not, no, I…' Alison began to stutter.

With a straight face, Frankie muttered. 'My mother wouldn't let me feed Liam a doner until he was nearly six months.'

For a second, Alison seemed frozen with wide-eyed disbelief before she realised. 'Oh, you're having me on…' She laughed, throwing her hand towards Frankie, before taking the notebook and pen up again to add Kate's resolution. 'Anyway, Kate – I think that sounds a lovely idea. Just because you've done it before—'

'Twice before,' Frankie corrected. 'She has *two* children, remember.'

'Yes, yes, twice before, doesn't mean it's any less amazing.'

Frankie shook her head. Kate was already a bit too perfect a mother for her liking. Any more dedicated and she wasn't sure they could be friends. 'What about you, Alison? What do you want from next year?'

'Oh, I've already made my list.'

'A list?' Frankie nearly spilt her wine.

'Yes, I like to have three or four targets for each year.' She flicked back through the notebook. 'Here it is. First one is to get Xander into some extra-curricular activities – I was thinking karate? Or football? Just something to channel all that energy of his.'

Frankie bit her lip to stop herself pointing out that Xander wasn't just energetic, he was a crazy devil-child. *See*, she thought, *I am not insulting him to his mum; I have grown as a person.*

'Then, secondly, I want to focus on our eating.'

'Whose?' Frankie asked, suddenly concerned that this might involve her.

'Mine and Xander's, and Simon's obviously, when he's here.' Frankie wondered if that was a bitter dig at Alison's husband's current absence, but Alison went on quickly, 'I was reading an article the other day about diet and behaviour and health and it struck me that Xander has far too much processed meat and we could all do with eating a bit more in the way of vegetables and pulses. I've ordered a new book online all about it, so I'm quite excited to start trying out the recipes – I'll let you know which ones are most popular.'

Frankie was glad to see Kate's face reflecting her own horror at the thought of cooking family meals of pulses and vegetables.

'And then the last one, I suppose, is all about me. I want to start doing a bit more exercise, you know, set a good example for Xander and get back to match fitness.'

'Did you used to play a lot of sport, then?' Kate asked.

Alison nodded. 'I was quite a gym bunny when I met Simon. I used to swim or do a fitness class almost every day before I went to work.' She looked down at her hands, twisting her engagement ring round on her finger. 'But, of course, that sort of thing gets dropped when you're trying for a baby. And then we moved here, where there aren't any gyms nearby, so I'll have to find another way to get fit.' She shook her head, then smoothed down the page in the notepad she'd been writing on and cleared her throat. 'So, anyway, resolutions done. Frankie is going to get a job – a better one, that she actually likes – Kate, you are going to try to be all "Zen" and enjoy this pregnancy, and I am going to get fit. They sound like a good set of plans.' She nodded. 'Ooh, it's like a little mum pact, isn't it?'

Kate held her glass out for a toast.

'Yes,' said Alison. 'We should definitely drink to the New Year and a new us. I mean, these are all things that will really improve our lives, aren't they? Make us happier and healthier. Here's to…' Her voice trailed off as she looked to the other two for input.

'To our New Year's resolutions?' Kate suggested.

'To not messing everything up?' Frankie muttered, then, seeing Alison's frown, said, 'To changing everything.'

'To our little Happiness Project,' Alison said, raising her glass.

'What could possibly go wrong?' Frankie said, clinking her glass against the other two.

JANUARY

CHAPTER TWO

Alison looked at the selection of folders, index cards, pens and magnets laid out on the table in front of her and felt a deep sense of satisfaction. This was the year she was going to be organised with meal planning. Each colour-coded index card had a meal written on it and would live in one of the slots of a plastic wallet in an appropriate section of the folder – organised by season and subdivided into different cuisines – until it was selected for that week's meals, when it would be transferred to the new magnetic whiteboard above the organisation station next to the fridge. She sighed in anticipation. With the right stationery, there was no task that couldn't be accomplished.

She picked out the first index card for this week's meal plan: red lentil lasagne. Containing four different vegetables, but all hidden so Xander wouldn't notice, it was vegetarian, but the online reviews claimed it was so tasty you'd never notice the lack of meat, so that should keep Simon happy. She used the magnets to secure the whole week's plan to the fridge.

Alison stepped back to admire her work.

She couldn't help it, she was feeling smug.

And so I should, she thought. It had taken several days of searching for recipes online and scouring her new recipe books to be able to fill in all the cards (cross-referenced so she could find the original recipes again) with meals that were guaranteed to be easy, healthy and tasty. And once she'd made her meal plan for the week, she would take Xander with her to the greengrocer's, so he could appreciate the colourful fruit and vegetables that would go into these meals.

He might even be interested enough to help her cook later and everybody knew kids who cooked were more adventurous eaters. Alison was already picturing the perfect dinnertime where she would reveal that the meal they had all adored was not only vegetarian, but also low in fat and high in fibre. Simon would be *so* impressed.

And yet, somehow, Simon was *not* impressed.

After dragging Xander round the greengrocer's as he whined about not being allowed to watch TV ('But Daddy *said* I could!'), he flatly refused to help with cooking, which turned out to be a good thing, given that the recipe's timings seemed entirely fictional and the finished product bore very little resemblance to the glossy pictures.

Xander began to pull faces as soon as Alison put his plate down in front of him.

'What is this you're trying to make us eat?' Simon asked, in a bemused tone, as she returned to the kitchen to get her own portion.

Alison took a deep breath and smiled in what she hoped was a winning way. 'This is a *different* sort of lasagne I'm trying.'

Simon nodded as he prodded at his dinner with his fork. 'What was wrong with the old lasagne?' he asked, running a hand over his silver-streaked hair, his dark eyes laughing as he smiled back at her.

'Well, nothing… just, it's not terribly healthy, is it? And we're trying to be a bit healthier this year.'

'Are we?'

'Yes, we are. It's our New Year's resolution.' Although in her head, Alison was already calling it her Happiness Project.

'Is it? I see. So, what makes this… healthy?' Simon persisted, tasting a tiny piece of it.

'Well,' Alison hesitated. She had hoped to win them over with the taste first, before admitting to the ingredients, but it really didn't look at all appetising. Just getting them to try it would be difficult and she wasn't feeling too confident about the taste any more. 'It's actually a vegetarian recipe, so lots of vegetables and the mince bit is red lentils, so good to get some pulses in there with all that protein and fibre, and the cheese sauce is actually made with cottage cheese, so lower in fat. But still *super* yummy.' As she finished, she took a large mouthful and began eating it enthusiastically despite her brain pointing out with every chew that this was in no way 'super yummy'. If she was honest with herself, it was, in fact, barely edible. The pasta was undercooked and chewy, the cheese sauce had a strange aftertaste, and nobody would ever believe the lumpy orange sauce was meat.

'Yuck!' Xander announced. 'It tastes like poo.'

Simon began to chuckle, and she looked up at him, a little hurt at his lack of support.

'What are you laughing at?'

'You.' He leaned over and kissed her cheek. 'I'm sorry, but this is not a success.' Smiling, he stood up, shaking his head slightly. 'I love that you try, but we can't eat that. Anyone fancy fish and chips?'

'Yay, Daddy! Me!' Xander shrieked, sliding down from his chair and running past his dad into the hallway.

'*Simon*,' Alison said, disliking the whine in her voice.

'Come on, Al, it's just not worked.'

'I think it's fine,' she lied.

Simon shrugged as he pulled his coat on and turned up the collar. 'I'll get enough for you just in case you change your mind.'

Alison sat at the table fuming. *In case you change your mind.* Unlikely. They hadn't even given it a chance. It just needed a few more mouthfuls to get used to the new taste. She took another forkful to prove her point and immediately wished she hadn't.

As Alison entered the Reception playground, she noticed Kate in her usual spot, waving frantically at her and made her way over to her.

'Hello,' Kate said, looking away to where Reuben stood a few feet away, watching some school kids (including his sister) climb over the timber trail. Alison turned to check on Xander, who was running over the little bridge, round the timber trail and back to the bridge to start again. In her world, it was going to be a hideous day, but in Xander's world, it was a day where he got to play at a friend's house after school.

'I've brought a change of clothes for this afternoon, just in case Xander…' Alison didn't want to spell out the numerous possibilities that could result in Xander needing new clothes. He was not a naturally clean child. 'Thank you again for doing this.'

'Of course, no worries. It'll be fine…' Kate took the bag she was handed. 'Are you all, er, ready for today?'

Alison nodded, at least partly to convince herself. Was anybody ever actually ready for a funeral? She hadn't been ready for Maggie's death even though she had seen it coming, because while Maggie's body slowly became frailer, her indomitable spirit never wavered. She made everyone laugh with her anecdotes and outlandish comments right up until the end and had even written long letters of instruction for her funeral, organising the celebrant, flowers, music and readings. There had been very little left for Alison to do to keep herself busy. And because of Maggie's involvement, she knew today's service at the crematorium would be all the more poignant.

'Do you have to do a reading or anything?'

Alison shook her head, then cleared her throat. 'Simon's uncle – the one down in Eastbourne – is reading a poem.'

'Is he Maggie's brother, then?'

'Brother-in-law.'

There was an awkward pause while Alison tried to think of something other than the impending funeral to talk about. 'I take it Frankie's not here yet,' she said, hoping her tone wasn't too critical. She was really starting to like the woman (in spite of her insistence on wearing heels even though she was already tall) but why on earth couldn't she manage to get anywhere on time?

'I've not seen her.'

The classroom door opened and Mr Armstrong appeared to welcome the children in. Alison turned to shout for Xander, but he had disappeared. She turned to search the other way and almost jumped to see that he had appeared right next to her.

'Goodbye, Xander,' she said, adding in a whisper, 'Remember to make good choices.' She doubted he heard it as he raced towards his teacher, but it made her feel better to say it.

'I hope it goes okay today, Alison,' Kate said, reaching across to place a hand on Alison's arm. 'Don't worry about Xander. He'll be fine with us until you're ready to come and get him.'

Alison found herself unable to do anything more than nod and smile gratefully.

When Alison returned home from dropping Xander at school, Simon was in the loft, moving boxes around.

'Simon, are you okay up there?' she shouted from the bottom of the ladder.

The shuffling of boxes stopped and his head appeared at the hatch. 'I need a black coat,' he said. 'Mine's blue.'

She avoided the temptation to tell him that he should have mentioned that earlier. 'Have you looked in the wardrobe in the spare room?'

He frowned. Clearly, he had not.

'I'll go and check.' She returned after a minute and held up his old black coat, under a plastic covering from the dry cleaners.

Alison went to get ready, changing into the outfit she had chosen a few days ago. Maggie, in her last few days, had been quite insistent that everyone had to wear at least a small splash of colour and while it felt absolutely wrong to do so, it would be more wrong to ignore her request. As a compromise, she had selected some jewellery Maggie had helped Simon to pick out as an anniversary present a few years ago. The earrings were flowers, with colourful enamel petals and a tiny diamond sparkling at the centre. She had guessed at Maggie's influence as soon as she opened the box and smiled at the happiness of the design. Putting them in her ears, Alison felt a wave of emotion rising, causing a lump in her throat. Today's aim, she reminded herself, was to get through it and be there for Simon.

When the cars arrived to collect them, she found him in the bathroom, standing at the toilet, staring at the inside of the cistern.

She wanted to ask what he was doing – the toilet hadn't been flushing right for months, DIY was not something he ever did – but it was obvious he was looking for a distraction. It didn't matter what that was. 'Simon?' she said. 'It's time.'

'What? Oh.' He glanced round briefly, not quite catching her eye before looking back at the cistern. 'I can't fix it,' he said, sighing. 'I can't fix it.'

'Come on.'

As he moved past her, she cast an eye over him, checking that his last-minute attempts at plumbing hadn't left marks or damp spots on his shirt. She helped him into his jacket and coat and ushered him out of the door.

Alison had tried to prepare herself as much as possible for the service. She had made herself listen to all the songs, she had read the readings, and she had spoken to the celebrant about what she would be saying. But the size of the line of people waiting outside the crematorium as they arrived caused a mental stumble. Of course she should have expected it; Maggie was friendly and everybody knew and loved her. She saw Simon staring down the line and wondered what was going through his mind.

Once they were sitting in the church and the service had started, Alison kept reminding herself not to listen. She tried to block out the music and the words and the stifled sobs around her. Beside her, Simon sat rigid. She had reached out to hold his hand at first, but he had waved her away. Slowly, she became aware of him slumping down in his seat, his shoulders rounding and his head falling forwards. He raised a hand to his face and Alison passed him the tissue she'd been keeping ready for him. This time when she offered her hand, he took it and pressed it gently.

Perhaps it was the relief that she'd finally been able to offer him some comfort that distracted her, allowing something to break through her barriers. Because, suddenly, she found herself really hearing the song that was playing as the curtain moved round to cover the coffin. She heard Morecambe & Wise singing about sunshine and joy and visions of Maggie laughing in a thousand different situations tumbled through her mind. And her carefully planned objectivity came crumbling down. Her vision blurred as the tears arrived, hampering her efforts to find another tissue in her handbag. A noisy sob was threatening and she put a hand across her mouth to stop it from escaping, realising too late that she had taken her hand from Simon's. Tears ran silently down her face and she felt disorientated in this new world without Maggie. She had played so many roles in their life; mother, grandmother, friend, always bringing warmth and laughter into their home. Without her, everything would change. Finally, she found the tissues and was able to dab her eyes and wipe her nose and regain her composure. She took a deep breath, ready to stand up and face everyone as they left the crematorium.

As they rose, she was aware that Simon's breathing sounded ragged and once they had passed through the exit into the bitterly cold Garden of Remembrance, he turned away from her.

'Sorry, I… just need a minute.' His voice was strained.

Alison fought the urge to follow him and fold him into an embrace. As she watched him out of the corner of her eye, trying to look as though she wasn't, she saw him struggling with his emotions. It must be very difficult, she thought, to go from an emotional even keel to having to cope with bereavement, and to feel the need to do it alone. *He knows I'm here.*

After another minute, he took a deep breath, sighed, shook his head and came back to stand beside her. Together, they turned to face the rest of the mourners.

CHAPTER THREE

Kate watched Alison's petite form walk quickly from the playground and wished there was something she could do. She had been so relieved when Alison had asked her to pick up Xander this afternoon, giving her a useful role, but she felt a little guilty that she wasn't going to Maggie's funeral. They hadn't been close, but, still, she had lived two doors up from Maggie for quite a few years now and it wasn't possible to know her, even a little, without feeling her friendship.

Although Kate doubted she'd have been able to cope with the emotion – yesterday she had cried over a TV advert for a furniture sale. She blamed the hormones. No, it was much better for her to stay away and be useful.

Frankie and Liam came running past her on their way into school as Kate was leaving. She smiled and stopped to wait for Frankie to come back. Reuben tugged at her arm, looking up at her as if she'd forgotten she was supposed to be walking.

'I'm just waiting to say hello to Frankie,' Kate explained. She wasn't sure why she felt it was so important to try and explain every little thing to him, but sometimes it worked, so she carried on.

Reuben frowned and went to take a step forward, accidentally sending a pebble skidding across the playground. He watched it go, then dropped his mum's hand to chase after it and kick it back.

'How am I always so sodding late?' Frankie shouted, coming towards them.

Kate smiled, waiting for her to reach them.

'We're nearly ready, then it takes him twenty minutes just to put his shoes on!'

'Hi,' said Kate, wondering whether Frankie was looking for advice or just sounding off. She decided it was probably the latter. 'What are you up to today?'

'More job hunting.' Frankie pulled a face at the folder she was carrying as they started heading out of the main entrance. 'You?'

'Dropping this one off at pre-school, then I'm meeting up with my friend Natalie for a cuppa.'

'Very nice.'

They walked along the road, Kate holding Reuben's hand again and trying to keep up with Frankie's long strides. She was concentrating so hard on the three of them walking together that she didn't notice Frankie was walking the wrong way – away from her house.

'Where are you headed to, then?' she asked, wondering if maybe Frankie was walking up to her mum's house to borrow the car.

'I'm going to the Hall. Interview at half nine.'

'Oh, fantastic! Good luck. What's it for?'

'Not sure,' Frankie grinned, shaking her head. 'Alison has worked wonders on my CV and when I was at hers the other day, she made me phone them and they asked me to come in for a chat today.'

She gave Kate a sideways glance, revealing her nervousness and Kate felt a rush of maternal feeling for her young friend.

'You'll do really well,' Kate said. 'I know you will. Just remember to smile… and breathe – that's quite important too.'

'Smile and breathe. Got it.'

'This is us.' Kate stopped at the gates to the church hall, wishing she had something profound to say. Words failed her, so she pulled Frankie in for a hug. 'Good luck.'

'Thanks. I'll let you know how it goes.'

Reuben was already through the gates and stood at the doorway, holding the door knob as if trying to open the heavy wooden door to the hall. Kate opened it for him, reminding herself again that his eagerness to go to pre-school and the fact that he didn't seem interested in saying goodbye were Good Things. As she turned and walked back home (a little quicker without Reuben at her side), she began to think about meeting up with Natalie.

As Natalie did not yet have kids, she was still under the impression that ten o'clock was quite early to meet up. When they'd been sending texts back and forth over Christmas to arrange getting together, Natalie had first suggested going out for lunch with Reuben as well. But Kate's idea of a good catch-up did not involve being interrupted every second sentence or having to bring along a bag of activities to keep a pre-schooler entertained. And she really wanted this to be a proper catch-up. So much had happened in the last few months and she hadn't seen Natalie since she and Nick broke up. Kate had only ever heard Nick's side of what happened with Natalie – mostly via Matthew – and now, here she was, living somewhere new, having a baby with a man Kate had never met.

The drive to Cheadbridge was down hedge-lined country lanes Kate had not driven before, and she concentrated on following the route she had worked out. She had never been to the village before, but its slightly ramshackle appearance struck her as perfect for Natalie, who loved all things homemade or repurposed. There was a pub at either end of the main road, with the café, a hairdresser's, post office and a florist spread out between them, each with houses either side. There was a parking space on the road right outside the café Natalie had suggested and as Kate got out of the car, she could already see her sat at a table in the window, waving.

Kate noticed the familiar way her thick dark hair fell over her shoulders onto an artfully thrown scarf. She was wearing the sort of long dangly earrings that babies loved to pull at. There was no sign of pregnancy until Natalie stood up to greet Kate and her dress revealed her neat little bump beneath.

'Oh my goodness, look how big you are!' Natalie exclaimed, throwing her arms around Kate, who was grateful that she was able to hide her face. 'I thought you were only about fifteen weeks.'

'Umm… you get bigger a lot quicker after the first one,' Kate said, taking off her layers before sitting down opposite Natalie. 'Do you remember with Amelia I didn't really get a bump until I was about twenty weeks?'

'Oh, that's like me!' Natalie said, placing both hands on her stomach. 'I couldn't wait for my bump to grow so I didn't just look like I'd been eating too much.'

Kate smiled and tried not to feel envious of how much Natalie seemed to be glowing with this pregnancy. 'Let me just get a drink.'

When she returned to the table, Natalie was holding her scan photo. Kate recognised it from the announcement on Facebook. She smiled. 'Oh, lovely! How many weeks are you now, then?'

Natalie stroked her stomach and said, 'I'll be twenty-three weeks on Tuesday. You?'

Kate felt her eyes widen and she knew her face was giving her away. 'Oh… I'm…' She didn't know how many weeks pregnant she was. *How could she not know?* 'I – I know – had my twelve-week scan last week, so I must be about thirteen weeks now.' Relieved that she wasn't completely clueless, Kate reached for her scan picture to pass it across.

A waitress arrived with the tray of tea and began to set it out on the table, clearing away Natalie's pot as she did so.

'Oh, d'you mind if I keep my cup? Thank you.' Natalie pulled it towards her and smiled at Kate. 'Can I steal some of yours?'

Kate nodded and began to pour. It was a huge pot of tea just for one person.

'I was so worried about cutting out caffeine, when I first heard I was pregnant,' Natalie said, stirring in milk. 'But I think I've managed to get used to the taste of decaff now, I can hardly tell the difference. I mean this…' she paused for a sip. 'This just doesn't taste any different from normal tea to me, now.'

Kate bit her lip and felt the guilt surge over her. 'Oh, it's not…' she stopped, looking at Natalie's raised eyebrows. How could she tell her the tea had caffeine in it? 'It's not… so bad once you get used to it.' She finished feebly. Somewhere, she could already hear how Frankie would laugh when she heard this.

It hadn't occurred to Kate to order decaffeinated tea. Now Natalie mentioned it, of course she shouldn't be drinking caffeine, and there were probably a hundred other things she should or shouldn't be doing while she was pregnant, but her whole Zen philosophy of 'being laid-back this time' meant she hadn't even glanced at the book of pregnancy advice she'd bought first time round. *I'm such a bad mum*, she thought, drinking the caffeine and making a mental note to buy some vitamins.

'So, how's work?' Kate asked, trying to move the conversation on, quickly. 'Are you still okay to teach like that… I mean, while you're pregnant?' When Kate had been friends with her, Natalie had been a yoga teacher, but (assuming her new life hadn't involved a career change as well) she couldn't imagine a pregnant yoga teacher.

Natalie was nodding. 'Yes, mostly – I've had to hand over some of my classes, but my smaller groups and one-to-ones don't mind and I've picked up a few more antenatal yoga classes to make up for it. You should come along to one – I'm sure I can find one to fit with Reuben's pre-school times. Yes! Do you remember the sessions we did before Amelia was born?'

Kate did remember those sessions. In Nick and Nat's front room, yoga mats on the laminate, a funny scented candle on the window sill and strange background music – harps mixed with the sound of waves, was it? – playing on the speakers. 'That sounds lovely,' she said, vaguely.

'We definitely should do some together. It would be so good for you.' Natalie paused, sipping her tea and staring dreamily at the sky out of the window. 'I'm finding it really powerful for my practice. I feel really... centred, y'know? It's so powerful, isn't it? My uterus is just amazing.'

Kate spluttered tea everywhere. 'Sorry,' she said between coughs. 'Just went down the wrong way.' Natalie had gone from slightly hippy to full-on earth mother, she thought, wiping her mouth with a napkin.

'Anyway, tell me all about your fiancé,' Kate said, searching for a new topic.

Natalie grinned and flicked her hair with one hand. 'River,' she sighed. 'Oh, you'd love him. He's very different to Nick.'

Natalie paused to take a sip of her tea and Kate tried to work out what she meant by that. The fact that he was called River told her that Nat's new boyfriend – sorry, fiancé – was nothing like her ex-boyfriend. 'Oh?' she prompted.

'He runs a sort of Fairtrade shop and he collects second-hand books and he does yoga. And he likes walking in the Peaks when he can and he is really tall and gorgeous.' Natalie rested her elbows on the table and leant forwards, looking like a teenager with a crush. 'He likes to be active all the time, so he never just sits around watching telly or drinking. And he's in a band – did I tell you that? Just a little folk band with some mates, but they gig at some of the local festivals. Wait – I have a photo on my phone.'

Kate tried to smile, but it felt false on her face. When had Natalie changed? Perhaps she had always been this way underneath, just constrained by her relationship with Nick? She looked at the picture Natalie produced, showing the pair laughing as they sheltered under an umbrella. He had long brown hair and smiling brown eyes set into a tanned and weathered face. She wondered briefly how old he was, but didn't like to ask.

'*And* he's great in bed too. Which is good because I'm finding myself insatiable at the moment – is that a normal pregnancy thing? It must be hormones.'

Kate nodded as though she was having an equally active sex life and was not in any way trying to recall the last time she and Matthew had made love. Could it actually have been when she conceived? There was no way she was admitting to that.

'We must invite you round sometime soon, I'd really like you to meet River before the wedding. Oh, speaking of the wedding…' Natalie pulled up her tote bag and dug around in it before passing Kate an envelope.

'Thanks,' said Kate. She wasn't sure of the etiquette of wedding invites. Should she open it now? She looked up at Natalie for a clue.

'You don't need to open it now,' she said, waving her hands. 'But I really hope you can make it – it's going to be such a small ceremony. We aren't really into the whole big white wedding thing, we just wanted to make it all a bit official before this one arrives.'

Not into the whole big white wedding thing?

Kate looked across at her friend, the one who had cried about Nick's refusal to get married; the woman who had once made a wedding scrapbook from magazine cuttings.

'Not official in the paperwork sense, of course. Just that River and I feel we need to demonstrate to Mother Nature how committed we are as a parental unit, you know?'

Kate didn't dare say out loud that she thought the two of them would probably have plenty of chances to demonstrate how committed they were as a parental unit once the baby had arrived.

CHAPTER FOUR

Frankie was, of course, late meeting her boyfriend at the Heppleton Arms. When she opened the door to the pub she could see Ben Carter sitting alone, staring intensely into the bottom of his pint. Even though they had been officially seeing each other for a while now, she still felt her stomach flip as he saw her and smiled.

'One day I'll be on time,' she said, finally sitting down in the window seat with her drink. 'And then you'll be completely freaked out.'

He looked across at her with a slight smile playing on his lips and both eyebrows raised incredulously. 'How did it go at the Hall?' he asked, clearly deciding it was safer to change the topic. 'Do they have a job for you?'

She shrugged. 'Kind of, but I don't think they really know exactly what, yet. They seem to be keeping some old staff and hiring some new staff and then just making it up as they go along. Apparently, they've done some work to the place, but at the moment it's really just the spa bit that's been done up – mostly treatment rooms and a little pool – and they have a café-type bit with a bar in it. I don't think they're doing anything with the bedrooms yet, although they've got about a dozen.' She paused, trying to remember what Erin, the manager, had said during the tour. She had been standing behind the reception desk when Frankie arrived at the Hall, and with her red hair pulled smoothly back into ballerina bun, dark-rimmed glasses and a frilly shirt under her dark blue suit, Frankie had assumed she was the receptionist. Even when she had come out from behind the desk she had seemed too slight and quiet and, well, too *young* to be in charge of a hotel. Erin had led the way around the building, pointing out the changes without seeming to have considered that Frankie had never stepped foot in the Hall before.

'Anyway, they mostly need more waitresses and bar staff, so that's where I'll start – I've got a uniform and everything – and, if I look halfway competent, they might put me on Reception or they might even have a supervisor role for me.' Frankie told Ben. 'The shifts will either be proper daytime hours or evening shifts, so Mum's said she could help out with some evenings if I have to do any of those, although I said I was really after the daytime ones.' When Frankie had outlined the hours she was looking for, Erin had nodded, as though it was ideal. Frankie had started to see the answer to her money problems.

'I'd never been before, it's much posher than I was expecting. Have you ever been in?'

Ben looked startled for a moment. 'Um, no. Well, I've picked Jo up from there a few times, she used to go a lot. I… I don't know if she still does.'

Frankie watched him panic and wondered if she should be more jealous of his ex-wife than she was. Why would she care if he was once in a relationship with someone who went for spa days? Given that she had never really *met* Jo – although she had been pointed out on the playground – Frankie found it hard to care much about her at all. Ben was scrupulous about never blaming Jo for anything and he bent over backwards to try and accommodate her for fear of being denied access to his son. Really all Frankie knew was that Jo hated her with all the anger and jealousy to be expected of an ex-wife.

'Well, anyway, the manager has put me down for working tomorrow, so my job search is over and I deserve a drink.'

Ben tipped his drink towards hers for a toast. 'Well done. Can you buy me a new camera with your first million?'

'Not even a little bit,' she said.

As she drank, another thought occurred to her. 'Alison will be very proud of me.'

'Why?'

'Because I've never had a New Year's resolution before and I've done it already.'

Ben looked down at the beer mat he was tapping against the table, trying to hide his smile. 'Do you not have to at least start the job… maybe keep it for a week before you start boasting?'

She frowned. 'What, you think I can't do it? It's not bloody rocket science, is it? Just working a bar and waiting on tables.'

He held his hands up defensively. 'Well, y'know, you're out drinking the night before your first day, which is potentially disastrous.' He smiled and reached a hand out to hers. 'Obviously, you'll be amazing at it, but what if you don't like it?'

Frankie flicked her long hair over her shoulder. 'Just so you know, all I heard there was that I'll be amazing. The rest was just noise.' Although he might, annoyingly, have a point about the drinking. 'On an unrelated note,' she said. 'I'll have to head home after this one.' She gestured to her half-finished wine glass. 'I need to go and prepare for tomorrow. It takes preparation, all that being amazing.'

Ben smiled in a *we both know you're agreeing with me but I won't say it* way, giving Frankie a slightly unfamiliar warm feeling in her chest. A job, a proper, nice boyfriend, her own house. She was totally smashing this year. Who needed a stupid Happiness Project?

'Did you hear back from Jeremy, yet?' Ben said, changing the subject and flushing away Frankie's smugness. She contemplated ignoring the question, but knew that, annoyingly, her proper, nice boyfriend wouldn't let her wriggle out of a conversation about her son's father even if it was awkward.

'Only every sodding day,' she said, sighing. 'I know I have to sort out him meeting Liam, but I haven't told Liam yet and I don't *wanna.*' Finishing with a whine, Frankie screwed up her face at her glass and avoided looking at Ben. It had only been a month or so since Jez had asked to meet his son and honestly, given that he had ignored the fact he *had* a son for so long, Frankie was surprised she was even contemplating letting him back into Liam's life. 'I'm already doing difficult things this week – can't I do it next week?'

Ben said nothing.

'I *know*, I said before Christmas he could meet Liam, but, well, it just all got too busy… I *will* organise it. I will. Just… I mean, he didn't care for the last four and half years, he can't demand instant access, can he?' She risked glancing up at Ben, who was looking surprisingly supportive.

'If it was my son,' he said, 'I'd be texting you every day too. I'd want to make sure I got to meet him as soon as possible.'

Misread that face, thought Frankie. All his support was clearly behind Jez.

'If it was your son, you wouldn't have bloody cut and run in the first place.'

Ben nodded and shrugged. 'Okay, true.'

Frankie doubted that would be the end of it. Between Ben's subtle guilt trips and Jez's daily texts she really had no choice but to introduce Liam to his dad, sooner rather than later.

As Frankie crunched up the gravel path towards Heppleton Hall, she held her hood up in an attempt to stop the rain from being whipped up underneath it.

She really wished she hadn't had to walk to work on her first day. Of course, she had no idea how she would have got there otherwise, but the rain and wind had ruined the sophisticated and together look she had been going for and she doubted that Erin would be impressed by the half-drowned style she was now sporting. She pulled open the heavy door and stopped just inside the main entrance, stooping slightly to check her reflection in the mirror behind the reception desk. Some of her hair had stayed where she had put it this morning, but most of it was now hanging down randomly. She sighed, removing the pins and holding them in her mouth while she pulled her fingers through her hair in an attempt to restore some order.

As she twisted her hair back up and secured it, she realised that someone was standing by the reception desk, watching her. Frankie straightened up. Erin was regarding her with a look of horror.

'Did I forget to show you the staff entrance?' Erin said. She stood perfectly still, not a hair out of place, holding a clipboard in her manicured hands.

'Oh, shit, no – sorry, no,' Frankie added, seeing her new boss's eyebrows shoot up at her language. 'I'm sorry, I forgot. Should I go back out?' *Please say no*, Frankie thought, *don't send me out into that again.*

Erin's face twitched back to neutral and managed a small, tight smile. 'No, don't worry about that now. Just remember for next time.'

'Yes, absolutely.' Frankie slipped behind the reception desk and headed to the staff area she had been shown under the stairs. This part of the Hall was very different to the public areas. It still had the high ceilings, but three of the walls were just stud walls, mostly covered in curling paper messages, dividing a once generously-sized room into several slightly cramped spaces. The only original wall now had dirty-beige coloured paint peeling from it. The space was filled by the sink, kettle and fridge on one side, a table with four chairs (all of the seats with ripped cushions) squashed in the middle and a bank of lockers on the other side. Frankie hung her jacket on the row of pegs behind the door and was wondering what to do with her bag – *why was it so big? What had she possibly needed to bring?* – when Erin appeared in the doorway, her clipboard still firmly in her grasp.

'Oh, good, you found your way alright. You can pick any locker for your bag.' Erin waved her arm in the general direction, while staring down at her clipboard. 'You'll be in Restore & Replenish today.'

'Umm, Restore and…?' *Why did the different parts of Hep Hall have to have such weird names?*

Erin looked up at her with a slight frown. 'Restore & Replenish. Our café bar.'

'Oh, yes, of course.'

'Adrian's already there, so he can show you the ropes. Do you remember where it is?'

'Umm…' Frankie really wanted to say she did, but she hadn't paid enough attention yesterday when Erin had given her the tour to be confident. Having made a less-than-favourable start, she didn't want to immediately get lost.

'Back out to Reception, round the stairs and turn left.'

Frankie nodded, 'Thanks.'

'And here's your name badge.' Erin handed it to her. 'Pin it to your waistcoat.'

Frankie began to attach it, but when she looked back, Erin had gone without making a sound. *It couldn't be good to have a boss who moved so stealthily*, she thought, making a mental note to double-check before she gossiped.

'You must be Frankie.' The man behind the bar wore the same striped waistcoat as her, but his shirt was white, unlike Frankie's blue one. He was older than her – late forties, maybe? – with very short dark hair and an arrogant stance.

'That's what it says,' Frankie said, pointing to her name tag and trying to smile, despite an immediate and irrational feeling of revulsion.

'I'm Adrian,' he said in a slightly bored voice.

'Hi.' She made herself walk towards him, her arm outstretched. *I want to keep this job*, she reminded herself, deciding not to point out to Adrian that her face was a few inches above where he was looking.

'You've worked in a bar before?'

She nodded.

He looked unimpressed and began to point out the basics ('optics here, till, glasses up there, wine in this fridge, soft drinks in that one') with a vague wave of his hand or nod of his head. 'Have you ever waitressed before?' he asked.

'A bit,' she lied.

He didn't look like he believed her, so she pushed her chin forward and her shoulders back, which had the unfortunate side effect of emphasising her chest. Adrian looked her up and down as he stepped out from behind the bar and came towards her.

'Kitchen,' he said, nodding his head to the swinging door beside her. 'Guests can order food anytime, but the waitress only works peak times, so take food orders at the bar, put them in the till and listen out for the bell – don't leave food waiting.'

'Okay.' Didn't this guy ever smile? In fact, did anyone in this whole place ever smile?

Adrian spent the next couple of hours telling her to do things ('clear that table', 'set up a table for eight', 'read the menu') as though he were testing her potential as a waitress. Only a few groups came in, all women wearing towelling robes and ordering pots of tea or bottles of champagne, but nothing in between, and Frankie wondered why Erin had bothered hiring her when Adrian was already there.

Just before midday a girl arrived, also in uniform, short hair falling out of the ponytail she had tried to force it into.

'Hello,' she said excitedly. 'You must be the new one.'

Finally, someone with a smile! 'I'm Frankie.'

'Hi, Frankie, I'm Tina, the other waitress.' She only seemed about twelve, but must be at least eighteen, Frankie thought, which in turn made Frankie feel old at twenty-eight.

'Tina,' Adrian said, coming out of the kitchen and spotting them together. He put an arm around Tina, and Frankie noticed the girl grimace slightly as he squeezed her against him. 'Tina, my girl, meet Frankie.'

'We've met,' Frankie said, disliking Adrian more with every passing minute.

Keeping this job was looking as though it was going to be more difficult than she had expected.

CHAPTER FIVE

Alison stood in the playground and went through her checklist one more time.

House tidied? Check.

Box of Lego in the lounge? Check.

Colouring books and pens out on the table? Check.

Toy cars and ramp on the floor in the corner of the kitchen? Check.

Pasta sauce with hidden vegetables (from previous day's batch-cooking session) in fridge ready to provide easy yet nutritious meal for kids? Check.

Ready for first afternoon with two children to look after? Umm…

No. She would be fine. She was braced and – most importantly – Liam always looked like such a quiet, well-behaved boy. Surely he would be a good influence on Xander? Alison did not like Xander's current preferred playmate, Torsten, who had a strange Mohican haircut, only ever wore shorts, even though it was freezing, and was somehow always around when Xander got into trouble.

Liam was a much better influence and therefore this was a bonus of being a good friend to Frankie and picking him up on a Wednesday afternoon.

'Hello,' Kate said, arriving next to her, half-hidden beneath a puffer coat and woolly hat. With so much padding around her, it was hard to tell she had a baby bump at all. 'Gosh, it's freezing, isn't it?'

Alison nodded, although she wasn't sure it was cold enough for Kate's Arctic attire. She was perfectly warm enough in her smart teal coat with the large checked scarf that Simon liked to joke could double as a picnic blanket. Somewhere, in the cupboard under the stairs in an organised box (although she wasn't sure which one), she had a cream hat with a fluffy bobble with brown and teal flecks in it that would be perfect for the school run when it got a little colder, she thought.

'How is *she* surviving in *those*?' Kate asked.

Alison followed her gaze to see the twins' mum, Emma, stepping from one foot to the other to keep warm while wearing cropped running tights with a hoodie over the top. As the mother of twins, Emma was already thought of as a superwoman by the other playground mums, a status only increased by the fact that she also worked, meaning her parents did most of the school pick-ups, and now she looked even more heroic in running clothes.

'Hi Emma,' she said brightly, taking a step towards her. Emma had not yet been persuaded to help out with the PTA, but Alison knew people found it so much harder to wriggle out of it when she approached them directly. 'Lovely to see you. Are you just off for a run, or have you just finished one?'

Emma smiled, that was a good sign. 'Hi, no, I'm just trying to get prepared. I've got to head out to netball as soon as my husband gets back tonight, and I didn't think I'd have a chance to get changed once the kids got home, so I did it before I came out.'

'How very organised of you,' Alison said, approvingly.

'Hmm... I'm sort of regretting it now, though – I hadn't realised quite how cold it was.'

'It *is* cold, isn't it?' Kate said. 'Where do you play netball?'

'Just in Millhurst – d'you know that little private school on the right as you drive through?'

Alison nodded.

'You should join us – we're always looking for new people.' Emma was still smiling and Alison was warming to her.

'I can't, I'm afraid,' Kate was saying. 'I'm pregnant. But Alison might like to join you – wouldn't that count for your New Year's resolution?'

'Oh, yes, I suppose it would…' Alison looked from Kate back to Emma. 'I'm supposed to be getting fitter. I suppose that's everyone's resolution, isn't it? Not very original.'

Emma was nodding enthusiastically. 'You should definitely come down, then. It's so much fun.'

The classroom door began to open and the sight of Mr Armstrong nodding at her distracted Alison – *what had Xander done now?* 'Absolutely,' she said, without realising.

'Great,' Emma said as she moved away to claim her kids. 'See you at seven fifteen sharp.'

'What?' But Emma had gone.

Beside her, Kate was beaming, Reuben stood silently next to her, while Amelia walked calmly from the classroom in the exact way Alison dreamed Xander would one day leave school.

'I'll see you later,' Kate called as she turned away. 'Have fun at netball.'

'See you later,' Alison replied, keeping her smile. She really wasn't sure she wanted to go to netball *tonight*. Except now Emma was expecting her. And at seven fifteen *sharp*? She'd have to text Simon to make sure he was home in time, because the only thing ruder than not turning up would be turning up late.

It would be fine. She had all afternoon to find something appropriately sporty to wear and to try to remember the rules of netball she had been taught at school. As Xander came running out of the classroom with Liam and Mr Armstrong in his wake (the latter once again carrying the accident book for her to sign), Alison realised that 'all afternoon' would actually be spent running around after two small boys (who would show no interest in the activities she'd put out for them), trying to stop them killing each other or breaking her house. There would be no time left over to prepare herself for netball. She took a deep breath and reapplied her smile.

'Come on, you two,' she said, taking the accident letter from Mr Armstrong and signing the book – there was no need for an explanation: it was the third time that week – before firmly taking one child's hand in each of hers. 'I thought we might go home and play with some Lego.'

Alison had managed to wrangle Xander into bed in record time after Frankie picked up Liam. Hurrying back into her own bedroom, she pulled on the cropped yoga pants she had found at the bottom of a drawer and a T-shirt she thought she had thrown out. When Simon arrived home, he found her searching amongst her shoes for some trainers.

'Hello, Sporty Spice,' he said. Even with her head in the wardrobe, Alison knew he was giving her his amused expression, reserved for times that would later lead to him having an *I told you so* moment.

Alison refused to answer to that name and continued the hunt for her trainers.

'Saw your message, so you're going to play netball tonight?' Simon continued when she emerged from the cupboard. 'Is it a match or a training session?'

'I don't know,' she admitted. 'It was a bit of a last-minute decision, to be honest, but exercise is good.'

He nodded in mock understanding. 'Oh yes, exercise is good.' He had stolen her words and added sarcasm.

'Thank you. Very supportive.' Still holding her trainers, she tried to flounce out of the bedroom, but Simon was closer to the door than she was and in just a couple of strides he had blocked the exit.

'Sorry – sorry,' he said, holding his arms up for a second, before reaching them around her waist. 'I love that you are constantly striving for improvements, Al. And I'm so happy this one doesn't affect my dinner.'

'Hey!' she said, pretending to be more offended than she was. He continued to smile down at her and she melted a little.

'What time do you need to leave?'

She checked her watch. It would probably take her another ten minutes to get out of the house between putting her shoes on and giving Simon instructions for his dinner. Then it was a five-minute drive to Millhurst, plus a bit extra for working out where to go, and a bit more because she wanted to be there a little early… 'Now.'

He held on to her for slightly longer than necessary, and in her head, Alison battled between enjoying the moment of closeness and the slight panic of not wanting to be late to netball.

Emma must have been looking out for her, because she was walking towards the car as soon as Alison had parked.

'You came!' she said, waving.

Alison looked past her at the floodlit court, where there were groups around each of the posts practising their shooting. As they walked over to the court, Alison noticed the other women all looked tall and athletic and were wearing proper Lycra sportswear, scoring one goal after another.

Emma must have seen the look of panic on Alison's face because she hastened to reassure her as she walked her over to the court that 'everyone is really friendly' and 'there's a huge range of ability, so don't worry if you haven't played for a while'. The coach, a tall, skinny woman with a booming voice, thrust a clipboard of forms under her nose as soon as she clocked eyes on Alison and sent everybody off for 'a few laps to get us warm'.

Alison filled in the forms slowly, allowing everyone to finish the first lap before she tried to join in. She watched the women talking as they jogged, trying to see if she recognised anyone. At the front, leading the pack was Becky, Queen of the PTA, with Jo to one side of her and Emma on the other. Becky nodded an acknowledgement to Alison – which felt less like a welcome and more like a challenge – as she passed. Jo turned away, apparently she was just going to ignore her, while Emma beckoned her to run with them. Not wanting to appear rude, (or like she cared that Jo and Becky had rejected her friendship), Alison dropped the clipboard on the pile of coats and joined them.

Keeping up with Becky and Jo's pace nearly killed Alison; her legs ached, her breathing tore at her throat and her heart threatened to explode inside her chest, but there was no way she was going to let them see how hard it was for her to keep up with them. As they returned to the start, she peeled off, motioning that she was getting a drink. She pretended to have to search for the bottle in her bag, while she took deep breaths and waited for the queasiness to subside.

It hadn't occurred to her that they might be here. She definitely wouldn't have come if she'd known. It was hard enough to face them at the school gates every day and she knew she'd have PTA meetings with them soon enough, but at least those times she was braced. She knew they would try to ignore or belittle her, and she would deflect their pettiness by not stooping to their level.

As she gulped down some water, Alison reminded herself that she was not here for *them*. She was here to improve her fitness and the fact that Becky and Jo were around was irrelevant.

'Okay,' the coach motioned for them to gather around her. 'This week we're going to be working on passing – quickly, accurately and repeatedly. Let's have two groups.' She divided the semicircle, grouping Alison with Jo, Becky, Emma and two other women. 'I want a line, with a feeder and two balls. Pass to the feeder, run out from the line to receive the ball, return it to the next in line. Okay? Off we go.'

Alison turned, expecting the faces around her to mirror her confusion, but they seemed to be organising themselves into a line with Becky facing Jo at the head.

'Don't worry,' Emma said, gently pulling her into line. 'It's always a bit confusing at first. Just watch and copy.'

Alison found herself moving up the line, watching as one after another the women darted out of the line, leaping to catch the ball, twisting in the air to land facing the line and pass the ball back.

'You're catching from Jackie,' Emma shouted to her as she threw the ball to Becky and ran to catch it back.

Who was Jackie? Alison looked for someone with a ball, but saw too late that it was hurtling through the air towards her already. She managed to bash it to the ground and make a grab at it before it got away.

'Now to me,' Becky said, patronisingly, holding her hands out for it.

Alison threw the ball as hard as she could and felt a small amount of satisfaction when Becky had to step back for the catch.

'Now you run.'

Alison had already started out to the side, but Becky threw the ball slightly ahead so she had to reach to get to it. It was no use: as she stretched to grab it the force of the ball caught the tips of her fingers and she gasped with the shock of pain on her cold hands as her fingers were pushed back. The ball bounced and rolled away.

'Nice try, Alison,' the coach shouted, scooping the ball up and sending it back to her. 'Becky – little bit less force next time, please.'

Alison squeezed the ball between her hands as she glanced at Becky, who looked unrepentant. Balancing the ball on one palm, she threw it high, hoping to make Becky have to stretch to reach too. Unfortunately, Alison realised too late that what was too high for *her* was only just above head height for Becky, who plucked it from the air easily.

'Oh dear,' Emma said, smiling apologetically as Alison re-joined the queue. 'Are you alright? Sorry about that – it's a bit of a vicious game sometimes.'

'I'm fine,' Alison lied, holding the fingers of her right hand protectively in her left hand, wondering how many more minutes were left of the session. What were the chances that she would survive without breaking anything? Because a couple of broken fingers would really mess up the whole Happiness Project thing.

CHAPTER SIX

Frankie was certain that if someone had asked her before her first shift if she'd like a job where there was hardly any work, she would have thought she'd reached the Promised Land. Now that she actually *had* a job that involved hardly any work, it was shit. Not only was she bored, but every moment she wasn't serving or cleaning up after guests was a moment she was alone with Adrian the Prick.

To begin with, he wasn't *so* bad. He seemed to be half-decent at his job. He was polite when Erin was around and he was good with the guests.

It was just in conversation with Frankie that he was a prick.

Frankie rang Alison's doorbell, having walked all the way back from Heppleton Hall to collect Liam. As Alison pulled the door open, she asked, 'How was your first week?'

Frankie shrugged. 'Mostly okay, my line manager's a bit… he's a…' she struggled to find a word to describe him with Liam in earshot, but had to settle with pulling a face to show what she meant.

'Ah,' Alison said, nodding. 'Still, maybe he'll improve with time. You don't want to get on the wrong side of colleagues this early on – no, Xander, *you're* not going out. Xander! Come back *here*.'

Annoyingly, Frankie knew Alison was right: she did not want to get on the wrong side of Adrian. At the start of her next shift, Frankie was ready with a smile for Adrian as she greeted him.

'What's up?' she said. But it did not have the desired effect.

'If I tell you, will you sit on it?' he replied, raising his eyebrows suggestively.

'Fuck off, prick.'

He laughed.

So much for that plan, Alison.

The rest of the week continued in a similar vein. Adrian had a habit of standing so close that she could feel his breath on her face, and he almost exclusively spoke to her chest. But worst of all, he had an unnerving ability to be able to make an innuendo about anything. After only a few hours with him, Frankie felt the need for a shower as soon as she got home.

During her second week at work, Erin asked if Frankie would mind looking after Reception for an hour and Frankie felt absurdly grateful to have an escape. Not that there was much more work to do on Reception. Mostly, she just had to point new arrivals towards the spa for their treatments. And there weren't many of them. How could the Hall possibly be making money with this few guests in it? Even if she managed not to completely lose control and punch Adrian the Prick, Frankie suspected her job would not last the year.

At least when Tina arrived at work for the non-existent lunch rush, there was respite from the monotony.

'Do you think it'll get busier in the summer?' Frankie asked as the pair of them took their time clearing the last table and wiping it down.

Tina put her head to one side. 'I don't know, I've not worked a summer, yet.'

'It'd be a great place for a summer party, though, wouldn't it?'

'I suppose that's why they've put that marquee up,' Tina said. 'I think they've got some summer weddings booked in.'

'Do they do other parties?' Frankie asked. 'I don't get why it's so quiet all the time when it's so nice inside… I'm just thinking, some of those mums up at the school with more money than they know what to do with, they'd love showing off with a birthday party here.'

Tina stared out of the window wistfully. 'With those little lights in the garden?'

'Sure.' The day had been grey with rain, the sky filled with dark clouds, hardly the best weather for showcasing the outdoor space. Frankie could only imagine how the garden would come to life in the summer, when the trees returned to green. The flowerbeds would be a riot of colour, the hedges thick and vibrant, the lawn path, dotted with lights, would lead down towards the marquee.

Tina sighed. 'With all the doors open so people could wander in and out?'

'It really would be beautiful… if anyone ever did it.'

Frankie felt the phone in her pocket vibrate. Quickly checking Adrian wasn't around, she took it out and looked at the text from Jez.

Just wanted to check tonight is still okay? I'll be at yours for 5.

Still fine, she replied, *Liam's expecting you. Don't be late.*

That second part probably wasn't necessary, Frankie admitted. Jeremy had been sending texts almost daily for the past week, sorting out plans to see Liam for the first time in four years. She wasn't even sure those cursory visits to hold his newborn baby counted as meeting him at all – this was essentially their first real meeting. At least his frequent texts gave her a little more confidence that Jez might manage to stick around a bit longer this time.

Frankie still wasn't convinced this was the right thing to do. In her head, there was an ongoing debate about it. At the moment the argument that Liam *deserved* to know his dad was winning, but her fear that he would get hurt if Jez was a dick was never far away.

She laid her phone on the table to wait for his reply while she re-laid the table.

'Frankie?' Erin's voice startled her and she whipped round, ready with a smile for her boss.

'Can you cover Reception for me now, just for an hour?'

'Of course,' Frankie replied. As she turned to go, she caught sight of Tina's face. The poor girl looked crestfallen. 'You okay?' she whispered.

'Fine,' Tina mumbled.

Frankie's mobile on the corner of the table rang out as it received a message.

'Whose phone is that?' Erin asked.

Shit.

'Oh, I think that lady left it.' Tina grabbed it and thrust it into her pocket, throwing Frankie a smile to show she knew who it really belonged to. 'I'll get it back to her,' she said, wandering out.

Frankie stood at Reception playing solitaire, wishing she had her phone to message Ben, or Kate, or even Alison. Not a single person arrived in the time she was there, and she could see from the bookings screen that only a handful were expected that afternoon.

After only forty minutes, Erin returned and sent her back to Replenish. Frankie was pleased to see the bar was empty. She didn't care where Adrian the Prick was, so long as he wasn't anywhere near her. She pushed open the kitchen door in search of Tina and her phone. Seeing as the lunch service had long since finished, she wasn't surprised there were no kitchen staff about – Tina would probably have gone too, although she hoped the girl hadn't taken her phone home.

She was about to leave when she realised there was somebody in there. Up at the far end, Adrian was standing facing the wall.

It took a second to notice Tina behind him. He stood with his back to Frankie, leaning over Tina, one arm stretched out to the wall, barring her way, while his other hand was stroking her hair. Frankie couldn't see Tina's face, but she could hear her giggling.

Adrian and Tina?

Adrian and Tina?

No. Frankie refused to believe it. And yet… here they were.

Frankie listened again to Tina's laughter and realised that it sounded wrong. It was too high-pitched, almost a little hysterical, the nervous laughter of someone in an uncomfortable situation.

'Tina?' Frankie called out.

Adrian turned, slipping his arm around Tina and giving her a squeeze. 'Frankie, you've caught me and my girl Tina having a quickie in the kitchen!' He laughed.

Frankie said nothing, but somehow her refusal to play along seemed to amuse him.

He released Tina and took a step forward. Now would be the time to punch him, she thought as he walked towards her. Seeing Tina's embarrassed face, she felt her hands tighten into fists.

'Sorry, I'd ask you to join in,' he said, as he paused halfway through the door, so close his breath was hot against her ear as he whispered, 'but you've been round the block a few too many times for me.'

He was gone before she could react.

'You okay, Tina?'

'I'm fine, it's fine, it's nothing – just messing around.' The girl was shrugging and shaking her head, carefully avoiding looking at Frankie. Who she was trying to convince?

'He is such a fucking prick,' Frankie said matter-of-factly.

Tina did a shocked little laugh. 'Don't say that, Erin might hear you.'

'If she doesn't already know, she must be blind or stupid.' Frankie left the doorway and went into the kitchen. 'Do you still have my phone?'

Tina handed it to her. Frankie looked down at a screen full of messages, but put it straight into her pocket, not wanting to get caught twice in one day. As she walked out of the kitchen, she was immediately grateful she had when she saw Erin behind the bar talking to Adrian.

He had his head on one side, looking as though he was listening, and Frankie couldn't help but notice that he was looking at Erin's face rather than her chest. They both turned to look at Frankie and Tina, then straightened up, nervously, exchanging a glance. It suddenly hit Frankie that their conversation was too informal for a discussion between colleagues. There was something intimate between them.

That's why Tina doesn't want Erin to know.

Oh, shit. Only a few shifts in and she was already swearing at her line manager, who happened to be the boss's boyfriend. *This is not going to end well*, Frankie thought.

Frankie kept replaying the scene between Adrian and Tina in her head and was ready to explode with frustration by the time she got to Ben's house to collect Liam.

Fucking Adrian.

It was one thing that he was generally a prick, but poor Tina was clearly bearing the brunt of it. And poor Erin seemed to have no idea. And Frankie had no idea what to do about any of it.

Keeping quiet didn't come naturally to Frankie, but when Ben opened the door, Liam came running at her to show her the sticker he'd earned at school for being a maths superstar and all her irritation was dissolved by his enthusiasm.

'Can I go and meet your friend now?' Liam asked, looking up at her with excited eyes.

'Okay.'

'You're sure you don't want me to come over too?' Ben asked.

'God, no. It's only Jez.' She did not need some sort of babysitter.

'Jez. That's a funny name. Jez. *Jez*. Jezjejezjez.' Liam repeated the name under his breath and Frankie fought the urge to tell him to shut up.

There was a car outside the house already. Twenty sodding minutes early. Frankie handed Liam the keys to open the front door and knocked on the car window.

'You're early,' she said, when Jeremy wound down the window. Just like the last time she'd seen him, when they'd met in the pub before Christmas, he was wearing a suit, although he had at least taken his tie off and was coiling it up.

'Sorry. We didn't want to be stuck in traffic.'

'We?' Frankie bent down and looked into the car. A neat-looking woman sat in the passenger seat wearing a green polo neck jumper and a dark checked shirt over the top. Who dressed like that?

'This is Mil – erm, Mariella, my fiancée.'

'Hello.' Mariella smiled, leaning forwards.

'No,' said Frankie. 'No, just you, Jez.'

There was no way Frankie was letting both of them in at once – it was too much. Let Liam get to know Jeremy, and then, in a few visits' time, he could meet Mariella and…

And then what? Weekends at the fancy house? Holidays with the rich grandparents? Frankie suddenly regretted ever agreeing to anything.

'Don't worry,' Mariella said. 'I'm just here for—'

'No,' Frankie said, trying to remember that this was about Liam, not her. As much as she might want to, she couldn't just send them packing. 'Not two of you. Give me five minutes before you knock.'

She stood up and went to Liam, who was still trying to get the key in the lock, and helped him to open the door. As she watched him abandon his coat, bag and shoes on the floor, she wondered how the hell she was going to explain this meeting to him. She was not ready for this.

'Okay, dude,' she said, following him into the kitchen. Was it too early for wine? Probably wouldn't look good. Chocolate digestives would have to do. 'Snack time. I'm breaking out the biscuits.'

Liam nodded eagerly.

There was a knock at the door as she was filling up the kettle. *Short five minutes*, she thought. Liam ran to the front door, standing so he could hide behind it when it opened.

'Jez,' Frankie said, letting him in, relieved to see he was alone.

'Hi, Frankie. Thanks for doing this.' Jeremy looked nervous. He ran his hand over his scalp, forehead to nape, emphasising his prematurely receding hairline. 'Is he around?'

'Come on out, dude,' she said, closing the door and revealing Liam behind it. 'Right – this is Jez— *Jeremy*, this is Liam.'

Liam took a step closer to her, leaning against her shyly, and Frankie reached a hand down to his shoulder.

'Erm, hi.' Jez bent his knees slightly and leant sideways to give an awkward wave, but Liam didn't respond. Each stared at the other without speaking. Frankie wondered what Jez had been expecting. Liam was treating him with the same level of suspicion he would anyone else who didn't have a child with them. Jez looked at her with an anxious expression. Be patient, she wanted to shout. It wouldn't take him long to warm up and then he'd go back to just being Liam and doing his own thing.

'Sorry to interrupt you two chatterboxes,' Frankie said sarcastically, hearing the kettle boil. 'I need my coffee. Drink, Jez?'

'Oh, okay, please. Tea?'

She nodded. 'Liam, get your reading book. You could read a couple of pages with Jez.' Jez looked up with an enthusiasm that suggested he'd never experienced the torture of a child reading aloud before. Well, if he wanted to be involved, she was damned if he was only getting the good bits of parenthood. There had to be some benefit to him being around.

CHAPTER SEVEN

When Kate had suggested a shopping trip for baby items, she had not been expecting Natalie to take her to a farm shop with a Fairtrade selection in one corner. It was a lovely, rustic shop, with beautiful views over the fields, just off the main road out of Cheadbridge, but it did not sell any of the products Kate needed.

'Aren't these simply wonderful?' Natalie said, holding up a bag of cloths. 'They're reusable wet wipes.' She fixed Kate with a serious look. 'I just couldn't be one of those mothers who was ruining the planet with those one-use ones.'

Kate tried to smile enthusiastically, shrugging off the feeling that Natalie was judging her. She thought of all the times she'd done battle with a nappy that had made her retch. The best thing about wet wipes was that you could throw them away. She did not point this out to Natalie. Nor the fact that she was about to move into a phase in her life that would be dominated by washing and the last thing she would need would be yet more stuff to wash.

No, this was important to Natalie and it was not up to Kate to tell her otherwise.

'Although, I was reading about how to make your own wet wipes the other day. Maybe that would be better.' Natalie put the pack down and turned to Kate. 'I was meaning to ask you – what were those nappies you used to have?'

Kate frowned. 'Nappies?'

'Yes… you remember you had those reusable ones?'

She nodded. Kate remembered well the saga of the reusable nappies. Someone had given them to her when Amelia was nine months old, but after a week of extra washing and clearing up after leaks and having just found out she was pregnant again, she had collapsed into a puddle of tears and Matthew had quietly taken the nappies away, never to be spoken of again.

'Obviously, we can't use disposables. Did you know newborn babies go through up to twelve nappies a day? Just imagine the waste! That's four or five thousand nappies before they're potty trained.'

It felt like more than that, Kate thought.

'So, we have to use cloth nappies,' Natalie continued. 'But I can't decide whether to get prefolds or pockets. What did you use again?'

'Umm,' she said, not wanting to remind Natalie about her failure to get to grips with reusables. 'It's been so long, I just don't remember, I'm afraid.'

'Oh, never mind. I'm going to one of those *nappocinos* next week. Nappies and coffee! You should come with me – it's at the café in Cheadbridge at three o'clock.'

Kate breathed a sigh of relief. 'Sorry – school run. Maybe another time.'

Natalie continued to browse, selecting some chemical-free plant-based organic disposable nappies 'just for emergencies', a goat-hair baby brush and a Fairtrade Indian hardwood rattle filled with some sort of special beads and coated in non-toxic, dye-free wax. All the while keeping up a commentary about the damage that mainstream alternatives were doing to the environment. Now Kate knew she was being judged.

'Look, Kate,' Natalie said, pointing to a catalogue picture of a nursery. 'Isn't this beautiful? That's the cot I want. Not yet, obviously. I think this little one will be in with me for a while, won't you?' she whispered to her bump.

Kate looked at the picture and tried to work out why this wooden cot was oval – did she need a different shaped cot now, too? Amelia and Reuben's rectangular cot was still in the attic at her dad's house, along with the other baby things she hadn't yet managed to get rid of. Matthew had accused her of hoarding at the time, although she had probably thought she would pass it on to Natalie when the time came (not that she'd want it now), but at least it meant they didn't have to buy a whole load of new stuff.

'Was there anything you wanted to look at?' Natalie asked.

'Oh, no, I think we've got most of what we need already,' Kate said. 'And it's a bit far from my due date to be buying nappies.' She did not add that when the time came she would be stocking up on disposable ones which weren't made from wood pulp.

'Great. Let's get to the tills, then, there's someone I want you to meet.'

Kate followed with trepidation as they headed to the checkout, where a man sat smiling at Natalie, who was smiling back. As they got closer, he stood up and leaned over the till to kiss Natalie.

'Kate, this is River. River, meet my friend Kate.'

'Hi there, Kate. Great to finally meet you.'

Kate nodded and joined the smiling party. *That explained why Natalie was so keen to come here, then.*

River was tall and broad with blonde-brown hair pulled back messily into a small ponytail. Everything about him was strong and masculine. His skin had a slight tan as though he had been working outside, his arm muscles were noticeable beneath his T-shirt. This was clearly a man at home with physical labour. And yet, he didn't have that air of arrogance or testosterone-filled aggression. He spoke quietly, pausing between phrases thoughtfully.

'Natalie has spoken of you a lot.' He turned to his fiancée. 'Did you ask her, yet?'

'Not yet, give me a chance,' she said, stroking his arm.

'Let me sort these out, then, while you ask her.' He took the basket and began to swipe the items through the till.

'Ask me…?' Kate prompted, as Natalie seemed to have gone into a daze.

'River…' Natalie put a hand on her pregnant stomach and he immediately reached for the same spot, the same dazed expression on his face, the shopping forgotten.

'Magical,' River declared after a moment. 'Thank you for sharing.' He looked at Kate. 'I do envy you women this incredible journey.'

'Being pregnant?' Kate blurted out.

'Oh yes. Us men are very jealous.'

Not all men, Kate wanted to say. She was fairly certain Matthew was much happier being the one who didn't have to give birth. But it seemed rude to disagree with River when he was being nice, so she just smiled and nodded.

'Anyway… I was about to say, we'd really like to see you *and* Matthew. Would you like to come round for dinner one evening?'

'Oh… yes, that sounds lovely.' On the inside, Kate's stomach sank. It was one thing for her to keep being friends with Nat, but she wasn't sure how Matthew would feel about a meal with his best friend's ex-girlfriend and her new partner. 'I'll need to check the calendar and sort out a babysitter…'

'We're fairly flexible on timings,' River said. 'As long as it's before the end of April.'

※

'I saw Natalie today,' Kate said.

'Uh huh.' Matthew didn't look up from the book he was marking, flicking the pages quickly, and occasionally pausing to tick or correct a word.

'And I met River.'

'Who's River?' Matthew threw the exercise book on the marked pile and picked up the next.

'Her fiancé.'

'Oh.' He paused and looked up at her, eyebrows raised. 'He's called *River*…'

'I need to reply to the wedding invite – it's only a couple of months away. What do you think?'

Matthew sighed. 'I think… I think River is a ridiculous name for a grown man, but yes, of course we can go. She's your friend, even if she did run out on *my* friend.'

'I know, sorry. But… River's really nice.' Even if he did use words like 'magical'.

Matthew rolled his eyes and began marking again.

'And also,' Kate said, determined to press on with the conversation, 'they've invited us to dinner.'

'Right.' Matthew raised his eyebrows again, but his pen didn't pause.

'I mean, I'll have to sort out a babysitter, but that's okay, isn't it?' Kate was fairly certain he wouldn't say no, even if he'd rather poke his eyes out.

'Okay.'

'Really?'

'Really,' he said. 'Although I can't promise not to make any jokes about his name.'

Kate hoped he was joking. River had seemed lovely, especially how attentive he was to Natalie. She deserved some looking after, having put up with Nick's selfishness for years. And maybe, after dinner with them, Kate would stop feeling so on edge around Natalie…

*

Frankie was still mostly asleep, her eyes firmly closed, when she felt Ben kiss her shoulder and begin to roll away from her.

She groaned. 'Stay,' she whispered, reaching for him.

For a moment he stopped, putting his arm around her. 'It's nearly seven,' he said. 'I've got to go.'

Giving in, she opened her eyes and struggled to sit up as he left the bed. 'Stay for breakfast.' She hadn't realised she was going to say it until the words were out, but as soon as they were, she meant them. 'And not just breakfast today…'

Ben turned to look at her as he zipped up his jeans. Frankie tried not to get distracted by the sight of his torso and the muscles underneath moving as he reached for his T-shirt.

'You're thinking again, aren't you?' she said. That was never a good sign. Ben overthought everything.

'*You* haven't thought about it at all, though,' he replied, sitting on the bed to pull on his socks. 'Hasn't Liam got enough changes going on at the moment?'

'Like what?'

'Like starting school and moving house and meeting his dad and—'

'Okay,' she interrupted, hating how reasonable he could be. 'But this isn't a real change, is it? He knows you and…' she sighed, wishing she wasn't having what was probably a very important conversation so early in the morning. 'Why are we making it complicated? If we're together, let's just be together. Like, all the time together, not sneaking around, like we're not really together… we *are* together, aren't we?'

'We are.' Ben leaned over to kiss her and she felt her body respond with the memory of last night. Pulling him closer, she wondered if they had time for a rerun. 'But, Charlie… and Jo… I can't just spring this on them.'

Frankie sighed. Too much thinking again.

He kissed her again before slipping away quietly. Two minutes later, Liam appeared, bleary-eyed, at the bedroom door, as if to prove Ben right.

CHAPTER EIGHT

Alison did not want to go to the PTA meeting, but the only thing worse than facing a smug Becky in her element would be letting her win. She chose her outfit with care – nothing with signs of wear, no last-season fashions, just classic, effortless style.

'You look nice,' Simon said as she came downstairs. 'Are you going out?'

'I've got a PTA meeting, remember? It's on the calendar.'

He nodded vaguely. 'Are you sure that's not a cover for meeting another man? You look far too gorgeous for a mums' get together.'

Alison was trying to put her coat on, but Simon's arms around her waist were hampering her efforts. 'I'm sure.' She sighed and kissed him. 'It's Thursday I meet my lover.'

He kissed her again before releasing her. 'I don't think you've put that on the calendar,' he called after her as she left, grinning at his silliness.

Kate was just leaving the alleyway to her house when Alison reached the High Street.

'Kate!' she called and was grateful to see Kate turn and wave. At least now she wouldn't be entering the lion's den on her own.

'Lovely to see you again,' Becky greeted them as they entered the Creative Café. While she was wearing her Chair of the PTA persona it was hard to see the hostility between them, but Alison was sure it was still there. There was no way Becky was going to forgive her for her twin crimes of helping Frankie get together with Jo's ex-husband *and* stopping Becky from turning the PTA's Christmas bazaar into a free event for her friends' businesses.

'I think we're about ready to start,' Becky called.

Everyone shuffled towards the rows of chairs that had been set up for the meeting. Alison headed for the front row, which had been turned round to face the rest of the crowd, where the committee sat, but only four seats had been put out and they were already taken. Becky was flanked by Jo and Rachel on one side and the headteacher Mrs Williams on the other. Kate had gone ahead and sat on the second row and was now waving to the spare seat beside her. Alison was damned sure she wouldn't go quietly. Becky, Jo and Rachel had rejected her once before, she wasn't going to let it happen again.

'Thanks,' Alison called across to her, far louder than she needed to. 'But I think the committee is supposed to sit together. I'll just get another chair.'

Becky looked stricken. 'That's okay,' she said hurriedly. 'We won't mind if you want to sit with your friend.'

Alison, chair in hand, stared directly at her with a smile they both knew she didn't mean. She was aware that a quiet had descended and they were now being watched by the other parents. 'Oh no. I think it's important to keep the committee together, don't you?' She dropped the chair the last few centimetres so that it clattered against the floor. 'Sorry about that. All ready now.' She tried not to think how different this meeting was from the first one, back in September, when she had sat with Rachel and Jo and been convinced they were at the start of an enduring friendship.

Becky turned away, picking up some papers from her chair before turning back to welcome everyone.

'We have some big events coming up this term,' she continued. 'The money we raised last year will pay for an author to visit on World Book Day and Years Four, Five and Six will have a theatre company coming in to do all sorts of workshops with them – and all because of the hard work we put into fundraising last academic year.' She paused, looking smug and nodding as she clapped patronisingly. 'Now we need to look ahead and use this meeting to decide what sort of thing we're going to do this term. Normally, we like to use either Valentine's Day or Mother's Day to have a big fundraising event. Obviously, if we wanted to do something for Valentine's Day, it is only a couple of weeks away.' She stopped to laugh. 'Luckily, I know we have some very dedicated people on our committee, so we really could manage that.' At this point, Becky briefly glanced left and right, avoiding Alison on the end of the row.

'Shall we start with the ideas? Rachel, over to you.'

Rachel stood and took a deep breath. When she began to speak, her voice quivered with nerves. 'I wondered about doing a Valentine's Day Ball, something to really get dressed up for. I have spoken to Heppleton Hall and they can do us a deal that works out at about £45 a head, or I think we can do something ourselves closer to £30 a head in the school hall, which would be good. I know that sounds like a lot of money, but we could offer discounts if people book a table for ten.'

There were murmurs around the room and Rachel's face began to drop a little. 'I think it would be really special,' she said a little petulantly.

Special and expensive, thought Alison, *especially if it was only in the school hall.*

'Thank you, Rachel,' Becky said. 'I think it's a wonderful idea, but it's not our only one. Jo?'

'Okay,' said Jo, standing up without even a pretence of a smile. Alison noticed she had not changed out of the suit she had obviously worn to work. Another reminder for the stay-at-home mums that she, as a working mother, was far busier than anyone else. 'I was thinking about focusing on Mother's Day instead and doing a pampering evening? We could set up the school's main hall doing some refreshments and some stalls and then do a few quick treatments, like nails or maybe a scalp massage, in some of the classrooms. I'd need volunteers to help pull in some providers, so if any of you know beauticians, make-up artists, that sort of thing…?' She looked around hopefully, but when no one in the audience said anything, Jo seemed to give up and sat down abruptly.

Alison frowned – there might be some merit in that idea, but it didn't sound fully thought through and she was sure Jo wouldn't be doing any of the work towards organising it.

'Thank you, Jo.' Becky was on her feet again. 'So those are our two ideas and you might want a few minutes to discuss them before we vote. Does anyone have any questions?'

Alison was not an impulsive person. She reached into her handbag and took out the notebook she had spent the week scribbling ideas down in. 'Becky?' she said, half-raising her hand.

But another mum was already pointing out the obvious: a Valentine's Ball was too expensive and surely too difficult to organise in a fortnight.

'Becky?' she tried again, but this time was drowned out by a dad on the third row complaining that a pamper evening only aimed at mums was sexist.

'Becky – I have another idea.' This time Alison stood up and stepped forward, successfully getting everyone's attention.

'Oh… Okay, sure.'

Alison was delighted to see Becky wrong-footed, reluctant to accept Alison's contribution but unable to ignore her.

'Yes. Well, a couple of ideas, actually. I'm afraid they're not quite as impressive as these events, but given that we've already had the quiz night and the Christmas bazaar, I wondered if it might be time for something smaller that doesn't take up so much time?' Alison looked from Becky to the parents, who looked hopeful. 'I wondered about doing a sort of shop for the children for Mother's Day so that parents – well, dads – can send in a couple of pounds and kids get to visit the shop and choose something to take home. But if that's a bit disruptive to the day, Mrs Williams,' she added, glancing at the teacher beside her, 'then we don't need to offer choice. Bulk-buy daffodils and we could make a pound profit on every bunch – we'd just need to tie a little ribbon around them with a label for the child's name or a little message, and I'm happy to sort that out (although if we had a little team of five, we'd be done in no time). Or we could do keyrings with the child's photograph on?'

'Wouldn't we need a photographer for that?' Becky interjected.

'I think we know a photographer who'd be willing to do it for free, don't we?' Alison said, thinking of Ben. Becky looked at Jo. Jo looked at Alison, her lip curling up in distaste. 'Or just do the flowers…'

Alison sat back down, aware that she wanted to appear reasonable to the rest of the parents, rather than petty and argumentative. The mention of Jo's ex-husband might have been a step too far. She didn't really want to drag Ben into this, especially if it caused more problems for him and Frankie.

'I like the flowers idea,' Kate said, adding quietly, 'I never get flowers.'

'And that would work for Fathers' Day too,' the dad on the third row pointed out. 'Maybe not flowers, but the key rings or something like that.'

As more parents added their support, Alison allowed herself a small smile.

'Very impressive,' Kate said as they left the café twenty minutes later.

'Thank you.' Alison felt it would be churlish to agree too loudly, but it was undoubtedly a victory. 'Now, not to sound like Frankie, but I could do with a drink.'

'Okay, let me just text Matthew.'

They crossed the road in silence.

'Do you think Frankie would like to join us?' Alison said, fairly certain of the answer.

'I'm not sure she can come out, though,' Kate said. 'I mean, she doesn't have anyone to watch Liam.'

'We'll just have to go to her, then, won't we?'

When she knocked on the door (quietly, so as not to wake a sleeping child), Alison worried a little that Frankie might already be dressed for bed – she wasn't sure she could take a onesie up close – and was relieved when the door was answered by a fully clothed Frankie.

'We fancied a drink,' Alison said when Frankie looked at them, confused. 'We thought you might have some.'

Frankie's frown changed into a grin and she opened the door wide to let them in. She still wore the black skirt, blue shirt and striped waistcoat of her uniform. Alison tried not to be bitter that such an outfit on her would have looked dowdy, while on Frankie it was extremely flattering.

'I'll get some more glasses,' Frankie said, disappearing into the kitchen, leaving the others in the lounge. 'Oi, Preggers, squash or orange juice?'

'Squash is fine,' Kate said, sitting on the futon. There was already a bottle of red and half a glass of wine on the little table in front of the futon. 'You started already.'

Alison tried to work out whether the beanbag or futon would be less uncomfortable. There was probably more chance she would be able to stand up again if she sat on the futon, she decided.

'Shit day at work,' Frankie explained, returning and pouring drinks before sinking onto the beanbag.

'How is the new job?' Kate asked.

'Boring. And my manager Adrian is a sleazy git.' Frankie sighed.

'Time for a new job?' Alison asked. If she was honest, she was a little disappointed that Frankie might give up on their Happiness Project so easily.

'No – I... I can't just leave.' Frankie looked up at her and Alison was surprised to see the uncertainty in her eyes. 'For one, that would prove to Mum that I can't hold down a sodding job and for two... I don't want Adrian to win.'

'What makes him such a... Why don't you like him?' Kate asked.

Frankie screwed up her face. 'He's all wandering hands and talking to my chest. But the best bit is, I just found out he's actually sleeping with the boss, so...'

'So, you're never going to win.'

'No, but...' She sighed again. 'I'm not going let him fucking win.' Frankie drained her glass and knelt at the table to fill it up again. 'Right, new topic. How was the PTA meeting? Did you guys have a punch-up?'

Kate laughed. 'They nearly did, you should have seen it. Alison stole the meeting and basically ended up running it.'

Alison liked this version of events. 'I didn't end up running it. It was just that we went with my idea of letting the kids buy little presents or flowers for Mother's Day and people asked me questions and I answered them.'

'It's okay, you're safe,' Kate added. 'You didn't get volunteered for anything.'

'Thank God,' Frankie said. 'My life is full enough right now.'

'How did it go with Liam's father?' Alison asked.

'Yeah, it was... okay.'

Alison stayed silent, waiting for her to continue.

'Jez was here for about an hour in the end. He played with Liam, heard him read, sat with him while he had tea.' She checked the activities off on her fingers. 'And he's coming back next week and I said he could bring his fiancée in with him this time. And if that goes well, I'm going to tell Liam who he is.'

Liam didn't even know Jeremy was his dad? Alison was glad she didn't have a mouthful of wine to splutter across the carpet.

'Why does he think Jeremy's visiting, then?' Kate asked.

Frankie gave them a look. 'He's four, for fuck's sake, he doesn't have any idea why anything's happening. He thinks the world revolves around him anyway. Don't give me that look, Alison.' She gestured with her glass, the wine dangerously close to spilling out. 'I'm not opening that can of worms until I'm sure Jez isn't just pissing about.'

Alison opened her mouth to argue back, but thought better of it. Lying to her child didn't *seem* a good idea, but at least Frankie was trying to look out for Liam.

'Did I tell you two I'm going to a wedding next month?' Kate said, timidly into the silence.

Alison shook her head, reaching for the bottle to top up her glass.

'My friend Nat's getting married.'

'She's Matthew's friend's ex?' Frankie asked. 'The pregnant one?'

Kate nodded. 'Yep. She's decided she wants to be married before the baby's born, so she and River—'

'I'm sorry, he's called River?' Frankie interrupted.

Alison was glad someone had said it.

'I know,' Kate laughed. 'But he seems really nice and they're so lovely together.' She sighed. 'I'm a bit jealous really. I remember when Matthew and I used to be like that.'

'Don't worry, she's just about to lose all dignity,' Frankie said. 'Then there'll be sleepless nights and leaking boobs and all the romance will be gone.'

'Frankie!' Kate was shocked.

'What she means,' Alison rushed to save the conversation, 'is that it's easy to be romantic without the added complications of children. But –' she saw Frankie about to disagree and held her hand up to stop her '– *but*, in a few months she will learn that true love is him making you a chocolate milkshake at three in the morning because it's the fifth feed of the night and you're so sleep-deprived, you can't stop crying.'

She watched Kate's eyes begin to well up. 'I got marmalade on toast,' she said, sniffing.

'You two are so sodding lucky,' Frankie said, sounding bitter. 'I just got a lecture on the dangers of unprotected sex from my mum.'

FEBRUARY

CHAPTER NINE

'I got your text,' Frankie said, opening the door to let Ben in. 'What's your plan?'

'Where's Liam?'

'Asleep, I think. Been quiet for the last half hour, anyway…'

'I've been thinking.'

'Again?' Frankie said, leaving Ben to shut the door while she headed to the kitchen. This would probably need a drink. 'I'm opening a bottle – do you want some?' she called back to him.

'Yeah, okay, just a small one.' He accepted the glass he was given without comment. *Really*, thought Frankie, *he should know I can't pour a small glass*. 'How was work?'

'Yuck.'

'Not loving it yet, then?'

She shook her head. She didn't go into detail, partly because she was sick of going over it in her head and not being able to come up with a solution, but mostly because she didn't want him to get outraged on her behalf or – worse – not get outraged at all.

'What have you been thinking about, anyway?' she prompted, noticing that he had brought a bag with him. 'What's that?'

'This,' he said, putting it on the table and taking out his laptop and opening it up, 'is what complicated looks like.'

'A spreadsheet?' She couldn't disagree – it definitely looked complicated.

He sat down and turned the screen to face her, gesturing at the colour-coded columns. 'This is what Jo does to organise when we each have Charlie, so there's no surprises.'

'Why are you bringing me complicated?'

'Because you're right, we're serious and the sooner we get this out in the open, the better. I'm going to add you and Liam to the spreadsheet. We'll do some things together, the four of us, and we could book in some time for just the two of us, and I'll add in picking up Liam on a Thursday for you – assuming you're okay with me still doing that?'

Frankie tried to tell herself that the mild feelings of panic were down to the spreadsheet rather than anything else. She reached out a hand to the table to steady herself.

'Umm…' she couldn't think what to say. It would be less terrifying to be presented with some sort of legal contract. 'You're going to add me to the spreadsheet?'

He smiled softly and reached out to her, pulling her onto his lap, his arm securely around her. 'It's okay, you don't have to deal with the actual spreadsheet.'

Well, that was something, at least.

He pointed at the screen. 'Here, this weekend Charlie is with me – why don't you and Liam come for tea and stay over?'

'Both of us?'

'Yes.'

'What will Jo say?' Frankie asked. Because there was no way Ben's ex-wife would want Frankie to have anything to do with Charlie.

'She isn't the biggest fan,' he admitted. 'But I was unrelentingly reasonable with her and she is willing to tolerate it. Not that she really has much choice.'

'Oh, so she already knows?' This was a done deal. Frankie couldn't work out why she seemed to be getting cold feet now – it must be the spreadsheet. 'Alright then.'

'And here,' Ben said, pointing to a green square on the screen. 'This is when I don't have Charlie, so I wondered if you could get a babysitter and I'll take you out for dinner.'

'Uh-huh.'

'And then this square here –' he pointed again, '– means I'll be asking if you could possibly pick up Charlie because I've agreed to photograph a Valentine's Day wedding and I got confused by the spreadsheet and thought Charlie was with Jo, but he's not and now I'm stuck.' He looked up, eyebrows raised hopefully.

Frankie looked at him and tipped her head to one side. 'Are you a little scared of the spreadsheet?'

'Hell, yes.'

She laughed with relief. 'Thank fuck for that.'

'Is that a yes?'

'That is a yes to this weekend and I'll find a babysitter and I'll sort out picking up Liam and Charlie – but please write the dates down and don't ever show me that spreadsheet again.'

He grinned and shut the laptop.

Putting her glass carefully on the table behind her, Frankie leaned in to kiss him, feeling her body tingle in response to his closeness. 'And you're staying tonight, right?'

Even though Ben had to sneak off before Liam woke up, Frankie started the day with a smile. This was new, this feeling of… happiness? … contentment? It gave her a sort of inner strength, like a secret only she knew that would make everything okay.

Of course, after three hours in a room with Adrian, there wasn't much of that feeling left.

They seemed to have reached a truce, where they mostly ignored each other as far as possible without being outwardly hostile. And when Erin appeared – silently, as always – The Prick would become charming to everyone around him. Then when she was gone he would lock eyes on Frankie with a smug, arrogant look that dared her to do something.

Frankie felt that she showed incredible self-control in not punching his face every time she saw the look. But she also felt ridiculously helpless every time she saw him standing a little too close to Tina.

Frankie spent much of the morning at Reception. In between welcoming guests – over ten, double figures felt worth celebrating – she found herself searching again for a solution that didn't involve being arrested for assaulting Adrian. Alison's stupid Happiness Project was bringing a whole new level of 'adulting' to her life that she just wasn't sure she was ready for.

The more she thought, the more she realised it had to come from Tina. Frankie needed to get Tina to go to Erin, then she could back her up and hope Erin would believe them. She would have to if they both said it, surely?

'Tina, can we talk?' Frankie asked, intercepting her just as she arrived for her shift.

Tina smiled, then sensed the tone and her face fell as she muttered something about being late.

'Just quickly.' Frankie reached out to the girl, who looked up, scared. 'Back here,' she said, gently leading her behind the reception desk.

Now that Tina was in front of her, Frankie wasn't quite sure where to start. *Best to just dive straight in*, she thought. 'We need to talk about Adrian.'

'What about him?'

'What he's doing.'

'Why? What's he doing?'

Frankie couldn't work out if Tina was being evasive on purpose or was genuinely clueless. 'The whole touchy-feely, grabby thing,' she said, hoping she didn't have to get too graphic. 'And the comments and the stares and everything. You shouldn't have to put up with it, you don't have to put up with it.'

'Oh, it's just how he is.' Tina waved her hand dismissively. 'He – it's no big deal. You know what blokes are like.'

'Are you fucking kidding me?' Frankie tried to keep her voice low, but it was hard when she was angry. 'It's not what blokes are like, it's not okay. We need to talk to Erin.'

'To Erin? About Adrian?' Now Tina looked more worried. How could she be more upset by the thought of talking to Erin than the thought of spending time with Adrian? 'No, I don't think Erin wouldn't like that. It's fine, it's fine. Every job has its downside, right?'

Frankie tried desperately to think of something to say, but as she watched Tina walk away, doubt began to sneak in. Maybe she hadn't seen what she thought she'd seen. Maybe Adrian was just a bit of a creep rather than a full-on groper. And if Tina didn't seem to mind… But she *had* minded. Frankie had seen her expression when Adrian put his arm around her, when he had stroked her hair, when she had heard Frankie was going to work on Reception for half an hour. Tina *did* mind, she was just too scared to say anything about it.

'Hi, Erin,' Tina said. Frankie looked to see the Silent Boss, as she had begun to think of Erin, walking towards them.

'Hi, Tina.'

Frankie smiled and stepped out from behind the desk to make room for Erin.

'Oh, actually, before you go,' Erin said, 'you're just the person I wanted to ask. I've got an evening booking next week – Adrian and Tina are already working, but I could do with an extra body. Can I put you down for that shift? On Thursday?'

'Yeah, sure.' Frankie might have to organise her mum to babysit in the evening, but there was no way she was leaving Tina working a whole shift alone with Adrian.

'By the way, what was Tina doing back here?'

'Oh – I was just showing her how to use the booking system in case she needs to cover Reception.'

'Hmm,' Erin said, with a half-smile. 'She's a sweet girl, Tina, but I'm not sure my niece has quite enough maturity yet to be the first impression people get when they arrive at Heppleton Hall.'

Her niece?

So, Adrian wasn't just Tina's boss's boyfriend, he was also her *aunt's* boyfriend. Her aunt who happened to be her boss. So, not *just* her job at stake if she made a fuss, then. Frankie could see how this added an extra layer of complication to the whole thing.

*

'Such a shame Ben couldn't make it today.'

Frankie tried not to hear the disappointment in her mum's voice as she repeated herself yet again. Ben joins them for Sunday lunch *one time* and suddenly the weekend is nothing without him.

'Maybe next week, Mum. I'll ask him.'

'That'd be nice, dear,' Paula said, handing Frankie her plate. 'He was very nice, wasn't he, Laura? We did like him.'

Frankie looked across the table to where her sister sat sulking next to her boyfriend and felt smug that it was finally *her* chance to be the one praised.

'At least he's better than *Jeremy,*' Laura said, reverting back to her *at least I didn't get pregnant and drop out of university* defence.

Frankie saw that Liam's head had popped up as he heard the now familiar name. She'd hoped he had been too distracted by the plate of food to have listened in on the conversation.

'Jeremy?' he said, looking from Laura to Frankie and back again. 'My friend Jeremy?'

Laura looked aghast, although Frankie couldn't tell whether it was because she was worried she'd put her foot in it or because she couldn't believe Frankie had allowed Liam to meet Jeremy. Probably the latter.

Frankie stared at her sister, trying to warn her not to say too much. 'Your Auntie Laura knows Jeremy from when I was friends with him before.'

Laura opened her mouth and closed it twice before looking at her mum, who shook her head. Beside Laura, Stuart, her lanky boyfriend, seemed to be trying to sink into his chair to escape from the tension.

'How's the house-hunting going?' Frankie asked.

'We went to see a house in Millhurst this morning,' Stuart said hurriedly, clearly pleased to be able to change the subject. 'Three bedrooms, but a bit pokey…'

Frankie sat eating in silence as Laura and Stuart spent the rest of the meal describing in detail the six houses they had viewed in the past week. In her head, inappropriate comments begged to be made about the mirrored wardrobes in the first house or the poles in the lounge of the house being renovated, but she bit them back, desperate not to make an enemy of Laura now. *This*, she thought, was why she had to tell Liam that Jeremy was his dad. She didn't really think her sister would be callous enough to tell Liam deliberately, but she could be utterly thoughtless and was likely to let it slip without realising.

When everyone had finished eating, Frankie jumped up to collect plates and take them to the kitchen. As expected, Laura, the dutiful daughter, followed behind with the serving dishes.

'Laura – please don't mention Jeremy to Liam,' Frankie said as soon as they reached the kitchen.

Her sister laid the dishes on the side then turned to face Frankie. 'I can't believe they've met. What were you thinking? You know he's just going to…' she dropped her voice, '*piss off* again, don't you?'

Frankie sighed. 'I think he's changed. He's getting married and his fiancée is really sweet. I think… I think Liam deserves to know his dad. Just – don't say anything about it. You can say *I told you so* if it all goes wrong, alright?'

Laura shook her head and seemed about to argue when their mum appeared with the last of the dishes. 'Everything okay in here, girls?' she said in the tone that made Frankie feel like a teenager caught smoking.

'Fine, Mum,' Laura muttered, picking up the dessert bowls and leaving.

'Actually, can I ask you a favour, Mum?' Frankie asked, remembering the extra shift she'd picked up at work. 'Next Thursday – the fourteenth – I've got to work the afternoon–evening shift, could you babysit Liam, please?'

'Fourteenth,' Paula repeated, checking the calendar on the fridge. 'Yes, I can. Valentine's Day. What a shame you have to work – aren't you doing something with Ben that night?'

'No, he's photographing a wedding that day – oh, no.' Frankie sighed, remembering the spreadsheet conversation.

'What's wrong?'

'I'd forgotten – Ben can't do pick-up after school, either because he's working and I'm supposed to be picking Charlie up that day, too.'

'I can get both boys after school, it's fine,' Paula said, writing it on the calendar.

Frankie breathed a sigh of relief at the crisis averted. She could totally do this without a crazy spreadsheet.

CHAPTER TEN

'Kate? What do you think?' Alison said, glaring at her.

They sat, balanced on the tiny chairs in the corridor just outside the classroom, going through the basket of reading books and organising them into different piles by stage.

'Sorry,' Kate said, trying to remember what they had been talking about. 'I… think about what?'

Alison sighed. 'The after-school clubs. Reception children can join after half term, I think. Are you signing Amelia up to anything?'

'Oh, I hadn't even thought. What clubs are there?'

'It was all on the letter we got last week.'

'There was a letter?' It didn't seem to matter how many times she asked Amelia about messages from school or how often she went through the school bag to check, Kate still felt she missed more messages than she caught.

Alison looked at her slightly pityingly. 'I'll take a photo of it and send it to you.'

'Thanks.'

'Although why they are still sending bits of paper home with unreliable children is beyond me. I think I might have a word with Mrs Williams, see if I can introduce her to email.'

Kate murmured in agreement, still distracted by the text she'd had from Natalie this morning.

Or rather, more accurately, she was distracted by the jealousy she was feeling as a result of that text.

She'd known it was Valentine's Day, of course, but it hadn't meant anything to her. Not like Nat, who was being whisked away for a romantic weekend to a surprise location, having been woken up with a large bunch of flowers and a handmade heart ornament.

Kate tried to think back to her pre-child life. Had she and Matthew ever been that romantic?

Matthew had bought her a small bunch of red flowers at Valentine's once or twice. Not roses, though. Which was fine, because roses were so expensive and she didn't mind. Not really. It's the thought that counts.

'Are you alright? You don't seem all there.'

'Oh, I'm… no, it's nothing.' Kate wished Alison hadn't asked such a direct question. She was the worst liar. 'Are you and Simon doing anything for Valentine's Day?'

Alison smiled. 'Of course. I've got a dinner booked at the new Thai restaurant in Millhurst.'

'Do you do cards and flowers and things, too?'

She nodded. 'But that's just us. It's not like we're romantic any other time of year, just one day to be nice to each other.'

Kate appreciated her trying to play it down.

'Are you planning anything?'

Kate shook her head. 'I hadn't thought… I don't think we've done anything since the kids were born. I don't know…'

'Doesn't mean you can't plan something last-minute. Why not cook a romantic meal for two?'

'He's got a parents' evening at his school tonight, so he won't be back till late. And also, I can't cook.'

Alison reached a hand out to Kate's arm and she looked up, surprised. 'I have the easiest ever recipe – you absolutely can't fail.'

Kate wasn't sure about that, but Alison looked too certain to argue with.

*

Having negotiated the after-school supermarket trip, Kate stood in the kitchen and stared at the instructions, trying to memorise them, but only managed to picture all the ways tagliatelle carbonara could go wrong.

The pancetta had to get crisp, but not burn. Remember to take out the garlic clove. Keep back some of the pasta water – a ladle? A mug? Most of it? Don't let the egg scramble, but make sure it's cooked.

Alison had been adamant that it was the ideal recipe. 'Only takes ten minutes – totally foolproof,' she'd promised. So Kate checked the ingredients and the instructions again. She had managed to get Amelia and Reuben into bed on time and had had time to change into cleaner jeans and her one 'going out' top. She was ready: if only Matthew would come home.

Having rushed to make sure everything was ready for seven thirty, she wasn't sure what to do now. She put another load of washing through the machine and did the washing-up. Then she sorted the recycling and put the bin out. Then she began writing a shopping list, which morphed into a 'things we need for the new baby' list, which was why she had abandoned her romantic meal preparation to take stock of the boxes of baby clothes in the loft. Which was where Matthew found her when he arrived home.

'What are you doing up here?' he said, his head and shoulders appearing from the loft hatch.

'Oh, I'm just – no, I should be cooking. Have you been home long?' She suddenly realised he was wearing a T-shirt, meaning he was already changed. He was supposed to get changed while she cooked, so she had it ready for him.

'Not long. It was a late one – several sets of parents panicking about the mocks and I had to take some of Mike's because he had to leave early. Thank goodness I ate beforehand or I would be starving by now.'

Kate was only half-listening as she approached the ladder and climbed down, trying to brush the dust off her.

'You look nice, are you going out?' he said.

'You've eaten?' she said, finally realising what he'd said.

'Yeah, grabbed a sandwich before parents' evening.'

'Oh.' She didn't know what else to say. It wasn't a big deal; it didn't normally matter because she ate with the kids. He didn't know she was planning a meal and it was her own fault for not saying anything, really. She could have sent him a text.

'Where are you going tonight, then?' he asked.

'Oh, nowhere. I mean, I'm not… going out, that is.'

He looked confused, but she left him upstairs and went down to the kitchen, trying desperately not to cry. She still needed to eat, but if Matthew didn't need dinner, she could cope with beans on toast.

'I didn't get to eat earlier,' she said, hearing him follow her. 'I was waiting for you.'

'Oh, sorry,' he said, sounding genuine. 'I assumed you would have eaten.'

'No, it's fine.' She dropped two slices of bread in the toaster and hunted for a tin in the cupboard. 'I'm not really hungry,' she lied.

While she cooked – not that it really involved much cooking, she admitted to herself – Matthew ran himself a glass of water and stood drinking it, surveying the ingredients on the side.

'You were going to make carbonara?' he asked, casually.

Kate nodded, wishing she'd hidden the evidence.

'Thank you,' he said, reaching his arm around her waist and kissing her cheek.

It helped. A little.

He came to sit with her at the table while she ate. She looked across at him and felt herself softening. Cooking for him would have been a disaster, and she would have been stressed, and she wouldn't have been able to enjoy it for fear of accidentally poisoning him. This way was much better.

Kate felt again the pleasure of knowing that this man – this attractive and kind man, she corrected herself – was her husband. *Hers*.

'What are you smiling at?' he asked, returning her grin.

She shook her head. 'Nothing.'

He held her gaze and for a second, she thought he was going to lean forward and kiss her, but he broke away to glance at the calendar.

'It's half term next week,' he said.

'Yes.' She had already started worrying about how to entertain two children without any school or pre-school. 'Are we still taking the kids to your parents' house?' she asked, hoping he had remembered to talk to them about that.

'Ah.' He looked guilty.

'Thing is, Mike's having a bit of a time of it at the moment – he's not well, although they don't know what it is – and he's asked if I can fill in for him on the Aberystwyth trip. I told him I'd have to check with you, but he's a bit stressed at the moment. It'd be good to be able to help him out with this.'

The trouble with marrying a nice man was that he was nice to everyone. He would help the colleague feeling overwhelmed, and the friend who just got dumped, the neighbour who needed their dog looking after.

'Of course.' What kind of wife would she be if she stamped her feet and said *she* wanted him? That she wanted to spend time with him and wanted him to look after the kids so she could have a break? And if she did, she knew he would drop everything to be there for her.

He smiled. 'Thanks. I knew you'd understand.' His phone beeped and he lifted it briefly to read the screen. 'Did I tell you Nick has a date tonight?'

'You did not.' Did that mean he was finally starting to get over losing Natalie? 'Who with?'

'He was a bit cagey about that. Some woman from work, I think.'

'Did you tell him we're going to have dinner with River and Nat?' she asked, finishing her meal.

He frowned. 'Not yet. Thought I'd wait and see how this date went. I'm hoping he'll care less if he's seeing someone.'

Kate stood up and carried her things to the sink, running the hot tap so she could wash up immediately rather than wake up to the job tomorrow.

Matthew picked up his phone and began replying to the earlier message as he wandered through to the lounge. Her hopes of an early night spent together dissolved as she returned to being invisible. She felt ridiculous having got dressed up.

As soon as she had finished drying the dishes and placed them in the cupboard, she went straight upstairs and got changed into her comfortable and utterly unsexy pyjamas. She lay in the dark, hoping that Matthew would wonder where she had gone and come to check on her, but she could hear him laughing at something on TV, clearly unconcerned.

Maybe this was what they were now, she thought – all missed signals and comfortable pyjamas. It was not a reassuring thought, but what could she do about it now?

CHAPTER ELEVEN

'It's sweet, isn't it?' Tina whispered to Frankie as they stood in the kitchen, peering out through the round windows to see the Valentine's Day high tea in full swing.

Frankie nodded, although in truth she wasn't sure 'sweet' was the right word. Surreal, maybe? She had not expected the dating event to be filled with old people. More women than men, and all of them looking like grandparents. She tried to imagine her mum at something like this, but given that Paula hadn't had a boyfriend in the twenty-odd years since Frankie's dad died, she just couldn't picture her dating.

The café was barely recognisable; the square tables that usually filled the space had been replaced with larger round ones covered in white tablecloths, with red napkins, confetti and vases of flowers on them. There was space for eight people around each table, but the hostess – a smiley woman with a clipboard and a loud voice – kept moving people on after their allotted twenty minutes conversation time, carrying their teacups and plates to the next table for them to talk to new people.

'Have they been here before?' Frankie asked. She hadn't seen anything like this afternoon tea at the Hall before, but it seemed exactly the sort of event they should be doing.

Tina shook her head. 'It's a trial to see if this would be a good venue for more events. Erin says this company organises parties and talks and meals and all sorts of things.'

They had been so busy staring at the collection of guests that Frankie didn't hear Adrian approach. She jumped as she felt his arm slip over her shoulder, his hand carelessly brushing against her breast.

'Hey,' she said, louder than she meant to, pushing his arm away and twisting back to stand facing him. He still had his arm around Tina, who hadn't made a sound. 'What the fuck, Adrian?'

He put his hand up apologetically. 'Whoa, sorry, missed the shoulder there. Lucky you haven't got much to grab, eh? Not like Tina here – now she'd be more than a handful. Honk, honk!' He mimed the squeeze, keeping his fingers millimetres away from Tina's blouse.

Don't punch him, don't punch him, don't punch him.

Tina giggled awkwardly, and didn't speak or move, paralysed by the situation.

Frankie had to do something, but – short of punching him – her options seemed limited. She stepped forward towards Tina, her hand out to lead her somewhere else – anywhere else – taking care to land the sharp heel of her shoe onto Adrian's foot, without looking at him.

'Ow,' he yelled, jumping back and releasing Tina as he clutched his foot.

'Oh, sorry,' Frankie said with mock innocence. 'Didn't see you were that close.' She took Tina's elbow and steered her through the kitchen and out of the back entrance.

'Bitch,' he hissed as they left, so quietly that Frankie wasn't entirely sure if she'd heard it.

In her hurry to get Tina away from Adrian, Frankie hadn't really thought about the fact that the back door only led to the bins, but she was not going back in until she was certain he had gone.

'Seriously, Tina,' Frankie said swinging round to face her, 'you can't just let that go.'

Tina was looking down at the cigarette butts on the floor, nudging one with the side of her shoe. She was so young, Frankie thought again. And caught between Adrian's groping and his girlfriend being her aunt.

Tina shrugged. 'S'okay, really. Mum says Adrian is good for Erin after her last boyfriend ran off with her bridesmaid. And she's all stressed with taking this place on, she doesn't need me making things worse.'

'You wouldn't be making it worse,' Frankie tried to reason, although her mind was still stuck on the words *he ran off with her bridesmaid*. Clearly, Erin had terrible taste in men.

Tina looked up at her with one eyebrow raised. 'I would.'

'No, Adrian is the one making all this worse. He's the one doing something wrong, not you. He's *not* good for her – he's a creep.'

'She wouldn't believe me, though.'

'Why not?'

'Well, it's… it's not much, is it? And Adrian is her boyfriend.'

'Yes, but also he's a prick. Erin's not stupid, she'll get it.'

Tina didn't say she agreed, but she didn't argue either, which Frankie decided to take as a good sign.

'Come on, they'll be needing the tables clearing.'

Adrian kept a low profile for the rest of the afternoon tea, staying behind the bar while Tina and Frankie brought the cakes and biscuits and more pots of tea to the tables. By four thirty, most of the guests were leaving, and Frankie found herself with less running around to do. She walked slowly round the room, picking up the odd crumb-strewn plate or empty teacup and taking them individually back to the kitchen, so she would look busier than she was.

'What do you think, Frankie?' Erin said, suddenly appearing at her side as she watched an elderly man transfer two slices of Battenberg to a napkin before wrapping them up and slipping them into his pocket.

'About the DIY doggy bag?' she asked.

'No.' Erin didn't even crack a smile. 'This. The event. Afternoon tea. Tina says you have ideas about functions. I'd like to hear them.'

'Oh.' For a second, Frankie wondered if she had misheard or misunderstood. Erin wanted *her* ideas? Why? And then she realised she didn't care why. 'I do. I have loads of ideas.' But where to start? 'I think we should do more with the marquee, not just weddings – maybe big birthday parties or christenings or anniversaries. And if we're trying to attract brides to hire the place for their wedding, we could organise a wedding fair to show it off. In fact, there needs to be more advertising and showing off in general, with competitions and promotions and deals and all sorts. Like offering group packages of a spa treatment and afternoon tea or a couple of treatments and lunch thrown in. What about Mother's Day and Easter and...' She faltered, not sure what else to add, and slightly surprised at herself sounding more like Alison than she ever had before.

'That is a lot of ideas,' Erin remarked, her face still expressionless. 'How would you organise something for Mother's Day?'

Frankie wasn't sure whether that was a rhetorical question, like her teachers used to ask her, when what they meant was '*you* couldn't'. Slightly defensively, wary of being told off, Frankie replied, 'I would have an offer – well, more than one – and I would advertise it in the *Hep Herald* and put up flyers in Spar and... y'know, that sort of thing.'

'And the wedding fair? What would that involve?'

'Well,' Frankie said, playing for time while she tried to think before she spoke. 'You'd want to get the marquee all dressed up to show how it would look. No, actually, just half of it and then in the rest you'd get some stalls for wedding things, like florists and cake makers and invitation designers, and you could get dress shops in to do a catwalk show and in here... in here, you could show our wedding food with canapés and stuff.' It wasn't the strongest ending, but Frankie couldn't think of anything to add. These ideas had sounded so good in her head, but once she said them out loud, she could only hear herself rambling.

'Hmm,' Erin said.

Frankie felt she was holding her breath, waiting for her boss to say something else.

'Do you fancy trying it?' Erin said at last.

'Trying what?'

'Bring me some actual ideas. Three different events – Mother's Day, Easter and a wedding fair. Realistic ones – nothing that's going to bankrupt us – and I'll take a look. If I think they'll work, we'll try them.'

'Really?'

'I don't have anyone organising events. If you can do it, the job's yours.'

'Alright, then.' So, she wasn't being told off. Frankie's defences were punctured and she was suddenly disorientated by the whole conversation.

Erin turned on her heel and left as silently as she had arrived.

Frankie grabbed the nearest dirty plate and nearly ran to the kitchen to tell Tina what Erin had said. She pushed the door open, dropped the dish on the side and was halfway into the room before she noticed Tina wasn't there. She checked the space out back by the bins, then went to check the bar. There was no sign of Adrian either.

Not caring if there were guests left that needed anything, Frankie broke into a run as she rounded the stairs and passed Reception, heading for the staff area. In her head, she was already punching the Prick while trying hard not to think about why he might deserve that.

As she opened the door to the tiny staffroom, she saw them.

Tina looked tiny as he towered over her, his body pressing hers against the wall, his finger stroking the side of her face as he sniggered.

Frankie saw Tina's expression and felt sick. Anger erupted within her and almost before she knew what she was doing, she was running into him, pushing him backwards as hard as she could, sending him crashing back into the table and chairs.

Tina shrieked.

'Crazy bitch.' Adrian scrambled to his feet, moving away from both of them. His eyes flashed past Frankie, staring at something behind her as he sank against the wall, rubbing at his chest where her hands had hit him, looking the innocent victim.

'What's going on?' Erin asked, quietly.

Frankie turned to see Silent Boss in the doorway, a slight frown on her face the only sign that she was anything but serene. *Well, there goes that job*, Frankie thought. She looked from Tina to Adrian, but both were avoiding her gaze.

'Fine,' Frankie said, turning to her locker to collect her things. She pulled her bag onto her shoulder and glanced at Tina again. The girl was still looking down, her face a mixture of guilt and sadness.

Frankie sighed. She wasn't getting the promotion, she was almost certainly losing her job, which meant it was quite likely she would also be losing her house, but right now she felt worse about leaving Tina. Apparently, all she could show her was that if you reacted to Adrian, you got sacked. Not the lesson she needed. She couldn't leave her like this.

'You know what?' Frankie said, turning back to Erin. 'It's not bloody *fine*.' She pointed behind her to Adrian. 'Because *he* is a creep and a prick and…'

'What?' Adrian managed to sound both horrified and innocent in just one word. 'Erin…'

Erin turned to Tina. 'Your shift has finished, hasn't it?'

Tina nodded and mumbled something Frankie couldn't quite catch.

'I'll see you later, then.' Erin said, standing to the side to let Tina pass.

'Adrian, shouldn't you be at the bar?' Erin said, her face still impossible to read.

'Yes, sorry, I was just, er, helping Tina with… I'd better get back there. Excuse me.'

'Great,' said Frankie sarcastically. 'So, you're just going to act like it's nothing? No wonder Tina was scared to tell you – she *knew* you wouldn't believe her.'

'Frankie…' Erin began hesitantly, but Frankie didn't want to hear it. After all, what else was there left to say?

'I know, I know, I'm going.' There was no way Frankie was going to wait and be told off like a small child. 'But just for the record, I'm *not* bloody sorry and I'm *not* going to apologise. Goodbye,' she said, storming off.

She was so livid that she was halfway down the drive before she realised her coat was still hung up in the staffroom. Well, she wasn't going to go back and get it now. Folding her arms across her chest and burying her hands in her armpits, she hurried forward, trying to ignore the viciously cold wind and the fact she had lost another job.

Frankie unscrewed the bottle and poured herself a large glass of wine to drink while she stared at the fridge, trying to work out what she could eat. She continued to stare even after a quick glance showed it to be empty. Was there a tin of beans in the cupboard? she wondered. She knew there hadn't been any bread when she'd left the house this morning, but she thought it was quite likely her mum had bought some to feed the two boys after school. Before she had a chance to check, there was a knock at the door.

Her insides jumped a little to see Ben as she opened the door. A Valentine's surprise, that's what she needed. To feel his arms around her and hear him tell her it would be okay. He would make jokes and they would laugh at it somehow. She smiled, expecting him to step forward to kiss her, but there was something wrong in his face.

He was frowning.

No, more than that.

He looked furious.

Frankie stepped back into her hallway, a thought occurring to her. 'Don't you have Charlie tonight?'

'Not any more,' he said, moving past her into the lounge, then turning to face her. 'Where were you? You said you'd pick him up from school.'

'I was working – my mum picked him up.' Frankie desperately tried to think back to the brief conversation she'd had when she arrived home. Charlie hadn't been here and her mum hadn't mentioned him. But she wouldn't have *forgotten* him. She didn't do things like that. 'She said she would.'

'Well, that's not the message I gave school – I said *you'd* be picking up.'

'What's the difference?' Frankie didn't understand.

'The difference is, they phoned Jo.'

'Oh, shit.'

'Exactly.' He nodded. 'I can't believe you just palmed the boys off on your mum and didn't even mention it to me.'

Frankie hadn't intended to not mention it. Although, now she thought about it, it had never occurred to her that he would need to know.

'Surprisingly, Jo didn't want her ex-husband's girlfriend's mother – *who she's never met* – to pick up her son. She left work and picked up Charlie and then phoned me and shouted for an hour.' He sighed, running both his hands through his hair in exasperation. 'So, no, I don't have Charlie tonight any more.'

Frankie desperately wanted to defend herself – how was she to know he hadn't told Jo? Why didn't he just tell school Charlie was going home with Liam? – but she knew none of that mattered. This was exactly why she had thought getting involved with Ben was a bad idea: Charlie was everything to him. 'God, I'm sorry,' she said, her voice sounding thin and pathetic even to her.

'You can't do this, Frankie. You can't just hand responsibility over to your mum when things get difficult – especially without telling me.' He sank down onto the futon. 'Why didn't you just say you couldn't do pick-up? Why would you take on an extra shift?'

She sat next to him, feeling panic banging around in her chest.

'I don't… I'm sorry,' she said, feeling useless, waiting for him to speak. After a moment, he stood up abruptly and headed for the front door. 'Ben?' she said, following him.

'I can't do this now, I need to think.' He didn't even turn to look at her as he pulled the door shut behind him.

Frankie leant against the door. She wanted him to come back. She wanted to fix the mess, but couldn't think of anything that wouldn't just make the whole thing worse.

She slid down the door until she was sat on the floor, hugging her legs and resting her head on her knees.

She was ruining everything.

It was bad enough that she had failed to help Tina and lost her job into the bargain, but that was nothing compared to this. She had failed to help Ben, which meant he might lose Charlie and she was going to lose him because of it.

Why was she always such a failure?

So much for Alison's sodding Happiness Project.

CHAPTER TWELVE

Alison was always slightly apprehensive about trying out a new restaurant, especially on a busy night like Valentine's Day, but she had checked the online reviews and asked around in the playground and everyone seemed very positive about Erawan. Especially about their pad Thai, which was really the most important thing.

'This seems nice,' she said as she and Simon were shown to their table.

'Uh-huh,' Simon said, pausing while she chose her seat, then taking the other one for himself. He glanced only briefly at the menu before putting it down. While Simon was fond of reminding people that he had spent a year travelling around Southeast Asia after university, Alison found it difficult to equate that with the man she knew who would only ever order a pad Thai. She looked over the menu, aware that while she was genuinely considering what to order, Simon had taken out his phone and was tapping away at the screen. She folded her menu and placed it in front of her, waiting for him to finish.

'Sorry,' he said, without looking up. 'Just replying to that email from the solicitor about Mum's house.'

Alison said nothing. She'd always found silence a far more effective weapon than complaining. She looked around the busy restaurant, taking in the white elephants painted on the walls, contrasting with the heavy wooden furniture. The entrance was a golden archway wrapped in fairy lights and Alison now noticed similar arches at various points around the main room, dividing it up and sheltering booths behind. She wished she'd asked for one of the booths around the edge, now. They looked quiet and intimate – perfect for a Valentine's Day meal. Their table was right in the middle and despite the best efforts of the nearest arch, it did not feel at all cosy.

'Okay, done.' He placed the phone on the table and looked around. 'Nice place. How did you find it?'

High praise from Simon. 'Someone at school mentioned it.'

'Those mums are like some kind of mafia,' he said. 'I bet you could find a number for a hitman from them if you wanted.'

Alison tutted. 'They're not all mums,' she said. 'Plenty of dads around.' Then she realised that sounded like a dig at his absence. 'But yes, I probably could. Best not to get on the wrong side of me, dear.'

He smiled.

A waitress appeared at their table with a plate of food. 'I've got one massaman and one fish cakes,' she said, looking at them expectantly.

Alison and Simon looked at each other and then back at the waitress.

'We haven't ordered yet,' Alison said.

'Oh,' the waitress said, looking confused. 'These aren't yours?'

Simon shook his head with a good-natured laugh and she turned and left.

'We should have taken them,' Simon said. 'They looked good.'

'But it wasn't a pad Thai,' Alison pointed out.

He shrugged. 'I would've survived.'

She was about to roll her eyes at him when the waitress reappeared, flustered. 'Sorry, what *did* you order?'

'We haven't ordered yet,' Alison said again. This didn't bode well. Nowhere in the reviews had it mentioned problems with customer service. She began to twist the rings on her left hand nervously.

'Oh, right, sorry.' The waitress flipped out her notebook and looked at Alison, poised to write down the order.

'I'll have the pork…' Alison tilted the menu to point to the unpronounceable name and the waitress nodded.

'I'm going to try the monkfish massaman,' Simon said avoiding Alison's look of surprise. 'And a bottle of the Pinot Gris, please.'

'Who are you and what have you done with my husband?' she whispered across the table once the waitress had left.

Simon smiled again. 'I am trying something new,' he said proudly. 'You can't go through life just being safe, can you? Life's boring if you always know what you're going to get.'

She frowned. This did not sound like Simon. He was the poster boy for being safe and only ordering things he knew. She looked at him, wondering if this was a new change brought on by his mum's death. He hadn't mentioned her since the funeral, doing a good job of pretending he was fine, but Alison knew he couldn't be, not really. Not after that.

'How's work?' she asked, knowing he wouldn't really talk about it, but hoping it would lead to a conversation about how he was coping.

'You know, same old…' he said, evasively, shaking his head. 'Anyway, how's netball going?'

It wasn't worth trying to push it, she thought, allowing him to change the conversation. 'I only went once.'

'Did you? Where were you on Tuesday, then?' He looked genuinely puzzled.

'That was the running club.'

Simon was about to say something when he was interrupted by the waitress appearing with the wine and beginning to pour it into the wine glasses on the table.

'But—'

'That's not—'

The waitress stopped pouring and looked from Simon to Alison and back again, eyes wide, reminding Alison of a startled cat.

'I don't think that's what we ordered,' Simon said, far more gently than Alison would have.

'Pinot Gris?'

'Pinot Gris is white,' he said, gesturing to the red wine she had poured into Alison's glass. 'I think that might be Pinot Noir?'

'Oh!' Her hand flew to her mouth as she twisted the bottle to take a closer look. 'I'm sorry, I… it is! I'm so sorry.' She snatched up the glass, turned and ran.

'Poor girl,' Simon said, looking after her.

'Incompetent waitress,' Alison corrected. 'Still feeling good about trying something new? Although I think there's quite a good chance you'll end up with a pad Thai anyway.'

He nodded a slight agreement. 'This running club, then. What's that about?'

'Well, I was chatting to a couple of mums at school and they mentioned this group was starting up and you know I'm trying to live a healthier lifestyle, so I thought this might be a good idea.' And it meant she could salvage that New Year's resolution and make real headway with her Happiness Project. Alison had read that most people's resolutions fail by the end of January, so she was feeling a little smug that she was not 'most people'.

'You just meet as a group to go running?'

She nodded. 'It's nice. There's a fast group and a beginners' group, and the route is already planned, so I don't have to worry about where we're going.'

Many of the women at the running group were familiar from the school gates, or faces she'd seen around the village. The woman looking after the beginners, who was short and broad, with such a strong Newcastle accent that Alison only caught the gist of what she was saying, had looked familiar and it had taken Alison most of the session to recognise her as working in the hairdresser's.

And Alison didn't seem to be hideously slower than anyone else.

And no one had mentioned Becky or Jo, so she was hopeful neither of them would get wind of it and turn up next week. The waitress approached again with a fresh bottle of wine and a glass and Alison and Simon exchanged a look. The bottle was held out for inspection this time and only once Simon had agreed it was the Pinot Gris did the waitress pour it.

'So, you'll go again?' asked Simon, once the waitress had gone.

'Yes, it's very sociable, actually.'

He laughed. 'You'd probably go faster if you weren't gossiping.'

'We're not gossiping,' she snapped back, stung. She'd been too out of breath to speak for most of the route. 'They're being encouraging and taking my mind off how much I hate running.'

He laughed. 'I'm sorry, I just… Why are you doing this again?'

'This is me "trying something new".' She decided to use his own words against him.

'It's hardly breaking out of your comfort zone, though, is it?' He smiled as he shook his head. 'I mean, running. Not *very* different.'

Why did that matter? she thought. She wasn't meant to be breaking out of her comfort zone, she was just trying to do some exercise.

Out of the corner of her eye, Alison saw the waitress approaching with a tray of dishes. *Please bring us the right food.* The waitress looked nervous as she placed the bowls and plates down on the table.

'The monkfish… and the pork… and your jasmine rice.' She picked up the tray, holding it like a shield against herself. 'Okay?'

'Yes,' said Alison, unable to keep the note of surprise out of her voice.

'Thank you,' Simon said.

Alison waited for the waitress to leave before looking across at Simon. 'Still glad you left your comfort zone?'

He said nothing but took a deep breath and began to spoon the rice and curry onto his plate. 'There's potato in this,' he said, frowning.

'Good to try something different,' she reminded him, trying not to sound too smug. 'Mine's delicious.' At least the reviews had been right about something.

He dug his fork into a mound of rice and sauce and ate it. She watched his expression as he chewed. She was torn between wanting a husband who was more adventurous in his food and one she was familiar with.

'S'good,' he said through his mouthful. 'You'd like this, Al.' He loaded up his fork for her and passed it across the table.

It was good. She passed back his fork with some of her pork dish for him to try.

'So, back to your running group,' he said, after a few moments of silence in which she had really hoped he'd forgotten about it. 'Are you setting yourself a challenge? Are you looking to run a marathon or anything?'

She shook her head. 'Not particularly. I just want to improve my fitness levels.'

'Oh, come on, Al – remember what my mum said at her funeral.'

Alison looked at him, confused. What his mum said *at her own funeral*? Although… Alison had put a *lot* of effort into not listening at Maggie's funeral, so it was entirely possible the celebrant had read something out from Maggie.

'Remember? "Life is for living, not repeating. Get out of your comfort zone and try new things".' He looked at her as though she should know what he was talking about. 'Well, here I am, trying new things – and liking them, too – now it's your turn.'

What could she say to that? 'Simon, I try new things all the time.' She began counting on her fingers. 'I joined the PTA, I'm trying all those new recipes, I went to netball and now I'm going to the running club…' What more did he want?

He sighed. 'Not exactly out there, though, are they?' He gestured with his fork. 'What would my mum have said about them?'

Alison felt herself becoming defensive. 'Maggie would have said lovely things about them. Maggie was never anything other than completely supportive of the things I was doing.' Tears had begun to sting in her eyes, but she blinked them away.

'Sorry, Al.' He reached under the table to place his hand on her knee. 'I didn't mean it like that. I'm just trying to be more like my mum… more *Maggie*. That's what she made me promise and that's what I want to do. For her.'

Alison covered his hand with her own and squeezed it in sympathy at what he was trying to do. And there was a part of her that agreed with him, that remembered Maggie, sitting in her kitchen wearing make-up to hide how ill she looked, imploring her daughter-in-law to 'stop trying to make life fit your ideas and start just living'. At the time, Alison hadn't made any promises. She had still believed that she would be able to do something to fix it all and there was no way she was going to give in and start making silly promises when she could be doing something more practical to help.

But it didn't feel like that now.

As much as she didn't want Simon to be right, he *was*. A running group, a new way of organising the week's meals, even organising the Mother's Day flowers – none of it was very Maggie. It wouldn't fit into the category of 'just living'. And it didn't matter that Alison hadn't actually promised… Maggie had still asked her.

And now she was dead, Alison couldn't argue with her.

CHAPTER THIRTEEN

Frankie was not hiding. She wasn't. She just didn't happen to see Ben on Friday because he was working. And she didn't go in to work because she had already booked Friday off to look after Liam for the inset day before half term. And anyway, given that she'd walked out, there might not be a job at all. And if she just ignored her problems, they might just go away…

Or, more likely, be drowned out by Liam's new game, which appeared to have no rules except saying the words 'poo', 'bum' or 'fart' as many times as possible in each sentence then collapsing with laughter. Frankie was fairly certain it was Xander who had come up with the game, and while quite annoying, it was at least tempered by the fact that Alison would have been horrified by it.

Frankie wondered how she was going to survive a whole day of this. School had made Liam much louder. And the smaller house didn't help. And the lack of Mum's presence.

I bet Alison has a plan for inset days, she thought, closely followed by, *how the hell does Kate do this with two children?* But then again, Frankie wasn't like Alison, with her organised fun, or Kate with her natural mothering skills. She was rubbish at all this. Maybe she should phone her mum and see if they could pop round there for lunch?

No.

She was Liam's mum and she could find a way to entertain him for one day.

'Fancy going to the playground?' she asked him as he came into the kitchen on all fours and growled at her. This pretending to be an animal thing he kept doing was new. Probably also from Xander.

'Woof,' he said, shaking his head. 'Woofy woof woof.'

'Good point.' She nodded, seriously, without any idea what he meant. 'What did you fancy doing, then?'

'Woof woof?'

This could go on a while. 'Yeah, I don't speak doggy, though, so…'

Liam looked confused and tried to rub his head against her ankles.

'How about some TV?'

'Woof!' He leapt up and ran into the lounge to throw himself onto the beanbag, lying on his front and staring expectantly at the TV screen.

'Don't worry, I'll turn it on for you.' Frankie passed him the remote and went to lie on the futon behind him and stare at her phone to drown out the sounds of *Octonauts*.

She'd already had a message from Jeremy to confirm the visit this weekend. This would be the fourth one in six weeks. He was definitely trying to show he was serious. Frankie's worry had changed from a fear he would drift away again to a fear that he wouldn't. That he and Millie would edge their way closer until there really wasn't much room left in Liam's life for a crappy mum like Frankie. Maybe that's why she still hadn't got round to telling Liam that Jez was his dad.

Frankie put her phone down and stared across at her son. He was giggling at something.

'Mum, look!' he said, pointing at the screen.

She grinned as he glanced up at her to check she was looking before returning his gaze to the TV. Frankie felt a strange tightening in her chest as her breath caught in her throat. This parenting thing was weird. At the same time as Liam was being annoying and frustrating and making her sit through mindless telly, he was somehow also awesome, and she didn't want to share him at all with Jez or anyone.

Liam started laughing harder, then farted loudly, which made him laugh even more.

'You're so gross,' said Frankie, shaking her head as she joined in the laughter.

She left him to his cartoons and went to the kitchen to make a coffee. Her phone beeped and she felt a rush of hope that Ben might have forgiven her but it was only her mum telling her about lunch on Sunday. She played with her hair as she tried to think of a way of explaining Ben's absence this time. Maybe Paula would forget she'd said she was going to bring him this week? This was definitely too much thinking.

Ignoring everything was a much better solution.

As she stared at the screen, it lit up with a message from Alison:

Hello! How's everyone's New Year's resolutions going?

Pretty much fucked up, thanks for asking, Frankie thought. Not trusting herself to reply, she deleted the message and went to fill the kettle.

She had only just put the phone down on the counter when it began ringing. There was no caller ID, so Frankie cancelled the call and carried on making her coffee. If only she had biscuits – chocolate Hobnobs solved so much.

Her phone beeped again to signify that someone had left a message.

'Frankie. Hello. It's, um, Erin here. I was just… Could you please give me a ring before your, erm… shift next week, please? Yes. I need to speak to you before you come in. Okay, bye.'

Frankie rolled her eyes. She'd heard that pause before Erin said 'shift', like 'it *would* be your next shift, but don't turn up because you don't have a job any more'. There was no way she was going to phone back just to hear Erin stuttering that she was fired. She'd got the picture; she didn't need telling explicitly.

And she really didn't want to spend time in this house thinking about it.

She sent Kate a text: *God I'm bored – U free this afternoon?*

The reply didn't come through until she had nearly finished her drink.

> *Children going stir crazy. Going to take them up to soft play*
> *– fancy it? I can fit us all in the car if you sit in the back.*

Frankie didn't fancy squeezing into the back of Kate's car, but Liam did love soft play and it would be a small improvement on spending the whole day inside these four walls. What were the chances of this soft play place selling gin, she wondered.

CHAPTER FOURTEEN

Kate spent most of the drive to Leapin' Leopold's looking in her rear-view mirror to where Frankie was squashed between Liam and Amelia and apologising for the size of her car.

'It's still better than my complete lack of car,' Frankie pointed out.

Kate wasn't convinced, though. She had just been trying to be helpful, but this was clearly a terrible idea. If only Frankie's text had arrived before she'd suggested the soft play place to the kids. They'd probably have been fine with just another child to play with. But she *had* already suggested it, and if she'd cancelled that they would have gone into meltdown.

She looked at Liam sitting quietly in the back. She couldn't imagine him ever having a meltdown. In fact, she was quite intrigued to see what he would be like at Leopold's. Was it wrong that she really hoped he would pretend not to hear his mother saying when it was time to go so she had to clamber in after him like Kate's kids did? Everything about Frankie just seemed so… cool. Like she just didn't care, and it all just worked out anyway. Kate felt a small twinge of jealousy and was instantly so consumed with guilt that she had to stop herself from apologising to Frankie again.

'Here we are,' she said instead, pulling into the car park.

They let the kids run off into the soft play, while Frankie bagged a table and Kate bought drinks.

'So, you're not working today, then?' Kate asked as she returned with two mugs.

Frankie grimaced. 'No.'

'Oh?' Kate waited for the rest of the story.

'Well… I was already off today and the start of next week, but there was a bit of a thing at work yesterday and I kind of assaulted my line manager, so I'm not working today or any other day…'

Kate gasped and her hand flew up to her mouth. 'Oh, Frankie!'

'No, no… it's fine, he totally had it coming.'

'Was it the… the one who was a bit of a *you-know-what*?' Kate just couldn't say it.

'Adrian the Prick?' Frankie nodded. 'Aargh. The thing is, I tried so hard not to punch him so many times, but now I wish I'd really punched him. I just pushed him and he barely even stumbled.'

'You don't mean that,' Kate said, shaking her head.

'I bloody do.' Frankie seemed quite vehement. 'Erin – the boss – had just offered me a sort of promotion as, like, an events organiser, and then I found him getting all handsy with the waitress and all I did was push him out of the way.'

Kate couldn't think of anything to say. She couldn't imagine what she would have done in that situation. No, worse, she knew she would probably have been too embarrassed to do anything.

She stared up at the soft play area to find the kids standing on the top level, waving from inside some sort of plastic bubble. As she waved back, she tried not to think about the thin plastic holding up the weight of all three of them. She glanced at Frankie to see if she had noticed the kids, but she had sighed and covered her face with her hands.

'And then, to make things worse, I think Ben and I have split up too.'

'Oh, no! When?'

'Same day. Worst Valentine's Day ever.' Frankie's voice began to crack.

'I'm sorry, Frankie.' Kate fished a tissue out of her bag and passed it across.

'No, I'm fine. I'm *fine*.' Frankie waved the tissue away, recovering herself.

'What happened?' Kate asked.

'I messed up.' Frankie shrugged, sniffed and took the tissue she'd rejected a moment ago. 'Should have picked Charlie up, didn't, Jo got called, she had a go at Ben.'

Kate stayed silent.

'I'm not just a rubbish mum to Liam, I'm a bad "dad's girlfriend" to Charlie.'

'No, of course you're not…'

'And Jez and Millie are coming again tomorrow and they'll be all fun and cheerful and rich.'

Kate cringed inwardly as she realised where this was going. 'No, Frankie, no.' She reached her hand out to grab Frankie's. Frankie turned to Kate, an exhausted expression etched over her face. This was too much for the poor girl, she looked completely overwhelmed. 'You are doing fine, it's just a bad week.' Kate smiled, trying to think what Frankie would say to her. 'It doesn't matter how rich and cheerful they are – you are *much* more fun.' She was rewarded by a grin from Frankie. 'And you're his mum. No one can replace you… No one could even *try*.'

She looked steadily at Frankie, hoping her words were sinking in.

'Would you like another coffee?' she asked, noticing Frankie looking wistfully at her empty cup.

'Yeah – my turn to get them. Another decaff for you?'

Kate nodded, watching Frankie slope off towards the counter, arms crossed tightly over her chest. She thought back to when she'd first met Frankie and found her confidence intimidating. Now she understood that hidden beneath her fierce attitude, Frankie was fragile.

'Here.' Frankie returned with the drinks and two bars of chocolate.

'Perfect,' Kate said, choosing the Flake and beginning to unwrap it immediately.

'Did you get the text from Alison earlier?' Frankie asked, rolling her eyes as she took her annoyance out on her Snickers.

'Don't be like that,' Kate said, gently. 'It's just her way of keeping us on track with her whole Happiness Project.'

'Yeah, but I'm not on track, am I?' Frankie laughed. 'I've crashed off at the corner and mown down several spectators on the way.'

Kate smiled, trying to avoid commenting.

'How's yours going, anyway?' Frankie asked, raising one eyebrow. 'Y'know, that whole more relaxed pregnancy thing?'

'Oh, it's okay.' Kate wasn't even sure if she was lying or not.

'What does that mean?'

Kate sighed. 'Well, I'm definitely more relaxed about this pregnancy, but my friend Natalie keeps reminding me of what I *should* be worrying about, so then I just feel bad about being *too* relaxed, if that makes sense?'

'Maybe you'd do better if you stopped seeing her?'

'I can't do that – she's my friend.'

Frankie laughed. 'Then you need to tell her to sod off when she starts spouting her chuffing rules about what you should be doing.'

Kate nodded, although both of them knew that she never would.

'Seriously,' Frankie continued, 'if she's shitting on your plans, you either need to tell her to stop or cut her loose.'

Now she just sounded like someone who had watched too much *Jeremy Kyle*.

'Y'know, in your own words, of course.' Frankie grinned.

Maybe she had a point? Kate thought. When she went to Natalie's for dinner tomorrow night, she would try and let the pregnancy talk just wash over her, rather than worry about whether she was getting it right or wrong.

'Should we reply to Alison, then?' Frankie looked worried again.

'I think we should…' *Although neither of us want to have to admit we're not up to Alison's high standards,* Kate thought. 'Just something vague – we're allowed to be struggling as long as we're still persevering, surely?' She fished in her bag for her phone. 'How about, *Not entirely going to plan, but…*'

'Back on track soon?' Frankie suggested.

'Yes,' Kate said, typing the message in and sending it. 'Because we will be, won't we? You'll sort out the job thing, or get another one, won't you? And I'm going to be totally Zen about the next five months and not get stressed about what Natalie says, *at all*.'

'Exactly.'

Kate smiled at Frankie, feeling a little lighter already.

CHAPTER FIFTEEN

Spending a day with Kate had put Frankie in a better mood. She woke up on Saturday with less of a sense of dread than she was expecting. When she saw Jez's car pull up outside the house mid-morning, she felt strangely Zen and wondered if perhaps Kate's New Year's resolution was rubbing off on her.

She had thought long and hard about how to approach the 'd-word', as she called it. Ideally, she would just drop it into conversation and Liam would start using it without realising, but Frankie knew it would never actually work like that.

'Liam,' she had said to him over breakfast that morning.

He pulled his gaze away from the cereal packet covered in cartoon animals to look up at her.

'Dude, do you know why Jez comes to see you?'

Liam looked confused. 'He's your friend.'

Well, that was a start. She took another mouthful of toast to put off the revelation. 'Okay, here's the thing: he's your dad.' She held her breath and waited.

Liam frowned and then shrugged and carried on eating his cereal.

Frankie had continued to wait, but Liam just carried on eating his breakfast and staring at the cereal box.

'Can I watch TV now?' he'd said once he'd finished.

'Okay.' Well, that was that, then. Maybe the questions would come later? Once again, Frankie wished she knew what she was doing. Perhaps she shouldn't have told him yet? Or maybe she should have told him when Jez first came to visit? How were you supposed to know what to do when it was all so complicated?

When Jez and Millie arrived, Liam seemed more reserved than usual. Frankie suggested going for a walk and was persuaded by Liam to make it a walk to the park. She watched closely as Liam and his dad walked in front, Jez reaching for his son's hand and uncertainly, withdrawing it quickly when Liam didn't immediately take it. A few minutes later, he tried again and this time Liam took his hand.

'This means a lot to Jeremy, you know,' said Millie, quietly, next to her.

Frankie felt that she should dislike this woman who would become Liam's… well, his dad's girlfriend, but it was hard to do when the woman was just so *nice*. Admittedly, she had a strange fashion sense, wearing polo neck tops under shirts, and a very posh accent, but once you got past that… She insisted on being called Millie, despite Jez introducing her as Mariella, and stayed quiet, just a sweet and inoffensive presence in the background.

'We were wondering…' Millie's voice was lost as Liam made a whooping noise and began running towards some figures on the playground.

Frankie squinted and then the outlines became clearer – it was Ben and Charlie. For a moment, she felt happy – a smile breaking out on her face – before she remembered. She felt a stinging pain in her chest as she looked at Ben and he looked at her and they said nothing.

Liam pulled Jez towards them, before announcing loudly, 'This is my dad.'

Ben's eyes flicked from Frankie to Jez and then back again, eyebrows raised, but she wasn't sure if his surprise was because he hadn't expected Jez to look like that or because he hadn't expected her to have told Liam yet.

'Hi, Jeremy Hawksworth.' He held out a hand, formally, as though they'd met at a meeting.

Ben took slightly longer than he should have done to reply, slowly turning to look at Jez and pulling his hand out of the pocket of his jacket to shake hands. 'Alright, *Jeremy*. I'm Ben. I'm… Charlie's dad.'

'He's mum's friend, too.' Liam looked solemnly at Jez as he spoke.

'Oh, I see.' Jez raised one eyebrow at her and nodded. He turned back to Ben and gave him a winning smile before gesturing to Millie to join him. 'Nice to meet you, then, Ben. And can I introduce my fiancée, Mariella Cresswell?'

'Millie, please.' She stepped forward and shook Ben's hand too.

Frankie wanted the ground to swallow her up. Now they had met Ben, they would ask if she was seeing him and she would have to tell them about that failure too. 'Dude, why don't you have a little play with Jez and Millie and I'll see you back at the house?'

Millie was nodding furiously, while Jez had his caught-in-the-headlights look. *If he wants to see his son, he should bloody well take a bit of responsibility for him*, Frankie thought. She spun round and headed out of the playground, ignoring Ben shouting her name. He only shouted twice. Probably felt he should. If he actually wanted to talk to her, he could have caught her up easily, but he didn't.

Frankie felt her insides ache as she left, stopping as soon as she was out of sight of the swings.

She shouldn't have left Liam with Jez. What if they didn't come home? Why had she been so stupid? Why couldn't she just cope with a few awkward minutes with Ben? So what if it hurt? Real mums did painful shit for their kids, didn't they?

Standing slightly hunched, next to the hedge, Frankie waited, shivering beneath her hoodie. Having left, she couldn't exactly go back, or even risk being seen hanging around, but she couldn't just abandon Liam. Every so often, she risked a quick peek over the top at the playground. Eventually, she saw the group of five separate as the men waved goodbye, Charlie and Ben heading towards the far gate while the other three came towards where she was standing. Not wanting to be caught, she walked quickly back towards her house, keen to be round the corner and out of sight before they emerged onto the pavement.

CHAPTER SIXTEEN

Despite what she had told Frankie yesterday, Kate was not feeling Zen about the meal at Natalie's. Instead, she found herself worrying over silly little things.

Earlier, worrying about what to wear, Kate had flicked through the items in her wardrobe, hoping to find something she'd forgotten, but there was only her mum uniform and much of that no longer fitted over her pregnant stomach anyway. So she was wearing a plain top and her cleanest maternity jeans with an old necklace and hoped that was good enough. *Of course it would be good enough for her friend*, she thought, giving herself a mental kick.

When he came upstairs to get changed, Matthew said, 'You look lovely tonight.'

See, she told herself, *you don't need to worry.*

'Are you sure you're okay doing this?' she asked him. She was also worried that asking Matthew to go for dinner with Nick's ex-girlfriend and her new fiancé was asking him to betray his friend. But, despite his initial reaction to River, he seemed keen to go.

'I'm sure,' he said, reassuringly.

Well, if she was honest with herself, it was Kate who wasn't sure how she would cope with the evening, given Natalie's recent behaviour. Kate wasn't looking forward to being judged. *Be Zen*, she reminded herself. It didn't matter if Nat had a different approach to her pregnancy, she would just let it wash over her.

At least it had been easy to find a babysitter. As soon as she had mentioned it, Alison had looked up the date on her phone and added it to the calendar. Admittedly, when Kate had told the kids who was looking after them, they had pulled faces and complained that Xander's mum was 'scary' and remained a bit sulky even after she had pointed out that they would be in bed before Alison arrived.

'Have a lovely time,' Alison said as she waved them out of the door.

Once they were sat in the car, Kate couldn't help but ask Matthew, 'You really don't think Nick will mind?'

'No… he's not mentioned Natalie for ages. He's still seeing that woman – Abigail, I think? – and it seems to be going well. Did I tell you he's ducked out of the last three training runs?'

'Oh… no.'

'Yeah. Honestly, he might not be up for the marathon now.'

Kate tried not to look too pleased. When Matthew had started running in the autumn, it had been a lot of short runs, supporting Nick while he was going through a tough time after his break-up with Natalie. But more recently he'd been out for hours at a time. Hours where children needed entertaining and feeding and cleaning up after.

Very soon, they were driving into the village of Cheadbridge. Natalie had described the location of River's cottage perfectly and they pulled onto the gravelled area to the side of the house next to an old Land Rover.

Taking a deep breath, Kate tried to will some positivity into her thoughts. After all, she reminded herself, her New Year's resolution was to try and enjoy this pregnancy, so an evening with Natalie might really help. She could almost see Alison nodding in agreement.

'How do we get in?' Matthew asked.

Kate shook her head. 'There's a gate round there.' She led the way back onto the pavement, through the little wooden gate and followed the path between the raised vegetable beds up to the white-painted stable door. *No backing out now*, she thought as she raised her hand and knocked.

The door was pulled open almost immediately and Natalie grabbed her and hugged her tightly, leaning forward to avoid bumping bumps, before Kate had a chance to say anything.

'Kate – you're here!' Natalie took her by the hands and led her into the room. 'River, they're here,' she called over her shoulder, before turning back to nod a greeting to Matthew.

They had come straight into a huge kitchen, with bifold doors opposite them running the length of the room. Next to the doors there was a huge yellow range in what must once have been a fireplace. In the middle of the room was a big scrubbed wooden table with mismatched chairs. Kate could see Nat's seemingly effortless style everywhere, from the botanical prints on the wall to the ceramic vases on the windowsill, and she wondered what the place had looked like before she moved in.

'This is lovely,' Kate said, shrugging off her coat as Matthew handed over a bottle of wine.

'Oh… thank you.' Nat's words were polite, but the tone and her frown screamed that their choice of gift was every kind of wrong.

'Sorry,' said Matthew. 'I never know what sort of wine to buy, but you can't go wrong with Australian, can you?'

'Australian what?' River said, appearing through a door just behind where Matthew had been standing.

'Oh, nothing,' Natalie said.

'Wine,' said Matthew at the same time.

'Oh, don't get me started on the air miles on Antipodean wine,' River said, smiling. Kate noticed Natalie place the wine on the counter behind her where River couldn't see it. 'I could rant all day. Sorry…' he waved an apology. 'I mean, hello, you must be Matthew.' They shook hands before River turned to Kate, embracing her with a kiss on both cheeks. 'And Kate, what a delight to see you again.'

'Hello, River,' she said. 'Sorry we're late.'

'What's time between friends?' he said, giving her an intense look before breaking into a smile. 'Let's get some drinks. Kate – we've got homemade lemonade, coconut water, carrot juice or almond milk. What do you fancy?'

A small glass of white wine? 'Oh, um… just normal water will be fine.'

'Okay. Matthew? We've also got wine and beer.'

'Beer sounds good.' He looked across at Kate, raising his eyebrows. It was a familiar look – *are you driving?* – and she nodded slightly.

'Good man. I've just got these bottles from a mate with an eco-brewery down the road. They use reed beds to filter the water back for reuse and it uses seaweed finings, so it's vegetarian.' As he spoke, River reached into a cupboard and retrieved a couple of bottles, pouring them carefully into the glasses Natalie had put out.

Kate watched her husband trying the beer and wondered what he was thinking. Was he really interested in an explanation of the brewery's ecological stance? He looked like he was listening and asking questions, making an effort to befriend River. That was good. *I need to be more like that*, she thought.

'Would you like to see the nursery?' Natalie asked, linking arms with Kate.

She nodded and allowed herself to be led through a door and up the stairs, leaving the two men deep in conversation over brewing methods. They went through the first door on the left into a little room with an oval-shaped cot against the middle of a wall that had been painted a soft grey. The big sash window was half-covered by a floor-length curtain with a pattern of dark grey and orange leaves falling down it, to match the white framed pictures of different safari animals silhouetted against an orange background.

'Orange and grey,' Kate said. 'That's just lovely.' It was not the usual choice of colours for a baby's room, but somehow Natalie's homemade additions made it look cheerful and relaxed.

She remembered all those times when they'd sat chatting and making things together – Kate sewing, Natalie upcycling some piece of old furniture. She missed having a friend to share those things with.

Natalie stood in the doorway, stroking her compact bump. 'We've only just finished it. I had to talk River into it. I think really,' she glanced at Kate with a slightly guilty expression, 'he wouldn't have bothered with a separate nursery, he'd have just had the baby in our room.'

'Oh?'

'He's keen on this contact parenting, where you try and maintain as much physical contact with your child as possible, so we're going to do co-sleeping and baby-wearing… and breastfeeding, obviously.'

Obviously.

Kate smiled and told herself that this was not Natalie making a statement about Amelia being bottle-fed. Maybe, with her new *laid-back about mothering* Zen, Kate would be inspired to try things like baby-wearing (once she'd found out what that was).

'And look at this.' Natalie proudly held up an almost blank sheet of paper on which Kate could read: *I don't need medical interventions. I can do this myself.*

'What's that?'

'That's our birth plan.'

'Oh.' Good for them. *Be Zen*, she reminded herself. *Maybe they would get exactly what they wanted.*

'Although, really I'd like to free birth. I mean, pregnancy and birth has become so *medicalised*, hasn't it? I don't want to be one of those mothers who just hands over control to doctors. Labour should be a verb. Labour*ing*. Active, you know?'

Kate couldn't think what to say. It was as though Natalie had forgotten she was talking to someone who had been through labour twice. And while Kate was well aware that there were many different ways women might end up giving birth, Natalie still seemed intent on telling her the 'right' way to do it.

'Umm, yes.'

'And free birthing is just a way to step back from all that interference and say, "I'm not a mum who's afraid of hard work".'

From downstairs came the sound of bells, preventing Kate from asking what free birthing actually was.

'Ah – time to eat.'

When they returned to the kitchen, Matthew was already sitting at the table with a plate of green leaves in front of him. Kate took the chair next to him, while Natalie and River sat down opposite, grinning at each other.

'Seeing as we have got two beautifully blooming bumps here today, we've gone all out pregnancy-friendly,' River said, taking Natalie's hand. She leaned forward and they kissed for slightly longer than Kate felt comfortable watching.

'This is a kale salad, with dried apricots, figs, barley and toasted almonds. Enjoy.' River brandished his fork and began to eat.

'Very nice.' Kate noticed Matthew had spoken before he ate anything.

Natalie and River smiled at each other as they ate, nodding in silent conversation. River brushed his hand gently against her arm and Natalie touched his knee.

'Kate tells me you work in a Fairtrade shop?' Matthew said.

'Well, I run Just Decent with a couple of mates, but we also have a band, so we do quite a few gigs with that, and I have a blog which keeps me busy too.'

'A blog?' Kate asked.

'"Living with the Earth", it's called,' Natalie said, placing her hand over River's and looking up at him proudly. 'It's all about how to try and make choices that not only don't damage the environment, but also help us to live in harmony with nature. It's got quite a big following, now. Companies have started sending him things to review.'

'Oh, that sounds… good.' Kate said.

'It must be great being able to find work that fits so completely with, erm… your values,' Matthew said and Kate was grateful that he was able to be pleasant to River, given the Nick situation.

The main course was also, as River called it, 'pregnancy-friendly', and Kate wondered if tonight was special, or if Natalie really had completely changed her diet.

'So, this pan-fried salmon has lots of healthy fats for you, and the leeks and lentil mix underneath is just packed full of fibre and protein,' River announced as he laid plates in front of Kate and Natalie.

'River caught this salmon himself.' Natalie turned to kiss him again as he put down the final plates and took his seat. 'Mostly we eat vegan food, but he does eat meat and fish he's killed himself, so he knows it left the world in a way that aligns with our values.'

'You won't be caught out with horse meat lasagne, then,' Matthew said, laughing.

'No, no, definitely not.' River smiled politely. 'So, Matthew, what is it you do?'

'I'm a teacher,' he replied.

'Oh, now that really is a calling. Well done, mate, well done. What do you teach?'

'Geography. In fact, I had some news at work this week.' Kate turned to look at him, surprised, but he gave her only the briefest of glances before he spoke again. 'One of my colleagues has unfortunately gone off on long-term sick leave, and I'm acting head of house for the next term. So now I'm a Geography teacher and a pastoral lead.'

Kate continued to stare at him, struggling to find her Zen. He seemed entirely unaware that he had dropped this news on her in front of people – well, *a* person at least – that she barely knew. Why wouldn't he have spoken to her about this before it was all finalised? *Surely he'd had time to think it over before he accepted the job?*

Finally, he turned and smiled at her and she gave small smile back (she didn't want Natalie and River to think they were arguing) before staring down at her plate.

'Congratulations, mate,' River said.

By the time dessert had appeared (an avocado and chocolate mousse that was apparently high in folate and potassium), Kate was barely clinging on to the last of her Zen and just wanted to go home to bed. She was beginning to feel incredibly tired.

'I can't believe next time I see you will be at the wedding,' Natalie said, hugging her again, while Matthew and River shook hands.

'Gosh, yes, I suppose it will be,' Kate said. 'Are you all organised for that?'

Natalie grinned. 'I think so. Not so much to do, really.' She readjusted her scarf slightly, 'I'm so glad you're going to be there.'

Kate smiled at her friend. This whole pregnancy and relationship were new to Natalie – *of course* she was going to be utterly absorbed by it. And maybe, sometimes, that sounded like Nat was judging her. But she was still the friend who'd been there to celebrate when Kate had first found out she was pregnant, and had listened to Kate's worries over everything. The least she should be doing now was offering Natalie the same support.

'If you need anything,' she said. 'Anything for the wedding or anything with the pregnancy, just ask. I'll help any way I can.' As she spoke, she realised that she really meant it. 'Any time. Absolutely. Just call.'

Kate followed Matthew back through the front garden and round to the car. She reversed off the drive without a word, not sure how to begin to explain how she was feeling, about the meal, or Natalie's determination to be an ultra-natural parent, or the fact that Matthew hadn't spoken to her about his promotion.

'You're very quiet,' Matthew said, warily.

She glanced across at him and realised that after all this time, he had learned how to read her.

'Well, this new job…' she started, still not sure exactly what to say.

'Umm…'

'You didn't mention it… before.' She was grateful to have to watch the road, unable to scrutinise his facial expressions and worry about what they might mean.

'Before what?'

He wasn't being deliberately obtuse, she reminded herself. 'Before you told Natalie and River. Or… before you took the job.'

'Ah, sorry.' He paused and she glanced across at him briefly. He was looking contrite. 'I couldn't say no, Kate.'

'I know.' And she did know. Everyone could rely on Matthew to do the right thing, to help out when someone was sick. He would never let his colleagues or students down. 'I just wish you'd mentioned it to me first.'

He twisted round in his seat so that he was facing her. 'But the extra money's good, right? I mean, we will need to start looking for a bigger house and buying baby bits again quite soon.'

She nodded.

'And it's only for a month or so,' he continued. 'Just until Mike is feeling better and then it'll get a bit less exhausting.'

She returned his smile, looking deeply into his pale blue eyes. She believed him. It was going to be hard work for a while, but it was the right decision. For both of them.

CHAPTER SEVENTEEN

Frankie stood staring at the aisle of costumes feeling entirely out of her depth. In the space of five seconds, she'd gone from feeling smug that she'd remembered to get a costume for World Book Day to realising she had no idea what the rules were about this. Liam was walking up and down, stroking the costumes with a thoughtful expression.

'Can I go as Ironman?' he asked, pulling on the leg of the costume.

'Is that a book?'

'Xander's got a book of Ironman.'

Did that count? Alison or Kate would know, she thought, getting out her phone to text them.

> *World Book Day – I remembered! – is it just any character from any book?*

'Mum, what's the one with the big ears?'

Kate would probably have made a costume. Alison would have been planning it for weeks, probably buying a costume and then adding accessories to make it amazing. For a moment, Frankie felt hideously jealous of the pair of them. How did they manage all this stuff? Keeping up with the letters from school, remembering all the dress-up days and the 'bring a cardboard tube into school' or 'take a photo of something for our display' requests. They probably never forgot to send something in for the cake sale. And they never left their boyfriend's son abandoned at school because they didn't have the relevant permission to ask someone else to collect him.

She felt the embarrassment of her stupidity surge through her again. How had she let it happen? Because she was shit at this. Who was she trying to kid? She was suddenly too hot, standing in the supermarket surrounded by synthetic fibres.

'I want this one.'

Frankie saw Liam pulling on a dragon costume. 'What book is that?'

He shrugged, but carried on trying to pull it down.

'Hey, dude, let it go.' She took it off him and hung it back up. 'How about Mr Twit?' she asked, reading the label on the next one. 'That's a book. Or... Tweedledum?'

Liam shook his head, screwing up his nose at both of her ideas.

Frankie's phone beeped to show Alison had replied to her text.

School says no Disney, no superheroes, preferably not from a film, must be an age-appropriate fiction book, ideally an animal character to fit the topic. No need to buy a costume (they say!) homemade is fine.

'Okay, there are some rules,' Frankie said, following Liam to where he was looking at a sparkly princess costume. 'Basically, you need to be an animal. Did you see any animals?'

'Paw Patrol,' he shouted, pointing at a dog in uniform costume.

'That's TV, not a book.'

'I've got a colouring book of Paw Patrol.' With his eyes wide, he nodded so vehemently his whole body moved.

'Not enough words in a colouring book, dude. How about this fox? Or a crocodile? Or...' As he continued to frown, she looked around desperately. 'Do you have a book with a dragon in?'

The unexpected negotiations, along with visits to the books section to try and find a book with a dragon in, meant the quick trip to the supermarket was not, in any way, actually quick. By the time they had got home and walked round to her mum's house, they were more than half an hour late for Sunday lunch.

'Here they are,' Paula said, opening the door in her apron. 'We knew you'd turn up eventually.'

'Sorry, Mum,' Frankie said, pushing Liam in front of her, partly as a shield, partly as a distraction. 'Liam's been choosing his World Book Day outfit.'

Paula beamed at her grandson. 'Liam, darling, how lovely to see you.' He hugged her legs with enough force to cause her to stumble before releasing her and running off into the lounge, leaving Frankie and her mother alone in the hallway.

'When we talked about Ben coming—' Paula began, just as Frankie remembered what she had meant to tell her.

'Oh, about that – I… forgot.' She had been doing such a good job of ignoring the Ben problem that she had failed to let her mum know he wouldn't be showing up at lunch.

'Well, I was a bit surprised you came separately,' Paula went on. 'But we've looked after him and Charlie, don't you worry.'

'What?'

Even out of the corner of her eye, she recognised his frame as he appeared in the doorway to the lounge. 'Hey, Frankie.'

'Ben, you're… here,' she said.

'Talk about stating the obvious,' Laura said from the kitchen doorway. 'Mum, something's beeping in here. Do I need to do anything?'

'That'll be the carrots. Excuse me,' Paula said, hurrying away, steering Laura into the kitchen ahead of her, leaving Ben and Frankie alone in the hallway.

Ben took a few steps towards Frankie, but stopped when he saw she had begun to step backwards towards the door. It wasn't that she didn't want to see him. In the three days since they had spoken – or rather since he had shouted at her for messing up – she had missed him constantly. But while she was still avoiding him, she could pretend that it wasn't over. She could pretend that he didn't hate her and she hadn't ruined everything.

'Frankie,' he said, moving closer again.

She turned away from him and was faced with the door. She couldn't run away from this. In fact, short of sticking her fingers in her ears, she couldn't think of any way of escaping what was coming. She took a deep breath and turned back to Ben.

'I didn't expect you'd be here after Thursday,' she said, honestly.

'No, well… I've been thinking a lot about that.'

He was so close she could smell his familiar scent. He filled her view and her mind and all she could think was, *God, this is going to hurt*. She closed her eyes. 'And?'

'Well, I… I realised that I'd been too harsh on you – I know you don't like having difficult conversations, or looking at scary spreadsheets, but if we're doing this, we will need to do both at some point.'

She opened her eyes to find him smiling at her. 'Oh,' she said, feeling the muscles she had tensed to brace against the pain relaxing a little. '*Oh*. I thought…'

'Yeah, you gave that impression.' He reached for her hand, intertwining his fingers with hers. 'You were right, this is… complicated. But we agreed we were going to do this, so we need to, y'know, do this.'

She couldn't help but laugh at the way he nodded his head as he spoke as though he was giving a motivational speech.

'You can laugh, but just so you know, after lunch, we're making you a spreadsheet.'

She shook her head, but he nodded and the only way she could think to argue back was by kissing him. As soon as they touched, she felt the familiar tingling spreading through her body, closely followed by a rush of desire. She pulled away, aware that they were standing in her mum's hall. She gazed into his eyes for reassurance, listening to the sound of his breathing.

'I've kinda missed you,' he whispered.

She frowned. '*Kind* of?'

'It has only been three days.' He smiled. 'But… yes.'

Frankie grinned, feeling a little giddy. 'It has been a fairly shit three days,' she agreed.

'Jeez, sis, get a room.'

At the sound of Laura's voice, Ben jumped backwards and began to blush, causing Frankie to laugh again.

Standing at the bottom of the stairs, they could hear Liam and Charlie in Liam's old room, mostly playing quietly except for the occasional thud and giggles. Ben raised his eyebrows at Frankie, who shrugged, her head to one side. 'I'm sure they're fine.'

Having greeted Laura and Stuart properly (that sort of thing was important to her mum), Frankie was sent to lay the table.

'Do you need a hand?' Ben asked, looking vaguely desperate. Frankie remembered that he'd just spent half an hour alone with her mum, her sister and her sister's boyfriend, and felt she should take pity on him.

'Come on, then.'

Frankie passed him the forks and he followed her around the table as she placed the knives at each setting.

'How's work going?' he asked, interrupting the quiet.

It was a casual question, just making conversation, and Frankie was tempted to gloss over the whole thing, but then remembered this was Ben and she didn't have to pretend with him.

'It's not,' she admitted. 'I sort of had a go at Adrian in front of Erin and now I'm fairly sure I've been sacked. I mean, you would, wouldn't you?'

She glanced up at him to see his reaction, but he seemed to be concentrating on straightening a fork on the table. 'Had a go at him?'

'Gave him a shove… well, sort of pushed him over. I wish I'd punched him, though.'

'This is the bar manager? The one you don't like?'

'Adrian the Prick. Yeah.'

Finally, he stopped fiddling with the forks and looked at her. 'Frankie, why did – what happened?'

'Because… he's a creep.'

'And?' He wasn't going to let her off that easily.

'And he's a bit… gropey.'

'What, with you?' Ben had clenched his jaw and stood very still.

'No – I mean, he tried it, and I stamped on his foot. In my heels.' She stood taller, chin up. 'I can look after myself.'

'I never doubted it.' He smiled, then frowned. 'So why did you have a go at him, then?'

Frankie broke off the eye contact, grabbing the pile of spoons and starting to lay them out. 'Tina came in to do the extra shift on Thursday too, and he's worse with her. He's also her aunt's boyfriend, so *she* didn't want to say anything. I've been trying not to leave her with him, but on Thursday, he followed her to the staffroom and I found him being all creepy and stroking her face and… I pushed him away. But I didn't realise Erin had just walked in too and then Adrian was all "*oh, she's attacked me*" and denying everything I said, so I left.'

'Frankie,' Ben said, but she wasn't ready for his reaction. She didn't want to be told off for acting without thinking or warned that he could press charges or be pitied for losing another job, she knew all that already. Avoiding looking at him, she took the glasses from the sideboard and began to put them on the table.

Much to her annoyance, saying it all out loud had ruined Frankie's plan to ignore the whole mess and a wave of panicked tears was now threatening to drown her. She stared up at the ceiling, willing them away, trying to regain control over her breathing.

'Frankie, are you okay? Wait, stop that a minute.' He came around the table to stand between her and the sideboard, his hand reaching out to her shoulder.

'Frankie, you need to talk to your boss.' She looked at him in surprise. That was not what she'd thought he'd say. He linked his arms behind her waist, gently holding her against him, speaking softly as though she were an animal that would startle easily. 'You can't just walk out, shouting insults. You need to go back and talk. Be… *rational* at her.'

'Rational is not my strong suit.'

He sighed. 'Okay, go and be caring, then.'

She pulled a sceptical face.

'You *are* – you're caring, you just hide it,' he said. 'I'll come with you, if you want.'

'I don't need you to hold my hand,' she snapped.

'No, you don't. That's not what I said.' His tone was sharper than she expected. 'If you want me to, I'll come with you. Or I could look after Liam while you go. But you can't just leave it like this.'

She looked at him, but his gaze was so open and direct it scared her. 'I hate it when you're right,' she said, pouting. Because she did need to make sure Erin heard her side, even though it probably wouldn't stop her getting sacked. And it wouldn't stop her leaving, if Adrian was staying.

Still not exactly winning at Alison's Happiness Project, she thought. This was why New Year's resolutions were a bad idea.

CHAPTER EIGHTEEN

After loading the dishwasher, washing up the pans from dinner and putting the clothes from the dryer into a basket to take upstairs and put away, Kate sat in her corner of the sofa with her sewing and angled the light next to her to shine in her lap.

'I thought you'd finished the dog tutu costume thingy,' Matthew said.

Kate glanced up at him.

He had a baffled expression on his face. No wonder really, she thought, if he was trying to work out how the small scrap of material covered with daisies fitted the rest of Amelia's costume for World Book Day.

'I have,' she said. Amelia had tried the whole outfit on to show him earlier and, to his credit, it only took a moment of him looking mildly panicked at the sight of the dog mask and pink tutu dress before he'd shouted, 'It's that one about the dancing dog!' much to Amelia's delight.

'So, what are you making now?' asked Matthew.

Kate finished pinning the material and held it up to show him. 'Amelia has a wobbly tooth so I was thinking that she'll need something to put it in when it falls out.'

He smiled. 'We can't just wrap them in a tissue?'

'It's just a little bag,' she shrugged. 'I thought it would be nice.'

And truthfully, she enjoyed sitting with needle and thread, concentrating on the tiny movements, with no brain left to worry.

Matthew went back to ticking the exercise book in front of him.

Kate threaded the needle and began to sew along the edge, leaning to the side to catch the light from the lamp. She had to concentrate to stitch neatly, but thoughts still began to whirr away in her mind.

Last night she had looked up River's blog, 'Living with the Earth', and had found herself surprised by just how real and official it all looked. There were different types of articles including reviews, opinions and general musings on life at the shop. She had stumbled upon an interview with one of the shop's stockists, who seemed to be called #isitnew? and who specialised in making dresses from recycled material. Following the links, Kate found their Instagram page, which was covered with before and after photos of not just dresses, but cushion covers, bags and baby blankets, all made from old clothes of some sort. It had been the tiny trinket bag that had caught her eye and she was immediately reminded that she had squirrelled away Amelia's old baby dresses in a box in the loft. She was certain Matthew wouldn't remember the daisy print dress, but with every stitch, Kate felt she was sewing memories into the bag. Every time it was used, it would remind her of the toddler Amelia had been.

She might… *might*, take a photo of it once she had finished.

And maybe, just maybe, she would post it on the Instagram page she'd created.

Kate smiled to herself as she thought, and sewed, silently.

She had almost forgotten she was not alone and jumped when Matthew spoke.

'Am I okay to go to the pub with Nick tomorrow night?' he asked.

'Yes,' said Kate.

'I'm going to tell him we're going to Natalie's wedding.' He looked up and Kate met his eyes in a silent understanding of all the awkwardness that would involve.

'Oh,' she said.

His eyes slid back to his marking.

Somewhere upstairs, Reuben began to cry. Kate looked up from her sewing and listened. He'd never slept as well as his older sister, but sometimes he just cried out in his sleep and then fell silent again. Not this time, though. As the noise continued, she put her sewing to one side and stood up. Matthew looked at her quizzically.

'I'm just going to see what's up with Reuben,' she said, wondering at Matthew's selective hearing.

Having reassured Reuben that his bad dream had gone and hugged him until he was calm enough to fall back to sleep, Kate stood for a moment, watching him. On the bunk above, Amelia rolled, her arm falling over the edge of the bed, and Kate kissed it as she gently placed it back onto the mattress, before heading back downstairs to Matthew.

When she went back into the lounge, he was still marking, occasionally glancing up and chuckling at something on TV before reaching for the next book.

Kate didn't like to interrupt his work, but she felt very lonely in the evenings at the moment. Matthew was still heading out on training runs a couple of times a week. And then there were parents' evenings or school trips or marking to do. The step up in his workload with his new head of house role was significant, but she knew she couldn't really complain about having less company or help at home when he was the one having to do the work to earn the money.

'Is it the weekend after next, the wedding?' Matthew asked, looking up as he peeled off a sticker to put on the page he was marking.

'No, the one after. Why?'

He shook his head. 'Oh, nothing. Just for when I speak to Nick.'

'How do you think he'll take it?'

Matthew shrugged, moving an exercise book to the marked pile and opening the next. 'Did I tell you he keeps ducking out of the runs?'

'Yes, you said you thought he might not do the marathon?'

'Yeah. No way he's gonna do that.'

'Would you still run it without him?' Kate asked.

Matthew shook his head. 'Probably not – when have I got time for that?'

Kate allowed herself a smile.

'I mean, I'd still like to go running…'

She glanced up to see he had stopped marking, pen hovering in mid-air, while he watched her face.

'Oh.'

'Just not… y'know, I'd be fine with just doing 5K round the village a couple of times a week. Maybe the odd longer run now and then?'

Kate realised he was asking for permission. Because although running was something he really wanted to do, he wanted it to be okay with her too. She nodded, smiling.

He's a good man, she thought. It wasn't the first time she'd thought it, but it felt like the first time in a while she'd really felt it. Alison was right: River and Natalie had a nauseating new-couple romance, but she and Matthew had something that had weathered the complications of children and that wasn't nothing.

Setting her sewing to one side for a moment, Kate moved to sit beside her husband, leaning gently against him as she tucked her feet up next to her. He turned to kiss her, before returning to his work with a soft sigh. This was her happy place.

CHAPTER NINETEEN

Frankie kept her head down, avoiding looking at the ivy-clad building as she approached. The sun was bright enough to cause her to squint, but the cold wind made her pull her hoodie tightly around her waist, folding her arms over to pin it in place. If nothing else, she thought, she would leave Heppleton Hall with her coat today and that was a win.

Doing something she didn't want to do did not come naturally to Frankie. She had spent all morning searching for an excuse to get out of going into work – or should that be ex-work? – but could think of nothing that would satisfy Ben.

Now she was so close to the front door, however, the urge to turn and run was stronger than ever and she had to ball her hands into fists to force herself forwards. She was just here to collect her coat. And see Erin. And tell Erin that… well, she was a bit hazy on exactly what she was going to tell Erin. She hoped the words would appear in a coherent form at the right moment.

Pushing the door open, she found Reception deserted. Frankie felt immediately wrong-footed: Erin had always been adamant the reception desk had to be covered, so why wouldn't there be someone there now?

Chewing her lip, she tried to think through her options.

She *could* sneak in, grab her coat and leave, but that didn't feel quite right.

She could just wait for Erin to appear, but who knew how long she'd have to wait for? She was too full of adrenaline to hang around doing nothing.

She could go looking for Erin, but there was a risk of bumping into Adrian, who would be unbearably smug, having won.

Frankie decided to check the small library behind Reception, and walk down to the spa for signs of Erin, but both were empty. It was possible she was somewhere upstairs sorting out the bedrooms, but the most logical next place to look would be the café and bar, where he was sure to be. Frankie took a deep breath, thrust her chin forward and marched with intent, ready to give as good as she got.

But it was Erin, not Adrian, who stood behind the bar.

Erin, who was now looking at her with eyebrows raised behind the dark-rimmed glasses.

Frankie looked back at her, frozen.

'Ah, Frankie,' Erin started, as Frankie said, 'Erm, I – coat…'

Erin gave a perfunctory smile, paused, then nodded. 'Shall we just talk here?' The way Erin spoke, Frankie knew it was not optional. She wanted to get her side of the story in first, but something about her boss's calm and controlled manner made her hesitate, then sit down at the table Erin indicated.

'Right, first of all,' Erin said, sitting down with a notebook that she flipped open to a blank page and a pen she held poised. 'Your actions on Thursday were obviously not acceptable—'

'Oh, fuck this.' Frankie felt the words explode from her as she stood up to leave. There was no way she was going to sit and be told off like this.

'Frankie, please.' Erin held up a hand and gestured for Frankie to take a seat again. 'Let me finish.'

But Frankie didn't sit down. Turning to face Erin, she said, 'I'll just get my coat and then I'll be out of your hair. You can tell Adrian he's won.'

'No, I can't.' Erin spoke quietly, but her tone caused Frankie to stop. 'Adrian… doesn't work here any more.'

The words took a moment to filter past her anger before Frankie actually heard them. 'What?'

'Adrian won't be back. Now, I need to talk to you about what happened on Thursday.'

At that moment, a group of women in dressing gowns appeared and Frankie moved aside to let them pass. Erin stood up to take their order. While she made and served the drinks Frankie moved behind the bar out of the way.

Adrian won't be back.

Why not?

Frankie felt uncertain how to react. Had Erin fired him? It didn't seem likely he'd simply left. Frankie had been all set to defend her actions and argue that Erin needed to do something about Adrian, but now…? Unsure of what to say, she waited for Erin to pick up the conversation when she came back.

'I don't condone violence or aggression, Frankie,' she said, opening the notebook again and using her finger to follow the notes she'd written, 'although I completely understand the motivation behind your actions. In future, I need you to come to me if you have problems with a member of staff, so I can deal with it in an appropriate manner.'

Frankie watched her, still a little in shock at the calm detachment with which she spoke.

'Adrian could have had you arrested for assault, which would have made him the victim, which he clearly was *not* in this case.' Erin looked over her glasses at Frankie. 'I wish you'd spoken to me. I wish Tina had said something… Honestly, I had no idea.'

Seeing the mixture of guilt and embarrassment on Erin's face, Frankie could well believe it.

'Tina said you'd looked out for her, so thank you for that.' She shut the notebook. 'I will need you to write down a statement for us, detailing some of the things you witnessed just in case he makes trouble for us.'

It really didn't sound to Frankie like she was losing her job, but she decided that she needed to be blunt if she wanted to know for certain. 'Have I still got a job or not?'

Erin half-smiled. 'Yes, you still have a job.'

'Which one?'

'Well, things are a bit up in the air at the moment. I still want you to look at those events, but for the next few days, you'll have to be based in here now we don't have a bar manager.' She frowned. 'You're not wearing your uniform.'

Frankie wrinkled her nose. 'I sort of assumed you'd sacked me.'

'I probably should have done.' Erin raised her eyebrows, as though she wasn't entirely certain she'd made the right decision. 'What are you wearing?'

Frankie unzipped her hoodie to reveal an electric blue top with a slash neck which fell over one shoulder to display the turquoise vest beneath. *It could have been worse*, she thought. Erin's face was still impassive, looking Frankie up and down. Finally, she nodded.

'That'll have to do.'

Picking up her notebook, she left Frankie alone in the bar, trying to work out what had happened. Not that she was complaining. Obviously, having a job was a good thing. And this wasn't just any job, it was one she already knew, made better now she would no longer have to put up with Adrian the Prick.

When Tina arrived just before lunch, she launched herself at Frankie, shrieking, 'You're back!'

'I am,' Frankie said, accepting the hug as she admitted that she was also pleased to see Tina again. 'Was there ever any doubt?'

Tina giggled. 'Erin wouldn't tell me whether you were coming back or not.'

'So, what happened with Adrian after I left on Thursday?' Frankie asked.

Tina clapped her hands and gave out a small squeal of excitement. 'Oh, I saw it all. I was supposed to leave, but I didn't want to miss anything. I saw you storm off and then Erin came to find Adrian to ask him what was going on, but he wouldn't really say much – obviously – although he did refer to you as a psycho bitch.'

Frankie considered the description before deciding she was alright with it.

'Then Erin saw me and at that point I thought you'd gone and Adrian was staying and so I got a bit upset and told her about… everything.' Tina looked up sheepishly. 'I'm sorry, I told her about you stamping on his foot that time.'

Frankie grinned. 'I'm quite proud of that.'

'Well, then she was really nice. I mean, she hugged me and everything.'

'Erin hugged you?' She couldn't picture that – she'd never seen the boss be anything other than professional and distant.

Tina nodded. 'Then she properly sent me away, so I missed a bit, but she turned up at Mum's on Friday night in tears. She'd split up with Adrian *and* sacked him.'

It was a hell of a thing to find out, Frankie thought, reassessing her opinion of Erin. Maybe the Tin Man did have a heart after all.

'She was talking about giving up on everything, but Mum talked her round – she's good like that. I guess it's a big sister's job.'

Frankie opened her mouth to ask more, when she saw Erin appear. She nudged Tina, who hurried out from behind the bar and off to the kitchen.

'Do you have that statement for me, Frankie?' Erin asked, eyebrows raised.

Frankie handed over what she'd written on the headed notepaper.

'Okay, thank you.' Erin tucked the sheets into her notebook. 'I've got a couple of people coming in this week about Adrian's old job – I'd like you to meet with them. And also, I wanted to ask if… if you would be interested in the position.'

'What, being in charge?'

Erin pushed her glasses up her nose. 'Yes.'

'Yes,' Frankie blurted out before she had a chance to think about it. 'Wait – what are the hours?'

Erin's blank face fixed her with a stare, giving nothing away. 'We'd need to talk about that, I suppose. Some daytime, but you'd need to cover more evenings, and quite a few weekends, too.'

'Okay,' Frankie said. 'I'll… think about it.'

As she watched Erin walk away she wondered who she was trying to kid. Having her friends pick Liam up once a week was one thing, trying to get cover for childcare at evenings and weekends was a whole different matter. She knew her mum would help out, but suddenly she could see herself being replaced by Paula on one side and Jez on the other – there would be no time left in Liam's life for her.

No, that was not a choice she could make.

The bar manager job would not be hers. Nor would the pay rise that would have gone with it. She sighed.

At least there was still a chance that she might be able to get this events post. Not that it was even a real post, just a possibility that would be a little closer if she could organise something amazing for Mother's Day to impress Erin. And that could change everything.

MARCH

CHAPTER TWENTY

By the time Simon came home, Alison was already in her running gear.

'You've got a stew keeping warm in the oven,' she said, pulling on her coat as she passed him in the hall.

'Hello,' he said, standing in her way to force her to stop. 'Traffic was a nightmare. But I am here before seven thirty, as instructed.' He dropped a kiss onto the top of her head as she ducked around him.

'Yes, dear. Well done.' Clearly, next time she shouldn't give him the absolute latest time she could leave and still get to the running club on time. 'See you later.'

'Okay,' he called after her as she left. 'Have fun at your totally new and life-changing hobby.'

The comment stayed in her head and she found herself silently arguing with him as she drove. Did he have a point about her just sticking to her comfort zone? Should she be attempting a bigger change? No. This *was* something new, and it *was* important, and being healthier would be life-improving, if not actually life-changing.

The thoughts continued to rattle around her brain as she parked up and joined the group who were already gathering in a huddle against the cool of the evening. After the polite greetings and a quick warm-up, they began to jog steadily down the lane, heading to the path through the woods. She had started off in the front with the faster group more by accident than design, but as the pair beside her pulled away and another few passed her, she felt a determination not to get left behind. Forcing herself to keep up with the next runners that caught her up, she didn't even try to join in with what they were saying, focusing only on breathing and running. They quickly reached the rocky path and the group slowed slightly as they watched their steps on the uneven ground. Alison was glad of the distraction: now there was no room in her brain to hear Simon's comments.

It was only once they had nearly finished the route that Alison began to tune back into the breathless chatter around her. After half an hour, they began to slow down and the thoughts crowded back in. Desperate to avoid them, she tried to join in the nearest conversation. The two women were a bit older than her, wearing loose-fitting T-shirts and cropped trousers, one with dyed blonde hair in a limp ponytail, the other with cropped dark hair. Alison had a vague recollection of being introduced to them last week, but couldn't remember their names now.

'It's only a month away now,' the blonde was saying, slowing to a brisk walk. 'I'm hoping it'll get a bit warmer – I don't fancy it in this weather.'

'Are you doing the Glorious too?' cropped hair said, looking to Alison.

'The Glorious?' Alison said.

Blonde hair nodded. 'There's a few of us from this group entering, we're trying to raise money for a cancer charity – you can sign up for it.'

'How far is it?'

'Oh, only 5K.'

Alison knew she could do that, although she'd never done it as part of a race. Maybe that would satisfy Simon's insistence that she *challenged* herself. And, obviously, it would help her to fit into the running group. And raising money for a cancer charity would definitely count as doing something in Simon's late mother's memory.

'I would like that. How do I sign up?'

'I'll get your name on the list when we get back. You'll need to fill in a form and because we're doing a group entry we get a discount; we get subsidised by the club so it's a bargain.'

When Alison arrived home she felt the satisfaction of someone who had managed to tick everything off the 'To do' list. As soon as she had showered, she went into the lounge and took out her Happiness Project notebook.

1. Enrol Xander into after-school clubs

Well, she hadn't known that Reception children weren't *actually* allowed to do the after-school clubs, so not her fault she hadn't managed that one, she thought, as she crossed it out.

2. Eat more fruit and veg, less processed meat, more pulses

She wasn't ready to give up on that one entirely, yet. Although most of her new recipes had been unqualified disasters, she had managed to get Xander to eat oranges, pears and melon, which was twice as many types of fruit as he used to eat. She'd also discovered that he would eat green beans and broccoli as long as he could dip them into tomato ketchup. Every time she saw him do it, she was torn between counting eating vegetables as a success and dying a little that she was the mother with the child who always asked for ketchup. *Maybe*, she thought, *I could make homemade tomato ketchup?*

3. Get fit

Now that one she really *was* winning on.

Her pen hovered over the next line. Should she add another one? Simon's words about *being more Maggie* kept repeating in her mind. No, she decided, putting the pen down. This was her Happiness Project, not his and it was going just fine.

'Quick, go and show Daddy before he leaves.' Alison propelled Xander down the stairs in his costume.

'Wow,' said Simon, coming into the hall and catching sight of Xander on the stairs. 'That is… quite some costume.'

Alison narrowed her eyes at him, trying to work out if he was laughing at her. 'It's World Book Day,' she prompted Xander. 'You're going as…'

'Roly-Poly Bird,' he shouted on cue, jumping the last three steps and trying to do a forward roll to the kitchen.

'No, Xander – get up. You'll ruin the costume.' Alison pulled him to his feet to inspect for damage.

'Impressive,' Simon said, landing a kiss on her lips. 'Have a good book day.'

Despite his words, Alison was not sure he was suitably impressed by the costume. She had bought the blue bird mask and mustard-coloured trousers specially, which had been quite an undertaking., but she was most proud of the way she'd added pink feathers to the top of the mask, and had sewn – without any help from Kate – blue scraps to the arms of a long-sleeved top to make wings. Her favourite part was the long stripy tail feathers she'd made by tying strips of material around a belt. Although right now, with Xander dancing into the kitchen, she suspected those tail feathers might not last the day.

'Let's get a photo of you before breakfast,' Alison called. 'Here, remember to hold the book.'

She positioned him against the kitchen door and took some pictures on her phone, making sure to turn him around to show the back, before uploading them to Facebook with a caption that suggested he had had a hand in both choosing and creating the outfit. Not an out-and-out lie, she reasoned; he hadn't argued when she'd told him he was going to be the Roly-Poly Bird and he *had* been enthusiastic about playing with the scraps of material she'd left on the table.

Alison was relieved to see it wasn't raining this morning. Every other day that week she had had to carry an umbrella on the school run and had already warned Xander that he couldn't get the feathery mask wet, so he wouldn't be able to wear it in the rain. He had subsequently shouted, curled up into a ball on the floor and cried for two minutes. It was definitely going to be easier without the rain.

As they walked to school, Alison looked out for the other costumes arriving. There were quite a few bought costumes, she noticed, with slight disapproval. It seemed a waste of money to spend ten pounds on a costume – and the letter had specified that homemade was fine. *No need to buy something new*, the school had said. Well, she had mostly made do with what they already had and it had only taken a few evenings to create something rather fabulous, even if she did say so herself.

As she arrived in the Reception playground, she saw a few generic animals (three mice, two dogs and four cats) and several *Fantastic Mr Fox* costumes. She waved to Kate, who had neither of her children next to her.

'Hello,' Kate said, looking over to the tyre park.

Alison followed her gaze and found Amelia wearing a tutu under her coat as she clambered over tyres, trailed by Reuben and now Xander.

'Morning,' Alison said. 'Happy World Book Day.'

'Oh, yes.' Kate waved the cardboard mask in her hand. 'Amelia's the dog from *Dogs Don't Do Ballet*,' she clarified.

Alison nodded, that explained the tutu. 'Xander is the Roly-Poly Bird,' she said. 'He just loves Roald Dahl books.' Well, he liked the pictures, anyway.

Kate smiled. 'You've certainly done an, um, amazing job on that costume.'

'Freaking hell, what's Xander come as – a blue dinosaur?' Frankie announced, as she arrived.

Alison stared at Frankie and then looked over to Xander, who had fallen off the tyres and was now shuffling on the muddy grass, undoubtedly destroying the tail feathers she had been so proud of. She looked back at Frankie and Liam standing next to her in a shop-bought dragon outfit and silently questioned which costume was the better choice.

'Have you seen Lily's outfit?' Kate asked, gesturing to where Becky had just entered the playground, holding her younger daughter's hand.

'What's she supposed to be?' Frankie whispered.

'The Cat in the Hat.' Alison couldn't help staring, trying not to let her jealousy show. The black and white body would have been simple, she told herself, the face paint was a nice touch, as were the ears on a headband, but the enormous red and white striped hat was particularly impressive. Taking a breath, she fixed a smile on her face which she really hoped said 'that's a nice effort, although I think you're trying a bit too hard', before turning away to stop Xander from getting more mud on him.

'Come on, Xander,' she said loudly, trying not to shout in front of the other mums.

He jumped up and grinned at her as he shook his head, waving his arms like wings as he pretended to fly around the playground.

She would not chase him: this was not a game.

As she stood trying to stop him with the power of a disapproving stare, Amelia ran past her, barking after Xander, followed by a roaring Liam and then two squeaking mice scampered along. Before she could blink it seemed the entire Reception class were chasing each other, making animal noises. Around her some of the parents were laughing, Frankie loudest of all, while others were shouting to their offspring to calm down and come back.

Oh, Xander – what have you started?

Alison looked down to avoid the other mums' glares and wished the ground would open up so she could disappear.

At that moment Mr Armstrong opened the classroom door to welcome in his pupils, and the children followed Xander into the classroom as though he were a Roly-Poly pied piper, still making the appropriate noises. Mr Armstrong looked bewildered and amused as he stepped back to allow them past.

'Well, at least they've got into the spirit of the day!' Frankie said, still laughing.

She wouldn't be laughing if Liam had started it, Alison thought, before immediately correcting herself. *Yes, she would.* Alison covered her face with her hands to hide her embarrassment.

'Lighten up, Alison,' Frankie said, throwing an arm around her as they started to leave the playground. 'Worse things happen at sea – argh! I sound like my mother!'

Once they reached the road, Kate turned to Alison, putting a hand on her arm. 'Would you like to pop round for a cuppa while Reuben's at pre-school?' she asked. 'We could get some of that wrapping done.'

'What are you wrapping?' Frankie asked.

Alison was almost surprised Frankie was still there. Usually she had to hurry off to work.

'Oh, it's just a PTA thing,' Alison said, knowing Frankie wouldn't be interested even if she had the time.

'Did you want to come and help?' Kate asked.

'Can't.' Frankie shook her head. 'Work. Those fancy-dress costumes don't pay for themselves, y'know.'

Alison watched Frankie marching off in front of them, crossing the road and disappearing down Church Street, alone. For a moment she wondered if she should have asked her to help out with the Mother's Day presents another time. No, she decided. Frankie wouldn't want to be involved in something like that. But, maybe… after all, it was always nicer to be asked than to be left out.

CHAPTER TWENTY-ONE

Kate looked at her reflection in the mirror and couldn't see a single thing she felt happy with.

She wiped the smudges from under her eyes and sighed. The maternity dress, which she had bought specially, thinking it was pretty and flowing, looked like a floral tent on her. Her hair was going flat at the front (despite her best efforts with the hair dryer) and her mascara had already smudged under her eyes. *No,* she reminded herself, *this is Natalie's wedding day, no one will care how I look.* And more importantly, perhaps, this level of worrying was really not very Zen. It would be fine. She pulled out the holdall of toys for the kids and dropped the invitation and her handbag inside.

'Time to go,' she said, to Matthew as much as the kids. 'Has everybody been to the toilet?'

She gathered another holdall with wellies and waterproofs, just in case, and brought both to the front door. Reuben was ready first, adorable in his new jeans, blue shirt and jacket. Although… he was looking pale and a bit peaky around the eyes. *Please don't be ill at the wedding,* she thought, as she helped him on with his coat.

Amelia was already putting on the sparkly shoes she had chosen – probably not the most practical choice, but they did go perfectly with the silver and white dress. Kate sighed, wondering if any of the outfits would survive the day unscathed.

Matthew took the bags and led the way to the car while Kate herded the children out and locked up behind them.

As he patiently waited for her to put the address into her phone to find directions, Matthew said, 'It'll be fine. You don't need to worry.'

Kate said nothing. She knew he believed his own words. She wondered if he would have changed his mind before the end of the afternoon.

No, this was her friend's special day. It would be lovely. The kids would behave well and she would be Zen *all day*.

There were large signposts announcing '*River and Natalie – Wedding*' for the last half-mile of country lanes. Relieved they hadn't got lost in what seemed to be the middle of nowhere, Kate pointed out the last sign, which read '*River and Natalie – Parking*' and directed them through an open gate.

'Are you sure?' Matthew asked, hesitating before he turned.

'That's what it says…' Kate really *wasn't* sure, but there wasn't anywhere else to try: the road was not wide enough to park on.

'Okay.'

The parking area was already a muddy swamp.

'Did you bring wellies?' Matthew asked, as he turned into the field.

Wearing more suitable footwear, with pretty shoes in the large bag just in case they were needed later, they left the car behind and followed more signs. The trees either side of the path had been decorated with colourful scraps of material tied to the tree trunks. Kate shivered, feeling the cold now they were out of the sunshine. Could she get away with keeping her coat on through the ceremony?

Reuben was walking even slower than usual, while Amelia was running from one side of the path to the other to make sure she had squelched her wellies through every bit of mud. Eventually, Matthew swung Reuben up onto his shoulders (trying unsuccessfully to keep the muddy wellies away from his jacket) to carry him the last few yards into a clearing. As they arrived, Kate looked ahead to see what looked like a group of festival goers, or hikers, up ahead.

The wedding guests were all wearing waterproof jackets and walking boots with gaiters.

'It's a bit… casual, isn't it?' Matthew whispered to her.

She nodded. It would seem she had got the dress code wrong. There were no other smart suits and the only dresses had a more bohemian feel. Even her woollen coat was wrong amongst all this serious stormwear.

'When will it start?' Amelia was asking.

'I don't know… soon.'

There was nowhere to hide the holdall of toys and shoes either, so Kate clung to it. She looked around for the table of presents, but could see nothing. As far as she could see, none of the other guests were clutching cards or gifts.

'Hello, everyone.' A voice with the authority of a headmistress broke through the sound of general chatter. 'Hello, please gather round. We are about to start the ceremony.'

Everyone shuffled closer to the voice until Kate could see that it came from a short, fierce-looking woman with long, straight grey hair brushed over her shoulders.

'Mummy, I need a wee,' Amelia whispered loudly, tugging at Kate's arm.

'Can you hold it?' Kate asked, fearing the answer.

'No, I'm desperate.' She bent slightly at the waist and began to wiggle from one foot to the other.

Kate looked around, hopeful that there would be some facilities she hadn't yet seen, but no, they were still in a forest, surrounded by trees. She dropped the bags on the ground and nodded, touching Matthew's arms and gesturing that she was taking Amelia. He nodded, Reuben still on his shoulders.

'Just before River and Natalie come to join us at this special place…' the celebrant continued.

Kate led Amelia back the way they came. *Please let us get back in time*, she thought, looking for a tree large enough to hide a five-year-old behind. The trees weren't quite close enough together to shield them from the view of the other guests yet. In the distance she could see Natalie floating towards the celebrant in a cream and green dress. *Definitely missing her big entrance, then.*

'Where's the loo?' Amelia asked.

'There isn't one, sweetheart,' Kate said, finally spotting a large trunk in the distance and making her way towards it. 'You'll have to do a nature wee.'

Amelia pulled a face.

'That's all there is. Here, behind this tree will do.' Checking around that nobody would see, Kate beckoned Amelia over from where she stood on the path.

'No, Mummy, I don't want to.'

'Do you need a wee or not?'

Amelia nodded.

'Well, then.'

'Can't we drive to somewhere with a toilet?' she tried. 'Like that time we went to that pub where we didn't have anything to eat, because Reuben needed the loo? We could do that, Mummy, we *could.*' As Amelia finished, she stamped her feet, clearly feeling hard done by.

'We can't,' Kate said, trying not to let her voice show her impatience. 'This is all there is. We can't drive anywhere because… Daddy has the car keys.' It wasn't exactly the main reason, but at least Amelia couldn't argue. 'Come on, let me help you, sweetheart.'

Pouting slightly, her daughter allowed herself to be manoeuvred into position and Kate held up the skirt of her dress.

'I've got you, now keep your legs apart. No… further. That's it, lean forward, right forwards… no, you're not going to fall, I've got you.' *This would be so much easier with Reuben*, she thought.

'Mummy, there's wee on my leg!' Amelia shouted, half-laughing, half-panicking.

'It's okay,' Kate said, handing her a tissue to wipe before helping her to pull up her pants and hoping no one watching the ceremony had heard.

'Here, have some hand wash,' she said, squirting the gel onto both of their palms and trying not to worry about how much of the ceremony they had missed.

Holding Amelia's hand, she made her way back to the clearing, where she could see Natalie and River were holding hands and beaming at each other, just in front of the celebrant.

'And now, having heard their vows, we would like to take a moment to reflect on the beauty of their love for one another in this place of natural beauty…' the celebrant was saying.

River, at least, had *tried* to dress up. He was wearing a creased brown suit with a green and yellow tie, although the outfit looked a little like he had worn it to do the gardening that morning already, Kate thought, and immediately felt uncharitable. Natalie, on the other hand, was glowing. The design of her dress was simple – V-neck, sleeveless, empire-line – but it seemed to be made from patches of material, all different shapes and patterns, going from pale cream at the shoulders to a dark green at the ankles. Her hair fell about her face in messy curls. She was beautiful. And… happy.

'So, we have come to the moment where the bride and groom can make a physical gesture of their emotional connection.'

Kate tried to suppress a giggle as Matthew raised his eyebrows at her in alarm. Natalie and River kissed and the rest of the guests began to clap. Amelia said loudly, 'Yuck, they're kissing!'

'You missed all the best bits,' Matthew said discreetly as they followed Natalie, River and the rest of the guests down another path away from the clearing. 'They tied their arms together with braided grasses as a symbol of their commitment and stuck twigs in their hair to honour Mother Nature.'

'Oh, how… lovely,' Kate said.

'And we all had to chant.'

'I see.'

'And hug trees.'

Kate frowned, twisting to look at him properly. 'Really?'

'No,' he admitted, 'only the tying.' He looked up at Reuben. 'Ready to come down and walk for a bit, Rubes?'

Reuben shook his head.

'Come on,' Kate said. 'Otherwise your legs will hurt, remember?' Sitting up on Matthew's shoulders for too long always made his feet go numb and he would cry and wail at the pins and needles as the feeling came back.

'Just a bit more,' he pleaded.

'Okay.' Matthew gave in too easily, Kate thought. 'But you're definitely coming down once we get to where we're going.'

'Where *is* that?' Kate asked.

'No idea,' he admitted.

Eventually, they arrived in a second clearing, far bigger than the first, dominated by a large yurt at one end, with fairy lights strung around the entrance. All around, colourful jars hung from branches and stands, with candles burning in them, bright decorations in the already-dimming late afternoon light. Mismatched tables (with more tealights in candles) and chairs were scattered around the grass, creating a chaotic, yet artistic scene. It was all very Natalie, Kate thought, feeling reassured that she had done the right thing by making their wedding present rather than buying it. As soon as she had found the cushion cover designs online, she knew the patchwork of blues and greens would be perfect in Natalie's lounge, and on the top corner, she had embroidered their initials and the wedding date. It had been a lot of effort, but looking around, Kate knew she would love it, and it was worth it to show Natalie how much she valued their friendship.

A large blackboard next to them read '*Friends, meet other friends! Sit, chat, eat. Here is where it starts!*'

'What do you think that means?' Matthew asked, nudging Kate.
'It means there's no seating plan,' she explained.

'Right, Reuben, down you come.' As Matthew lifted his son
from his shoulders, Reuben began to cry and once he was on the
floor, he sat on the grass, pulling his legs to him, wailing about
them hurting. That was the problem with Matthew giving in and
carrying Reuben for longer: they all knew it would end like this.

'Come on, Amelia, let's find a table.' Still carrying the bag for
all eventualities (except, invariably, the one that would *actually*
happen) and holding Amelia's hand, Kate tried not to look like
she was hurrying as she made a beeline for a little table at the edge
of the space. She left Matthew with the kids as she went in search
of drinks for them all.

After a little investigation, Kate found that the yurt had drinks
at one end of it. There was a large variety of fruit juices in one
large ice bucket and vegan white wine in the next, with three kegs
sitting up on a bar with a blackboard declaring 'homebrew' leaning
against them. Beside the drinks, an enormous collection of large
jam jars sat on a table, each labelled with a name. Upon an easel,
a blackboard explained, '*No plastic here! Find your cup, fill it up…
again and again and again. From us to you with love, R+N*'.

Kate was starting to develop an irrational dislike of blackboards,
especially those with cheery (yet patronising) instructions and
hand-drawn hearts on them. Was this reaction Frankie's influence?
She saw another message next to the bins outside reminding guests
that they were trying to avoid waste and would appreciate them
recycling or taking rubbish home with them.

The other end of the yurt was set up with large bowls of food.
Kate's heart sank as she looked desperately for something child-
friendly. There was bread next to some homemade ras-el-hannout
hummus, but it was dark brown in colour and looked filled with
what Reuben referred to as 'seedy, beady bits'. She counted six
different types of salad, a further five different vegetable dishes

and three whole fish (with a sign declaring that River had caught them and thanked them before despatching them), but nothing she would be able to persuade her kids to try. No matter, this was why she had packed breadsticks, she reminded herself.

When she reached the table, clutching two jars of apple juice for the kids, Matthew was standing talking to River, holding onto the back of Amelia's chair while she added stickers to her magazine. Reuben sat slumped holding a pencil crayon, but not actually colouring. He didn't look quite right – definitely sickening for something.

'Kate?' Matthew turned to her. 'Are you okay here if I just go and look at River's homebrew?'

She smiled. 'Of course. That's fine.' She settled into the chair beside Reuben and he immediately climbed across onto her lap, trapping her. 'I'll be fine here,' she said, possibly to convince herself.

Matthew reached across and stroked the top of her arm with the back of his hand before walking away just as Amelia began to ask her for help with a spot-the-difference puzzle. Reuben nuzzled into her shoulder and Kate resigned herself to watching the wedding celebrations from afar rather than actually being involved in them. It didn't matter, she was still here, she was still happy for her friend.

Kate twisted round in her chair to watch Matthew standing beside River, holding up a glass of beer to inspect the colour. She continued to stare, willing him to turn and see her, but he looked from the glass to River and back again.

'Mummy, *look*,' Amelia whined, tugging at her arm for attention.

Reuben squirmed on Kate's lap and she wished she could just unhook her bump for a while to give him more space.

She dragged her eyes back to the puzzle in the magazine. 'Have you seen the pandas' faces?' she asked helpfully, waiting while Amelia compared the expressions on both pandas and noticed that one had a smile and the other a frown.

Amelia finished the puzzle and sighed. 'I'm *bored*.'

'Oh dear,' Kate said with a smile. 'You can go and play if you want?' There was a handful of children running around in the trees shrieking with laughter, looking like an advert for a happy childhood.

Amelia shook her head. 'I'm hungry…'

Kate didn't really want to break out the snacks just yet, but given that she didn't know how long it would be until people started eating, she also didn't want to risk the kids reaching a meltdown that could be averted by a quick food fix.

'Have a drink first, sweetheart,' Kate suggested, pushing a jar of juice towards her before leaning over and fishing around in the large bag, pulling out a couple of fruit-based cereal bars that masqueraded as healthy.

Amelia screwed her nose up.

'It's apple juice.' Kate wasn't sure if it was the cloudy liquid or the jam jar that her daughter didn't trust.

Looking suspicious, Amelia sipped a little before pursing her lips. 'Yuck! It's got bits in.'

Of course, Kate thought, *River probably made it from fresh apples this morning.*

'Shall I get you some water?' she asked, passing her the water bottle from the bag.

'Are you okay there, Reuben?' she said quietly, stroking his hair back from his forehead. 'You feel a bit hot…' She kissed his forehead. Definitely warmer than it should be. 'Do you feel a bit poorly?'

He nodded, looking up at her from under heavily lidded eyes. 'My tummy hurts,' he said, pulling on his ear.

'Would you like some Calpol?'

Reuben didn't respond for a moment, so Kate sat him upright so she could rummage deeper into the large bag of provisions.

'I'm still bored,' Amelia complained.

Kate didn't have enough energy to argue with her while she was trying to sort out Reuben. Feeling a surge of bad mum guilt, she handed over her phone for Amelia to play on.

'Here we go, Reuben.' She held up two sachets and tried to read the dosage information on the back. 'And then do you want a drink to wash it down? I've got your water bottle, or apple juice?'

He looked over pathetically, then reached for the water.

Kate had just torn the sachet open when Natalie came over. 'Hello, hello, hello,' she said to each of them in turn. Kate's heart fell as she realised that Natalie wouldn't get a spontaneous response from either child.

'Hello,' she said, nudging Amelia with the toe of her shoe under the table, but she only scowled and moved her feet away, without looking up at either adult. 'We were just saying what a beautiful spot this is.'

'It *is* perfect, isn't it?' Natalie agreed, either not noticing or not drawing attention to the fact that both children had ignored her. 'River's brother's friend owns it and he does all sorts of retreats here, so when we said we were looking for a natural venue, he offered us this one.'

Kate nodded, looking around. 'And I love the way you've dressed it up with the tea lights and everything. It's just lovely, really, Natalie. You've done a great job.'

'Aw, thanks, although we did have a lot of help. River's sister Idoya spent ages painting all these jars for the candles.'

'And your dress is just lovely, too.' Kate reached out a hand to touch the material, then realised it was now sticky with Calpol and snatched it away again.

'Thank you – there's this woman who works at the shop with River who makes dresses from recycled materials and she is so talented, don't you think?'

Kate nodded, wondering how she was going to get Reuben to take the medicine while she talked to Nat.

'We managed to get almost everything from sustainable or recycled sources in the end. My dress is made from plastic dredged from the local rivers,' Natalie went on with a self-satisfied tone that Kate was trying not to find irritating. 'The only thing we bought as new were the wedding rings, I think. Oh, and the cups – but they are also our favours and so much better than the alternative. You know, those plastic disposable glasses – we just *couldn't* have had those, could we?'

'No, I suppose not.' Kate decided to just go for it and held up the sachet for Reuben. She didn't have to stop chatting to her friend just because he needed a little medicine. 'Here you go, sweetheart, here's the first one.'

'My goodness, what's that?' Natalie sounded shocked.

'This is the wonder of Calpol,' Kate replied, smiling.

'Is he really ill?'

Kate finished with the second sachet and looked round for somewhere to put the rubbish. 'Just a temperature. I'm sure he'll be fine in half an hour.' Leaning over, she dug around in the holdall until she found a tissue to wrap it in.

'Does Reuben really *need* the drugs, then?' Natalie's patronising tone irritated Kate. 'Have you thought he might do better without all those extra chemicals? I mean, you just don't know the long-term effects of that stuff, do you?'

Avoiding looking at her friend, Kate gathered the empty snack wrappers from the table. 'Oh, he's… it's just Calpol.'

She wished Matthew were here. He'd have some quip to stop Nat's needling without it getting serious. Kate glanced over her shoulder to see him standing with a jar of beer, talking to River and his friends. She stared at him for a moment, but he still didn't look over.

'Oh, you didn't have to bring your *own* snacks, Kate. We've got a whole load of food in the yurt. And it's all fresh and healthy – none of this processed nonsense. You should try it sometime.

Our little one certainly isn't going to have anything unnatural. And, you know, it's shown to be linked to fussy eating. The more you give in to those sort of snacks, the less they will eat real food.'

Kate smiled, but didn't trust herself to speak. It was hard to stay Zen, but she had to keep trying. Why was Matthew taking so long?

'Amelia, you don't have to play on that phone, you know.' Natalie put her hand out as if to take it away and Amelia twisted away from her, eyes still glued to the screen. 'Oh, come on, there's a real world here you can play in!' Natalie looked at Kate and rolled her eyes. 'Honestly…'

'She's fine, Nat.' It sounded lame to Kate's own ears.

'Doesn't she know that nature is the best playground?'

Why wouldn't she just let it go? 'Really, it doesn't matter.'

'But it *does* matter, Kate. I remember when we used to talk about how you wanted to raise your kids and I'm not sure this is you, is it? Drugging your children at the drop of a hat and letting them play on screens just to keep them quiet?' She leaned in and dropped her voice to a whisper. 'Do you worry about where you went wrong?'

Kate felt hot tears pricking at her eyes. 'Wrong?'

Natalie tilted her head to the side and nodded slowly, seemingly unaware of how hurtful her words were. Kate's stomach was twisting with guilt and worry, hearing Natalie voice her deepest fears. *She was a terrible mother. She was doing everything wrong.*

'I mean… it's like you just *gave up.*'

The words stung.

Natalie sighed. 'Come on, Kate. You're sitting here not talking to anyone, drugging one child with chemicals and the other with a screen. If you three weren't going to really get involved in the day, why did you bother coming in the first place? I mean, is there really any point in you being here?'

'I'm sorry, Natalie.' Kate wondered how she could get Amelia to join in with the other kids. 'Come on, Amelia, put that down.'

Kate reached for the phone, but Amelia turned away and made a growling noise.

'No, Amelia…' She tried again, but this time when her daughter jerked away, Kate was ready and snatched the phone back, already feeling guilty, given all the times she had told Amelia not to snatch.

'No, I just need to…' Amelia screeched.

Kate flinched at the tone of the noise. On her lap, Reuben began to wail, his hands clamped over his ears. She wished they were anywhere but here.

Natalie looked horrified. 'Oh my goodness,' she said. 'Kate, it's important that we maintain the good energy around this place.'

Easier said than done, Kate thought, trying to soothe Reuben while giving Amelia a look.

'Wow… I think it might be for the best if you leave if you're going to let your kids act like that.'

'Oh.' Kate took a deep breath, trying to blink away the tears. 'Right.' She began pulling the magazine, colouring book, pens and water bottles towards her, throwing them messily into the bag, feeling too humiliated to argue that they were just acting like children.

'I'm sorry, but I don't want all this to ruin the happiness of the day. You do understand, don't you?' Natalie said as Kate took Reuben off her lap and stood up.

'Of course… Um, here's your present.' Kate tried to force a smile onto her face as she handed the present over.

Natalie nodded as she accepted it.

Not even a thank you, Kate noticed, grabbing the bag in one hand and taking Reuben's in the other. They had to walk around the edge of the clearing to get back to the path they had arrived on and Kate was painfully aware of eyes following her progress. She daren't look up to see where Matthew had got to, she just had to hope that he would see they had gone and come after them.

'Why are we leaving?' Amelia asked sulkily.

Kate sniffed, tears blurring her vision. 'Well, Reuben is poorly…'
Although looking at him now, you wouldn't know it, she thought,
watching him begin to skip as the Calpol kicked in. 'It's just time
for us to be going.'

'But what about Daddy?'

Good question, Kate thought. 'Oh, he'll be along in a minute.'

As they reached the site of the ceremony, she heard Matthew
calling from the path behind them.

'Kate?' He jogged the last few steps. 'What's up? Natalie said
you had to leave?'

She turned to face him and his face creased with worry as he
saw her.

'Oh, hey, it's okay.' He slipped an arm around her shoulder.

'Nat asked me to leave – she said…' Kate tried and failed to
explain what had happened as she cried and hiccoughed into his
shoulder while he patted her back reassuringly.

'Well, it's probably for the best,' Matthew said when she finally
calmed down enough to talk. He took the bag to carry and walked
ahead of her, calling over his shoulder, 'There's only so long I can
talk about vegan brewing techniques.'

She smiled. It was true to say that none of them had been
having a fun day.

But, still.

I can't believe Nat told me to leave.

Kate thought of all the things she should have said to Nat. She
wished she'd told her that giving Reuben Calpol wasn't the same
as giving him crack cocaine and that letting Amelia play on her
phone was not the worst thing a parent could do.

But most of all, she wished she'd told Nat to stop *judging* her
as a mum.

Trying to keep a friendship going was one thing, but it wasn't worth
being made to feel like this. Right now, Kate wasn't even sure there
was a way to stay friends with Nat without losing her Zen for good.

CHAPTER TWENTY-TWO

Frankie knew she was sulking and acting like a child. Even though, with all those evening and weekend hours, she knew she couldn't have done the bar manager job, she had still *wanted* it. It would have meant more money, but more than that, it would have been actual evidence that she could do a good job, despite what her mother said.

It's not fair, the voice inside her head kept saying. She'd been so happy to be out of Mum's house and in her own place, but now that meant that she couldn't have this job.

'I've gone with Ruth,' Erin said, as Frankie stood wiping down the optics bottles behind the bar.

'Ruth,' she said, blankly, without bothering to turn around. Had she met anyone called Ruth?

'Yes, she's starting on Thursday. She seems very capable and no-nonsense.'

'Okay, then.'

'I don't see it taking her long to get the hang of it, so can you have those ideas for a Mother's Day event and so on ready to pitch to me on Wednesday afternoon?'

'Pitch the ideas… yeah – totally,' Frankie said, trying to sound as though she was completely on top of it. As soon as Erin disappeared back to Reception, she pulled out the notebook she had started writing in last week and flicked through it. There were several pages of thoughts and suggestions, but she had no idea what to do with them all now. Erin wouldn't want anything vague, she would want proper plans. So, she was focusing on something easy and quick for Mother's Day – that was only a couple of weeks away; a wedding fair – which should be fairly straightforward; and something for Easter. That was the one she had no idea about, but at least it was further into the future.

She unlocked her phone and began to Google 'Spa events for Mother's Day'.

For the rest of the afternoon, she spent the time in between serving customers surfing the internet, bookmarking websites and saving useful-looking images on her phone. The main problem she could now see was that she simply didn't know enough about the business as a whole. She could see that the café and bar were consistently underused and she knew there was only a handful of weddings booked over the summer, but she had no idea what was going on with the bedrooms or how busy the spa was. By the end of her shift, her brain was hurting from thinking and Frankie didn't even feel she'd made that much progress.

'Sorry I'm late,' she said, when Ben answered the door, stepping forward to kiss him. She had no idea what time it was – once she'd realised she was late leaving work, she had avoided looking at clocks.

He sighed. 'Well, I was fairly sure you'd turn up eventually. They're both in the bath.'

'The bath?' Oh God, she really was late. She followed him as he headed back to the bathroom, where she could hear the sounds of splashing and giggling.

'Yeah, Liam can borrow some of Charlie's pyjamas to go home in.'

'Thanks.'

Ben stopped just before the doorway, turning to face Frankie with a frown. 'Frankie, I need to have a word.'

'I know, I know…' She tilted her head and made an apologetic face. 'It's too late. I really am sorry. I just had to try and sort out these promotional ideas for Erin and there's so much to do – I'm going to have to sit down tonight and do some more. It won't happen again, Scout's honour.' She held up her hand and tried to look solemn, but it was hard to be serious with a chorus of 'splish, splash, bathy bath' coming from behind him.

He smiled. 'Yeah, it will – but it's not that.' Lowering his voice, he went on, 'Mr Armstrong wanted to have a quick word with you about Liam. Just that he had an *accident* today at school.'

Frankie raised her eyebrows quizzically. 'An *accident*?' Was that supposed to mean something to her?

'He's in trousers from lost property and the wet ones are in a plastic bag in his schoolbag.'

Oh, *that* kind of accident. Great.

'And it's the second time this month, so Mr Armstrong just wanted to speak to you. Can you give him a ring tomorrow?'

Frankie didn't like the sound of that. It sounded too much like she was about to be told off. She nodded, although she had no intention of calling him.

'Oh, also – I bought you a present.' He disappeared into the bedroom and came back bearing a large flat rectangular envelope.

He was looking so pleased with himself that Frankie worried about what it might be and opened the envelope with trepidation. 'A calendar?' she said, having only pulled the spiral top out a couple of centimetres. 'Thanks… but, *really*?'

'Look, it's instead of a spreadsheet. Trust me, you'll like it.'

Frankie pulled a face at him, but carried on pulling out the calendar, smiling when she saw the name of it. 'The Sarcastic Mum's Attempt at Organising,' she read out. 'They made a calendar just for me?'

'See? Not so bad.'

She reached an arm around him. 'Okay, thanks,' she said and kissed him.

Ben pulled away from her for a moment to speak. 'It needs to go up in your house and I'm going to add stuff from the spreadsheet.' He moved back in for another kiss, but this time it was Frankie who stepped back.

'Not the spreadsheet.'

'Don't worry, you won't have to see the spreadsheet. I'll do it when you're not looking.'

'Okay. Just so we're clear on that.' She nodded and moved towards him to accept the kiss just at the moment when Liam began to shriek.

'I think that's probably the end of bathtime, then,' said Ben.

'What do you think of Ruth, then?' Frankie asked Tina quietly, helping her to clear the last table.

Tina wrinkled her nose and shrugged. 'Better than Adrian,' she said, stacking the plates. 'What do *you* think?'

'Yeah, she's alright.' And she was. She was fine. When Frankie had been introduced, she had smiled and said hello. When they'd been left to work the bar together, Ruth had made small talk, uninhibited by Frankie's monosyllabic answers. Okay, so the nonstop talking was a bit annoying, but Tina was right, it could be worse. It could be Adrian.

'Don't know why she didn't just get you to do it, though.' Tina was pouting slightly, and Frankie felt both pleased that Tina thought so highly of her and annoyed again that the hours had stopped her from going after that promotion. No, she had to stop thinking about it. There could be a whole new role for her, if this afternoon's meeting went well.

'Right, wish me luck,' Frankie said, changing the subject as she picked up the tray. 'As soon as I've dealt with these, I'm off to pitch my ideas to Erin.'

Tina grinned. Frankie had spent most of the morning trying out her ideas on her, feeding on her enthusiasm for everything. 'You'll do great.'

'Thanks.'

As Frankie left the tray in the kitchen and set off to find Erin in Reception, she could feel her breath starting to get away from her. *I'll be fine*, she told herself. *I have good ideas. I can do this.* But with every step the self-doubt began to creep in. It wasn't like she'd ever done anything like this before. Why had she even thought she wanted to?

'Ah, Frankie.' Erin looked up from the computer as she approached. 'Are you all set? What have you got?'

'Okay, erm…' Frankie joined her behind the desk, pulling out her mobile. 'Sorry, I – I have it all on here.' She gestured to her phone.

Erin looked as unimpressed as ever, but pulled her notebook towards her, ready to write on. 'Shall we start with Mothering Sunday, seeing as that's the closest?'

'Right. Yes. So,' Frankie felt herself stutter and tried to mentally punch herself back to making sense. 'Mother's Day. I checked the spa slots and saw we're pretty full for treatments already, but there's almost nothing booked in for lunch, so I was thinking about this…' She turned the screen of her phone to Erin to show her an ad she had mocked up. 'A voucher for a discount on drinks or meals in Restore & Replenish to be used on the day for anyone who has a treatment. We can have them here on Reception and down near the treatment rooms and we could even email them out the week before. Or,' she swiped to the next photo, 'this might be better – a voucher they can buy on or before Mother's Day for afternoon tea, maybe with a discount to come back to the spa another day? We could advertise it as "Mum and Me", so customers could add it to an existing treatment booking or as a separate treat.'

'Uh-huh.' Erin frowned, passing the phone back and scribbling on her pad.

Frankie paused, not sure whether to carry on or wait.

Looking up, Erin prompted, 'And Easter?'

'Okay, Easter.' Frankie angled the phone again to show Erin her idea. 'I think we should make it a weekend of celebrations. We can lay on a set menu for lunch on Saturday, Sunday and Monday and encourage families by having an Easter egg hunt in the garden and maybe some outdoor games. We have enough time to advertise it in the paper and we could print flyers and put them up around the town, or send out an email shot to all our customers and put it on our Facebook page. It would make people think of it as a venue for events, not just a spa. And we could have a raffle, maybe?' Frankie stopped to breathe and tried to slow down. Erin was still frowning and scribbling, and Frankie had no idea if her ideas were being well received or not.

'Oh, I nearly forgot,' Frankie swiped to the next picture. 'I was also thinking that we could do one of those pop-up photo booths, with Easter props, like this, to encourage people to post their photos online with our hashtag as free advertising. I mean, I think Heppleton Hall has a really good reputation as a spa, but people think it's a bit posh and fancy and, like, old-fashioned, but if they saw people having fun, I think they'd be more likely to come here.'

'Did you get anywhere with the wedding fair?'

'I did.' Frankie scrolled to the last image and turned the phone to show a landscape view of the table she had typed out. 'I don't know how much you'll be able to read that, but I can email it to you.' She waited while Erin lowered her glasses and peered over them at the screen. 'I tried to list all the local wedding suppliers in each category, so you could see the sort of people we could invite – not just obvious ones like florists, but we can invite bands or singers to perform at different slots in the afternoon. There's a wine shop in Millhurst that specialises in personalised cases of wine as wedding presents, and the vintage cars place in Cheadbridge could show off its less traditional wedding transport.'

'How much do you think something like this will cost?' Erin asked.

Frankie winced slightly, she didn't have figures. And if Erin was just thinking about the cost, she wasn't seeing the bigger picture.

'Well, I mean, it *will* cost us, because I think we should give everyone a drink as they arrive and have some canapés going round…'

'And we can't have anything else going on that day,' Erin added.

'Yes, but the bar can still be open, so they can order drinks too. And we can charge the exhibitors. And it will end up making us money in the long run. Even if people don't decide to get married here, they might still think of us for other events and maybe they'll suggest us as a possible venue to others. It'll be all about getting a buzz about what we can do here.'

Frankie stopped talking as Erin passed her back the phone and nodded.

That was a good sign, right?

'I like these ideas,' she said. 'This is exactly what we need to be doing, but I just don't have time to organise any of it.'

Frankie held her breath – was this Erin's way of turning her down? 'I see,' she said, not seeing at all.

'Firstly, don't ever present anything on a phone again. It's far too small and it looks completely unprofessional.'

Erin raised her eyebrows at Frankie, who nodded hopefully.

'I want you to cut back on your time in the bar now Ruth's here and I need you on Reception more. When you're here, you can use this computer and phone to plan and organise the events. If you need to go out and meet people, I can cover the desk, but you'll need to check ahead of time.'

'I can totally do that.'

'You'll work closely with me on the Mother's Day promotion and get everything checked by me. Until that is finished, everything is provisional, but assuming the event works well, there'll be a new role for you organising events like this in addition to working on Reception and in Restore & Replenish, as required.'

Frankie felt her chest lift and realised she was grinning like an idiot. 'Cool,' she said, flicking her hair as if she didn't care. She noticed Erin smile briefly.

After a further hour of more specific planning, Erin left Frankie to begin working through her list. Having made sure she was really gone, Frankie pulled her phone towards her, desperate to tell someone about her new job, but hesitating over who. It wasn't like anyone was waiting to hear – she hadn't mentioned the meeting with Erin, unwilling to risk having to admit she'd messed up her chance if it didn't go well.

So, I just got a promotion she typed, sending the text simultaneously to Ben, Kate and Alison, then tucked the phone away in her pocket to avoid staring at the screen while she waited for replies. As she began the planning document Erin had told her to create, her phone vibrated. She wondered who had replied so quickly, but it was 'Jez' that had popped up on the screen.

> *Hi Frankie. Thanks for letting us be a part of Liam's life over the past few weeks. He means a lot to us and we'd really like to give him a special role as ring bearer in our wedding. Would that be okay? We'll bring the invite and ask him properly this weekend. J&M.*

Frankie felt her body react even before she had finished reading it, tensing up and holding her breath.

No, she thought, *it's not okay*. Liam was *hers*, not *theirs*.

She imagined their wedding in some stunning country house with every detail perfect, even down to the adorable ring bearer that Jez would loudly claim as his son who 'meant a lot to him' even though this was the same son he'd ignored for four years. Well, she had to hand it to Jez, he certainly was working hard to secure a ring bearer for his wedding. The question was, would he remember Liam once the honeymoon was over and he didn't need him any more?

Frankie was so busy being angry at Jez that when the first congratulatory text arrived from Alison, it took her a moment to remember what she had to be happy about.

I got a promotion, she reminded herself, forcefully, pushing Jez out of her mind. *Erin liked my ideas and I am going to be awesome at this.*

CHAPTER TWENTY-THREE

Alison nearly jumped as Kate stepped out from the alleyway as she passed.

'Sorry,' Kate said, falling into step as they walked up the High Street.

Alison smiled. 'It's alright. Have you been waiting long?'

'No, I saw you coming and thought I'd rather go in with you.'

Alison didn't blame her. The PTA meetings had become increasingly hostile this term. Obviously, Alison hadn't exactly helped matters by criticising Jo and Rachel's suggestions, but she was not going to be quiet just for an easy life. This PTA deserved better.

'Have you heard anything from Frankie lately?' Alison asked.

'No… she's always in such a rush when I see her.'

'I wanted to ask her about Mother's Day – do you think the Hall might be doing some special offers for it? I was wondering if we could do a bit of a promotion – the PTA with the Hall – and get some kind of cashback or something to raise money?' Alison hadn't quite thought the idea through, but it felt intuitively right to use their connection to the Hall and any Mother's Day spa promotions to benefit the PTA. If only Frankie came to these meetings, she could have asked her directly. Or if she wasn't always so late dropping Liam off or picking him up, then she'd be able to have a proper conversation with her. Alison made a mental note to organise a get-together.

As they reached the café, Alison held the door open for Kate and watched her go in. She seemed a little flat, somehow. She was never the loudest, but even for Kate she appeared muted.

'How was your friend's wedding?' Alison asked as they approached the counter, trying not to draw attention to the way they were avoiding Becky's side of the room.

'Oh… well,' Kate paused as they got to the counter to order.

'Not much fun then,' Alison prompted, as they picked up their tea and turned to find a seat.

'It was a lovely setting…'

'A forest, wasn't it?' *A brave choice in March*, Alison thought.

'Yes. I missed the ceremony because Amelia needed the toilet, but then we went to this other bit, where they had lots of tables set up and a yurt with food and drink in and…' She sighed, putting a hand over her face. 'Oh, it was awful! Reuben had a temperature and the kids wouldn't eat any of the weird vegan food and we didn't know anyone. Then Natalie said how terrible it was that I let my kids have processed snacks and play on screens all the time and she was horrified that I gave Reuben Calpol.'

'*No.* That's ridiculous!' Alison didn't know which was worse, that someone would say that out loud to a mum or that anyone would even *think* that of Kate. 'What did you do?'

'I left.'

'You mean you stormed off?' She couldn't quite imagine it.

'Not quite – she said if we weren't going to get into the wedding properly we should leave. She didn't want any… *negativity* in the forest.' Kate was shaking her head with a shame-filled expression.

'Wow. That is unbelievable.' Alison wasn't sure what to say – Natalie sounded nasty. 'Can you imagine the scene Frankie would have made if she'd heard her?'

Kate laughed so hard that her teacup, almost at her lips, spilled tea into the saucer and then onto the floor.

'Right – are we all ready to start, then?' Becky announced from the front, then paused while the last few parents stopped talking and settled down. 'It should be a quick one tonight. First, Alison, are you all set for Mother's Day?'

'We are.' Alison fought the urge to stand up. She didn't want to be seen as taking over. 'There is a choice of three gifts and we've left one of each unwrapped, so the kids can see what they're choosing, but the rest are being wrapped and will have a tag on for the child to write their name. We're charging three pounds per gift, so we will make a couple of pounds profit on each one.'

'And they'll all be ready for the kids to choose next week?' Becky looked sceptical. 'Because we've already sent parents an email about it. The kids will be bringing money in and hoping to choose gifts on Wednesday and Thursday.'

Alison tried to maintain the moral high ground. She was not going to be drawn into a public argument. 'They will be ready.' She smiled.

'Okay, then.' Becky ticked the list on her clipboard. 'Rachel – you were going to look into those fundraising ideas you mentioned the other week?'

The meeting moved on through Rachel's explanation of cash-back websites to a long complaint from Becky about the decrease in the number of volunteers before Jo stood up and talked about the accounts in an unnecessarily confusing way. Finally, Becky took to her feet to give a short, smug speech about how much the children were benefitting from the money the PTA raised.

'After Mother's Day, we'll be about halfway through our fund-raising year, so in the next meeting, we'll be looking for ideas for the summer term. I think it's probably best,' Becky said, looking directly at Alison for just a moment, 'if people email me any ideas *before* the next meeting so I can see what might work in advance and save you any unnecessary research.'

Alison supposed she should be annoyed by the dig at her, but mostly she was pleased Becky was that worried about her inter-rupting with good ideas. *Oh well*, she thought, *get ready, because it's going to happen again.*

'Are you off running now?' Kate asked Alison.

'I am – I've got training to fit in for this charity 5K.' Alison waited as Kate struggled into her padded coat. 'Which reminds me – will you sponsor me?'

'Of course.'

'Great. I'll email you the link to the sponsorship page. I think it's called The Glorious Race,' said Alison as they reached the door.

'You're doing the Glorious?'

Alison hadn't registered Becky standing by the door, but now she turned to find herself face to face with her. She didn't know what had prompted Becky's incredulous tone, but she was certainly not going to rise to it. 'I am.'

Becky laughed. 'Wow, I didn't think *you* would go for *that*. All that mud!' She shuddered. 'Jo – did you hear?' she called across the café. 'Alison's doing The Glorious Race?'

Jo laughed unpleasantly.

Alison kept her disinterested smile on her face even while her brain began to panic. There was no way she was going to show her surprise to Becky. 'Goodnight, Becky,' she said, heading out into the cool evening air.

'What did she mean, "all that mud"?' Kate asked quietly, as she hurried along the pavement to keep up.

'I don't know,' Alison admitted, pulling her phone from her pocket to Google the race. 'Oh, no…' As she found the event's website and she saw the images from the race her heart sank. Why hadn't she looked it up before? She carried on scrolling, reading the description in the desperate hope that her run wasn't like these even though she knew it would be. 'Glorious mud,' she said. 'It's one of those muddy obstacle courses.' She held up the phone for Kate to see.

'Uh-oh. Is it too late to back out?'

Alison looked at her friend's wide eyes. 'Well, technically, no. But I can't, can I? Not *now*. I mean, I've told everyone I'm doing it… and I've got sponsorship.' *And I've told Simon I'm doing it.*

Kate smiled reassuringly. 'I'm sure it'll be fine,' she said. 'It's just a bit of mud. You'll be great.'

'Absolutely. Running in mud. How tough can it be?'

CHAPTER TWENTY-FOUR

Kate watched the heavily pregnant woman rush from the scan room straight for the toilets, just like the previous three women had done. Not that Kate could blame any of them. As instructed, she'd made sure she had a full bladder for the scan, but had now been sitting in the waiting area for twenty-five minutes.

Beside her, Matthew had stopped checking work emails on his phone and, as she watched, he locked the screen and slipped the phone into his pocket before reaching across to hold her hand.

'Alright?' he asked.

Kate nodded. Obviously, she was battling with a hundred 'what if's', but third time around, she did feel a little calmer than she had with either Amelia or Reuben. Although that might be partly because they hadn't brought the children with them: Reuben was at pre-school and Amelia was at school. Kate smiled as she remembered how, when they'd gone for Reuben's dating scan, a newly walking Amelia had spent the whole time squirming in Matthew's arms, desperate to get to the floor and start exploring.

'Kate Lambert?'

They both looked up to see a woman with Kate's notes gesturing for them to go into the room and, still holding hands, they immediately stood and followed her.

'So, this is your twenty-week scan…' the sonographer said as she tucked paper towels into Kate's clothing either side of her bump.

'I think I'm actually more like twenty-three weeks,' Kate said, trying not to flinch at the cool gel being spread over her stomach.

'Okay.'

'I'm sorry, we should have booked in earlier, but…' Kate gave up trying to think of a good excuse. Life had just got in the way.

'That's fine.'

Matthew stood behind the sonographer, staring at the screen Kate couldn't see with a frown on his face. She wondered what he could see, feeling fear beginning to steal across her.

'Is it okay?' she asked, trying not to sink into panic.

'Here we go…' The sonographer began moving the handheld probe across Kate's stomach, pausing to tap at the keyboard. 'So, we're just taking some measurements and checking everything is developing as you would expect.'

'And is it?' Matthew asked, still looking uncertain.

'Uh-huh,' she said, concentrating on the screen. 'I'll just take these measurements and then I'll turn this screen around so you and your wife can get a good view.'

'Is that its heart beating?' Matthew said, pointing.

She nodded.

'Wow, Kate, it's like this little pulsing heart. Look!'

But Kate knew she couldn't twist her head far enough round to see the screen. She watched the joy on his face and wished she could share it. Inside, she felt a flutter as the baby kicked as if to show annoyance at the intrusion.

'Was that – did it just punch? Did you feel that, Kate?'

She nodded, grinning.

'I saw that!' He looked across at her with a look of amazement.

'And did you want to know the sex of the baby?'

'Oh no,' Kate said.

'Yeah,' Matthew said.

The sonographer looked from one to the other, then discreetly turned her attention back to the screen and carried on working quietly.

Kate looked at Matthew in surprise. They'd never found out before, it hadn't even occurred to her to do it differently this time.

'Go on,' he said. 'It's our last chance to find out – we're not going to have another baby, are we?'

'No.' As she said the word, Kate realised she felt more strongly about this than she had realised. 'I don't want to know until… I want it to be a surprise.' She shook her head again. 'No.'

Matthew looked slightly taken aback by her response. 'Are you sure?'

'Sure.'

'We don't want to know, then,' he said to the sonographer, who smiled and nodded.

Matthew dropped Kate back at home before he raced back to work for the rest of the afternoon. She had twenty minutes to spare before she had to collect Reuben from pre-school, so she immediately headed upstairs to fetch another load of washing to put on.

In Amelia's room, the tutu Kate had made her for her World Book Day costume was currently being worn by her giant penguin teddy, a present from Nick and Nat for her first birthday. Kate wondered how Natalie would react to someone giving her baby such a toy now. The way they had parted at the wedding was still a source of embarrassment for Kate, but more and more, she was starting to feel annoyed at her friend.

If they could even still be called friends.

They hadn't spoken in the five days since it had happened and Kate wasn't sure how much she wanted to. She might have missed Nat when she left Nick and ran off with River, but she wasn't sure she would miss this new Natalie.

Dropping to her knees beside the penguin, Kate tried to straighten the teddy and fluffed out the tutu before taking a photo on her phone. It only took a moment to post it on her Instagram account with the caption '*Homemade tutu originally for WBD, now modelled by Penpen the Penguin*'.

That made five photos on there so far. No big deal. She was just using it to store the pictures of the things she'd made. Not really for anyone else to see.

Last night she'd noticed someone had commented on the photo of the tooth bag.

'What a great idea! Def gonna do this.'

The compliment from a stranger had made her smile and now she found herself thinking about what she might make next.

CHAPTER TWENTY-FIVE

Frankie felt rather pleased with herself as she walked Liam up to school, enjoying the March sunshine. She was not rushing. She was not late. She was like a proper grown-up who got to places on time. Who knew setting the alarm ten minutes earlier would make such a difference?

'Well, here she is,' Alison said, not quite managing to hide her surprise at seeing Frankie in the school playground on time. 'The high-flyer, the career woman. How's the new job?'

'Oh, y'know, it pays the bills,' she said, pretending the literal truth was a flippant answer.

'Well done you,' Kate said, arms open for a hug. 'Congratulations, you'll be running the place before long.'

'Piss off, that looks like far too much hard work,' Frankie laughed, secretly delighted. 'Anyway, I've only had it a week, it won't be much longer before they realise I have no idea what I'm doing and I'll be out looking for something else.'

'Gosh, has it been a week already?' Kate said. 'We really need to get together so I can hear all about this properly.'

Alison tutted, seeing Xander rolling on the grass. 'Xander!' she hissed, heading towards him. 'Get *up* – before you get grass stains on those trousers.' She pulled him to his feet and dragged him back to wait with her.

Frankie watched Jo arriving, in her running kit as always, holding Charlie's hand as she chatted to Boden-clad Becky, followed by her daughters, Lily and Rose. both with their perfectly parted hair pulled back into low ponytails, walking calmly and quietly. They were a catalogue advert for motherhood.

She was willing to bet Becky had never had a call from one of her girls' teachers to discuss – what was it Mr Armstrong called it? – some 'concerning behaviour'. Frankie had put off returning his call for as long as she could, but after the third reminder, she gave in and listened, dying a little as he explained how Liam had now had three tantrums in the classroom this term, not to mention his accidents. Frankie didn't know what to say to that. She couldn't exactly do anything about it while she was at work, could she? He'd asked, patronisingly, if there had been anything in Liam's home life that might have unsettled him, and she'd resisted the urge to tell him to piss off, not really paying attention to the rest of the conversation, just desperate to end it as soon as possible.

'Did you see what *she* put in the PTA newsletter?' Alison said, turning back to Frankie and nodding towards Becky, dragging her back to the present.

'There was a newsletter?'

'Yes – you must have got it.'

'Let's pretend I did,' said Frankie. 'Remind me what was in it?'

Alison sighed. 'It just talked about how much we've raised, what it will be spent on, what our target is for this term… that sort of stuff. But she also put a note in about wanting all ideas to be emailed to her a minimum of two days before the next meeting. *Obviously* aimed at me so she can veto my ideas or pass them off as her own.' Alison shook her head, clearly still riled. 'No, Xander, no… come back here!' She went striding after him as he slipped from her grasp and raced to the other end of the playground.

'Oh dear,' said Kate.

Frankie watched the pair of mums as they stood, chatting, Jo deliberately turning her back to them. 'Jo's being a right pain in the arse with Ben, too,' Frankie said. 'She's gone all weird about Sunday, whether she wants Charlie or not, how long she wants him for. Ben's tiptoeing around her like she might explode at any moment.'

'Well, I suppose you don't want to make an enemy of her, do you?' Kate said, with an annoying wisdom.

'I've threatened to have a word with her if he doesn't sort it out.'

'Frankie, you mustn't!' Kate was horrified, putting a hand on Frankie's arm as if to physically restrain her.

'I know *that*.'

'What do you know?' Alison said, slightly out of breath as she rejoined the group without Xander, but staring at him as he balanced on the tyres.

'She's threatening to talk to Jo,' Kate explained. 'To tell her off about how she's treating Ben.'

'No – not really. But first she says she wants Charlie all day, then she says she's going out for a treat, so Ben needs to pick him up in the morning and drop him off mid-afternoon, then she says she's away all weekend, so Ben needs to keep Charlie the whole time and now she's back to wanting him all day.'

'It *is* Mother's Day, I suppose…' Kate looked slightly apologetic, so Frankie forgave her for trying to be reasonable.

'Yes, but…' Frankie hated the way she was sounding. 'It's the chopping and changing, like she wants to make everything so freaking difficult. He's made three different plans and now… who knows? I just want her to see it's not *fair*. Ben shouldn't have to be constantly doing whatever she wants in case she takes Charlie away from him.' She crossed her arms over her chest and resisted the urge to take out her irritation on the world. Ben had planned to take Charlie to visit his mum, but kept having to phone her to rearrange every time Jo's mood changed.

'She'll get bored of messing him around eventually,' Alison said, just as Mr Armstrong opened the classroom door to welcome in his pupils.

'God, I hope so.' Frankie gave Liam their customary fist bump before he went in. 'And she'd better keep the hell away from me in the meantime otherwise I'll probably fuck it up royally.'

'I think it's time to put the rest of these out.' Erin put a box down on the reception desk in front of Frankie, picked up the scissors to open it and took out a stack of glossy leaflets advertising the Mother's Day offer. 'The others have already gone and I think we might still have a last-minute surge.'

'We are getting pretty full for the afternoon tea now,' Frankie said. 'But I'd say about half of the vouchers I've sold haven't booked in yet, so hopefully we'll see more customers over the next few weeks too.'

Erin nodded. 'Good. I'll take some of these flyers down to the spa. Can you sort out some for here and take some to Restore & Replenish when you go?'

'Yep.' Frankie took a stack and began filling the leaflet stand by the door.

'Frankie, have you seen Erin?' Tina appeared round the corner.

'She's just gone over to the treatment rooms to put these out,' Frankie said, holding out a flyer for her to see.

'Oh, this is so exciting,' Tina said, clapping.

'Is it?' It was sweet to see the girl so enthusiastic, but Frankie was not sure exactly why she was.

'Oh, yes. I mean, not just this, but the whole events thing – the Easter party and the wedding fair. Erin's so *animated* about it.'

'She *is*?' Frankie didn't think the word animated could ever be applied to her boss. She thought she'd once seen a hint of a smile, but now she even doubted that. '*Really*? Animated?'

Tina rolled her eyes. 'Well, she's…' She leaned forwards and dropped her voice to a whisper. 'I don't think her taking on the

Hall was going so well, and then the whole thing with Adrian…
I think she just wanted to give up and walk away, but last night
she told Mum she thinks she can turn it around.'

Seeing Erin approaching, Frankie hastily stood upright and
nodded in her direction. 'Yes, she's just there, Tina.'

Unfortunately, Tina was not so quick and still had a guilty
expression when she turned to face Erin. 'Oh, yes, um, Ruth has
the menus for you.'

'Right,' Erin said, turning to head back to the bar with Tina
hurrying after her.

When she walked back behind the reception desk, Frankie
checked her phone, where it lay next to the keyboard, hidden from
view. There was a message from Alison to her and Kate. Quickly
glancing around to make sure they had gone, she read it.

> *We need to arrange a date to get together. When are you*
> *free? Alison*

Never, thought Frankie. Between working and sorting out
Liam and trying to find time to see Ben and arranging Jez's visits
there was barely enough time to keep on top of the never-ending
washing and cooking and cleaning. This weekend Jez and Millie
were staying overnight at hers to experience the joy of bedtime and
breakfasts with Liam, and next weekend was Mother's Day, which
would involve the double joys of half a day at work followed by
an afternoon at her mum's.

It depressed her most that she could remember all this without
looking it up in the calendar app on her phone. Had she really begun
to morph into something approaching a real grown-up? She was
getting Liam to school on time more often than not, after all. And
she had a proper grown-up job which paid her enough to keep her
under her overdraft limit. *And* it had been weeks since they last ran
out of clean clothes or loo roll or some other item vital to everyday life.

Maybe I could actually do this, she thought, *maybe I could be all serious and mature.*

In a surge of motivation, she began typing, then hit send without hesitating to think it over.

Come 2 mine for lunch. April 8th. Bring kids and husbands.

Shit.

What had she done?

Six adults and five kids – she didn't own anything like enough plates or chairs… and she'd never cooked for that many people before. As she stared at her phone, wishing there was a way to unsend, the replies flew in.

Great! We'll be there. Kate x

Looking forward to it – it's already on the calendar! Alison.

Too late, it was already on Alison's calendar. Now there was no chance of backing out.

CHAPTER TWENTY-SIX

Kate tried to wait patiently in bed, but at six months pregnant it was not as comfortable as it used to be and she had to keep shifting around and stealing pillows from Matthew's side to prop herself up. She could hear noises downstairs – a crash here, a shriek there – that suggested Matthew was not entirely in control and she began to feel anxious about the state the kitchen would be left in. Throwing the covers back, she eased out of bed and stood up to stretch out her back. Her bump had grown to that inconvenient size where sitting or standing or lying for too long were all equally uncomfortable. Earlier in the week she had turned sideways to squeeze between cars in a car park and suddenly realised that she was now bigger that way round.

With a thud, the door at the bottom of the stairs was flung open and Kate hurriedly got back into bed, listening.

'Careful with that, Amelia,' Matthew was saying quietly. 'Use two hands… two hands, Amelia – *two hands*. Don't worry, I caught it. Here, try again… two hands, remember.'

When they finally came to the bedroom door, Matthew was bent low over Amelia, his hands hovering below hers as she carried a plate with toast perilously close to slipping onto the floor.

'Happy Mother's Day,' she said, proudly handing it across. 'Marmalade toast – I did it myself.'

Yes, you did, thought Kate, amused at the thick layer of marmalade. 'It looks lovely, sweetheart. Thank you.'

Matthew sat back on his side of the bed and Amelia crawled onto the foot of the bed. 'Erm,' Kate said, looking from one to the other. 'Did you forget Reuben?'

'No,' Matthew said, swinging his legs off the bed and heading back downstairs. 'Reuben, are you coming?'

Kate caught sight of Amelia rolling her eyes and couldn't help laughing.

Reuben ran into the bedroom carrying a small bunch of daffodils and a card which he threw at Kate. 'Happy birthday,' he said, giggling.

'It's not her *birthday*,' said Amelia in her exasperated big sister voice. 'It's *Mother's Day*.'

'Thank you, Reuben.' Kate smiled across at him, drinking in the sight of his happy little face. His soft brown hair had grown a little too long, curling over his ears. She opened the envelope, and pulled out the card, which had a picture of a vase of flowers on it. Inside, the kids had scrawled their names across one side and there was a folded piece of paper.

'I drew you a picture,' said Amelia, snatching the card and unfolding the paper. 'Look, it's you!'

'Oh, lovely.' The picture was of a very fat woman, but she was smiling, so Kate decided to focus on that. 'I look very happy.'

Kate took the card from the bed where Amelia had discarded it and set it on the bedside table.

'And a cup of tea,' Matthew said, re-entering the bedroom, holding a large steaming mug.

'Thank you,' said Kate for the third time, but really meaning it this time as she wrapped her hands around the warm mug.

'Come on now, kids, let's leave Mum to enjoy her breakfast in peace.' Matthew herded them out. 'Let's go and sort out the kitchen, shall we?'

Kate sank back into the quiet, sipping her tea, feeling uncertain about what she should be doing. The washing basket was full, she'd not managed to finish the washing-up from last night, and she'd noticed Reuben's trousers were looking a bit short so his wardrobe probably needed a sort out to find out what still fitted, but she wasn't sure if she was allowed to do any of that today. And if she didn't do it, it probably wouldn't get done – it just wasn't on Matthew's radar.

No, she thought, finishing her tea and taking a bit of over-marmaladed toast. It needed doing, so that's what she would do. She put on her dressing gown, collected a load of washing and took it downstairs to sneak into the machine while Matthew was in the lounge watching *Paw Patrol* with the kids. By the time he appeared in the kitchen to tell her off she was filling the sink with hot soapy water.

'What are you doing?' he asked, stopping in the doorway.

'I'm just washing up,' she said, collecting the kids' breakfast things from the table to add them to the pile.

'Don't you need to be going soon?'

Kate looked at him, confused. 'Going where?'

'You didn't read the card, did you? The message in it.' He took her hand and began to lead her back up the stairs. 'Here.'

She took the card he handed her and as she opened it, she saw the note that had been hidden behind Amelia's drawing.

You have been booked in for a pedicure at 9:30 at Heppleton Hall.

'Half nine,' she said, looking at the clock on the bedside table showing that it was already after nine. 'That's…'

'I know – that's why I thought you might want to get a move on.'

'But… I need a shower.' She looked up at him, panicked.

'Better get a move on, then,' he said, chuckling as she raced past him to the bathroom.

Kate left the house with her hair still wet from the shower and made it to the Hall only a few minutes before her appointment.

'Hello, stranger.' Frankie stood behind the reception desk, looking smart and efficient in a green shirt and navy jacket, her hair pulled back into some kind of bun. She certainly looked a far cry from the dishevelled mess that had once turned up to drop Liam off at school wearing a onesie. Kate had a surge of pride at how *together* her friend looked.

'Hi, Frankie,' Kate said, smiling. 'I didn't expect to see you here.'

'Yeah, never expect to see someone where they work,' Frankie replied, sarcastically.

'Oh, well, no, I… I thought you were at your mum's today – I didn't know you worked at the weekend.' Kate was now flustered as well as anxious about being late.

Frankie smiled, shrugging. 'I don't, normally. I've just come in for the morning because it's a bit busier than usual. Liam's already at Mum's and I'm going to head over there for a late lunch when I'm done here.'

'Oh.' That made sense.

'What are you in for?' Frankie prompted her.

'Me? Yes – I've got a pedicure at… well, now.'

'That's fine – I'll take you down to the treatment rooms.' Frankie stepped out from behind the desk and Kate was a little relieved to see that she was still wearing big heels: she hadn't changed completely, then.

Kate heard her phone beep and she saw Matthew had sent her a message.

'Everything okay?' Frankie asked.

'Yes… no.' Kate sighed. 'Just Matthew asking where the kids' wellies are and what snacks he should take for a walk in the woods.' She couldn't help the feeling of annoyance that crept over her. For a start, that washing-up still needed doing and now she knew it would be waiting for her when she got back, and for another, why hadn't he asked her earlier if he knew he was taking the kids to the woods? Stupid question. Of course it would be a spur-of-the-moment decision. 'I should probably give him a ring.'

'Don't you dare,' said Frankie, stopping in the corridor and turning to face her. 'It's not going to kill him to have to work it out himself.'

Kate wasn't convinced. 'It's fine… I'll just do it quickly.'

As Kate scrolled to find his number, Frankie snatched the phone from her and turned it off. 'It'll be fine,' she said in a tone that would not accept argument. 'I mean, *he* might not be, but the kids will be. And maybe then he'll think twice about last-minute texts.'

It must be liberating to think like that, Kate thought, not entirely convinced by Frankie's argument, but certainly not going to disagree.

'Good.' Frankie nodded and pointed to a chair under the window. 'I'd better get back, we're looking to be pretty busy today. Have a seat and Jade will be out in just a moment to take you through for your treatment. In the meantime, can you fill out one of these cards?'

'Okay. Thanks.'

Left alone, Kate eyed the chair, but decided it was too low to risk sitting in only to have to stand a moment later. As she leant against the window sill, filling in the health card, the door in front of her opened and a young blonde girl in a pale blue uniform appeared, her high ponytail bobbing behind her.

'Mrs Lambert? I'm Jade. Do you want to… oh!'

Kate noticed the girl's eyes drop to her bump.

'Sorry, I didn't… erm, nobody mentioned pregnancy.' She looked terrified. 'I … let me just chat to my colleague for a moment.'

As Kate watched the panic on Jade's face, she felt sorry for her. Jade began to back away and entered the next door along. Unsure quite what that meant, she returned to filling in the card. A few moments passed before Jade reappeared, followed by an older woman who was dressed identically, but smiling reassuringly.

'Hello, Mrs Lambert, my name's Sonia. I'm going to be doing your pedicure this morning.'

Sonia took the card to check and ushered Kate into the treatment room. The air was heavily scented with aromatherapy oils and Kate took shallow breaths through her mouth to try to avoid choking on the smells.

'Well, this all looks straightforward,' Sonia said. 'Do have a seat for me. And if you want to take your shoes and socks off…'

Kate sat down obediently and began undoing her laces.

Sonia sat on a stool beside her feet. 'Sorry about that, Jade hasn't done her pregnancy care training, yet, so she was a bit unsure about it all.'

'All what?' Kate asked.

'Well, as I'm sure you're aware, there are some modifications that we do for a pedicure in pregnancy.'

Kate's eyes widened in bewilderment. She was not aware. 'Oh,' she said.

'We have to be careful to avoid the ankles as those are key acupressure points which can actually bring on early labour, and there are certain essential oils we need to avoid because they can be harmful to you or baby. We also use nail polish that is formaldehyde-free and toluene-free because that can irritate your eyes and throat and even affect baby.' Sonia smiled again. 'Don't worry, we'll take good care of you.'

It's a good thing someone's looking out for these things, thought Kate.

The sensation of warm oils being gently rubbed on her feet was not unpleasant, and Kate found herself beginning to relax.

Her thoughts returned to Natalie. She must be approaching her due date soon, although they hadn't spoken since the wedding. She should probably phone… or at least text. Maybe invite them round for a pregnancy-friendly vegan meal?

No. Kate wasn't at all sure she could cope with a rerun of *that* meal. It wasn't just the food, which would definitely be a stretch, it was having to watch River and Natalie being all touchy-feely and unburdened by the stress of parenthood. It was their foolish naivete. It was their superiority, their assumption that they had thought more about their child and therefore would be able to do it right. Unlike everyone else. Or more specifically, unlike *her*.

But maybe… if they just had a baby that was a fussy eater, or preferred watching TV screens to basket-weaving… Maybe then they'd understand…

'Okay, would you like to choose a colour?' Sonia asked, breaking into Kate's thoughts as she gestured to a row of nail polishes.

When Sonia had finished applying the polish, Kate bent forward to see her shiny, gold toenails. She sat admiring them for a moment, while Sonia collected up the various products she had used and tidied them away into the cupboards.

'Don't put your socks on until they're dry,' Sonia instructed.

Kate nodded.

'Have you ever been into our café?'

'No… I've never been here before at all.' Kate felt a little embarrassed by this confession. Real mums probably came to places like this all the time to relax.

Sonia smiled. 'Oh, it's lovely! It's called Restore & Replenish, just back towards Reception, but then straight ahead of you instead of turning left at the stairs. And we've got a special offer on today.' She pressed a small voucher into Kate's hand. 'If you wanted to get yourself a drink, we'll treat you to a slice of cake.'

'Thanks.' A quiet cup of tea definitely sounded more appealing than returning to housework, with or without children present.

'You'll just need to pop some of our flip-flops on for hygiene reasons,' she said, passing two white, flat, foam ovals to Kate before turning to sort out some towels.

Kate stared at what must be the flip-flops, wondering what she was supposed to do with them. They were very wide, with cuts around the outline of the heel, and in the middle of where the toes would go, a curved T shape was cut out. Placing the soles on the floor, she stepped onto them uncertainly, pulling the back section up to make a sling-back and slotting the front section between her big and second toe. She frowned as she tried to shuffle towards her bag and shoes. The flip-flops didn't want to stay on. She tried going slower, attempting to really grip the T bar between her toes, which helped, but she doubted she'd get all the way to the café like this (not to mention the fact she looked ridiculous).

'Oh, Mrs Lambert,' Sonia said, clearly fighting to keep a straight face. 'Sorry, I should have…please, let me.'

Kneeling beside Kate, Sonia took the flip-flop and deftly pulled the back section all the way to the front, then slotted the T shape through to form a strap.

'Oh.' Of course. 'Well, that makes it easier to walk in them,' she admitted.

She walked down the corridor in the now-properly-constructed flip-flops, holding her shoes in her hand, and found an empty table next to the window. When the waitress came over to take her order, Kate handed over the card and asked for tea with a slice of lemon drizzle cake and then relaxed back against the upholstered chair and looked around at the busy café.

It wasn't what she had expected when Sonia had used the word 'café'. There was a bar down one wall and huge Georgian windows hung with dark duck egg blue curtains down the adjacent wall. The high-backed chairs were nearly all full of women of varying ages.

When her tea arrived, Kate tried to sip it slowly and enjoy not having anything to do, but she wasn't very good at it. She ate her cake too hurriedly and was annoyed at herself for not appreciating it enough. The more she tried to ignore the phone that still lay switched off in her bag, the more guilt piled on her until she couldn't bear it any longer and put her cup down to see what she had missed in the last forty minutes.

It seemed to take forever for her phone to turn on, as though punishing her for snubbing it, but finally it came to life, beeping repeatedly to inform her that she had two answerphone messages and three texts, all from Matthew. She sighed, wondering for a second what would happen if she had Frankie's ability to shrug and walk away. *No*, she corrected herself, *that's not fair*.

She sighed and started reading the text.

> *Hi – guessing you can't answer your phone – ignore the messages I left, it's all good here! Mx*

Kate hesitated. Even though Matthew had said everything was okay, she couldn't help feeling guilty for not answering. She wondered what was she supposed to do now. Maybe she should listen to the messages, after all, he might still need her help?

She sighed and reached for her socks to pull them on. Her spell of relaxation was clearly up, now it was time to get home and see what had happened. She paid for her drink and bent down to put her shoes on before easing herself out of her chair and heading back to the entrance.

As Kate was leaving the café, she saw Frankie coming towards her, this time wearing a striped waistcoat instead of the navy jacket.

'Hello,' she said. 'You weren't wearing that earlier.'

Frankie grinned. 'That was Frankie the receptionist, this is Frankie the waitress.' Leaning in, she whispered, 'I think all staff should just wear onesies, then I wouldn't even have to get dressed in the morning.'

Over Frankie's shoulder, Kate saw Jo walk past from Reception to the treatment rooms. *Of course*, she thought, *she's* exactly *the sort of person who would be at a spa on Mother's Day.* And then immediately panicked, *don't let Frankie see her* and in her nervousness she laughed far too loudly at Frankie's comment.

'All right, calm down, it wasn't that funny.'

'Sorry, it's the pedicure and the cake… they've made me giddy.' Jo had gone, but Kate was gripped by fear of what Frankie might do if confronted with Jo without warning.

'If I tell you something, promise you won't do anything stupid,' she said.

'Yeah, I'm not sure that's a promise I can make, but go on.'

'I just saw Jo arrive.'

'Here?'

Kate nodded.

'And you're worried I'll have a go at her for messing Ben about so much over this weekend?'

Kate nodded again, feeling that she might have made the wrong decision.

'I'm so over that,' Frankie said, gesturing with her hand. 'I'm chilled and grown-up about the whole thing now. I'm in my professional work persona. I'm not about to make a scene just because she's not even spending time with the son she *demanded* she have all weekend.' She took a deep breath and blew it out of her pursed lips. 'See? Chilled Frankie.'

'Good, that's good.' Kate was not entirely convinced, but at least Frankie was pre-warned. And she was right, she was at work, so hopefully would be more careful if she did say anything.

'Right, back to work – see you next week.'

Kate watched Frankie stop at a table to speak to a customer, nodding and smiling, before heading into the kitchen. She did look different at work. It wasn't just her appearance, it was the way she held herself; she seemed to walk taller, less defensively.

If Frankie can change that much, so can I.

Reaching into her bag, Kate unlocked her phone and deleted the answerphone messages without listening to them. *A definite step towards more laid-back parenting*, she thought, remembering her New Year's resolution. Alison would be proud of her progress on their little Happiness Project.

CHAPTER TWENTY-SEVEN

Hearing Simon and Xander on the landing, Alison closed her eyes and pretended to be asleep. Xander wriggled into the bed next to her and threw his arm over her to wake her up with a big hug.

'Mummy – I got you a card,' he said, twisting next to her, jabbing her in the stomach with his elbow. 'Look, Mummy.'

Alison sat up as she was presented with the card he had made at school, the front decorated with circles of tissue paper, which might have been balloons or possibly flowers.

'That's just lovely, dear,' she said. 'I can see you've put so much effort into it.'

'And that's not all,' Simon said from the doorway, carrying a tray of breakfast with orange juice, tea and a plate of crumpets with butter melting over them, which he placed on her lap. She mentally gave him a gold star. 'Come on, Xander, let's leave her in peace.'

Alison watched Xander bound out of the room, followed by Simon, who turned in the doorway to close the door behind him. She caught his eye and nodded, but he made no comment and she could see a slight strain on his face.

As she rearranged the pillows behind her and began to eat the crumpets, Alison wondered if Simon had realised how hard today would be. This time last year, Maggie had come over for lunch. It had been unexpectedly warm, so she had commandeered some gardening tools and set about weeding the garden while Alison cooked the roast. *None of us had known it would be her last Mother's Day*, she thought. How could they? Her mother-in-law had been as full of energy and life as always, making everyone laugh with anecdotes from her cycling holiday in Holland.

She felt tears begin to well and sniffed them away. She couldn't do this, not today. She had to be ready to support Simon.

Since Christmas, Simon's work schedule had been hectic, with meetings in New York, Paris and Berlin this month alone, and Alison suspected that he was working hard to distract himself from his feelings. But that couldn't last forever. Especially on a day as significant as Mother's Day.

That was what she had to do. Stop him from hiding. Make this day all about Maggie.

She still wasn't entirely convinced about her plan – it was definitely out of her comfort zone – but she was convinced that she had to do something. She finished her crumpets, checked the duvet for crumbs, then got up decisively. She had time for a quick shower before making the picnic.

'Umm, what are you wearing?' Simon said, when he caught sight of her in the kitchen, chopping cucumber sticks. He was still wearing his pyjamas and one side of his black and silver hair was flattened where he'd slept on it. She tried to work out timings in her head: if he went for a shower now, she could manage to get Xander dressed so they weren't leaving too late.

'Walking clothes,' she said with deliberate vagueness. 'I thought we could go for a walk somewhere. I'm making a picnic.'

He looked at her quizzically. 'You don't want to go and get your nails done, or have a coffee with one of your friends?'

'No.' Alison said, placing the cucumber in a bag and beginning to peel carrots. 'I want to go on a little walk. In the Peak District. The three of us.'

'Really?' He frowned. 'Is it not a bit cold?'

Admittedly, she had thought he would be more enthusiastic than this, but Alison had a plan and was not going to be deterred.

'We'll just need to wrap up warm,' she said, transferring the carrot sticks to a small plastic pot. 'We could take a flask of hot chocolate.'

'Okay, then. I'll go and dig out my thermals.'

She turned, to see if he was joking, but he had already gone. He was *probably* joking, she decided.

Once she'd finished making the picnic and packing it into a couple of rucksacks, Alison called Xander to come and get dressed in the clothes she'd laid out for him.

'Where is it that we're going for this walk?' Simon asked, seeing her lining up both sets of walking boots alongside Xander's wellies in the hall.

'Mawsdale,' she said, watching for his response.

'Oh.'

Alison had chosen this walk specifically because it was where he and Maggie had spent the day only a few weeks before she died, but she also knew it was an area of the Peak District that Simon and his parents had visited many times during his childhood. And while Simon had been doing a good job of not thinking about his mother, Alison could see that it was taking effort. He didn't ask any more questions or even raise his eyebrows at her. He just looked at her and repeated, 'Oh,' his jaw clenching with the effort of keeping it all in.

She could see he knew what she was doing.

The drive was beautiful once they had left the motorway, leading through forests and then opening out to give a scenic view across a valley to the hills beyond. She had the directions printed out, just to be prepared, but he didn't need them. It took over an hour to get there, so by the time they neared their destination, Alison was already feeling slightly frazzled from playing Xander's version of 'I Spy', which made no sense, but always resulted in her losing, much to his amusement.

'Are we actually going into Mawsdale, or parking in Bakewell and walking that way?' Simon asked.

'Mawsdale,' she said, confidently.

'There isn't a car park there. Do you have a plan for parking?'

She did not. 'There should be some parking on the road, I think,' she said, less confidently. The way he'd said it suggested that only an idiot would try and park there.

They entered the village and while she checked road names to get her bearings, Alison noticed the lack of space along the roads to park.

'The walk starts at the bottom of the road on the left, there.'

'This dead end?' he asked.

'Yes. There's bound to be space down there.'

There was not.

The road quickly began to narrow between drystone walls. With nowhere to turn around, they had no choice but to carry straight on. Just as Alison began to fear that the whole outing was doomed, she saw a paved area on one side of the road big enough for a few cars.

'There,' she said, pointing.

'Are you sure that isn't someone's driveway?'

She wasn't at all sure. 'It's fine,' she said, looking for signs just in case.

'Okay.'

While Simon parked, she glanced up out of the window at the sky. The early morning sun had been replaced by thick clouds. At least they were pale grey, not rainclouds. As she got out of the car, the cold wind hit her, but she braced into it. 'We'll soon get warm walking,' she said, hoping she sounded convincing.

Pulling one of the rucksacks onto her back, she set off determinedly, hoping to set a positive tone. She was relieved to see Xander shoot past her at once, clearly enthusiastic.

'Xander, wait, we're still on the road, you need to stay with us,' she called after him.

Simon fell into step beside her, chuckling to himself.

'What are you laughing at?'

He shook his head slightly. 'It's just what us Lund boys do.' He spoke softly, almost to himself, and Alison saw he recognised himself in Xander. She wondered if he was remembering walks with his parents. Probably. Her plan was working.

The road wandered gently downhill, a roof of overhanging branches with new leaves blocking out any sunlight that might appear. Alison tried to hide her shiver, walking more briskly and reminding herself that she would warm up in no time, just as soon as they were out of this wind that was flicking her hair around – why hadn't she thought to bring a hat? They passed the last few houses and finally reached the small trickle of river at the bottom of the hill. There was a signpost indicating a footpath to the left, running alongside the river, and another leading straight on across a wooden bridge that did not seem entirely trustworthy, before disappearing into the fields beyond.

Alison paused to check the map, although she knew that the route she had planned was a little walk next to the river before looping back into the village, with options to cut the walk short if Simon was too upset, or extend it, if needed. Xander ran onto the bridge and jumped up and down in his wellies. 'Hello, trolls!' he shouted.

'Xander, don't do that,' Alison called, worried the bridge might collapse. *No*, she thought, *this is* not *positive parenting*. She tried to smile and said in a more enthusiastic voice, 'Come on, we're going this way.'

'That way looks much more fun,' Simon said, following Xander onto the bridge.

'Umm… I thought we'd go this way,' Alison said, not wishing to divert from the route so early on.

'I think that way just loops back into the village,' he countered. 'Why don't we explore this way? We can always come back if we don't like it.' He turned to look at her and raised his eyebrows in mock horror. 'Let's go crazy and deviate from the plan.'

'Oh, okay,' she said, trying to sound reasonable. 'I mean, from the map, it just looks like a path across a field to the next road – it doesn't go anywhere, so we'll have to come straight back.' She gestured left. 'Or, if we go this way, we get to walk next to the river and past some nice picnic spots and then we can either head into the village for a drink at the pub or head over the fields that way, if we fancy it.' She shrugged as though she was entirely capable of being flexible and had no particular view on the matter. 'But it's up to you.'

Simon narrowed his eyes and she could see that he was torn between wanting to rebel against the plan and actually liking the plan. 'Okay, Xander – looks like your mum has a plan. Let's go that way.'

'Only if you're sure,' Alison said as they both trotted past her, heads down.

It wasn't long before Xander had found a stick from somewhere to hit the ground with as he walked. Alison reached for Simon's hand as they walked along behind their son. Her other hand was pushed deep into the pocket of her coat to protect it from the cold. She wondered whether to wait for Simon to bring up his mum, which might never happen, or if she should just go for it.

'What made you want to go walking, then?' Simon asked, making the decision for her.

'Maggie.'

'Maggie?'

'Yes. You know, you were talking about me trying something new and being more Maggie. And it is Mother's Day, so…'

'I see.' He seemed to be trying to stifle a laugh.

'What do you see?' she said, sharply, looking across at him. 'This is you trying something new?'

Alison let go of his hand and turned to frown at him. 'Yes.'

He seemed to pause before he replied. 'Good for you.'

That wasn't what he was going to say. She wanted to question him further, but out of the corner of her eye, she saw a coloured blur fall into the water with a splash and snapped her head round to see what was going on. It took her a second to realise that Xander was still standing on the path and it was a large Labrador that had jumped into the river and was now paddling about. She looked about for the owner and saw a man in a black puffer jacket with gloves and a hat on, carrying a stick, which he waved at the dog, who scrambled out of the water and ran to him, shaking itself dry as it went.

Alison felt drops of water on her face and grimaced. 'Yuck.'

'What's up?' Simon asked as they continued to walk.

'That dog just flicked me with water.' And then she felt some more drops.

'I don't think that was the dog,' Simon said, looking up at the sky.

The pale clouds had darkened and begun to spit rain.

'I'm hungry,' Xander moaned. 'When are we eating?'

'Not really the weather for a picnic, now,' said Simon, quickening his pace as the rain began to fall more heavily.

This had definitely not been on the weather forecast, Alison thought as they hurried to reach the cover of the trees further ahead. But once there, she discovered that they did not give nearly as much shelter as she had hoped. As they cowered in the hope that the rain would soon stop, she also discovered that while her jacket was waterproof, her trousers were not and where the front of them had become wet, the moisture seeped quickly through the material to her skin, making her colder than the earlier wind had.

'We can't stay here all day,' Simon said, frowning at the sky. 'And I'm not sure it's much wetter out there anyway.'

The three of them made their way out from under the trees, walking single file along the footpath, heads bowed against the rain. Even Xander was walking without his usual bounce, the stick trailing behind him. They followed the curve of the river without talking. Alison couldn't even find it in herself to comment when the trees opened up to give an impressive view of the hills ahead. All she could think was that this damp, cold walk was not what she had planned. As long as they kept moving, it was not too cold, but there was no way they would be able to stop and get out the picnic she'd packed in this rain. She handed Xander an apple and then a cereal bar in an attempt to stave off hunger, but she could tell his mood was dipping and all of them would need to stop for food at some point.

When they finally reached the bridge she had intended for them to cross over, Alison paused. 'Let's head left up here,' she said, pointing away from the bridge to the stile leading back to the road. From here, according to her map, they could head up the hill to the pub at the top. It wasn't her original route, admittedly, but it was one of her possible back-ups if Simon had been overcome with emotion. Not that *that* looked likely now – unless 'hunger' counted as an emotion.

For once, he didn't answer. She walked ahead, marching now she had a purpose and an end in sight. The rain continued to fall, a little heavier now, gathering in the creases of her waterproof before rolling down to her trousers. The wind blew droplets in her face and hair, while others found a way under the waterproof so that she couldn't quite tell what was sweat and what was rain. All she could tell was that the dampness was without end.

'Are you thinking they might do a hot drink?' Simon asked, catching up with her. He nodded towards the pub, which had just come into sight.

Alison nodded, then, realising that wasn't easy for him to see with her hood up, added, 'And maybe lunch in the dry?'

'Hmm.' He didn't sound convinced. 'Come on, Xander – I'll race you to that road sign.'

Alison felt, rather than saw, Xander as he raced past them.

'You've remembered it's Mother's Day, haven't you?' Simon said, then ran after Xander, leaving her behind.

Of course she knew what day it was. And it had crossed her mind that any decent pub would be fairly full, but she was still hopeful that there would be a little table in a corner she could squeeze them onto. They looked so pathetic and bedraggled, surely a kindly landlord would take pity on them?

They did not.

Alison did not do well with refusal, however, so she persevered. 'It's so wet out there, we've had to have a change of plans. And we were just hoping that you might be able to do us a hot meal so we could get some feeling back in our feet. Is there any way you could just fit us in somewhere?'

The woman behind the bar smiled sympathetically and nodded. 'I'm sorry, we just don't have any more room. But, if it's just something hot to eat you're after, we can do you a takeaway? Here,' she said, producing a card from the side of the till.

'How long will that take?' Alison asked.

Simon reached past Alison to grab the menu, as though worried she would turn it down.

'About ten minutes – they're pretty quick dishes.'

'Three scampi and chips,' Simon said, handing the card back.

Alison looked at him in surprise.

'Trust me.' He winked. 'Are you okay to pay if I take him out? I saw a playground outside.'

She was not going to argue with that split of labour. Xander would happily run around outside even in pouring rain, and Alison much preferred sitting in a warm and dry pub. In the end, she barely had time to stare around the bar and judge the customers before the barmaid appeared with three boxes in a plastic bag. Without an excuse to stay any longer, Alison headed back outside, hugging the warm parcel. The rain had stopped. The view from the pub stretched away into the valley and up the hills the other side, all vibrant shades of green in the foreground, dimming to greys under the veil of rain in the distance. Simon stood in the smoking shelter, staring at his phone, immune to the view, while only Xander's bottom half was visible as he disappeared over the top of the climbing wall.

'Who wants food?' she shouted. *That* got their attention.

As they walked back to the car, Simon carried the bag of food to eat in the car. 'Thanks for, erm, the walk,' he said.

She shrugged. 'Well, I'm trying to get out of my comfort zone. "Be more Maggie" as you said.'

He laughed, holding out the keys and pressing the button to unlock the doors. 'This is *not* out of your comfort zone.'

Alison stared at him as he opened the back door for Xander to climb in and shut it behind him before going round to his side of the car. *How did he not see that this* was *out of her comfort zone?*

Leaning over the car, she whispered loudly, 'Me, walking? In the rain?'

He stopped with his hand on the door handle. 'Al, think about it. You thoroughly planned and organised this in an effort to fix me or something. It's you all over.' And then he got into the car, leaving her fuming in the rain.

She opened the door and fought to get her waterproof off before sitting down, the soaked coat balled up under her feet, and slamming the door shut. She wanted to argue, or at least explain, but was too angry to find the words, especially with Xander sat behind her.

'Here,' Simon said, passing her a polystyrene container. 'There's those little wooden fork things if you want one, too?'

On principle, Alison nodded. It might be takeaway, but scampi and chips wasn't *really* finger food. She waited while Simon opened Xander's food parcel and squeezed the contents of a sachet of ketchup on top of the chips before handing them back to him.

The windows steamed up as they sat and ate in silence.

'Thank you,' Simon said, eventually, turning to look at her.

'For what?' she asked, surprised.

'For this.' He gestured out of the window with the chip he was holding. 'For trying. For coming here instead of booking in to the Hall for a facial or something.'

She felt the corners of her mouth start to lift despite her irritation. 'A spa day would have been both warm and dry, I think I made the wrong choice.'

He smiled across at her. 'I'm okay, you know. I mean, I wish Mum was still here… but I don't need *fixing*, I'm doing okay.'

A knock on her window made Alison jump, almost causing her to throw her food down her lap. An angry-looking man was pointing at something on the wall behind them and gesturing them to move.

'Al, I'm not sure this is a parking space.' Simon passed her his tray and turned the key in the ignition.

She turned to look at what the man was pointing at. 'Oh, no, there *is* a sign. Just there – no parking. We should probably move.'

'Good plan.' He looked at her as he put the car into gear, laughter playing around his eyes as they silently shared their amusement at the ridiculousness of the situation.

CHAPTER TWENTY-EIGHT

Frankie supposed it was a good thing for the Hall to be this busy, but right now, as she rushed to get the tray of sandwiches to one table, while another asked for the bill and a third needed clearing for the group waiting at the bar, it just felt like hard work. It didn't help that her stomach was beginning to rumble. She should probably have had breakfast, but between getting ready for work and dropping Liam at her mum's, there just hadn't been time.

She pretended not to notice Jo arriving and heading straight to the bar for a drink. Because Frankie had meant it. She was not going to get into it with Jo today. Jo was Ben's problem and the less involved she got, the easier it would be for him to sort it out. Even if Ben was currently visiting his own mother without Charlie, who Jo 'couldn't do without' this weekend, despite appearing to be coping quite well as she began to sip a prosecco cocktail she had just bought.

Realising she was staring, Frankie finished wiping the table, then turned to hurry back to the kitchen with the tray of dirty dishes without looking back at the bar.

Don't get annoyed. Don't interfere. *How hard could it be to ignore someone?*

And she had a lot to distract her from Jo. Yet even as she ran between the tables, the bar and the kitchen, she couldn't help but notice Jo checking her phone. *Was she flirting by text?* The smiles, the little hair flicks as she tapped away made Frankie think she might be.

Maybe she was seeing someone. That would explain the indecision over Charlie, if she wasn't sure whether her date was going to work out or not.

Stay out of it, Frankie.

'You were right,' Ruth said as Frankie picked up a tray of drinks from the bar. 'Those prosecco cocktails are very popular. I'm just going to have to grab some more – be as quick as I can.'

'Okay,' Frankie said. The cocktails had actually been Ruth's suggestion – a sort of updated Buck's Fizz with three different flavours – and as soon as she'd mentioned them, Frankie knew they'd be a hit. So far almost every table had ordered at least one.

In fact, Jo had already finished hers. Frankie hoped Ruth would hurry back to serve her so Frankie could continue to pretend she hadn't noticed her. Moving away from the bar, she cleared the big table by the window and laid down the little blackboard with 'reserved' written on it, so no one would take it in the next half hour before the booking.

It was as Frankie turned back towards the bar that she noticed the man arrive. He was undeniably attractive, with artistically messy blonde hair, and he headed straight for Jo.

No way. Jo *was* actually meeting a man. And not just meeting, she'd thrown her arms around him with a shriek as he'd lifted her off the ground.

All this time Jo was making life difficult for Ben and Frankie when she was also seeing someone else. How could she do that to Ben?

No. Stay out of it, Frankie.

'You *need* one of these cocktails,' Jo was saying to him, looking round for someone to serve her.

Taking a deep breath against her annoyance, Frankie stepped behind the bar and along to Jo's end with a smile.

'Oh, it's you.' Jo's eyes narrowed, then flicked from side to side as if trying to work out if there was anyone else who could serve her.

'Hello, Jo,' Frankie said, determined to use her newly found professional face. She thought of Alison with her fixed smile and tried to copy it.

'I didn't know you worked here.'

'Evidently.' *Because otherwise you probably wouldn't have arranged to meet your new boyfriend here.*

'What? Never mind.' She waved her hand dismissively. 'I'll have the pear and prosecco cocktail and… what do you want, Guy?' As Jo laid her hand on the man's forearm, Frankie fought to stop herself rolling her eyes and shaking her head, but apparently failed.

'What is your problem?' Jo snapped at her, clearly noticing the scowl.

'Nothing,' she replied, then, unable to keep it in any longer, she added, 'I was just wondering where Charlie was while you were… here?' *On a sodding date*, she added in her head.

Jo's face froze, and for a second Frankie enjoyed what she assumed was a guilty look.

Then, shaking her head, her lip curling with contempt, Jo said, 'Not that it's any of your sodding business, but this is my brother Guy and we are waiting for my mum, who is currently having a massage, and my dad, who is babysitting Charlie, to come and join us for a Mother's Day lunch. Does that answer your question?'

Shit.

Stupid, stupid, stupid. *This is why I should have stayed out of it.*

Out of the corner of her eye, Frankie could see Ruth returning with a crate of bottles and was fairly certain that Jo would gladly throw such a strop that Ruth would have to step in. Frankie cast around wildly for something that would keep Jo quiet.

'I see. Well, I hope you have a lovely meal,' she lied, forcing a congenial smile onto her face. 'Please let me get you those cocktails on the house. Anther pear and…?'

'Oh, elderflower, please.' Frankie was grateful that at least Guy had manners.

'Certainly.'

The cost was worth it to keep Jo from taking this out on Ben, Frankie told herself.

'Well, that's a start,' Jo said. 'But I think you forgot the part where you apologise for being rude and making moves on Ben when we were still married and—'

'Jo,' Guy said in a warning voice.

'Guy, this is *Frankie*. This is the – what are you, like twenty-five? – the twenty-something barmaid that Ben is currently shagging, *and has practically moved in with*.' Jo raised her voice until she was almost shouting.

Frankie clenched her jaw to try and stop herself defending her relationship with Ben – it would only get her into trouble at this point. They *both* knew Ben and Frankie hadn't even met until months after he and Jo had separated and she wanted to shout it back in Jo's face, but the rational, Kate-like voice in her head was loud enough to stop her. If she didn't hold onto her thoughts and try to grovel her way through this, it would all come back on Ben and while Frankie could handle a slanging match, she refused to be responsible for standing between Ben and his son.

With great difficulty and trying to sound as though she did mean it, Frankie said, 'I'm sorry.'

'Like *you* care, you stupid bitch.'

'Jo, come on,' Guy took his sister's arm and steered her away.

Frankie stood still, shocked by the venom. She knew Jo didn't like her – and who was really going to *like* their ex-husband's new girlfriend, anyway? – but she hadn't been ready for such hatred. She realised that her heart was racing and she was actually holding her breath.

'What was all that about?' Ruth asked, arriving next to her.

'Nothing, really. Just my boyfriend's ex-wife,' Frankie said, deciding she didn't need all the details. 'I don't think she likes me very much.'

Ruth let out low whistle. 'I'll say! You okay?'

Frankie nodded.

'Let's get Tina to wait on that table. You stay behind the bar for a bit.'

'Thanks,' said Frankie, gratefully.

'Hello, you,' Ben said.

Frankie was walking quickly against the rain, holding the phone to her ear with one hand and clutching her bag to her chest with the other as she walked out of the grounds of Heppleton Hall and down Church Street. The sound of his voice made her smile at the same time as it pricked the guilt in her stomach.

'Frankie? Are you there or are you just sitting on your phone?'

'I'm here.' She wanted to just hear him talk and joke and not have to tell him how she'd gone and put her foot in it with Jo again. 'How's it going at your mum's?'

'Great. We've had the baby photos out to reminisce about my childhood. I treated her to lunch out, which she thoroughly enjoyed criticising. Oh, and she's been grilling me about this new girlfriend of mine.'

'Oh? What's the verdict? Too good for you?'

'Ha! You've not met Mum yet, so you wouldn't know it, but there'll never be a woman good enough for me, and she's a little scarred by the last girl I brought home.'

'Who was that? Jo?'

'Yeah. Let's just say they didn't exactly see eye to eye on, well, anything. But this new girlfriend… I think this one has potential.'

She laughed, causing a man walking his dog on the other side of the road to turn and stare at her.

'How's it going with your mum?' he asked.

'I'm not there yet, so it's great at the moment.'

'Are you walking?'

'Yeah, just finished work, so you're keeping me company while I get rained on. I've just gone past the church,' she said, hoping he was imagining walking next to her.

'How was work?'

'Umm… not great.' Here was the opener. Here was where she needed to tell him… and yet, she didn't. 'It was properly busy.'

'That's good, isn't it? Do you think it's because of that promotion you did?'

She nodded, then, realising he couldn't see her, she said, 'I think so. There were a lot of those vouchers coming in.'

'Great. Where have you got to now?'

'I've just crossed over School Lane,' she said, trying to distract herself from the fact she hadn't told him about Jo yet.

'Ah, thanks. Frankie, I'll have to go in a sec – Mum's just brought the biscuits in, which means the tea tray is on its way. I'll speak to you later, okay?'

'I saw Jo at work,' Frankie blurted out, half-hoping he'd already hung up.

'You saw Jo?' He had not hung up.

'Yeah, and…' She sighed. 'I'm sorry, it didn't go well. I thought she was on a date, but it was her brother and she ended up shouting at me and – she really hates me, doesn't she?'

On the other end of the phone, Ben was silent. Frankie wiped the rain from her face and tried to guess his reaction.

'Are you okay?' he said eventually.

'Yeah, I'm fine, but she was…'

'I can imagine. Sorry, I should have thought… she always used to go to the Hall. If I'd thought about it, I could have warned you.' His voice sounded strained.

'Yeah, really not your fault she's some crazy shouty woman,' Frankie said quickly. It was bad enough that Jo might have a go at him about it, he shouldn't be feeling guilty too. 'I mean, I assume she wasn't such a loon when you married her.'

'I think she just hid it better.' His voice had lost its lighter tone and Frankie's animosity towards Jo grew.

'I'm really sorry – I gave her a drink on the house and her brother sort of calmed her down and then I just stayed out of her way, so it wasn't too bad,' Frankie said, trying to convince herself as much as him.

'Yeah, Guy's alright and they're close, so he'll have been able to…' She heard him sigh. 'It'll be fine, I shouldn't worry about it.'

Frankie didn't believe him, but talking about it any more wouldn't help. 'Is your mum waiting with the teapot, now?' she asked. 'Are you going to get in trouble for being on the phone too long?'

'No, I'll just blame my new girlfriend. Didn't I mention I could do no wrong?'

'Hey!' she said with mock outrage. 'You get back in there and tell her I'm awesome.'

He laughed. 'Are you nearly at your mum's now?'

'Yep. Just at the bottom of the crescent now.'

Frankie waited at the end of the road even after he'd hung up, holding the phone tightly in her hand, and wished it was all just a little different. Why couldn't she have met Ben a year later, once Jo was happily divorced and cared less about who he was seeing?

And once they'd come to a less precarious custody arrangement.

Frankie thought about how hard she was finding sharing Liam with Jez and Millie. How much harder would it have been if she didn't like Millie? Or if she was still in love with Jez?

The thin seam of sympathy made her feel faintly uncomfortable. It was much easier just to think about how unreasonable Jo was when she was just shouting insults.

She sighed. Why did it have to be this complicated?

APRIL

CHAPTER TWENTY-NINE

Kate had managed to tidy away the breakfast things and wipe down the surfaces before Alison knocked on the door. She put out the broom so at least it looked as though she was in the process of sorting the toast crumbs and cereal scattered on the floor around the table. She didn't think Alison would actually judge her, it was more that Kate really wanted it to look as though she had a handle on her life, and a floor that crunched when you stepped on it didn't suggest that.

'Hello,' Kate said as Alison swept in, carrying an IKEA bag in one hand and a wooden high chair in the other.

'Here we go – this is the chair I was talking about.' Alison looked up and down the narrow hall, apparently trying to work out where to put it. 'Shall I take it straight through to the kitchen? Here, it goes right up to the table, so it hardly takes up any room, and it's adjustable, so Reuben could probably use it until you add the baby bits and then it'll be perfect for the baby.'

Kate had followed Alison as she took the chair to the table in the kitchen to demonstrate it and now stood staring at it, not quite sure what to say. It certainly looked better than the plastic one they'd got rid of once Reuben had outgrown it. And it took up less room – they'd be able to get all five of them round the table without a problem. And Alison seemed determined to give it to them… it just didn't seem right to be giving away such an expensive brand for free.

'Are you sure you don't mind?' she said.

'Oh no, of course not. Don't be silly. It's not like I'm going to need it again – it would be good to see someone else getting some use out of it.'

'Well, okay, then. Thank you.' She turned to put the kettle on. 'Cup of tea?'

'Yes, please.'

'Let me just sort this out,' she said quietly, sweeping up under the table while she waited for the kettle to boil.

'Here, let me get this for you.' Alison picked up the dustpan and brush from the work surface and crouched down to finish up.

Kate tried to push the guilty feeling away. 'Thanks.' For all her bluster, Alison was very kind and suddenly Kate felt lucky to have her as a friend. She sniffed the tears away before they became obvious, blaming the hormones.

'Would you like some birthday cake with your tea?' Kate asked, pouring water into the mugs.

'Whose birthday was it?'

'Reuben's.'

'Happy birthday, Reuben. Did he have a party?'

'No, not really. Well, I mean, we had a little birthday tea and a cake and some balloons. But, no, not really.'

'How lovely! Cake and balloons – what more do you need when you're four years old?' Alison said.

I hope you're right.

'What sort of cake was it?'

Kate lifted the silver foil from the plate to expose what was left of the cake.

'Very nice,' Alison said, inspecting it. 'Did you…?'

Kate smiled. 'It was a joint effort with Matthew.' Kate had learnt from Amelia's party not to attempt anything too complicated. Matthew had baked the cakes and sandwiched them together, then the pair of them had attempted to cover them with the ready-made yellow icing before she carefully placed one of Reuben's little Pokémon toys on top. The birthday boy had loved it and she had not had a meltdown. This was undoubtedly the way forward.

They took their tea and cake through to the lounge, Alison still carrying her IKEA bag.

'I'm glad Matthew can't see us now. This is what he thinks I spend all day doing,' Kate confided.

Alison nodded. 'Simon probably thinks the same, he just has too much self-preservation to say it out loud.'

Kate chuckled.

'Anyway, when I was getting the chair out of the loft, I came across some other baby things and I thought – given that you said you'd got rid of so much – they might be useful. So, here they are.' Alison pulled the bag open and began pulling out vests, babygros, sleepsuits, blankets and towels.

'Oh, wow, there's so much.' Kate felt herself in danger of becoming overwhelmed again.

'Well, I thought maybe Simon might change his mind about having more kids, in which case we'd need it all again.' Alison stared into the bag as she spoke.

Kate had heard Alison speak before about wanting more children and wondered again if she'd actually made her peace with just having the one. Not that it was any of her business.

'Do you know if you're having a boy or a girl?' Alison asked, replacing the items she'd taken out and pushing the bag closer to Kate.

'No, we didn't find out. I don't want to know until he or she is actually here.'

'Ah, well, we found out with Xander, so I'm afraid most of this is boy stuff.'

Kate shrugged. 'I don't think the baby will mind.' From the look on Alison's face, it seemed that this was a shocking idea. *Perhaps I won't tell her how often Reuben was dressed in Amelia's mostly pink hand-me-downs.* 'Thank you,' she said, taking the bag. 'Are you looking forward to this weekend?'

'You mean Frankie's big meal?' Alison grimaced slightly.

'Is that a no?'

'No, no… It'll be nice to have a proper catch-up. After all, we don't exactly get to see much of Frankie any more, do we?'

Kate smiled at Alison's attempt at diplomacy. It was true that although they technically saw Frankie most mornings at drop-off, she was always in a rush to get to work afterwards and even when she picked Liam up from Kate's on a Tuesday, she was usually so late there was no time for small talk. 'It will be nice to say more than "hello, goodbye",' Kate agreed.

'Although I do worry that she is perhaps biting off a little more than she can chew… I don't think she thought it through.'

'Frankie? Not thinking something through?' Kate feigned shock.

Alison laughed. 'But, *eleven* people – that's a lot! And she's never done anything like this before. I really want to help her, but I don't want her thinking I'm taking over.'

Kate nodded. 'I think we have to wait until she asks. She might end up being really good at all this. I mean, look at her getting that job at the Hall and then getting a promotion and working on these events.'

'Hmm… True.'

Kate sipped her tea, waiting for Alison to elaborate.

'She is doing really well, but… she's always in a rush, isn't she?'

'I think that's just Frankie.'

'Yes, but you know she's working such long hours – it's nearly half six before she picks Liam up *and* I've heard her talking about bringing work home with her. And then she's trying to juggle him seeing his dad and her seeing Ben and… when is she going to have time to plan and cook this meal?'

Kate tried to avoid Alison's questioning glare by staring down into the last dregs of tea in her mug. 'Poor Frankie.' It was a lot to do, she had to admit.

Although, being at work did get Frankie out of being on the reading rota, and the parent helpers' rota and every 'can you help us to walk the kids to somewhere we've decided might be educational?' request. Sometimes, Kate thought, working sounded like an easier option.

No, that wasn't fair, she corrected herself.

In amongst the drudgery of those things were the sweet moments when Amelia saw her mum doing them and beamed at her with pride. And one smile could wipe out hours of irritation, making anything seem utterly worth it.

When it came to parenting, there really wasn't any easier option.

CHAPTER THIRTY

Frankie stared at the screen in front of her, barely seeing the Easter menu she was meant to be checking. She was supposed to have taken it through to Erin half an hour ago, but every time she tried to read it, she lost focus and her mind switched back to panicking about her stupid lunch.

How could she have left it this late?

It was only three days until everyone was coming over and she had done nothing about it. She needed to borrow so much stuff, cook the food – not that she'd worked out what yet – and buy drinks (of the alcoholic and non-alcoholic variety), and… napkins? Did people (other than her mother) really use napkins? And music – she definitely needed to do a playlist…

This was going to be the worst party ever.

Her only experience of parties so far were the drunken ones at university, none of which she could really remember, and her mum's dry (in more than one way) New Year's Eve parties. Frankie bit her lip. Ben and Jo had probably had grown-up dinner parties. Alison almost certainly hosted social events immaculately, complete with themed menus, matching décor and choreographed conversations.

For the thousandth time, she wondered why she had suggested it.

Overconfidence in her culinary skills or masochistic tendencies?

'Is there something wrong with the Easter menu?'

Frankie jumped, hearing Erin's voice, and desperately tried to remember what her train of thought had been before she became distracted. 'Oh, no… it looks fine. I was just…' *What had she been doing?* 'Yep, everything's okay, so…' she let her voice trail off, lamely, but Erin was writing something in her notebook and seemed unaware of Frankie's wittering.

'And where are we with the bouncy castle and face painter?' she asked, finally looking up.

'Booked. I'm just waiting for confirmation on the party games hire place and then I think the Easter weekend's all sorted.'

'Once you get that,' Erin said, gesturing with her pencil, 'we'll need to go out into the grounds and pace out where everything will go.'

Frankie nodded, although with the huge grounds, she knew fitting it all in was not going to be a problem.

Erin turned over the pages of the notebook. 'Which brings us to the wedding fair.'

Frankie's days at work had definitely become more hectic over the last month. There were noticeably more clients visiting Restore & Replenish before or after their treatments, meaning she had less time to sit at the laptop Erin had given her to research and organise the wedding fair. The café tended to be quieter later in the afternoon, at which point she would set up the laptop at one of the tables and sometimes managed up to an hour without interruptions, before Erin would move her to Reception. It was also understandable that her work on an event as big as the wedding fair would be tightly scrutinised, but that didn't stop Frankie being irritated at having to tell Erin everything she was going to do and then tell her again once she'd done it – it was like having to do the work three times over.

It was worth it, though, just to be able to prove she could do this.

As Frankie came to the footpath that led down to the end of Potters Lane, she pushed herself to walk faster. Alison's house was not far from the Hall, but Frankie was late. *How had it happened again?* She had actually put effort into trying to keep an eye on the time and leave promptly today, only to suddenly realise that the last forty minutes had flown by without her noticing and it was after five thirty, but she still had to finish emailing the florists about the wedding fair. And even as she was trying to leave, she was stopped by Erin asking for an update. So now it was ten past six and she was late. Again.

The door was opened before Frankie had a chance to knock.

'Here she is, Liam,' Alison said, smiling briefly as she pulled the door fully open to reveal Liam sitting in his coat, his shoes already on, school bag beside him.

Frankie felt guilt pull at her insides. How long had he been waiting for her? He shrugged on his rucksack and pushed past her without a word. Not knowing what to do, Frankie looked back to Alison, eyebrows raised in a question she couldn't find the words for.

Alison smiled and shook her head. 'You all planned for this weekend, then?'

Not even a little bit. 'Well…' Frankie found herself not wanting to admit to Alison, Queen of Organising, that she hadn't really had time to sort anything out. As she looked at Alison's expectant face, she realised how pathetic she would sound.

'If you need me to do anything, just shout. You know, if you need some nibbles or an extra salad or pudding or anything.'

An extra *salad?* What sort of meal was Alison expecting?

'No – don't worry, I'm *totally* all over the multiple courses with many, many salads.' Frankie had a sudden desire to serve doner kebabs with a chip salad. She turned to follow Liam down the driveway. His shoulders were pulled down and hunched forward as he stared at the ground, kicking a stone as he walked.

Frankie sighed. Alison clearly viewed her as incapable and the more she thought about it, the more Frankie was riled by her smug, patronising, self-satisfied attitude.

It wasn't until she was nearly home that she felt her mobile vibrate with a new message from Alison.

Sorry – totally forgot to mention. Mr Armstrong wanted to speak to you after school about Liam. He will phone you, tomorrow. Or you could you ring him in the afternoon. Alison.

Frankie pictured Mr Armstrong – Paul, as he'd always asked her to call him. Tall and attractive, with chiselled cheekbones and blonde sweeping hair, he looked as though he belonged in a nineties boy band.

And she *so* didn't want to speak to him.

'Here you go,' Frankie said, handing Ben the holdall of overnight gear.

He smiled. 'I was worried you'd changed your mind,' he said.

'You worry too much.'

Around them the school playground was beginning to empty, most of the children having gone into the classrooms already. Frankie turned to Liam beside her and crouched down to speak to him. 'Okay, dude, so tonight we're having the big, but very sensible, sleepover, yeah?'

He shrugged, nodded and stared at anything except her.

'Right, see you later.' She held her hand out, ready for their customary fist bump, but Liam turned and ran off immediately, leaving her fist raised, stranded in mid-air. Frankie stood up, brushing down the front of her trousers as if she didn't care. 'God, my son's a freak,' she said. 'That boy is too damn keen to be in school.'

Ben laughed. 'Don't worry.'

'I'm not worried. Anyway, I can't stand here chatting, I've got to get to work.' She leant forwards and kissed him. 'See you later.'

As she strode away, she felt a shiver of excitement run down her back. Tonight, after work, she would be heading straight for Ben's house and staying for breakfast. It was, admittedly, a risky strategy, first sleepover on a school night, but trying to find a night when none of them had something important that day (and when Charlie was also staying with Ben) seemed to take them all the way to the summer holidays. Ben had stared at his spreadsheet and Frankie's calendar for hours trying to find a slot, finally covering his face with his hands and announcing it would have to be this Thursday.

'Okay,' she'd shrugged. *What difference did it make what day it was?*

'We'll have to be really strict about bedtime routine, though. I might start early, before you get home. And I'll talk to Liam about what happens in the morning at my house, so he knows what to expect – if that's alright?'

'What happens at your house?' she asked, bemused.

'We're a little less… laid-back,' he said, seeming to struggle to find the right words. 'I don't want Charlie telling him off. No TV, eating in the kitchen, dressed before breakfast—'

Frankie laughed at the thought of some sort of military morning plan. 'Do those rules apply to me too?'

'Well, er…' His face screwed itself up with the effort of working out how to say it. 'Yeah, they kinda have to, don't they?'

To his credit, Liam was now so knowledgeable about the Carter morning routine, he'd started telling her, 'when we stay at Charlie's house, we have to get dressed before we're allowed to have breakfast,' or 'did you know Charlie doesn't watch telly before school?' in his serious voice.

Not that there had been any of that this morning.

It wasn't just the lack of a goodbye that had been missing. Ever since pick-up last night, Liam had acknowledged her only in monosyllabic responses or grunts. He seemed to have lost all his excitement about the sleepover, but when she asked if he was okay, he'd shrugged and said 'yeah' like some sort of moody teenager.

Frankie tried to imagine what her mother would say about Liam's recent shift in tune. (Not that she was about to admit any worries to her mum.) She'd probably say he was just feeling a little under the weather.

Oh God, don't get ill for the weekend, she thought.

Then she changed her mind. That would be the perfect excuse to have to cancel the lunch without admitting defeat.

Shit, Frankie. You just wished your child was ill. You are a bad mother.

When Frankie began covering Reception at two o'clock, it was her first chance to start working on the list of local wedding dress shops, but even as she began researching them, her phone vibrated loudly on the desk. She answered without thinking.

'Good afternoon, Heppleton Hall.' And then her brain engaged and she mentally kicked herself. 'No, sorry, hello, just Frankie.'

There was a pause on the other end of the line. 'Hello, this is Mr Armstrong calling from Heppleton Primary School, is that Liam Wood's, er, mum?'

'It is,' she replied, simultaneously annoyed that he had hesitated as though even *he* didn't think it was likely Frankie would have parental responsibility, while also wishing that she actually didn't have parental responsibility. Maybe she should start putting Jez's name down on the forms, so he got the uncomfortable calls. *No, scratch that*, she thought, she wasn't ready to go down that route anytime soon.

'Hello, I hope you got my message from Xander's mum that I'd be calling?'

'Uh-huh.'

'Well, it's not really anything to worry about. I just wanted a quick word about Liam's behaviour recently.'

'His behaviour?' *Oh, God – what had he done?*

She heard Mr Armstrong clearing his throat. 'I know we spoke a little while ago about him acting out, and that seems to have settled down.'

That was good, wasn't it?

'It's just that he's been very quiet at school recently, he seems a little anxious and he is still having these accidents…'

'Right,' Frankie said, waiting for him to go on, but he seemed to have got to the end of what he wanted to say. She sighed and tried to work out how she was supposed to respond. What would Alison or Kate say? That didn't help: Alison would go on the offensive and Kate would collapse with worry. 'Thanks, but I think maybe he's just feeling a bit under the weather at the moment,' she said, channelling her mum instead.

'Well, I'll certainly keep an eye on him this end. Like I said, I just wanted to make you aware of his behavioural changes in case there was anything going on at home that was causing it… Has he experienced any changes that might have unsettled him at all?'

Just a few, she thought, not wanting to start a list. 'We've moved house,' Frankie said. 'We used to live with my mum and now… we don't. Maybe that's it?'

'Could be, could be. That might seem like quite a big change to Liam.'

Frankie felt herself sigh with relief, as though she had passed some sort of parenting exam.

By the time Frankie got to Ben's the two boys were in the bath, splashing and shrieking.

'This is your calming pre-bed routine, is it?' Frankie said as she stood with Ben just outside the bathroom door, watching. *So much for Liam being quiet and anxious*, she thought.

'It was always going to be a bit more exciting, the first time.' Ben ventured into the bathroom to put a towel on the floor to mop up the excess water. 'Right, you two, last minute before you need to get out.'

Frankie noticed that there were already two towels waiting, folded, on the lid of the toilet seat. She leant back to look into Charlie's bedroom and saw, as she had suspected, that the two beds (Charlie's and an air mattress on the floor) had the covers drawn back and a set of pyjamas laid out ready. Ben had put serious time into thinking this night through. Frankie felt a twinge of guilt that she hadn't spent longer thinking about it. A real mum probably wouldn't have left all the organising to someone else.

Once they were in their PJs, Charlie sat on his bed for a story with his dad, while Liam and Frankie cuddled up in Ben's bed to read his latest favourite, *Lost and Found*, which she had now read for ten consecutive nights. She was fairly sure he had memorised it by now, as he turned the pages for her without her having to prompt him.

'It looks like Charlie's already finished,' she said as they got up off the bed, 'so we'll have to sneak in quietly, okay?'

Liam nodded. 'Are you staying too, Mummy?'

'Sure thing, dude. I'll be right in there.' She pointed back to the room they'd just come from.

'All night?'

She squatted down to his level and looked him squarely in the eye. 'All night,' she promised. 'Now, get into bed and make sure you don't have any wild parties, okay? Not a peep from either of you.'

He accepted her hug and she watched him tiptoe into the dim bedroom and pull the covers over him.

She paused on the landing for a moment, hearing Ben tapping away at his laptop downstairs, and stifled giggles from the boys' room, wondering if this was how it would feel if they were actually a proper living-together family.

The question felt a little unsettling but at the same time terrifyingly wonderful.

CHAPTER THIRTY-ONE

Alison could feel her legs complaining as she continued running up the long, slow hill, but she reminded herself she had to keep going. *Shut up, legs.* She pulled air in through her nose and out through her mouth, breathing as deeply as she could, focusing on keeping the momentum going forwards. Once she had passed the next right turn, she would be halfway up. Then, once she had reached that road sign, she would sprint to the top, just to show the world she could.

It was her second run that week, and she was proud to have managed to fit three sessions in each week since she'd signed up for The Glorious. If she couldn't back out of this race, she certainly wasn't going to let herself down by not being able to finish it, so training was essential. To begin with she had just copied the routes the running club had taken, but last week Simon had put a new app on her phone which helped her to plan routes of the lengths she wanted, and she had found footpaths around the woods and back along a brook that she had never known existed.

She was nearly at the sign. It was only a couple of hundred yards to the top of the hill and once she was over the top, she would find the footpath and have to slow down to get over the stile.

Come on, you can do this.

Legs aching, she forced herself to take longer strides, swinging her arms for momentum, fists clenched with the effort. As she did so, she gasped for air and felt her breath tearing at her throat.

Don't think, just keep going.

As she reached the top, she slowed, feeling a smile of satisfaction spread across her sweaty face. She was barely moving faster than a walk now, taking the opportunity to shake out her arms and stretch her fingers before pushing her shoulders back and chest out to breathe more deeply.

Once she had clambered over the stile, she allowed herself to settle into a gentle jog as she made her way through the trees, watching the path carefully for rocks or roots. Even as she concentrated on her steps, her mind began to wander.

She was still feeling uncertain about last night's conversation with Frankie. Despite what Kate had said, Alison was still finding it hard to imagine Frankie being able to produce lunch for three families in her little house. And yet, when she'd tried to offer help, Frankie hadn't wanted it. Maybe she was just caught off guard? *Perhaps,* Alison thought, *I should offer again at pick-up tomorrow?*

Taking the left fork, Alison began the long loop around the woods that would lead her down the hill and then round and back up to here again, when she would be allowed to take the other fork back down to the brook. Downhill was the easy bit, the rest phase: as long as she kept moving her legs, gravity would help her. Uphill was when she got to push herself, when she fought against her legs and every other muscle that wanted to give up. And only when she reached the top without stopping or slowing did she really know she could do it.

The route was quiet. Sometimes she passed a couple of dog walkers or runners, but so far tonight, she had seen no one. She could hear the wind rustling in the leaves overhead and the birds chirping. Now that the weather had turned, there were signs of daffodils and violets; it felt as though spring had arrived. Alison turned her face up to look for the birds amongst the branches, but wherever they were, they were well hidden.

Up ahead, the path began to turn into what Alison always thought of as the muddy corner. Even when it hadn't rained, this part of the path never seemed to fully dry out. She kept to the side, trying to avoid the muddiest section, slowing right down as she stepped over a fallen branch. The sound of laughter carried towards her from somewhere ahead on the path. It sounded familiar and after a moment it was accompanied by two voices she recognised.

Picking up her speed again, Alison rounded the corner to see Becky and Jo jogging towards her. She had often seen Jo in her running gear, but Becky also looked utterly at home in her dark, multi-coloured three-quarter-length leggings, and a fashionable two-layer top, as she ran. If she was sweating or tired, there was no sign of it on her face. Alison fixed them both with a smile, *you can't make me feel bad,* and crossed the still-muddy path to avoid them.

She didn't see the rock, but her toe found the edge of it, causing her to stumble, and she hadn't quite righted herself before she was caught out by the root of a tree hidden in the mud. Unable to keep her balance, Alison felt her arms wave ineffectually as she fell, landing on her side in the dirt, the mud squelching as she turned to sit up.

She heard Jo howl with laughter.

'I don't think you actually have to fall into mud to practise for The Glorious,' Becky sneered, sounding barely out of breath. 'Do you need a hand getting up?'

Alison struggled to her feet as quickly as she could, ignoring the pain in her hip. 'No, I'm fine thanks, just a little trip.' She couldn't look at them, but she heard their sniggers as she ran away.

Of all the times to fall.

Of all the people to witness it.

Now the ache in her muscles was joined by the pain of the fall. Having made sure Becky and Jo were nowhere to be seen, Alison slowed to inspect the damage. Her right side, ribs to knee, was covered in mud, as were her hands. She wiped the muck off on the left side of her T-shirt, noticing as she did so a stinging pain, and looked down to see a graze on her right elbow, and a small trickle of blood.

How would she ever live this down?

The shock, the pain, the humiliation, it all suddenly felt overwhelming and she felt the tears spill over. Automatically, she wiped them away with her hand and then realised she probably now had mud streaked across her face too.

It was too much.

It was not fair.

She tried to be a good person. She worked hard. She prioritised the important things in life. She put other people first. She tried so hard. So how did the likes of Becky and Jo always come out on top? With their well-behaved kids and their perfectly styled lives… Where was the justice in that?

Alison took a deep breath and tried to get a grip on herself.

Chin up.

Deep breath.

Carry on running.

It only took a few minutes of putting one foot in front of the other before she felt her head start to clear. By the time the path had finished the downhill loop and begun to climb again, she felt in charge of herself once again.

She had been silly to compare herself to Becky and Jo. It didn't matter what it looked like on the outside, she had no idea what their lives were like on the inside.

And she might be sweaty and muddy and out of breath, but that probably meant she was working harder than them.

Although… maybe next time, she'd find a new route to run.

CHAPTER THIRTY-TWO

Ben took the takeaway tubs from the plastic bag and laid them on the counter next to the plates.

'Have they gone quiet yet?' he asked Frankie, accepting the glass of wine she passed him.

'Yeah – just checked. Spark out.' This wasn't entirely true. Charlie was asleep, but Liam had complained the room was too dark, and he was too hot, and he needed a glass of water, and his leg hurt, and finally asked, 'how do corners work?' After getting his drink, rearranging his duvet, putting the bathroom light on and refusing to debate ridiculous questions after bedtime, Frankie had sat at the top of the stairs with her wine, waiting for Ben to return with the takeaway and hoping that Liam would just go to sleep.

'Mum-my,' Liam whined from upstairs.

'Or maybe not.' Frankie took a gulp of wine and left Ben to divide up the Indian takeaway between the two plates.

'What now?' she whispered as she got to the bedroom doorway. 'I'm still too hot.'

'Right, take your PJs off.' She knelt down to help pull the T-shirt over his head.

'I don't want no bottoms on,' he said in such a small worried tone that Frankie found herself feeling bad for being annoyed.

'Here,' she said, passing him his pants. 'Wear these.' She waited while he changed. 'Better?'

He nodded.

'Okay, then. Go to sleep.' She leant forward to kiss his cheek. 'Goodnight,' she said in what she hoped was a *seriously, I'm out of patience, just go the fuck to sleep, and remember I love you,* tone.

When she returned downstairs, she met Ben carrying the plates through to the table in the corner of the lounge. This house was a definite step up from his old flat. It wasn't huge, but it had an extra bedroom for Charlie and a garden too. The only downside was that it was past the other end of the High Street from her house, although that still only made it a fifteen-minute walk (or twenty, with Liam in tow).

'I suppose it'll take a while for the boys to get used to this,' Ben said as they sat down.

'Hmm,' said Frankie. She didn't really want to talk about that. The idea of getting used to staying at Ben's was a bit too close to the idea of moving in together full-time and much as that sounded fantastic, it still scared the bejesus out of her. It would have been big and scary enough if it had just been about her and Ben – with the exception of Jez at university, she'd never had a serious boyfriend. But this wasn't just about her and Ben. It was hideously complicated by children and their other parents.

'How did the big sleepover with Jez and Millie go last weekend?' Ben asked.

'Alright, I think.' *Better than this*, she thought. 'They came over in the afternoon and we all had pasta together, which was a bit weird, but Liam loved it. They both went and chatted to him while he had a bath, then Jez read his bedtime story and the three of us had a couple of awkward hours watching telly before they made their excuses and went to bed.'

'Where did they sleep in the end?'

'Liam's room – he came into my bed.'

Ben looked at her as though he was trying to weigh up whether to ask her something or not. Finally, he speared a piece of chicken dopiaza and asked, 'Did they ask you about the wedding again?'

Frankie's shoulders sagged. 'Yes. And I told them I was still thinking about it and they said I could come too – but I couldn't think of anything worse.'

'Wouldn't that be better?'

Her eyebrows shot up. 'Seriously? A whole day surrounded by his friends and family? Me on my own, just watching Liam being made a fuss of by his new, rich and exciting family? Sounds great!' Her words dripped with sarcasm.

'Would it help if you weren't on your own? Would you like me to come too?'

She looked up at him, surprised. That was not what she had expected him to say. 'What?'

'I mean, you don't have to, I just thought—'

'Yes,' she said, before he could take it back. 'Yes. I still don't *wanna* go, but…'

Ben nodded slowly as he mixed the rice with the remaining sauce.

'Would you go? If it was the other way around? Like, if Jo remarried – would you go to their wedding?'

'It's not the same thing.' He shook his head. 'Charlie's been with his mum and not me loads of times, and he knows her family and friends and he'd play with our – her – friends' kids.'

'Oh.' Frankie shrugged. That hadn't been much help.

'But for Liam, he won't know anyone except his dad, well, and his step-mum-to-be, I suppose.'

His dad and step-mum. Frankie had never thought of them like that before, like a whole family ready for a child. 'Just call them Jez and Millie.' Suddenly feeling nauseous, she dropped her fork onto her plate and sat back in her chair.

'Sorry,' Ben said, watching her.

In her mind, the wedding of Jez and Millie morphed into the wedding of Liam's other parents and a fear she couldn't quite name tightened her chest.

'He seemed like a nice guy, Jeremy,' Ben said quietly. 'And Millie, too.'

Traitor.

'Although they're both really nervous.'

Her head shot up. 'Nervous?'

He smiled. 'Frankie, they have no idea what they're doing with Liam and they must be terrified that they'll do something wrong and you won't let them back.'

'I wouldn't do that.' Even as she said it, Frankie realised it probably wasn't true.

'Frankie, I know it must be difficult… it's hard enough sharing Charlie, but it's all for Liam, isn't it?'

'Fine,' she said, wanting him to stop talking. 'Fine, I'll take him to the stupid wedding.' She fixed him with a look. 'And you – you're not getting out of it.'

Ben smiled. 'I'd love to.' And she couldn't work out whether he meant it or not.

'You're so bloody annoying,' she said, unable to stop the smile creeping across her face.

'Mummy?' a voice whispered.

Frankie opened her eyes to find Liam's face two inches from her own in the darkness.

'Christ.' She jerked her head back, trying to remember where she was. The bedside clock on Ben's side of the bed pointed out that it was only half past midnight. 'What is it?' she said, struggling to keep her eyes open.

'Mummy, I can't sleep.'

'Go back to bed, Liam.' Frankie was never at her best in the middle of the night.

He shook his head, looking scared. 'It's too dark.'

'Okay, I'll put the bathroom light on for you.'

As she began to climb out of bed, hoping she wasn't disturbing Ben, Liam grabbed her hand, clinging so hard it was difficult to keep her balance.

'Hey, dude, careful.'

Frankie led the way back to his room, pausing at the bathroom to reach in and pull the cord. The sudden light was so bright, she closed her eyes, feeling for the door to close it at least a little bit.

'No, I need the light,' Liam protested.

'It's still light. Come on.' She waited while he got into his bed, then turned to go.

'No, Mummy, stay… please?'

She sighed. 'Where?' Charlie's room was not big to begin with and with an air mattress on the floor, there was no space left for her.

'In my bed?' He shuffled across a little and held the duvet open for her.

'Just a few minutes,' she warned, getting in.

But he snuggled in next to her, holding tightly, and she knew it wouldn't be easy to leave. She tried to remember when she'd last shared a bed with him not counting last weekend. She had a memory of bringing him into her bed as a baby after she had fed him. He had been warm and soft; she could still feel his fuzzy hair against her cheek as she drifted off to sleep only to be woken by her mother and lectured on the dangers of sharing a bed with an infant. Once he was three months old, he had moved into a cot in his own room on the first floor, next to her mum's, so it became his nana he went to in the night while Frankie was left alone with unbroken nights of sleep.

It all seemed so long ago.

Right now, though, Frankie's arm was losing feeling and Liam's elbow was digging into her side. Having heard the minutes tick by and Liam's breathing become slow and steady, she eased herself away from his warm little body, rolling gently onto the sliver of floor, before standing up.

As she got back into Ben's bed, she felt his arm go around her. 'Alright?' he murmured.

'Yeah, sorry.'

It seemed that she had only just closed her eyes when a hand gently shook her arm. 'Mummy?'

'Mmm, yeah… what?' She opened one eye.

'I still can't sleep. Can I get into your bed?'

She shook her head and sat up. 'No, Liam, there's no room here. Come on, back to your bed.'

'Will you stay with me?'

Once again, she climbed in next to him, counting the seconds until she could slip away. She'd always thought of him as a good sleeper, but was that just because she'd been up in her little attic room at her mother's, separated from the details of his night-time routine?

This time she waited until she was certain he was out for the count before she moved, trying to slip into Ben's bed without waking him and falling asleep within seconds of pulling the duvet over her.

'Mummy, I've got a tummy ache. And I wanted to tell you something…'

Desperate to return to sleep, Frankie forced herself to sit up and look at him through blurry eyes.

'No, Liam, back to bed.'

'Will you stay with me all night?' It might not be comfortable, but if it meant not being woken up every twenty minutes, it would be worth it. 'Okay,' she said as she stood up to follow him back to bed.

'Frankie, wait,' Ben said, sitting up in bed. 'You and Liam take this bed. I'll go in Charlie's room.' He pushed back the covers and left before Frankie could thank him.

Without a word, Liam crawled into the bed, curled up and closed his eyes.

Frankie rolled towards him and stared at the red digits on the bedside clock: two fifteen. It was no use. The interruptions had left her wide awake.

And awake in the dark the fears she had been hiding from stormed into her mind.

She couldn't pretend any longer.

Liam was obviously struggling.

She didn't know whether it was because of the move, or the meetings with Jez or even what was happening between her and Ben. But it didn't matter, because whichever it was, she was the cause of all of those things.

She was a terrible mum in three different ways.

But what else could she do?

CHAPTER THIRTY-THREE

Kate found herself awake, listening to the sound of the water running through the pipes and realising Matthew must have got up early again. She rolled over and tried to enjoy the novelty of lying in bed without feeling guilty, but thoughts and worries began to gather in her mind and by the time Matthew came back into the bedroom, she had sat up and was trying to arrange them into a 'To Do' list she could work through.

'Sorry, did I wake you?' he said, coming over to kiss her. 'Morning.'

She watched as he took off his towel and threw it on the bed before searching for pants in the pile of clean washing she had not yet put away.

'Anything exciting planned for today?' he asked as he began to get dressed.

'I need to sort out the baby things Alison gave us,' she said, thinking back to the list. 'This morning Reuben's at pre-school, so I should get a chance to do that and wash the sheets and change the beds, put some of this washing away. And it's Friday, so this afternoon I'll take Reuben to the reading group at the library. And while I'm in the village, I could do with going to the post office and seeing if they've got a birthday card for your mum. And I think Amelia's grown again, her pinafore was looking a bit short yesterday. I'll see if I can take the hem down. And if I've got time, I could do with popping to the butcher to pick up sausages for lunch.'

'Wow, rock 'n' roll.' He chose a tie and turned to the mirror to do it up.

'How about you?' she asked, watching him concentrating.

'I'm meeting with the Head first thing about that boy who had surgery on his heart – about him starting back next week – then I'm on gate duty before school, I'm teaching all day and have to set cover for Monday when I go on this training.' He checked his tie was straight, then turned to face her as he pulled his collar down. 'Oh, and I have three detainees after school.'

No wonder he was getting up early, she thought. 'You win.'

He smiled at her. 'It's not a competition,' he said, kissing the top of Kate's forehead. 'I'm going to have breakfast at work. Have a good day.'

She listened to the sound of his footsteps down the stairs, the jangle of keys, the rustle of material as he picked up his coat and then the door opening and shutting behind him. The house was silent around her for a second before she heard the floorboards creaking as Amelia sneaked along the hall to the bathroom, marking the real start to her day.

As ever, they arrived first at the Reception playground for pick-up. The sun had finally made an appearance and although the wind was cool, Kate was feeling too warm in her coat, having walked up from the library with a large bag of books. She put the books on the ground next to her and Reuben immediately began pulling them out of the bag as he searched for the one he wanted. She watched him, trying to work out how long to leave it before she began tidying away after him. Finally, he seized *The Smartest Giant in Town* with both hands and sat cross-legged on the tarmac, flicking through the pages. Kate put the rest of the books back in the bag and worried about what the other mums on the playground would be thinking.

I can't believe she lets him sit on the floor.
Showing off her child reading already.

Why isn't he running around playing like a normal boy?
I would never let my child treat books like that.

She glanced around, but nobody seemed to be looking. Maybe no one was thinking those things. Her mood lifted as she saw Frankie appear at the gate, arms folded as she marched across the playground. *She wouldn't care what anyone else might be thinking,* Kate told herself. *Be more Frankie.*

'Hey,' Frankie said, coming to stand next to her. 'How's it going?'

'Good, thanks.' Kate smiled. 'You're early today.' It was more common for Frankie to be running in as everyone else was leaving, and Kate always felt stressed on a Tuesday when it got to bath time without Liam having been picked up.

'Yeah, it's a new thing I'm trying – I call it *getting to places on time.*'

There was something different about Frankie. 'Oh, how's that going?'

'Well, today is the first day I've managed it this week, so…' Frankie sighed. 'Not the best.'

'Still, well done,' Kate offered, hoping to encourage her. 'How did you manage it?'

'I set alarms and I brought work home.' She tapped her tote bag. 'Fun weekend ahead.'

As the classroom door opened, Kate realised she only had a few seconds before they would have claimed their children and gone their separate ways, but she was loath to leave Frankie when she looked so low.

'Do you think it's warm enough for the park?' Kate asked.

Frankie sighed and smiled. 'Yeah – fancy it?'

Kate nodded.

They followed the now over-excited kids as they ran across the field to the back entrance and up to the High Street.

'Hold my hands while we cross the road,' Kate said, taking a grip on Amelia and Reuben. She didn't dare look at Frankie as she began the road crossing rhyme, knowing how ridiculous it must sound. 'Look both ways, left, right, left, Mummy says…'

'Safe to go!' Reuben shouted.

'Safe to go,' Kate agreed as they crossed the road.

As soon as they got to the pavement Amelia dropped her hand and raced to the gap in the hedge that led to the playground. Reuben followed her and Kate tried to walk faster to keep an eye on them. She noticed that Frankie had headed straight for the bench, and Kate stopped, torn between wanting to join her friend and wanting to be closer to her children, who were busy climbing up the slide, just in case. *You're worrying too much*, she told herself, turning to join Frankie.

'All set for tomorrow, then?' Kate asked.

'God, no.' Frankie pulled a face. 'Work has been stupid busy – I haven't had a chance to do anything.'

'Oh dear.' Kate felt her fingers wrap themselves together as she took on some of Frankie's worry.

Liam stood near the bench, playing with his zip, his head turning to stare at his mum, then his friend and back again. 'You alright, dude?' Frankie asked, and Liam nodded, finally turning towards the swings.

Kate watched him go, slowly, glancing back at Frankie. Liam was usually such an independent little boy, running off to play with Amelia on the climbing frame or slide without a backward glance. 'Do you need some help with tomorrow, then?' she asked.

Frankie sighed. 'No, I'll figure something out. Actually – I might need some plates…'

'I can help with that,' she said, pleased to be given an easy task. 'Just plates, or bowls and cutlery and glasses too?'

'Like, everything…'

'How many?'

Frankie looked desperate. 'I don't freaking know. Can I text you tomorrow?'

'Okay.' She nodded. 'You know, you should ask Alison,' Kate suggested. 'She's bound to have ideas about food you could do last minute. I bet she'd even do the cooking for you if you asked.'

'No,' Frankie snapped, almost causing Kate to jump in surprise. 'No, I just… she's… I can do this myself.'

What's going on there? Kate wondered. Frankie and Alison had been getting on so much better since the Christmas bazaar, why did Frankie seem to be so annoyed at Alison now?

'Mummy!' Liam yelled, holding the chain of the swing. 'Mu-ummy!'

Frankie looked up, surprised. 'What's up, dude?'

'Push me.'

'Okay.' As Frankie passed Kate, she shrugged and whispered, 'Well, this is new.'

Kate could see Reuben staring at the swings with a frown on his face. 'Did you want to go on the swing?' she called to him.

He nodded and slid down, running to meet her at the swing.

After a moment of silence in which they pushed their children on the swing, Frankie turned her face to Kate. 'So, I heard about what thingy said to you at the whatsit.'

Kate tried not to laugh at Frankie's effort to be subtle. 'Can I have a clue of who or where?'

'Y'know, at the wedding.'

'Ah. Yes. It was not great.' Kate felt the pangs of guilt once again.

'I think you did well not to deck her. She sounds freaking annoying.'

Kate sighed. 'She's just… unrealistic. I bet we were like that before we had kids, with all these things we thought we could do better.'

'Speak for yourself.'

'Even you, Frankie. You had one idea about what it would be like to have a child and then it turned out not to be so easy?'

'Hmm.' Clearly, Frankie was not ready to admit that she might once have felt like that.

'I just feel so guilty. I mean, it was her *wedding day*.' The last words were whispered.

'No, she was way out of order, Kate. Have you heard from her since?' She sounded so certain.

Kate shook her head. 'I should probably phone her. It's been nearly a month.'

'Yeah, but *she's* the one who needs to apologise. Why hasn't *she* called *you* yet?'

Part of Kate agreed with Frankie, but the bigger part disagreed. Natalie's life had changed so much in the past year, and she was going through pregnancy for the first time, not to mention the stress of organising a wedding so quickly. Maybe she should be a bit more supportive? 'I might text her later.'

But later, after the kids had gone to sleep and dinner had been cleared away, an exhausted Kate stared at her phone, struggling to find the words.

I'm really sorry about what happened at the wedding.

But she wasn't really that sorry, she didn't really think she'd done anything wrong.

Hello! Just wondering how you're doing?

No, that totally ignored what had happened and glossing over it wouldn't help.

Sorry about how we left things – how are you?

She yawned. That was probably as good as anything. She hit send before she could change her mind. Now she just had to worry about whether or not Natalie replied.

CHAPTER THIRTY-FOUR

Frankie couldn't remember a time when she had been awake earlier than Liam. The sun wasn't even up yet, there was just a haze visible through the gap in the curtains. She rolled over onto her right side to face Ben's sleeping figure and contemplated waking him up, but decided he probably wouldn't be much use in his early morning grumpiness.

She sighed and turned away. Her bed was uncomfortable, the duvet twisting around her, the pillows all fluffy in the wrong places. It was no good: she would have to get up.

Sighing, she went downstairs to make herself a coffee in an attempt to come up with a solution to the looming problem of today's big lunch. As she waited for the kettle to boil, she tapped her fingernails on the counter and wondered if she could invent a small emergency that meant she would have to cancel. Nothing too big.

A health scare for her mum? No, they would probably see her at some point and ask about it.

A fictitious rash for Liam? No, they would ask too many questions and then he'd end up having to be off school in case it was infectious or something.

A migraine! Perfect. She could legitimately spend all day in bed – she could get her mum or Ben to look after Liam – and best of all, no one would have any way of proving it was fake.

Even as she felt pleased with her solution, the guilt began to wash over her. It was not a familiar emotion and Frankie did not like it. This was a perfectly good plan and now it was ruined by some stupid sense of right and wrong.

She sat up on the worktop and hugged her coffee cup to her chest, gently blowing on it. Next to her was the work bag she'd abandoned last night, her notebook spilling out of it.

Maybe she had been looking at this all wrong.

If this was an event at work, she wouldn't be able to get out of organising it. She'd pulled off a Mother's Day promotion in just two weeks and that had involved loads more people.

Frankie put down her coffee and pulled the notebook out, finding a blank page and a pen. At work, she would start by brainstorming ideas and problems, just to get it all out of her head so she could see what she was dealing with. That was what she needed to do now.

After ten minutes of scribbling, crossing out, annotating and rearranging, she had a prioritised list to start working through:

1. Choose food and buy enough for six adults and five children. Cook it.
2. Sort drinks and glasses/cups.
3. Buy napkins?
4. Tidy and clean downstairs.

The first item was obviously the biggest difficulty. She checked her watch: it was now half past six, which meant she had six hours at the most, including getting dressed. She still had to buy ingredients and cook something, but given that she didn't have much in the way of pots and pans, she'd probably end up having to cook in batches, which would take even longer. Maybe a bolognaise or chicken curry? But she didn't have anywhere for people to sit down and eat a meal so it had to be finger food.

Did hot dogs count as finger food?

No, you can't serve hot dogs, Frankie.

She was ready to throw the pen across the room and give up when Ben came in, yawning.

'You're up early,' he said, wrapping an arm around her as he reached to turn the kettle on with the other.

'I'm just trying to sort crap out for later,' she said.

'What did you decide to do for lunch in the end?'

'Erm… hot dogs?'

He laughed. 'Seriously?'

'No, of course not seriously.' She grimaced.

'You mean you still don't know?'

'No, I know,' she lied. 'I've got it all worked out. I've decided to go with finger food that I don't need a hundred pans to cook.'

He frowned. 'What sort of finger food?'

Good question.

Pizza.

'I thought pizza?' she half said, half asked.

He nodded. 'Good plan. With salad?'

No, you needed bowls or plates and forks for a salad. 'Do I have to?'

He hesitated. 'I can't see Alison eating pizza without salad. But I bet she brings spare carrot sticks for Xander in case you don't do healthy options,' he said, laughing.

'Fine. I can do carrot sticks.'

'And cucumber sticks? Maybe some red or yellow peppers? Or cherry tomatoes?'

'Yeah, alright.' She pushed him away playfully. 'Been planning this long, have you?'

'And pudding?' he asked.

'You got a suggestion?'

'Well, I'd always go with a chocolate brownie and bowl of fruit.'

'Oh, would you?' Why hadn't she asked Ben before? He seemed to have an answer for everything.

He shrugged, moving to the side to make his cup of tea. 'That many people, you've got to go for the crowd pleasers.'

Frankie looked at her list again and decided the first thing she needed to do was go shopping for pizzas and drinks and food in general. And while she was waiting for Liam to wake up and have breakfast with her, she would have a go at tidying up downstairs.

It was after nine when Frankie and Liam left for the supermarket. Ben dropped them off before going home to change and pick up Charlie from Jo's. Frankie began piling the trolley with fruit, salad and pizzas before heading to the drinks aisle, where she added wine and some Shloer for Kate. Her hand paused on a bottle of Coke, but she decided she couldn't risk a lecture from Alison, so she picked up some cartons of apple juice for the kids. In order to get to the tills they had to go past the party aisle, where Frankie spotted napkins and paper plates.

'Okay, Liam, you get to choose the napkins,' she said, picking up the plates. Without hesitating, he picked up a packet with silver and purple unicorns on and threw it into the trolley. Frankie stared at him for a moment before deciding she didn't have time to ask about that choice now.

It was only once they got back home and began to unload that she realised she had forgotten about the non-fruit dessert. Ben had suggested making chocolate brownies, but without the skill or equipment for baking, Frankie had been thinking about buying one of those tubs full of mini brownies or rocky road bites that her mum always had in the cupboard in case of emergencies. She looked at the shopping bags on the kitchen counter and the clock on the wall that reminded her she had only a couple of hours remaining before people would start arriving. Ben was still out collecting Charlie from Jo's and she couldn't face another taxi journey to the shop. The café in the village sold individual brownie slices, but it would cost a fortune to buy eleven of them.

There was just one other place she could think of to get them. Someone who would always have something in the cupboard.

And she wasn't asking for a handout. She would offer to buy them, fair and square. Or at the very least she would offer to replace them next time she went shopping.

'Come on, Liam,' she said, trying to sound exciting enough to avoid the meltdown that turning off the TV usually led to. 'Let's go visit Nana.'

Frankie sent her mum a text as they walked down School Lane and round to the crescent, trying to keep the message vague to avoid Paula sighing in her passive-aggressive way. She spotted her sister's car in the driveway and groaned inwardly. She did not need an audience for this; Laura would spot what she was here for a mile off and would shout about it until everyone was well aware of Frankie's failings.

'Hi, Mum,' Frankie said as the front door opened.

'Francesca,' Paula said, nodding at Frankie before she bent forward and beamed at Liam, opening her arms for a hug. 'And how's my little Liam? It feels so long since I've seen you.'

'It's not even a week, Mum.'

'It feels *so* long, now you don't live here.' Releasing Liam, Paula turned and ushered them inside. 'This is such a nice surprise, though. I was feeling so sad that I wouldn't see anyone for lunch tomorrow, and now you're all here unexpectedly.'

Frankie bit her lip to stop herself pointing out that the lack of a family lunch tomorrow was because her mum was going to her friends' wedding anniversary party. For once, not Frankie's fault.

'Hey, Frankie!' Laura came out of the lounge, leading her boyfriend, Stuart, by the hand.

'Hey, Loz. What are you doing here?' She was always suspicious of her sister's motives, but there was something in her smile that seemed particularly fishy.

'Come on, let's go into the lounge, I'll just get an extra cup for the tea. Liam, can I get you a Ribena?' Paula ushered them out of the hallway and Frankie found herself sitting on one sofa with Liam, while Laura and Stuart sat on the other one, holding hands and giggling.

'It's a good job you're here, too, Frankie,' Laura said, smiling before turning away to exchange a meaningful look with her boyfriend.

Something was definitely up and Frankie had a hunch she knew what it was.

As Paula came in and fussed around the teapot, Frankie tried to glance subtly at Laura's left hand, but it was clasped in Stuart's, her ring finger hidden from view. A knot of dread formed in her stomach.

'Well, isn't this nice?'

Frankie accepted the tea from her mum and waited for whatever it was that Laura had come to gloat about.

'Would you like a biscuit?'

For God's sake, just get on with it.

'Has everybody got a drink?'

'Yes, Mum. Just chuffing sit down.'

'Alright, alright.' Paula settled into her armchair, turning to face Laura. 'So, you were telling me about last night,' she prompted.

'Well, I thought we were just going out for dinner in town –'

'To Le Bistrot Pierre,' Stuart supplied.

'Yes – and I would have been perfectly happy there,' Laura said, beaming up at him. 'But then, yesterday afternoon, he said he'd got a cancellation at La Taberna – you know, that Spanish one that's had all the great reviews that I was saying I wanted to go to, but it was booked solid for months?'

Frankie nodded, pretending she cared.

'And it was a-ma-*zing*, wasn't it?'

'It was,' Stuart agreed. 'Very much worth booking three months in advance.'

'How lovely,' Paula said.

Frankie could feel Liam beginning to fidget next to her, having finished his biscuit. She wanted to change the subject, but could tell they weren't finished with the story.

'But that wasn't even the best bit,' Laura said, her voice rising. 'Just before the last course, Stuart got down on one knee and asked… asked…' Her voice broke as her eyes filled with tears.

Such a bloody drama queen.

'Shall I finish the story?' Stuart asked politely, putting his arm around her. She nodded and, still looking at her, he continued, 'I asked Laura to marry me, and luckily, she said "yes". And the whole restaurant clapped, and they brought us champagne to celebrate, didn't they?'

'Look, look!' She held out her hand to flash the diamond ring.

'Congratulations,' Frankie said, watching her mum and her sister moving closer to hug.

Liam turned to Frankie and leaned into her. 'Why is Nana crying?' he asked.

'Because she's so happy,' Frankie replied. 'Because Auntie Laura is going to get married to Stuart and that makes her happy.' *Because Miss-Bloody-Perfect has got it right, yet again.*

She sat watching them, trying to work out if she should just steal the brownie bites while her mum was distracted, rather than admit that her excuse for coming round was really not as impressive as Laura's.

Right now, comparisons between her and her sister wouldn't do her any good.

No, now was not the time to wallow. Now was the time to pick herself up and get lunch organised.

CHAPTER THIRTY-FIVE

Alison laid out all the ingredients and equipment she would need to bake the biscuits *before* asking Xander if he wanted to help.

'What are you making?' Simon asked, coming into the kitchen as she was trying to restrain Xander with a sieve full of flour.

'Careful,' she said, 'try and get it in the bowl… No, this way just a bit more. No, don't shake it so much.'

'Is this for Frankie's lunch?' Simon stood at a safe distance, the other side of the counter.

'Yes,' Alison said. 'It doesn't feel right to turn up empty-handed.'

'Can I put the chocolate in now, Mummy?' Xander threw down the sieve and grabbed the bowl of chocolate chips and as he held it over the mixing bowl a few began to fall in.

Alison retrieved the sieve from where it had been abandoned on the work surface. 'Okay, then mix it all together,' she said, holding the bowl for him as he held the wooden spoon with both hands and stirred a little too forcefully.

'So, is it a jeans and T-shirt sort of lunch, or jeans and a shirt sort of lunch?' Simon asked.

'Umm…' Alison was concentrating on watching for the moment when Xander would get bored and she could take over to mix it properly. 'Jeans and T-shirt, probably.' Xander stopped mixing and she took the spoon from him.

She heard Simon sigh lightly. 'Well, what are *you* wearing?' he asked.

'Mummy – I was mixing!'

'I know, I'm just checking. You've done a great job!' she stirred frantically for a few seconds before passing the bowl back. 'Right, now can you get those trays we lined earlier?' She paused, looking at Simon and trying to remember his question. 'I am wearing my new shirtdress with leggings – it's all laid out on the bed upstairs if you want to see.' Turning back to where Xander was sliding the trays onto the work surface, she pulled the teaspoons out of the way before they were pushed onto the floor and passed one to him. 'Right, time to scoop.'

An hour later, with the kitchen and Xander cleaned of cookie dough, Alison was ready to go. Leaving Simon to put his shoes on, she shrugged on her coat and ushered Xander out of the house.

'Are we walking?' Simon asked, locking up behind them.

'Of course we're walking,' she replied, then reminded herself that he had never been to Frankie's house before. 'It's not far, Frankie lives on that estate behind the Heppleton Arms.'

'And what time are we supposed to get there?'

'Half past twelve.' Alison checked her watch. Perfect, they should arrive exactly on time.

'And can you just remind me who they all are?'

She watched Xander skipping ahead down the footpath. 'Okay, there's Frankie and her son Liam, and she's actually the sister of Laura Wood – d'you remember her, from Accounts?'

He nodded, although Alison suspected it was only because the name was vaguely familiar. Back in the time before Xander, when they had both worked for the same company, it had always been Alison who knew their colleagues' names.

'Actually, that probably won't help you much because they're nothing alike. And there'll be Frankie's boyfriend Ben there – he's a photographer – with *his* son Charlie. Kate will be with her husband Matthew – he's a teacher – and their daughter Amelia, who is in the same class as Xander, Charlie and Ben, and their youngest, Reuben, who will go into Reception next year. Oh, and Kate's pregnant.'

'How pregnant?'

She shrugged slightly. 'About six months or so? But she looks quite big.'

Alison felt a little surprised to feel him reach for her hand to hold as they walked round to Frankie's. She had forgotten that he didn't really know these people at all. She was confident he would like them, though.

When they reached Frankie's front door, Alison knocked while Simon attempted to persuade Xander to stop kicking the gravel from the driveway onto the pavement. She watched him, wondering whether she should intervene, but decided to see how long it would take him without her. Just as she was raising her hand to knock on the door again, Ben came walking up the road with Charlie.

'Hello,' Alison said, stepping away from the door to greet him as he turned into the driveway.

He gave her the same rabbit-in-the-headlights look he always did, but Charlie ran up to Xander and began to join him investigating the gravel with his toes.

'Ben, this is Simon, my husband. Simon, this is Ben and Charlie.'

'Hello,' they said, nodding and shaking hands in a surprisingly formal exchange.

'Is she not back, yet?' Ben said, gesturing at the door as he walked towards it.

'I don't know, I've only knocked the once.'

He knocked again, then tried the door handle. 'Ah, it's open, she must be here.' He opened the door, letting Charlie and Xander run in ahead of him. Alison followed him, turning to make sure Simon shut the front door behind him. The two boys found Liam sitting on the futon in the lounge, watching *Power Rangers* on TV and made themselves at home either side of him, their eyes already glued to the screen.

'Oh my God, you're early,' Frankie said when Alison arrived in the kitchen to find her ripping open the packaging around some shop-bought pizzas. On the work surface there were three plastic bags of shopping, a pot of rocky road bites and a glass of white wine.

Alison checked her watch. 'You said twelve thirty, didn't you?' It didn't look as though guests were expected for at least half an hour.

'Sorry, I mean "oh my God, you're exactly on time".'

Alison tried to ignore the sarcasm, stepping forward with the Tupperware box of biscuits. 'Hello, Frankie. I've brought you a little something.'

'Thanks.' She took it and immediately opened the lid. 'Home-made… of course. Wonderful.'

'I made them with Xander this morning,' Alison said. 'They're still warm.'

Frankie smiled, but it seemed to border on a grimace, her jaw clenched, and Alison suspected she had been right to think that Frankie had bitten off more than she could chew with this meal.

'What can I do to help?' she asked, ready to step in and save lunch.

'Nothing. I'm fine.' Frankie snapped.

This time she was definitely grimacing, Alison decided. 'Okay, well… just shout if you need anything.' She stepped backwards, but found a foot beneath her own and turned to see Simon hovering awkwardly just behind her. 'Oh, sorry, Frankie, this is Simon, I don't think you've met, have you?'

'No, we haven't,' Simon smiled, moving forwards for a London-style greeting, kissing either side of Frankie's slightly surprised face.

'Hi,' Frankie said, and Alison could tell she was biting back some inappropriate comment.

'So, I see you already started on the wine… Do you want me to sort out some drinks for the rest of us?' Ben asked and Alison was slightly irked when Frankie nodded.

It was as Ben was pouring the requested wine, beer and squash that Kate arrived.

'Why is no one *late*?' Frankie muttered as she went to answer the door.

The kitchen was a little crowded with six adults in it, but with the children occupying the other room, they had no choice but to manoeuvre around each other to make introductions.

'Okay, Matthew, this is Ben, Frankie, you met briefly – I don't know if you remember? – and you've not met Alison or…'

'This is my husband Simon,' Alison supplied. She stood, leaning back against the fridge freezer, watching Frankie hack away first at carrots, then cucumber, while she sipped her wine.

'We've brought the glasses you asked for, and plates for the kids,' Kate said, motioning for Matthew to give the bag he was carrying to Frankie.

'Thanks.'

'I'll just put them over here, shall I?'

'How's training going?' Kate asked Alison, who was so busy trying to work out why everyone else was allowed to help except her that Kate had to repeat the question.

'It's going well, I've kept to the schedule and done all the training runs. Just one last run tomorrow evening – that'll be the last one before the actual race.'

'And how are you feeling about The Glorious, now?' Kate was nodding sympathetically, making Alison feel utterly pathetic.

'I don't think it's going to be my finest hour,' she admitted. 'But sometimes you just need to push yourself out of your comfort zone. There's all that sponsorship, for one. And I really couldn't face PTA meetings if Jo and Becky found out I'd wimped out. I'm hoping it'll be a good lesson for Xander, too, y'know, doing something challenging.'

'Well, I think it's very impressive,' Kate said.

'It's certainly not your average 5K,' Simon added.

'It's not?' Matthew asked.

Kate tutted. 'Remember I told you – it's this muddy obstacle race.'

'Oh yeah – they look like great fun.'

Alison laughed. 'Well, you're welcome to join us – we're a bit short on numbers – although I suspect it'll be a bit different to your usual runs.'

'Next weekend? Shame, I've got a GCSE revision day at school. Maybe next time?'

Kate gave him a playful dig in the ribs. 'Don't you go taking on anything else, Matthew.' She turned back to Alison. 'Don't worry, we'll all be there to cheer you on, won't we, Frankie?'

Frankie didn't answer for a moment and Alison wasn't sure if it was because she was counting pizzas or trying to think of an excuse not to come.

Kate reached out to place a hand on Alison's arm. 'We will. And I'll get the kids to make a banner.'

Alison smiled. 'Thanks.' She felt the blast of hot air as Frankie opened the oven and then turned away to pick up the pizza. At the same time, she felt something brush past her leg and looked down to see Liam heading straight for his mum, one hand already out as if to push at or lean on the open oven door. Trying not to panic him, she reached forward and grabbed his shoulders, pulling him back. 'Wait, Liam. Hot oven.'

Hearing Alison, followed immediately by Liam's complaining, Frankie turned round. 'What are you doing?' she asked, sharply.

'Just… the oven,' Alison said, feeling defensive now. *Surely the danger was obvious?*

Frankie kicked the oven door shut before crouching down to see Liam. 'Alright, dude?' she said, as if nothing had happened.

Alison swallowed, feeling embarrassed, releasing her grip on the child. *Had she overreacted?* 'I'm just going to check on Xander,' she said, making her way to the door without looking at anyone.

In the lounge, Xander and Amelia were still sitting on the futon, while Reuben had taken the space left by Liam and lay on his back with his head dangling over the edge. Charlie was sitting on the floor with Xander's bag of toys, looking through his set of Top Trumps.

Yes, they were all doing fine. Electronic babysitter working well. But now she had checked on them, she didn't want to go back into the kitchen. She felt an arm around her shoulders and the familiar scent of Simon's aftershave. She sank back against him a little. 'Is it just me,' she whispered, 'or is Frankie annoyed at me?'

He squeezed her, reassuringly. 'I don't think it's you,' he replied. 'She does seem a bit grumpy, though.'

Alison did not offer to help again and she accepted her slice of pizza on a napkin with as much grace as she could muster. If only Frankie had asked, she could have brought enough plates for everyone – she could even have brought the old table and chairs that were still stacked up in a corner of their garage. But she mentioned none of this, at the risk of provoking Frankie further.

'More pizza, anyone?' Frankie shouted, getting another one out of the oven. 'I've got one chicken and bacon and one veggie here – and another plain one on the way too, kids.'

Alison watched as she sliced the pizzas and began handing them out. Part of her softened a little, realising that feeding this many people from a fairly small kitchen and with very little in the way of equipment must have actually taken quite a lot of effort and thought.

Taking her extra slice into the lounge, she heard her phone beep with a new message. She was starting to regret joining the running group's WhatsApp group. For every message that had useful information about the run next weekend, there were ten or twenty inane ones just saying thank you or wishing everyone a good run.

> *Two spare spaces for Glorious – anyone got a friend who could fill in?*

Alison sighed. That meant they were down to just three runners. So much for 'most of the group are signing up'. There was no way that Kate could run, obviously, and she was fairly sure she knew what Frankie would say if she was asked to join The Glorious.

'Mummy, why is everyone on their phone?' Liam asked loudly, standing next to Frankie as he had done for most of the last hour.

Alison hurriedly put her phone away, noticing Simon doing the same thing with a scowl on his face that meant he was thinking about work. Not wanting to discuss whatever bad news she was about to get – it would invariably be him having to work away or put in some longer hours – she turned to Kate, who was standing the other side of her, frowning at her phone.

'You okay?'

'Yeah, I…' She sighed, passing Alison the phone. 'I finally heard from Nat.'

Hi – are you free? Can you ring me?

'Well, it's not an apology,' Alison began, but then saw the look on Kate's face and decided not to make it more difficult for her. 'Maybe she just wants to wipe the slate clean and start again?'

'Hmm.' Kate seemed unconvinced as she put her phone away. 'Frankie, do you need a hand getting the pudding out?' she said, moving away.

Alison watched her go, not wanting to offer Frankie help only for it to be rejected again. Maybe Frankie was just in a bad mood, like Simon said, but why did she only seem to be taking it out on her? Unless she had misjudged Frankie, and her first impression of her as an immature and selfish mum had been closer to the truth. Either way, right now, Alison really didn't feel like staying around all afternoon to find out. She checked her watch: not quite two o'clock. How long before they would be able to leave, she wondered.

CHAPTER THIRTY-SIX

As Kate peeled the satsuma for Reuben, she carried on worrying about Natalie's text.

'Here you are, sweetheart,' she said, passing the fruit to Reuben before going back into the kitchen to find the bin.

'There's these for pudding too,' Frankie said, opening the rocky road bites and offering one to Kate.

'Thanks, but I'm still a bit full from the pizza.' She couldn't eat too much in one go any more without risking heartburn.

'I can help you out with those,' Matthew said, appearing next to her, his hand already outstretched. 'Do you want me to take them next door, too?'

'Yeah, I suppose the kids will want some.' Frankie handed him the whole tub.

'They've all disappeared upstairs, even Reuben,' Matthew said, as they walked through to the lounge. 'Do you think we should worry?'

'Not until we hear crying,' Simon said, as Matthew offered him some rocky road. He sat on the futon, seemingly relaxed, next to Alison who was bolt upright, her hands clasped tightly on her lap.

Kate had noticed the atmosphere between Alison and Frankie, but hoped it was just down to Frankie getting stressed about doing lunch for everyone. On the one hand, she wanted to smooth the whole thing over, but on the other, she wanted to stay well out of it.

'It all seems quiet up there at the moment,' Ben said, coming back in from the hall. 'I just had a listen and they seem to be playing schools. I think Amelia was being the teacher and Liam was being the teaching assistant and it's possible that Xander just got sent to the head teacher.'

Simon laughed. 'That sounds about right! Any idea what he'd done?'

Ben looked sheepish. 'Um… Amelia was busy saying he shouted "duck" at someone, which was very rude, apparently.'

'Oh no, that's me – Amelia asked me yesterday if "duck" was a bad word.' Kate felt her toes curl with embarrassment.

'But you *never* swear,' Alison said, looking shocked.

'I know, we were coming out of the library and getting in the car when some woman came past, shouting on a mobile phone – every other word was the F word. I just sort of ignored it, then Amelia came out with *that*!'

'What did you say?'

'I didn't know what to say,' Kate admitted. 'So, I said it was only bad if you said it when you were angry and shouty.'

'Sort of true…' Matthew smiled at her. 'She does come out with some great questions, doesn't she? My favourite was when Amelia asked you when Reuben's willy would fall off – d'you remember? I think you were changing his nappy at the time.'

Kate nodded and sighed. 'She asks so many questions. I mean, obviously it's wonderful that she's so curious, but some of the things she asks…'

'Charlie's the same,' Ben said. 'We saw a dead bird on the way to school last week and Charlie started asking if we could take it home. When I said no, because it was dead, he kept asking if it had gone to heaven, and if it had, was it watching us right now? *And* what should he do if he wanted not to be watched?'

'How did you get out of that one?' Simon asked, a slight look of panic on his face.

'I changed the subject – pointed to some random child in the distance and claimed it was one of his friends that we should run to catch up.'

There was a general nod of agreement that distraction and avoidance were really the only way to deal with such awkward questions. Footsteps thundered down the stairs and they all turned to see the children, led by Liam and Charlie, burst into the room.

'We didn't get any pudding!'

'Is there pudding?'

'Mu-um – I want pudding!'

Kate was watching Matthew and the children trying to teach Simon and Ben to do 'the floss' when she felt her phone buzz with another message from Natalie.

Please, Kate. Are you free?

Kate began to worry.

It didn't sound like just a friendly catch-up or a casual text: this read more like a cry for help.

Kate had known Natalie a long time and despite the difference in their parenting philosophies, they had a history of being there for each other. Looking at the message one more time, Kate made the decision: if Natalie needed her, she would absolutely be there for her.

'Frankie, I was just… would you mind if I popped upstairs and phoned Nat?'

'As long as you're going to give her an earful for all that sh– erm, rubbish, she said at the wedding.'

Kate smiled, knowing she would do no such thing, but not wanting an argument with Frankie. She seemed particularly prickly today.

'Kate – hi!' Natalie answered before Kate had even got to the top of the stairs.

'Hello,' she said, going into Frankie's bedroom and pulling the door shut behind her. 'I got your text. How are you?'

'I… I don't know.'

Kate heard her friend's voice crack and waited for her to go on.

'It's probably nothing, but River's not here and I'm not feeling well and…'

So she didn't want to apologise, she wanted to ask for help. 'Unwell?' Kate asked. 'Is it the baby?'

'Oh, I don't think so… I've just got another one of these headaches.'

Kate could hear her friend trying to downplay it, but she was clearly concerned. It must be worrying her more than she was letting on if she had called the woman she had practically kicked out of her own wedding. 'Are you at home?'

'Yeah.'

'I'm coming over.' Kate didn't ask in case Natalie said no.

'Could you? Oh, that would be lovely. You're not busy?' The relief in her voice was clear.

'No,' Kate lied. 'I'll come straight away.'

She made her way down the stairs. Reuben and Charlie had brought down a box of Lego, which they had overturned and were now searching through. Amelia and Xander seemed to be having a dance-off without music as they showed off how quickly they could do 'the floss'. Liam stood next to his mum, his hand outstretched for a piece of rocky road. Kate couldn't see Alison, but Matthew was chatting with Simon and Ben, each with a beer in hand.

'Matthew,' Kate said. 'Nat's not feeling well, and I want to go over and check on her. Are you alright with the kids if I go?'

He was already nodding. 'We'll be fine – don't worry about us, just go.'

She hesitated. 'I don't know how long I'll be, but for tea—'

He stepped away from the other two men and slipped his hand into hers, giving it a gentle, reassuring squeeze. 'Seriously, just go, sort things out – we'll be fine.'

She looked at his face, and realised he was right: it would be fine. He wasn't perfect, but he would do whatever was needed to make it okay. She leant forward and kissed him, lingering in the moment. When she finally pulled back, Matthew was smiling. 'Go on,' he said. 'Keep me posted.'

She walked home to collect the car, before driving over to Cheadbridge. The journey took longer than she expected, giving her too much time to worry about Natalie and the baby. It wasn't long until her due date, but still, there were so many dangers. When Kate had been pregnant with Amelia, Matthew had started hiding the pregnancy books after he found her crying over all the things that could go wrong. *Don't think about it,* she told herself. *It might be nothing.*

She parked on the gravel drive, taking the steps down to the front door, nerves causing her to knock a little too loudly.

'Hello, thank you for this,' Natalie said, ushering her into the kitchen and lowering herself into a chair at the table.

'What's the matter?'

'Oh, I really think it's nothing. If River was here he'd be telling me to trust in Mother Nature, I know, but he's just headed to a folk festival this weekend for a gig and I don't want to distract him…'

'Nat – it may be nothing, but what *is* it?' Kate held onto her friend's hand to try and focus her.

'I've been having a few headaches over the last couple of days – and you know I don't get migraines, but I see these weird, like, zig-zaggy lines across everything.' She waved her fingers in front of her eyes. 'And a bit of pain here, which I thought was indigestion, but it can't be because I've hardly eaten anything this morning.' She began to rub the top of her bump absentmindedly. 'What do you think?'

'Well, I don't know,' Kate said, honestly. 'What did your midwife say?'

Natalie looked slightly guilty. 'I haven't seen one recently.'

'What do you mean?' Kate felt sure she should have seen one in the last couple of weeks. She couldn't remember exactly, but she did know that the appointments became more frequent as you approached your due date.

'Okay, don't get all… I didn't tell you this earlier, because we thought you might not understand it, but we really want a calm, natural homebirth, so I told the midwife I'd moved to a new area so I didn't have to do the whole hospital thing.'

'*Nat!*' Kate was surprised by the strength of her annoyance. 'You don't have to lie to them, you just say you want a home birth. Don't you remember, I was going to do that with Reuben? It's not like you're not allowed.'

'You *didn't* have Reuben at home, though, did you?' Natalie had a triumphant look on her face.

'No, but that's because it wasn't safe for *my* pregnancy – and it was *my* decision. I talked to my midwife about it loads, I knew what I was doing.' Kate shook her head. This was not the time to argue. What Natalie needed was to speak to a midwife. 'Where are your notes?' she asked.

Natalie shrugged and pointed to a cupboard. 'I think they're in there somewhere.' As Kate began searching, she added, 'This is probably all nothing, anyway. Pregnancy has just become so medicalised – women have been giving birth for *centuries* without doctors telling them how to.'

Kate didn't think now was the time to point out the obvious: that medical knowledge had made childbirth a whole lot safer. And where was she getting all this from? It sounded like something River would say. Kate felt herself getting annoyed at him for encouraging Natalie to do something so stupid.

'Here they are.' She pulled the booklet out from under a stack of leaflets. 'And there's the number on the back to phone – are you going to call them or should I?'

'It's just a few headaches and a bit of indigestion, Kate. Honestly, I feel better already for having some company.'

Kate paused, looked at Natalie and tried to work out what to do. This was her pregnancy and if she felt okay, surely it was not up to her to go against what she wanted? But on the other hand, if she hadn't seen a midwife, she *couldn't* know everything was okay. Kate had to do this.

'I'll just give them a ring for you.' She used her own mobile to dial the Maternity Assessment Unit, feeling nervous as a midwife answered. 'Oh, hello, I'm, er, calling for my friend who is thirty…' covering the phone and whispering to Nat, 'How many weeks are you?'

'Thirty-seven.'

'She's thirty-seven weeks pregnant, but hasn't seen a midwife since her first scan, I think. And she's been having some headaches, like migraines with fuzzy vision, if that makes sense?' She stopped speaking as she tried to remember if Natalie had mentioned anything else. 'Oh, and indigestion.'

'Are you with your friend at the moment?' the midwife asked.

'I am.'

'It's probably best for her to come in so we can get her checked out – could I have a word with her?'

Kate handed the phone over and watched as Natalie listened with the occasional 'uh-huh' or 'yeah, I suppose so', her face still frowning. Even after she had hung up the phone, she didn't speak to, or look at, Kate.

'Shall I drive you?'

Natalie nodded.

'You should take some things with you in case they keep you overnight.'

Natalie nodded again, still staring at the table, unmoving.

'Come on, let's go upstairs and find you some PJs and a change of clothes,' Kate said, reaching a hand out to help her up, taking a step back to create enough room for both their bumps.

Kate wondered what was happening back at Frankie's house. If she was still there, she would have been starting to think about leaving to make sure the kids were home in time for tea. They'd probably need a bit of a countdown to avoid a meltdown… And she hadn't managed to tell Matthew what there was for tea. *No*, she reminded herself, *I'm not there. I don't need to worry about it. He'll be fine.*

She herded Natalie into her bedroom – a beautiful room decorated in shades of green and cream – and prompted her as she began to pack. She had to hold her hands to stop herself from taking over when Natalie faltered. It wasn't so different to getting the kids packed and out of the house, really.

CHAPTER THIRTY-SEVEN

Frankie was jealous of the kids lying on the floor in the lounge. Between the shopping, loading and unloading pizzas into the oven and chopping cucumber and carrot sticks (that had hardly been touched), she felt like she'd been on her feet all day. Alison was sitting on the beanbag, playing idly with the Lego while Reuben watched. On the futon, Ben, Simon and Matthew chatted as they drank their bottles of beer. Earlier, Frankie was sure they had been talking about football, but the conversation had moved on to seeing family over Easter with each of them offering anecdotes about their relatives.

Frankie listened for a moment before turning away from the doorway and going to the sink to run a bowl of washing-up water. Another day, she would have been happy to join in, but today, she was just too tired. And too pissed off with sodding Laura for being annoying. This whole day had been a stupid idea.

'Can I help?'

Frankie jumped at the sound of Alison's voice behind her.

'If you pass me a tea towel, I could dry up for you. Or it might be better for me to wash, so you can put things away as you dry.'

'I was just going to let them dry on the draining board,' Frankie said, knowing this answer showed yet another way she did things wrong. She felt certain Alison dried and put away everything immediately. *God, she was annoying, just like Laura – both so bloody perfect.*

'Well, this way you won't be left with another job later.'

It was as though Alison couldn't take a hint. 'I'll be fine, Alison.'

'Oh… okay.'

Frankie picked up the first glasses to wash and put them in the water. Out of the corner of her eye, she saw Alison take the plates she'd stacked haphazardly on the side and scrape the pizza crusts and rejected salad into the bin.

'Oh, for God's sake!' Frankie turned, a glass still in her hand. 'Just bloody leave it – I can do this, I don't *need* your help.' The glass slipped from her soapy hand, smashing against the tiled floor, giving her words more anger than she'd meant. Alison looked close to tears.

'Are you alright in here?' Ben asked from the doorway. He looked from the broken glass on the floor to Alison then Frankie, and down to her bare feet. 'Not really, then. Stay there, I'll get the broom.'

He moved past them, seemingly oblivious to the frozen atmosphere.

'I've had a text!' Matthew shouted from the lounge. Appearing in the doorway, holding his phone, he went on, 'Kate's still at the hospital. Looks like it might be a while and she's going to stay until River gets there.'

'Right,' Alison said, quietly.

'Are we having a smashing time in the kitchen?' Simon asked from over Matthew's shoulder.

Ben groaned at the joke as he began to sweep the glass away.

'I think we need to be leaving,' Alison said, ignoring the attempt at humour, stepping carefully over the shards. 'Simon?'

'Oh, yes, ready when you are.'

'Come on, Xander, it's time to go. Come and get your shoes on.'

Frankie heard the strain in Alison's voice. She stepped forward, 'Alison, wait…'

'Frankie – don't move, there's glass everywhere.' Ben caught her with his arm and she felt trapped.

She heard Alison in the lounge. 'No, Xander, *everyone* is leaving – just put that down or I will take it off you.'

'Alison…' Frankie called, trying to push Ben's arm away to escape, but before she could move, he grabbed her waist and lifted her up.

'Just let her go for now,' he whispered in her ear as he placed her down on the mat at the back door.

'Right, that's us off. Thanks for everything, Frankie,' Simon said, waving his goodbye from the doorway.

'Actually, we should probably get going, too,' Matthew said, putting the phone back into his pocket. 'I should really think about getting tea ready for the kids and stuff if Kate's going to be late home.'

Frankie stayed marooned on the mat while Ben saw them all to the door and waved them off. She heard the voices fading to silence and was just left with the sense that everything was falling apart.

When Ben came back, he said nothing, picking the broom up and sweeping the broken glass into the centre of the room, then fetching the dustpan and brush to finish the job.

'Well, that was shit,' Frankie said, eventually, unable to cope with the silence any longer.

He looked up, surprised. 'I thought it went quite well – I like Simon and Matt, and even Alison wasn't too scary, up close. Although that wasn't exactly the way I thought it was going to end.' He grinned at her, which just made her feel worse.

'I didn't mean to throw a glass.'

'You *threw* it?'

'No. I… it just slipped out of my hand.'

'Well, that'll stand up in court,' he said, concentrating on emptying the contents of the dustpan into the bin.

She watched him put the broom away, feeling unable to move from the mat.

'What's up with you, then?' he asked, casually.

'Nothing.'

'Oh, that bad.'

She looked at him, knowing she wanted to tell him about the mess of thoughts swirling around in her head, but with no idea which thread to start pulling at first.

'Alison?' he prompted.

'Well, she's just bloody annoying. Like, bringing the sodding cookies and always offering to help – I don't need her help. I can totally do this.'

He took a step towards her. 'She wasn't *that* annoying,' he said. 'Just average for Alison, I would have said.'

Frankie felt her shoulders sag a little. She wasn't willing to admit it out loud, but he was probably right: it wasn't really Alison she was mad at.

'You were alright when I left you this morning,' Ben continued, moving closer to her. 'And then when I got back with Charlie, you were in a foul mood. I don't *think* I did anything. Was it the supermarket?'

She accepted the hand he held out and laced her fingers between his. 'I went to Mum's after we got back.'

'Oh?'

'That's where I got those mini-pudding things from. Anyway, Laura was there too, because she's just got engaged.'

'To Stuart?'

'To Stuart.'

'And this is bad because…'

Frankie took a deep breath, suspecting it would sound pathetic once she actually said it. 'It's just… she's done it again. She's done what she's supposed to. Laura always does everything right – better grades at school, her friends were more polite, better university – don't even mention the *not dropping out* – really good job, which she then left to retrain as a teacher so now she can be all "it's not about the money, I just want to make a difference to the children", and then she's gone and snagged this boyfriend that Mum loves and now they're getting married and next thing you know, she'll be dropping perfect little sprogs…' *And they won't be accidents that Mum has to deal with.* The only thing she'd ever had over Laura was that she had given her mum a grandchild, and even that was done in the wrong way. Once her sister started having children, she'd win the favourite daughter accolade hands down.

Her voice trailed off and she risked looking at Ben, terrified he'd be wanting to back away.

'It must be exhausting in your head,' he said. 'Seriously. All that from an engagement you could have predicted – in fact, you did predict it a few weeks ago, didn't you?'

'Knowing they were probably going to get married is different to it actually happening.' She heard how lame that sounded and hated herself for it. 'I'm sorry, I know I shouldn't feel like this…'

He moved his head to one side and narrowed his eyes at her. 'Wait… now it all makes sense – you're jealous. A-ha! You secretly have the hots for Stuart and now you're heartbroken you have to make do with me?'

She couldn't help but laugh. It was about as ridiculous as what she was feeling. 'Oh no, you guessed!'

He smiled, leaning forward to kiss her as his arm wrapped around her waist. She sank into the moment, feeling as though at least a small weight had been lifted. Even if sodding Laura achieved sainted status, it wouldn't really change very much, after all.

Now all she had to do was think of a way to try and make it up to Alison.

Later, once the house had been put back together and Ben had taken Charlie home, Frankie put Liam's plate down in front of him and wondered how he could possibly find room for more food after all that pizza. He picked up the jam sandwich, prodding it thoughtfully before licking the jam from his finger.

'So, y'know Jez and Millie are getting married,' Frankie said. 'They wondered if you'd like to do a special job at the wedding. It'll be like a big party and I'll be there and so will Ben. And you'll get all dressed up and follow Millie up the aisle of the church to Jez. Would you like that?'

He frowned, folded his arms and shook his head.

This was not the response Frankie had expected. Liam loved it when Jez visited. And he loved new clothes. As she was wondering why he'd had such a negative response, Liam moved around to try and climb onto Frankie's lap, holding her arm tightly as he clambered up.

'Ouch, Liam. What are you doing? Sit on your own chair, get off.'

But he held on.

'Liam, dude, what is going on?'

'Don't want to leave you,' he said in a baby voice.

Frankie frowned. 'You can't eat on my lap – go on. I'm not leaving.'

But he shook his head again. 'I don't wanna go to Jez,' he said.

She pulled him round so that they were face to face, trying to make sense of his words. 'You mean at the wedding? But I'll be there too.'

He sighed, looking away. '*After* the wedding. I don't wanna go to Jez *after*.'

Frankie pulled him closer, wrapping her arms tightly around him, leaning her cheek on his hair and closing her eyes. As she realised what he meant, she felt terror clutching at her insides. 'You're not going anywhere, Liam. You are stuck with me. After the wedding you will come back here and carry on seeing Jez, just like you do now.' *I'm not letting you go*, she added to herself.

'Amelia says once mummies and daddies get married, they get children,' Liam said quietly.

Thanks, Amelia.

Frankie groped for words to try and make sense without explaining so much she confused him. 'Okay, sometimes – usually – they do. But they tend to start with babies. And this isn't your mummy and daddy, it's your daddy and his girlfriend. And, well, we do things differently… we're a sort of complicated family.'

Liam looked up at her and she was pleased to see he looked relieved, although still as serious as ever. 'Why are we comp-lated?'

She smiled. 'Because we're so freaking awesome, *everybody* wants to be part of our family.'

He nodded, seemingly satisfied with that answer.

'Mummy,' he said, sliding off her lap and picking up his sandwich.

'Yes?' she answered, bracing herself for another difficult question.

'Can I have crisps, too?'

CHAPTER THIRTY-EIGHT

'Do you want me to phone River and see where he is?' Kate asked, sitting beside Natalie as she lay propped up in bed in the Assessment Unit. Natalie had sent him a text on the way here, and he'd replied that he would come straight away. The festival was somewhere in Leicestershire, so not that local, but even so he should have been here by now.

Natalie shook her head.

Kate tried to think of something else to talk about. Over the past two hours, she'd tried to make small talk about the weather, the hospital's blue and purple colour scheme and every article in the magazines she had bought from the hospital shop. Natalie had avoided talking about the baby, so Kate didn't bring it up. Even when they had been seen by a midwife when they first arrived, Natalie had barely spoken while she had taken blood and measured her pulse and blood pressure. When the midwife went to strap the CTG belts to her, explaining that they wanted to monitor the baby's heart rate, Kate was worried for a moment that Natalie would refuse, but after a brief hesitation she moved her arm and sat up slightly to make way for the belt to be strapped on.

'I'll just text Matthew, to let him know what's going on,' Kate said, getting her phone out. She'd already told him they were up at the hospital, but he was probably wondering where she was now.

'It's very quiet here, isn't it?' Kate said vaguely as she put her phone back in her bag.

Natalie frowned at her and Kate realised that there were beeping sounds coming from the monitors, the lights were buzzing and she could hear several people talking in the corridor beyond the curtain.

'Yeah, okay. I probably just meant it was quieter than my house with the children in it.'

'A house with quiet kids is a house with too many screens,' Nat said, with the wisdom of someone without children. Then, as if realising how that must have sounded, she turned to look at Kate and added, 'Sorry, I didn't mean… Look, I'm sorry about what happened, y'know, at the wedding.'

'I'm sorry too,' Kate said without hesitation, biting back any resentment caused by Nat's screen comment. It felt good to clear the air. 'I was having such a bad day. I hope you still got to enjoy the rest of the wedding.'

She smiled. 'Oh, it was fantastic! I had the best time. Not long after you left, River and his band got playing and we were still singing and dancing when the sun went down. It was magical. I'm so sorry you couldn't stay, the kids would have loved it.'

No, they wouldn't, Kate thought, *that was why you made us leave in the first place*. But that really wasn't the point. The important part was that they were both sorry.

Without warning, the curtain was drawn back and the midwife came in. It was the same woman who had spoken to them when they had first arrived. She had introduced herself, but Kate had immediately forgotten her name as she was too busy trying to listen to all the information.

'How are we doing in here?' the midwife asked. 'I just wanted to come in and let you know we're going to send you down for a quick scan while we wait for your blood test results to come back.'

Natalie said nothing.

'What is that for?' Kate asked.

'We're just trying to build up a picture of your symptoms,' she said. 'As I said before, it's a bit harder without any history, and we don't have an anomaly scan, but doing this one now can just help us to check the baby's growth.' She paused, looking between Kate and Nat, who still hadn't acknowledged her, finally seeming to settle on Kate to explain things to. 'Usually you would have your urine checked for protein at every midwife appointment, so although we've checked it now and we know it *is* present, we don't know whether this is a new thing or something that has been going on for a little while. We will book you in for a detailed growth scan on Monday, but we are getting someone to do a more informal one this afternoon, just to let us know.'

'And what does the protein mean, again?' Kate asked, hoping Natalie was listening, despite the fact she was apparently just staring at the ceiling.

'It can be a sign of pre-eclampsia, especially with your high blood pressure,' the midwife said.

'Do you think that's what's causing the headaches?'

The midwife pressed her lips together and nodded slightly. 'I think so, probably, but we'll know for definite once the blood results come back.'

'So, if it is that, what happens next?'

'Well, we'll make a decision once we've got all the results back – the registrar will come and talk to you, she'll probably put you up on the ward to monitor you overnight. And you're very close to your due date, so the best thing would probably be to get you induced and deliver the baby just a little early.'

'But I'm having a home birth,' Natalie snapped, glaring at Kate.

Kate took a deep breath, trying to work out how to make her understand. She looked back at Natalie, seeing the panic in her eyes. She looked up and smiled at the midwife. 'She had her heart set on a home birth,' she said. 'And she stopped seeing her midwife because she was scared she wouldn't be allowed one.'

The midwife smiled back, nodding. 'Well, we don't know what we're dealing with yet, but we can talk about the birth when the registrar comes down. If it is pre-eclampsia – and at the moment that seems quite likely – that can be very serious, both for you and the baby, but we can talk you through all the different options and you can decide what is right for you and the baby. It's important that you make your decisions based on all the information.'

Natalie sank back further into the pillows as the midwife closed the curtain behind her. 'They're not going to let me out, are they?' she said, petulantly. 'Well, they can't make me stay. When River gets here, I want to go home.'

Kate tried not to let her horror at that suggestion show. 'Why?'

'Because we want to have this baby at home… *naturally*.'

'We?'

'Yes. Me and River. We don't want the start of this baby's life to be all *medical*. Idoya says…'

'Idoya?' The name sounded familiar, but Kate couldn't place it.

'River's sister. She agrees with me and River that birth should be a *natural* process.'

Kate imagined Alison or Frankie's reaction to Idoya and tried to channel their strength of opinion. 'Nat, this isn't about what you and River – or even Idoya – *want*. This is about you and this baby *not dying*. The midwife isn't trying to make you stay in hospital for fun, she's just trying to keep you two healthy. And I *know* it's not what you want, but for heaven's sake, don't go home because of some ideal birth imagined. Just talk to the doctor and the midwife, *listen* to them.'

Natalie seemed to hesitate. 'Don't you regret going to hospital with Reuben? Wouldn't it have been better if you'd been allowed to stay at home?'

'Oh, Nat. They didn't *make* me go, I *chose* to because he was breech.'

'So, you don't regret it?'

'Not even a little bit. I'd do exactly the same again.' Kate shifted position in her chair to look directly at Nat. 'Look, motherhood isn't all about how you give birth, it's about a thousand tiny choices you make every day for their whole life. And you can't start with a selfish decision – you've got to think about what's right for the baby.'

Natalie chewed her lip and looked away, tears filling her eyes. 'I've not even had this baby yet and I'm already a bad mum,' she whispered.

Welcome to the club, Kate thought.

The curtain swished back to reveal an out-of-breath River, looking worried. 'Natalie, what's happening? Are you okay? And the baby?' he asked, reaching for Nat's hand with one of his, the other resting on her pregnant stomach.

'I'm really sorry,' she said. 'Kate thought I should come in and… I'm sorry.'

'You don't have to be sorry. Why are you sorry?' he asked, but Natalie had dissolved into sobs, her shoulders shaking. 'Why is she sorry?' he asked Kate.

'Because she knows you wanted a *natural* birth.' Kate found it difficult to hide her irritation at him. 'Because she knows you don't want her in a hospital – even though she might have pre-eclampsia, which is *really* serious. And because she knows you'll think she's a failure if she stays here.'

He looked startled. 'But, I… No, Natalie, *Natalie*, I won't…' He looked between the two women. 'Why would you…? Oh, wait.' He closed his eyes and sighed. 'Have you been talking to Idoya?'

Natalie looked up at him guiltily and he shook his head gently.

'Has the doctor – or whatever – been in yet? What did they say?'

Kate felt reassured that he had asked. 'They're just waiting for some results, then the registrar will come and talk to you. The midwife said they'd probably want to keep her on the ward at least overnight, for observation, but they might end up inducing.'

'Oh.' He turned back to Natalie. 'Oh. Okay, well, let's just wait and see what they say, shall we?'

Kate saw the look that passed between them and realised that she might have judged River too harshly. He didn't seem about to let Natalie storm out of the hospital. She stood up, collecting her bag and coat from the back of the chair.

'Now you're here, I'll go,' she said to River, edging round the bed towards the curtain.

'Okay, thanks.'

She hesitated, wanting to be certain that they weren't about to do something risky. She looked at River looking at Natalie and tried to pluck up the courage to say something. 'River?'

'Uh-huh?' He turned to look at her and she felt her stomach churn at the thought of a confrontation.

'It could be really serious, you know. Don't leave… wait for the registrar and stay, if you have to, overnight.'

He looked surprised. 'Well, yes,' he said, beginning to nod. 'We need to make sure everything's okay, don't we?' He turned back to Nat. 'I'll get Idoya to pick up a bag of things for you – and I'll get her working on some scents and things, so even if you give birth here, it'll be *like* we're in the forest.'

Kate coughed to hide her laughter. *Don't judge*, she thought, *pretending a labour room is actually a forest glade is a lot better than leaving the hospital to find a real one.*

'Kate?' Natalie sniffed and wiped her eyes on the back of her hand. 'Thank you, for… everything. I knew you'd know what to do. You're so *good* at all this… I hope I'm as good a mum as you.' She smiled weakly.

Knowing this was probably as close to an apology as she would get, Kate smiled. 'Don't worry about it, Nat. You'll be a wonderful mum!'

CHAPTER THIRTY-NINE

Alison took two towels from the cupboard, refolded them and put them into the IKEA bag. She sighed. *Was that enough?* She had no way of knowing how muddy it would get. Too many was better than too few, she decided, adding another couple of towels on top.

Carrying the bag to the bedroom, she took her spare clothes – with extra layers – and shoes and put them in as well. *What else would she need?*

If Simon was here, he would be laughing at her taking this much stuff to a run. And she would argue back that this wasn't just any run, this was a hideous muddy course, which would undoubtedly ruin her trainers and kit and quite possibly get mud all over the car too, if she wasn't careful. And then… she frowned, unable to imagine his comeback to that.

Although, right now, she didn't care what he'd say. Having pressured her into 'breaking out of her comfort zone', he wasn't even around to look after Xander while she did it; he was off working in New York again. Thank goodness Kate had agreed to help out.

Deep down, Alison knew Simon didn't have a huge amount of choice about where he worked and she was used to him flying to meetings each month in New York, and more frequently, to ones in Europe. But, still. This was something that was important to *her* and she had hoped he would make the effort to be there. Because if it was important to her, it should be important to him too. Surely he could have done something about it?

And it wasn't like he had given her much notice. Wimp that he was, he had only told her the day before he'd flown to New

York, because he 'didn't want to worry her unnecessarily' in case it didn't happen.

Except it *had* happened.

He'd been away for most of the week and she hadn't had any time to prepare for his absence. She'd already planned the week's food, and now there was far too much for just her and Xander to eat.

And there was no Maggie.

Maggie, alone for so many years after her husband died, had always been quick to invite her over or to come and keep her company while Simon was away. Alison felt something catch in her throat, threatening tears. She wondered what Maggie would say if she could see her now and felt herself smile as she imagined her mother-in-law's enthusiasm for something as ridiculous as The Glorious.

'This is for you, Maggie,' she said quietly. 'So far out of my comfort zone, I'll need a map to find my way back.'

Alison heaved the bag off the bed and made her way downstairs to pick up the little rucksack she would ask Kate to hold while she ran. A text message from Simon came through just before she dropped the phone in her bag.

> *Back in the country just in time to wish you luck! See you later.*

Well, there was a first time for everything, she thought, struggling to remember him ever texting from the airport before. When he had first admitted he wouldn't be flying back until the weekend, he had claimed he was sorry not to be able to make it to The Glorious. Perhaps he actually *was*.

'Nearly time to go, Xander!' she shouted from the bottom of the stairs, hoping he would hear her even while he was engrossed in Minecraft.

It was colder than she had expected outside. The sun was shining weakly through the clouds, but giving very little warmth. Over the week, the weather forecast for today had gone from 'sunny but cold' to 'cold with a chance of rain', and seeing the sun now gave her hope that it might not rain after all. As she put her bags in the car, she double-checked her list: purse, phone, safety pins, water bottle, tissues and wet wipes, cereal bar, bin bags, thermos of hot chocolate.

Xander spent the drive giggling at a Horrid Henry CD, but Alison was unable to concentrate on the story, the same thoughts chasing round and round in her mind. *How can I get out of this? I'll be fine, I can survive an hour of mud. But, I really, really don't want to do this…*

After forty-five minutes' driving, she saw the first sign, bright green with 'The Glorious' written on it in brown, along with some mud splats.

'Nearly there, Xander – can you help me look out for the green signs?'

'There's one!' he shouted, pointing to the one she'd already spotted.

She turned into the long driveway of a stately home and followed more signposts away from the usual car park to the other end of the estate, where she was directed to a space by the marshals.

'So many cars!' Xander shouted, pointing.

Alison looked at the field that had been turned into a temporary car park and couldn't disagree. This was clearly a much bigger event than she'd expected. There must have been hundreds of cars. Suddenly she felt sick, her mind sticking on just one thought: *I really, really don't want to do this…*

'Come on,' she said, attempting a bright and carefree tone that in no way matched her mood. 'Let's go and find Kate.'

'And Amelia,' Xander reminded her. '*And* Liam.'

'I'm not sure… I don't know if Liam and his mum are coming,' Alison said, taking his hand to stop him wandering off, certain that she would never find him again if he did. In fact, now she thought about it, she wasn't really sure where she would find Kate. When she'd seen her yesterday, they'd just agreed to 'meet by the entrance'.

'*Yes*, Liam.' Xander was nodding with so much force it seemed that his head might fall off.

Alison didn't have the strength to argue with him, but she was doubtful Frankie would show up. They'd missed each other in the school playground all week – Alison assumed Frankie was back to being late again – and on Wednesday, Alison hadn't collected Liam from school as usual, because Xander had a dentist appointment, so she hadn't seen Frankie since her outburst last weekend.

They walked down the gently sloping field towards the flags either side of the entrance banner. Beyond, she could see two lines of food vans leading towards a big marquee, probably where she needed to register.

'We're heading to the big tent,' she explained to Xander, who had begun running and skipping alongside her. 'I've got to register to get my numbers, then we'll go looking for my running friends and Kate. Okay?'

He nodded.

Alison hung back at the edge of the marquee, watching the other runners to see what to do. She spotted several groups in matching T-shirts and wished her running group had something like that to make them easier to find. She was surprised by how cheerful the other runners seemed to be – some were wearing fancy dress, others were wandering around with food or drinks as though it were a family outing.

Finally plucking up the courage to move, Alison took a disclaimer form from the nearest table and signed it without reading about all the potential dangers of the race. She took it over to the other side of the marquee and gave her name to a man standing behind the table, who leafed through the box in front of him before handing her an envelope. She checked inside – there were her numbers and a wristband for emergency contact and medical details – then left the tent, motioning for Xander to follow as her phone beeped.

Are you here yet? We're next to the gin van – Gin and Bear It.

Alison looked around and spotted the dark green campervan that had been revamped as a mobile gin bar with, inexplicably, a giant teddy bear on the roof.

'Head for the green van there,' she told Xander, as she began to type out a reply on her phone, not watching where she was going. Before she could send it, a message arrived on the running WhatsApp group.

Really sorry – both kids have vomiting bug, I'm not going to make it. Do us proud, guys!

Alison couldn't remember which runner that was, but they were the second person this morning to pull out, leaving just three runners, including her. Why had she ever let herself be persuaded to sign up for this? Why hadn't she pulled out weeks ago? No one else seemed bothered about going through with it. But now she was here, with Kate to cheer her on, she was trapped. A 'not great' day just kept getting worse.

'Hi, Alison!' Kate shouted.

Alison looked up from her phone and waved to her. She was standing with her kids and another runner, who was crouching to do her shoelace up. Alison really hoped it was a replacement for the two who had dropped out last weekend.

'Hello,' Alison said, pulling the numbers from the envelope and holding them out. 'Any chance you could help me put these on my back?'

As she spoke, the woman tying her shoelaces stood up and Alison realised with a start that it was Frankie, wearing trainers, leggings and a hoodie. 'Hey, looking good, Mrs Lund – all ready for the mud?'

Alison clenched her jaw as she looked up at her. *How could Frankie just stand there and act like last weekend hadn't happened?* With Kate there, and pinning her numbers on, she couldn't very well leave, even though that is what she most wanted to do. Instead, she took a deep breath and nodded, aiming for an *I'll be civil but I'm not forgiving you* smile and began attaching the number to her front. 'Frankie. You look like you should be the one running.'

Frankie laughed. 'Yeah, I don't *do* running. Not even for a bus. I just wanted to look the part to cheer you on.'

'There, all done.' Kate patted her back gently.

'It's a bigger event than I thought it would be,' Alison admitted to Kate, pretending Frankie wasn't there. 'And a bit further away, too, with all that driving through the grounds.'

Kate nodded. 'I was so glad Matthew looked the route up for me last night. I had to get up extra early to fit in my visit to meet baby Hazel before picking up Frankie this morning.'

'Hazel? Is that Natalie's baby?' Alison asked. Kate had mentioned on Tuesday that Natalie had given birth to a baby girl in the hospital, but also that the new parents had decided not to name her until they could take her to the forest to hear the name Mother Nature had destined for her. 'They're calling her Hazel? What a lovely name.'

'I know, I was a bit worried what name they'd go for, if I'm honest. Nat said her middle name is going to be Brooke, after her dad, to keep the whole water theme.'

Alison stifled a laugh. 'Oh, that's nice – thank goodness they didn't go for Hazel *Swamp*! But she's okay, then?'

'Yes,' Kate said, nodding. 'They're both back home and doing fine.'

With a start, Alison realised she had lost track of Xander, but he was playing tag with Liam, running around Frankie. 'Careful,

Xander,' she said. 'Don't go knocking anyone over.' She turned to Kate. 'Are you sure you'll be alright with him while I race?'

'We'll be fine,' she said. 'What time do you start?'

'Ten past twelve.' She looked at her watch before taking it off and dropping it into her rucksack, which she handed to Kate for safekeeping. 'I probably need to be going to the warm-up in a few minutes.' She held up her phone. 'I would say I need to find the rest of my team, but I'm not sure if there's anyone else *to* find. Another runner just cancelled, so I think there's only two here.'

It was then that she saw them, crossing the field towards her. 'Oh, no,' she said under her breath. Kate and Frankie turned to follow her gaze.

'Shit,' said Frankie.

'Are they running?' Kate asked.

Jo and Becky were striding towards her with big smiles. 'Hello, teammate,' Becky said. 'We thought we should come and find you – we just got Annie Becker's message. Looks like it's only going to be the three of us.'

Alison felt her chest tighten, pushing the air out of her lungs and leaving her without any breath to reply. This could not be happening. How could it have got any worse?

'Hello,' Kate said, sounding friendlier than Alison could have managed. 'Are you running?'

'We are,' Becky replied. 'We have been inspired by Alison here, and when our friend said there were a couple of spare places, we grabbed the chance to come and show her how The Glorious is really done.'

'Wh— I…' But Alison could not find words to speak.

'Don't tell anyone, but I'm running as Gina and Becky has Clare's numbers,' Jo mock-whispered.

'Can you do that?' Kate asked, eyes wide.

'Well, we have.' Jo frowned at her, clearly irritated that she hadn't been impressed.

'They're not going to care as long as you've signed the form and paid the money,' Becky said dismissively. 'Right, time for the warm-up. Ready, Alison?'

Alison nodded, still unable to speak. Avoiding looking at Kate or Frankie, she allowed herself to be herded towards the warm-up area by Becky. She felt somebody – Kate? – take the mobile from her hand and heard someone else shout, 'good luck', as she went.

Just an hour of my life, she thought. *I will survive this and then I'll never have to do it again.*

CHAPTER FORTY

Frankie watched Alison being led away.

'Fuck,' she said, as quietly as she could. Suddenly, it didn't matter that Alison had irritated her last weekend, or that she had just ignored her for the last five minutes. All she could see was her friend about to be humiliated. She had to do something. 'Could you cope with Liam, too?' she asked Kate.

'Umm, yeah, sure… why? Where are you going?' Far from looking panicked, Kate looked at Frankie with a smile, as if she had just worked out her plan.

'Who did they say hadn't turned up – was it Annie Beckett?'

'Becker – like Boris,' Kate answered.

'Come on, kids,' Frankie shouted, feeling the adrenaline kick in. 'We've got a change of plan.'

The six of them ran across to the marquee, where Frankie hurried to claim Annie's numbers, taking off her hoodie so that Kate could pin them to her.

'Liam, hold these.' Frankie passed him her phone, wallet, keys and hoodie. 'I'm off to roll in some mud. Wish me luck, everyone.'

'Are you sure you want to do this?' Kate asked, taking Frankie's valuables from Liam and putting them in her bag.

'God, no! But we can't leave her on her own, and you're *really* not allowed to do an obstacle course.'

She nodded. 'I *have* got a good excuse, but…'

'She'd do the same for me,' Frankie reasoned. 'Well, no, she'd think of something smarter, but I've got nothing else, so I'm going in.'

'Okay, then. Good luck catching her.'

'Good luck, Mummy!' Liam shouted, waving to her.

'Be good!' Frankie shouted back as she ran towards the area for warm-ups. For a moment she watched as Alison, with at least fifty other runners, jogged from one end of the enclosure to the other under the watchful eye of an instructor.

'And back – high knees this time, everyone!' he shouted. 'Are you all ready for this? Come on, let's go. And again – side step now. Don't forget to turn halfway.'

The area was only fenced off by a rope, but Frankie couldn't see how she would make it from where she was standing to where the runners were without being spotted by the instructor. Not willing to give up so early, she skirted around the boundary.

'And back to jogging, this time, let's see those front-crawl arms!'

As the joggers got near, Frankie watched the instructor, waiting for the moment when he would turn around, so that she could slip under the rope and join in without being spotted.

'And let's have some heel kicks this time. Yeah!' He watched the front of the group and as soon as his head had turned to follow them, Frankie ducked under the rope and slotted in behind the back row.

'Okay, hit the floor,' he said. 'Let's have some crawling – try to bring those heels up to your elbows and get those hips opening!'

Frankie copied the runners next to her and just about managed to keep up with them, but doing this, there was no way she could catch up with Alison. The ground beneath her fingers was cold and damp, reminding her that she was likely to get a lot colder and muddier very soon.

'And jump up – reach up high, ready for the jumping high ten at the finish line! And we are all done!' the instructor shouted. 'Let's head into that first obstacle. You're gonna have a great race – enjoy it!'

At the back of the crowd, Frankie couldn't see what the first obstacle was until the line in front of her disappeared with a shriek and she was left staring at a ditch filled with water. She looked down at the trainers she had bought at the supermarket yesterday, took a deep breath and jumped in.

'Shit, shit, shit…'

The cold water came up to mid-thigh, taking her breath away, while her feet slid about in the mud at the bottom. She pushed through the water. Just three steps took her to the opposite bank, most of which had been turned into a mud slide by the previous runners. Grabbing a rope hanging down, she began trying to pull herself out, her feet unable to find anything to push against.

'Here, grab on,' she heard someone say. Grateful, she took the hand that was offered and as she was hoisted up, her knee found the top of the bank and she was able to crawl out.

'Thanks,' she said, twisting to see who had helped her and finding herself in a group of men and women all wearing orange T-shirts with 'Legs Eleven' written on them.

'First time?' the nearest woman asked as they began to jog across a patch of grass.

Frankie nodded, already out of breath.

'It's hard going on your own.'

'Not… on my own…' Frankie tried to say as she gasped for breath. 'My friend's… up there.' She looked forward as she pointed, to see a wall made from logs in front of her. *How was she going to get over that?*

'Here's where you need a team!' The woman smiled.

As Frankie watched, the first of the team, a bearded man wearing a sweatband, reached the wall and went down on one knee to give a tall, wiry man a leg-up. The second man hoisted himself onto the wall, sitting astride it to reach down and help another team member up.

'Go on,' the woman said, nodding.

Frankie didn't wait to make sure she really could. She had to get over the sodding wall. Trying not to think about how Alison had managed this with Becky and Jo, she stepped onto the man's hands and reached up to pull herself over, feeling an arm hooking under one shoulder to help her.

'Cheers,' she said, as she swung her legs over and lowered herself down the other side, ready to run again.

The route led into a wood, the path twisting around, meaning she couldn't see very far ahead at all. Staying on her feet took all of her attention as the uneven path threatened to trip her up with stones, roots and the occasional log. Now that her trainers had been completely soaked, she didn't think twice about splashing through the puddles that dotted the path. Turning yet another corner, she found a clearing with netting strung up just below waist height over a muddy patch about ten metres long. She scanned the runners in front of her, searching for Alison, and became aware of a soft drizzle starting to fall. There, already at the other end of the netting, crawling slowly, was Alison. Not wanting to fall any further behind, Frankie threw herself down, moving as fast as she could on hands and knees, feeling the mud squelching between her fingers and pulling at her shoes. As she reached the end, she tucked a stray hair behind her ear and wiped her face with her muddy hand, trying not to think about the state she must now look.

Alison's slow-moving shape was not too far ahead now and although Frankie's legs were already aching, she pushed herself into a faster run. She left the trees, heading across another field of damp grass, this one sloping upwards towards the grey sky. With no trees to provide shelter, she could feel the wind, brutal against her wet legs.

Becky and Jo must have gone ahead, leaving Alison alone, and Frankie was close enough now to see her faltering. *Don't give up,* she willed her. Less than five metres to go. She slowed a little, reaching out, ready to scoop Alison up.

'Keep going,' Frankie said. One arm reaching around Alison's waist, the other grabbing her nearest arm, she pushed Alison along. 'Come on, fuck's sake, don't stop now!'

Alison turned, staring at her in surprise, her face covered in mud spatter, her eyes blinking back tears. 'Frankie? What are you doing here?'

'We couldn't let you do this alone, you idiot. No – don't stop, get moving!'

Alison added a burst of speed that Frankie struggled to match uphill. She saw Becky and Jo another ten metres or so further on, looking back over their shoulders.

'Have you done all that?' Alison asked, gesturing behind her.

Frankie raised an eyebrow. 'No, I just decided to bathe in mud and paint my face red before I got to you.'

Alison laughed. 'Do I look as ridiculous as you?'

Utterly out of breath, feeling at the same time both hot and sweaty *and* cold and damp, Frankie smiled. 'Probably.' Having never seen her anything other than perfectly turned out, Frankie thought there was something quite satisfying about seeing Alison's face streaked in mud, stray hairs blowing about, having escaped from her ponytail.

They had nearly made it to the top of the hill and Alison was looking at the view over the fields to the left. 'Have you seen that?' she asked, pointing to the dark clouds heading their way with a curtain of rain falling beneath them.

'Never mind that,' Frankie said as they reached the summit. 'What the shag is that?'

There were three giant steps with several runners just standing at the top. Alison shrugged, reaching for the rope to start hauling herself up. Frankie tried not to laugh at the sight of her petite friend barely reaching the top of the first step, even with her arms outstretched.

'Here,' she said, grabbing Alison's waist to pick her up, but misjudging the lift and knocking her off balance instead, so that she staggered sideways, letting go of the rope and falling to her knees. 'Oh, sorry!'

'First, you throw a glass at me, now you just throw me over?'

Frankie laughed, hoping Alison was joking. 'Yeah… Try this,' she said, linking her hands together and bending to get them low enough for her to stand on. As Alison stepped on, Frankie pushed, straightening her legs and propelling her onto the first step.

'How are you going to get up?' Alison asked, turning to hold a hand out.

'By being tall.' Frankie jumped up, getting her elbows onto the top of the step and pulling at the rope while Alison grabbed one of her legs and swung it up so that Frankie could clamber onto the platform. 'See? Easy,' Frankie said, lying flat on her back, panting, her arms aching already. 'Just, y'know, two more to go… in a sec.'

Alison had already begun to pull at the rope for the next step, clearly forgetting that Frankie had not done any training for this and was therefore vastly more knackered than she was.

'Okay, okay,' Frankie said, slowly getting to her feet and into position for another leg-up. Either this step was slightly shorter, or they were getting better at it. This time, she didn't lie back, but jumped up to help Alison up to the last one immediately before clambering up herself.

It was only when she stood up next to Alison on the last step that Frankie saw what was ahead of them: stretching out in front of them was the longest waterslide she'd ever seen. Four lanes of red plastic ran all the way down the slope, each one with a stream of brown water sloshing down it already. At the far end, she could see people splashing into a giant muddy puddle at the bottom.

'Wait here,' said the marshal next to them, wearing a hi-vis tabard over his coat, one arm out to stop them while the four runners ahead of them threw themselves down.

'Oh, *flipping heck*,' Alison said.

'Jesus, if there was ever a time for real swear words, this would be it.' Frankie said, lining up next to her. 'Wait – before we do this… sorry I was such a cow on Saturday. I was just a bit mardy and took it out on you. But doing this totally makes up for me throwing a glass at you, okay?'

'Head first – arms up!' shouted the marshal as he motioned them forwards. 'Go!'

Alison raised her eyebrows at her. 'I'll forgive you if you go first?'

'Piss off,' laughed Frankie. 'We go together on three. One, two… three!'

Before she could think too deeply about what she was about to do, Frankie closed her eyes and dived onto the slide. Keeping her arms up, she felt herself whooshing down, the cold water rushing around her. She lifted her head up and risked opening her eyes, looking left to see Alison slightly ahead of her, swearing as she went down.

'Woohoo!' she shouted as she whizzed down the flume, the adrenaline roaring in her ears.

Frankie plunged into the pool of sludge-brown water at the bottom. Somehow her body had got twisted and her feet were pointing upwards. She struggled to turn herself round, the shock of the freezing water making it difficult for her to work out how to put her feet down. Suddenly she felt hands pulling her up and she was able to push her feet down and propel herself out of the water to a standing position, wiping the water from her eyes.

'God, that's cold,' she said, finding Alison next to her, holding her arm.

'Keep it moving!' shouted yet another marshal, offering them a hand to climb over the plastic edge of the pool and out onto the slippery path.

'It's alright for him,' Frankie said, gulping for air as they set off at a jog again. 'He's wrapped up in a coat!'

'You'll warm up if you run,' Alison said.

Frankie scowled, knowing she was probably right.

By now, they had looped back to the wood, the path criss-crossing back and forth, at times becoming too crowded to keep running, and Frankie was grateful for the respite. She wasn't even sure if she was halfway yet and already her body felt as though she had been thrown around in a washing machine. On a cold spin. 'What happened to the other two, anyway?'

'Becky and Jo? I lost them at that bit where you crawl through the mud. I went under the net first and the pair of them raced around the outside, to skip it and lose me.' Alison bent her head forward and used the edge of her soaking wet T-shirt to dab at her cheek. 'To be honest, when you caught me up I was wondering how on earth I was going to do this on my own… If it wasn't… well, I probably would have given up.'

Frankie noticed how Alison was looking away and worried she was about to get a little too emotional. 'Whoa – hold on a sodding minute! We didn't have to crawl under the net? Are you shitting me?'

Alison laughed. 'Well, no, I mean, of course you *should*, but you don't *have* to.'

Frankie grinned. 'Obviously, we're more hardcore than them.'

'Obviously.'

CHAPTER FORTY-ONE

Kate handed hotdogs out to each of the children as they pressed towards her to claim their food.

'Can I have ketchup?' Xander shouted.

'I don't want ketchup,' Amelia said, shaking her head.

'Ketchup!'

'We'll sort out ketchup in a minute, let me pay.' Handing over the notes, Kate headed to the table next to the food van, stocking up on napkins from her bag and helping those who wanted it to ketchup.

'Right,' she said. 'We're going to sit at that bench there – go and grab it, kids.' They ran ahead of her to claim the seats and she winced, waiting for one of them to fall over and drop their hotdog. She did not want to have to queue up for another one.

For the first fifteen minutes or so after Frankie left, Kate had distracted the kids, first, by making them follow the warm-up, and then by letting them run loose on the grass behind the food vans. But when they grew tired of chasing each other, and began complaining they were cold, she suggested hotdogs to help warm up again. And once these were eaten, she was hoping it would be nearly time to head round to the finish line and start looking out for Frankie and Alison.

Beside her, Reuben began to giggle.

'Mummy, your bag's tickling.'

'Oh, my phone!' she said, startled, digging her way through her bag to find her mobile, but it wasn't hers that was ringing, it was Alison's. There was silence for a moment, then the ringing started again and she was able to find the phone in the front of her rucksack. She hesitated, seeing that it was Simon calling, but she had met him and it might be important.

'Hello? Umm… Alison's phone?' she said, suddenly certain this was the wrong thing to do.

'Hello? Who is this, then?' Simon asked.

'It's Kate – Alison gave me her phone to look after.'

'She's still out running, then?'

'She is.'

There was a pause in which Kate wondered what else she was supposed to say.

'Good. Right, well… Where are you?' he said eventually.

Kate frowned. 'We're just waiting at The Glorious while she does it.'

'Yes, but where *exactly*? I'm heading towards the flags from the car park – where are you?'

Simon was *here*? Kate turned and looked around her, trying to find some sort of landmark. 'We're at a picnic bench near the start point, on the left as you come in, the other side of the food vans.'

Within a couple of minutes, he had appeared, standing out like a sore thumb in his suit and raincoat, carrying a small suitcase in his hand and laptop bag over his shoulder. As he walked towards them, his shoes slid on the wet grass.

'Look, there's Xander's daddy,' Kate said, waving. Xander jumped up and ran to him, and Simon caught him under one arm and half carried, half dragged him back towards the bench.

'Hello,' he said. 'Is it just you? No Frankie?'

'Ah, well, she's doing the run as well now.'

His eyes widened. 'Wow. So, you've got the crèche.'

Kate smiled, wondering if she should stand up to talk to him. 'Yeah, it's okay, they've been fine.'

He laughed, knowingly. 'I struggle one-to-one with Xander, and then here you are with four children, just sitting and eating calmly. Matthew said you were great at this sort of thing.'

Kate blushed a little at the compliment. *Did Matthew really say that?*

'Right, let's go near the end to see if we can spot them coming over the last few obstacles,' Kate said. 'How does that sound, kids?'

They cheered, Xander running around the table as he did so.

Kate took out wet wipes to sort out greasy or ketchup-y hands and faces, then began to collect up bags and herd the kids.

'Here, let me take those,' Simon said, taking Alison's rucksack and her own huge handbag before she had a chance to say it wasn't necessary.

He walked beside her, looking down as he did so, clearly concentrating on each step.

'If you don't mind me saying, you don't look dressed for the outdoors,' Kate said, worrying that this might be a bit intrusive.

He laughed. 'No. If I'd had a bit more time I'd have gone home and changed, but I came straight from the airport, got the driver to drop me at the entrance to here – which he thought was a bit odd to start with, but when I explained, he understood.'

Kate wanted to know *what* he'd explained, but Simon didn't elaborate, so she stayed quiet.

'Good God, is it all like that?' he exclaimed as they walked past the start, where another wave of runners was leaping into the water.

Kate nodded. 'There's a map up that way,' she said, nodding towards the marquee, 'showing the whole route. There's only a couple of bits in the stream, but there's all sorts of things they have to climb over or slide down or crawl under, and *lots* of muddy bits.' She'd shuddered when she saw it, wondering why all these people seemed so happy about taking part.

He shook his head.

Kate held a hand out to see if she had imagined those few spots of rain. No, she definitely hadn't. 'It's raining – hoods up!' she called to the kids, as she pulled up her own and tried to sink inside the coat a little more.

Despite wearing a raincoat, Simon had no hood and no umbrella. As the rain came down, drops fell against his face, but he didn't shrink away from it. Instead, he smiled and rolled his eyes. 'Oh, Alison, what have you got yourself into?'

'Mud, glorious mud,' Kate said with a wry smile.

CHAPTER FORTY-TWO

At least before it had started raining, some parts of the path had been dry. *Why didn't I appreciate that earlier?* Alison thought, splashing and sliding her way through the wood. Behind her, Frankie had slowed to walking pace and while Alison didn't mind slowing down, she was now more determined than ever not to stop. She had said she would do this and so she would. Even if Simon didn't think it counted as being 'out of her comfort zone'. Even if every other runner dropped out.

Except Becky and Jo.

She could see the pair of them now, just up ahead. If Frankie would only go a little faster, it would be easy to catch up with them, show them she could do it despite their laughing.

Not that she could really criticise Frankie. Who would have thought she would jump in and rescue her like that? Without her turning up, Alison knew she wouldn't have got this far. She consciously slowed her pace a little to allow Frankie to keep up, losing sight of Becky and Jo through the trees.

'Are you okay back there?' she asked Frankie, turning to see her.

Frankie nodded, breathing heavily, wiping the rain from her forehead and smearing the mud further down her face.

The path split, and Alison took the left fork, checking that Frankie followed. After only a hundred yards, it turned into a swamp, with two rows of planks zigzagging across it. There were a few people trying to force their way through the mud at the edges of the swamp, one man reaching back to reclaim his trainer, laughing as he pulled it out, now so caked in mud it was unrecognisable as footwear. Clearly, the makeshift bridges were the way to go, Alison decided. Although they were shiny wet and worryingly narrow.

Grabbing Frankie's hand, she stepped gingerly onto the nearest plank. Frankie nodded in understanding, treading on the second one. As they edged their way along, she felt her arm tense as she tried to use Frankie for balance and vice versa. Looking across, she realised that Frankie was shaking with silent laughter.

'What's so funny?' she asked.

'Oh, God, what *isn't* funny?' Frankie chuckled. 'I'm an *actual* grown-up with a son and a proper job, and here I am covered in mud, my clothes are absolutely soaking and I'm trying to balance on a tiny piece of wood. This is the most ridiculous thing in the world!'

'You're not a proper grown-up,' Alison argued. 'You're not even thirty, yet.'

Frankie laughed so hard she wobbled, threatening to take them both down. 'You're doing alright, old lady.'

'Hey, I may be a little older, but at least I'm wise enough to bring a towel and a change of clothes in the car.'

Frankie looked up with a smile. 'Yeah, but I'm betting you brought spares.' She jerked her arm as she lost and then regained her balance.

'Just concentrate on the flipping wood,' Alison admonished her, trying and failing to keep a straight face.

At the end of the wooden bridges there was around two metres of bog without any way to get across. Alison scanned ahead. There was no way she would be able to jump all the way across, but if she could just make it most of the way… Her thoughts faltered as she realised that there was no way of avoiding crawling through at least some of that mud. And given that she was already wearing quite a lot of mud, a little more wouldn't hurt.

'Do you think we should jump?' Alison asked.

'I might try flying,' Frankie looked up with a smile.

Alison ignored the sarcasm and focused on the leap she would need to do. 'Right, let's do this.' Taking a deep breath, she bent her knees and hurled herself forwards, arms flung out in front, still holding Frankie's hand.

'Argh!' Frankie yelled as they landed on their feet before being thrown forwards onto their hands and knees. 'Bloody hell, woman, give me some notice next time.'

'Stop your moaning,' Alison replied, grinning. She reached forwards, leaning on her forearms to try and crawl, but mostly sliding through the mud. Frankie was right, this was utterly ridiculous and yet she couldn't wipe the smile off her face. She could feel the mud pulling at her clothes – it would take several showers before she felt clean again. As she reached solid ground, she turned to check Frankie was behind her.

'Ha, take that, mud!' Frankie said, gasping for breath as she staggered upright, leaning against a tree trunk for support.

'You tell it!' said a woman behind them in a T-shirt that must have started life bright orange, but was now mostly brown. 'Hey, you found your friend!' She nodded at Frankie as if she knew her.

'I did,' Frankie said, proudly. 'Alison, this is the team that got me over that first wall thing.'

Alison realised that they were now surrounded by half a dozen runners wearing the mud-streaked orange T-shirts, helping the last few out of the bog before they set off again. This would be so much easier in a group, she thought. Two was definitely better than one, but next time... She checked herself: *why on earth would there be a next time?*

'Come on,' Frankie said, standing upright. 'Gotta keep going.'

Alison nodded, falling into a gentle jog while Frankie walked. 'Am I allowed to ask...' Frankie was already breathless, so Alison went as slowly as she could without actually walking. 'Are we nearly there yet?'

Alison rolled her eyes and increased her speed just enough that Frankie had to change her walk into a jog.

'Hey!'

'Frankie, haven't you seen any of the signs?'

'Um, no.'

'We're on the last kilometre.'

'Thank fuck for that!'

The route left the wood and headed across another field, uphill at first, then over the brow and down the other side. Out of the trees, there was no shelter from the wind and rain that now hit them, stinging against their cold skin. Beyond the trees at the bottom of the hill, Alison could see some of the food vans and the registration marquee. Somewhere down there, Kate was trying to corral their children in this weather. Alison wasn't sure which of them was doing the harder task.

'Is that… Can you see…?' Frankie panted as she ran, pointing towards two figures at the bottom of the hill.

'Becky and Jo?' Alison supplied. 'I think it might be.' The two women had stopped at the side of the path. Becky stood on one leg, holding onto Jo for support as she emptied mud from her trainer.

Frankie and Alison exchanged a look and Alison raised an eyebrow.

'Hell, yes!' said Frankie. 'Come on.'

Alison was surprised to discover that Frankie was able to match her speed as she increased it, racing down the hill. Ahead of them, the other two women had seen them approaching and were now hurrying to get Becky's trainer back on and done up, clearly panicked, only just managing to do so in time.

As soon as she reached the bottom of the hill, Alison followed the route through the trees before heading back out into the open and coming face to face with a wide, shallow, muddy ditch. She paused for a second at the top, considering the slopes down and back up. The left-hand side had a large brown puddle, the middle section looked like it had thick mud, but the right-hand side seemed passable.

'Go, go, go!' Frankie yelled, half stepping, half slipping down the side.

'Keep right!' Alison shouted after her as she started to run after Jo and Becky. 'Go right!' She scrambled down, reaching for Frankie's arm to pull her to the side before she could be caught in the mud.

Frankie and Alison held their arms out for balance as they took the first few steps, sinking into the mud immediately. Alison reached back to help Frankie pull each foot clear, taking huge steps before twisting back to Alison, holding her hands out in return. Taking it in turns to pull the other out, they made their way across to the other side, where ropes hung down to help their climb.

'You first,' Frankie said, gesturing to Alison to take the rope.

Alison braced herself for a moment, then pulled as hard as she could, trying and failing to find purchase on the muddy slope. She felt Frankie's hands grabbing at her legs, giving her something to push against. It was enough. Alison heaved herself up the rope with Frankie's shoulder wedging itself against her butt, shoving her higher. Staying low, she turned to help pull Frankie up, her mud-covered fingers slipping as they tried to grip under her shoulders.

'Where are they?' Frankie asked as they stood up and surveyed the next ditch, longer than the one they had just managed to cross.

'There,' Alison pointed to the pair who were crawling in the middle, their hands and feet sunk deep into the mud. They were making very slow progress, their whole bodies straining as they pulled each limb out of the mud in turn before moving on to the next.

'God, that looks difficult,' Frankie said.

Alison nodded. She was surprised she didn't feel more satisfaction seeing them stuck and so obviously not enjoying the run they had only signed up to out of spite. 'Keep right again,' she said, taking a deep breath and stepping out first.

'Okay, I was watching that last team,' Alison said, once Frankie was down next to her. 'They did a weird crawl thing – like this…'

She crouched down, reaching her fingers out into the mud and keeping low to the ground as she crept forwards on hands and feet, keeping her knees just above the mud.

Alison kept turning to watch Becky and Jo attempting to get out of the mud. Neither of them seemed to be getting very far. Becky was slightly ahead, kneeling up, grasping one of her thighs, trying to pull her foot out.

Frankie laughed. 'Becky doesn't look too happy right now,' she said.

As they watched, Becky managed to wrestle her foot from the mud, losing her trainer in the process.

'Oh, no!' said Alison, then remembered how much she disliked Becky. *Serves her right*, she thought.

The crawling technique was working and they were now more than halfway across the ditch, although her wrists were complaining. They had drawn level with Jo, who was still making slow progress, while Becky had reached relatively dry land, and was now shouting and gesturing to the marshal who stood on top of the bank. He shook his head.

'Don't tell me... she wants him to... get her sodding shoe back!' Frankie panted.

'It does look like that.' *What on earth made her think that somebody else should dive into the bog to save her shoe?*

At that moment, Becky looked in their direction and scowled. She threw her arms into the air and shouted something back to Jo.

'Woohoo!' Frankie yelled, reaching the bank just ahead of Alison and leaning against it. 'Okay, when you're ready, old lady,' she said, holding her hands out to give her a leg-up.

Alison couldn't help but smile. Frankie's enthusiasm didn't seem to be waning. 'Older and wiser,' she muttered, stepping up and grabbing the rope.

Once they had both made it to the top of the bank, Alison turned back to see Jo still fighting the mud and Becky hauling herself up on the rope. She wasn't sure what made her move across to Becky.

'Need a hand?' she asked, reaching down to her.

Becky didn't even look in her direction. She raised her chin and pulled harder on the rope. As she reached the top, she threw an evil glance at Alison and muttered, 'Ridiculous event… you can't even run it properly.'

Alison bit her lip to stop herself from laughing as Becky stormed off towards the marshal as best she could, wearing only one shoe.

CHAPTER FORTY-THREE

Frankie watched Becky go, then turned back to where Jo seemed to have been abandoned in the mud. Somehow this didn't feel like a victory.

'Alison!' she called, waiting for her to look round before she nodded towards where Jo was still squirming.

Alison raised her eyebrows as if to say *Really?*

Frankie shrugged. She was pretty sure if it was the other way around, Jo would leave her. She sighed, thinking about how Ben ran around in circles trying to keep Jo happy for fear of losing Charlie. And while Ben was part of her life, so was Charlie, and, by extension, Jo.

It was all stupidly complicated unless you just made it simple.

Jo was important to Charlie.

Jo should not be left alone for someone else to help.

Frankie nodded decisively at Alison before sliding back down the bank and taking a couple of steps towards where Jo lay. The mud was thick, Frankie's feet sank in to the ankle and were held firm when she tried to move them.

'Frankie, are you stuck too, now?' Alison whispered, stopping just behind her on the last of the mostly firm ground.

Frankie shook her head. 'No,' she lied. That didn't matter for the moment. Jo was now only a couple of feet from her, completely submerged from the waist down. 'Need a hand?' she shouted to her.

Jo looked at her, utterly defeated. Frankie could see that tears were very near the surface and while she didn't mind helping her, dealing with a sobbing Jo was more than she could cope with.

'This mud's a bitch, isn't it?' Frankie said. 'How far can you reach?' she asked, her hands outstretched, grateful that with her feet held firmly by the mud there was no chance she would slip, but a little concerned that she might now be quite stuck.

Jo looked sullen and continued wriggling ineffectually on her own.

'*Jesus*, just give me your chuffing hand, Jo!'

'I'll be fine,' she replied, heaving herself a centimetre or two further forward before sliding back a little.

'Yeah, no,' Frankie said, shaking her head. 'I'm too scared of our sons to leave you here. They'd shout at me for abandoning you. Or worse, they'd, like, sing the *Go Jetters* theme tune on a loop. Oh, God, my ears!'

She saw the corner of Jo's mouth tweak into a tiny smile. 'Charlie keeps singing that annoying "baby shark" song,' she said.

'Nooo, anything but that!' Frankie accepted the temporary truce, reaching out again to grab Jo's wrist and feeling Jo's fingers gripping tightly around her own. 'Ready?'

Jo nodded. Frankie bent her knees and pulled as hard as she could, leaning back as far as she dared. Alison appeared next to her and took Jo's left arm to join in as they dragged her slowly towards them. After a moment of effort, Frankie paused, gasping for breath. Jo had definitely moved, if only by a foot or so.

'Again?' Frankie said and they both nodded.

Jo was still twisting and wriggling as they hauled her closer still.

'We need to move back,' Alison said, as they paused a second time. Holding Frankie's arm with one hand, she used the other to tug her feet free one at a time to step backwards a little.

Frankie found she could wiggle her feet a bit, although the mud still dragged at her trainers. Alison reached forwards, gripping Jo's calf with both hands while Frankie clutched at Jo's arm and between them, they managed to pull Jo's feet free from the mud.

'Okay, ready?' Frankie said, once they had taken up positions on firmer ground.

Each with one hand around Jo's wrist and the other gripping her upper arm, Frankie and Alison heaved once more. Jo writhed and squirmed, dragging her legs from the mud one at a time to step towards them.

'Woohoo! Take that, you stinky, sodding mud!' Frankie spun round to Alison, both hands raised. Alison grinned as she accepted the high ten with an *I'm too old for that sort of thing* look. Without thinking, Frankie turned to Jo, her hands still raised. Jo looked at her, eyes wide, then sighed. Frankie froze with the awkwardness of being left hanging. Almost in slow motion, Jo raised her hands, smacking her palms against Frankie's.

'Thanks,' she said. 'I suppose I'm glad you're so scared of Charlie and his singing.'

Frankie grinned.

They stood for a moment, Jo holding onto the rope, Alison and Frankie leaning against each other for support, while they got their breath back. Frankie looked up towards the marshal, half-expecting to see Becky next to him still, but she was nowhere to be seen.

Had she even waited to make sure her friend was out of the mud before she went?

Alison held out a hand. 'I think the rain has stopped,' she said.

Frankie nodded.

There were more runners now coming across the mud towards them: the next wave must have reached them.

'Come on, Alison,' she said, offering up her hands. And once she was up, Frankie nodded to Jo: 'Your turn.' She hoped her tone showed she was not to be argued with, but Jo hesitated.

'I'm not getting you out of the mud to leave you down here,' Frankie said simply.

Jo rolled her eyes, then put her mud-covered foot on Frankie's hand and propelled herself up towards the bank. Frankie had fully expected her to go without a second glance, but once she had made it up, Jo dropped to her knees beside Alison, reaching back to help Frankie.

'Don't think this makes us friends,' she said, once Frankie was standing next to her. 'You're still my ex's new girlfriend.'

Frankie shrugged. 'I'll settle for not hating each other.'

Jo's mouth twitched once more and Frankie wondered if she ever really smiled. 'I'll take that.'

'Look – the finish line!' Alison squealed, sounding more excited than a kid finding presents from Santa.

Frankie looked to where she was pointing. Once they had gone down this bank, there was a short run to an area where people seemed to be climbing over tyres, then just beyond that a big red banner with '*Finish*' written on it.

'Let's do it!' Frankie said, punching the air before launching herself down the bank. If you took away the fact that she was struggling to feel her fingers, and that her arms and legs ached from the unexpected exertion, rolling around in mud was stupidly fun.

CHAPTER FORTY-FOUR

Now that she could see the end, Alison finally believed, for the first time that day, that she would survive to finish the race. Not that it was much of a race; as they jogged towards the tyres, they passed several groups of runners who were just ambling along as though they weren't all that bothered about finishing. Several of them were even smiling and laughing and for a moment Alison wondered if they had been on some alternate course that didn't involve strength-sapping mud and freezing rain, but they were just as muddy as she was.

Frankie ran beside her, just about managing to keep up, with Jo next to her. Alison glanced across to see Frankie's ridiculous grin and was surprised to feel the corners of her own lips lifting in response. This was not how she had expected this day to go.

The tyres were lying flat, five across, squashed close together, each with mud smeared over them and brown puddles in their centre. Cautiously, Alison stepped onto the closest, arms out for balance. Beside her, the other two did the same. Wobbling only slightly, she moved onto the next one, slipping slightly on the muddy rubber, her hand grasping for something to hold onto and finding Frankie's hand. Regaining her composure, she edged a little further round and reached her foot out again.

'Is anyone else thinking their kids would go mad for this?' Frankie said.

Jo laughed. 'Charlie loves that tyre park at school.'

'Xander would have loved the whole course,' Alison said. Climbing, splashing, mud… all his favourite things. All, ironically, her least favourite things. Weakened by physical exertion, she began to giggle.

'What's got you?' Frankie asked.

Alison shook her head and wiped her eyes, trying to control the laughter that seemed to have hold of her. 'How did I get a son who loves mess?' she finally managed to say.

'You're loving it, really,' Frankie said. 'You just hide it well. I bet you want to do this again, don't you?'

'Not even a little bit.'

'Crap – I did not see that,' Frankie said, as they made it to the end of the tyres to find a hidden ditch between them and the finish line.

'At least it'll wash off some of the mud,' Alison said, determined not to slow down now she was this close to the end.

'We can just go round it,' Jo suggested.

Alison and Frankie both looked at her and frowned. 'Er, no,' Frankie said.

Alison moved round to the other side of Jo and took her hand. 'If we're doing this, we're doing it right,' she said.

Jo looked doubtful and Alison wondered exactly how many obstacles she and Becky had skipped. It certainly explained why they'd had so much difficulty in the muddy swamps, where there had been no options to avoid the obstacles.

'Ready?' she said, then without waiting for an answer she began to clamber down into the water, still holding Jo's hand.

The cold water was less of a surprise than it had been at the start, but it still took her breath away. Letting go of Jo, she waved her hands in the water to rinse them, splashing it up her chest and leaning forwards to wash her face. It wasn't worth doing her hair – that could wait until she got home and had a lovely long hot shower. Somehow Jo was out of the water and on the bank before them. For a second, Alison thought she might just run off, but then she turned back and reached out a hand. In turn, Alison reached to help Frankie.

'Come on,' she said, setting off on the last few metres, seeing Jo disappearing ahead of them.

Thank God it's nearly over, she thought, then *I've made it!*

As she took the last steps over the finish line, something began to swell up in her chest, threatening to spill over into tears.

'You did it!' Frankie shouted, grabbing Alison's arm and raising it victoriously. 'Woohoo!'

Alison nodded and sniffed, unable to speak.

'Wait – are you crying?'

Alison wiped at her eyes and shook her head.

'Come on, I can see Kate and the kids. And…'

Taking a deep breath, Alison looked up to see Kate and the kids on the other side of the rope, waving frantically.

And Simon.

He was standing in a muddy field in his work suit, his suitcase at his feet, beaming at her.

'This way for your goodie bags!' shouted the nearest marshal, herding them towards a gazebo.

Right now, Alison couldn't have cared less about a goodie bag. She wanted nothing else but to collapse into Simon's arms.

'But…'

Frankie pulled her away to the gazebo, Simon following. The rope was still between them, but his eyes never left hers.

Alison walked through the gazebo without stopping to collect a bag, and straight to Simon. 'You're *here*,' she said in disbelief. 'You're really here.'

He nodded, folding her into a bear hug, and as she felt the strength go from her legs, he held her tightly, holding her up.

'I came straight from the airport,' he whispered. 'I'm sorry I wasn't here earlier.'

'You're here now,' she said. 'You're here when I need you.'

'You didn't need me,' he disagreed, softly. 'You did just fine on your own.'

'MUMMY!'

Alison staggered as Xander threw himself at her, arms wide.

'Careful,' Simon said. 'I suspect Mummy might be a little delicate for the next couple of days.'

'You're all wet,' Xander said, letting go. 'And *dirty*. And you *smell…*'

'Thanks,' Alison said. Then she stepped back, suddenly realising Simon was still in his suit. 'Oh no, you're all wet and muddy now!'

He shook his head as though he didn't care. 'Al, I can't believe you did that,' he said. 'You are amazing.'

She looked up at him. 'I hated pretty much every minute,' she admitted.

'Mmm.' He smiled. 'Definitely out of your comfort zone, I'd say.'

Alison felt the warmth of his words and understood their significance as she held his gaze, losing herself in his eyes.

'It's very Maggie,' he added. 'She'd have loved doing something like this.'

'*That's* where Xander gets it from,' Alison said, wondering how she hadn't seen that before.

'I think I'll have to double my sponsorship,' he said.

'You haven't sponsored me, yet,' she pointed out.

'Fine… I'll *more* than double my sponsorship,' he said, laughing.

'Can I get some of that?' Frankie asked, making Alison jump. She'd almost forgotten they weren't alone.

'Of course,' Simon said.

'You see, you were wrong,' Alison said to him. 'I didn't do fine on my *own*.'

'Yes, I saw. I hadn't realised you were going to do it too, Frankie.'

'I wasn't. It was a bit of a last-minute decision.'

Alison turned to Kate. 'Thanks for watching all the kids, Kate. I hope they were alright?'

'Oh, yes, they were fine.' Kate was glancing at where the four children were now clambering over a fallen tree not far from them.

'Next time,' Frankie said, 'we'll get the boys to take the kids and then we can all do it – assuming you're not preggo again.'

'No, no…' Kate protested.

'Are you kidding?' Alison said. 'You want to do that again?'

Frankie grinned. 'Well…'

Alison shook her head, but when she glanced across at Frankie, she had to admit there had been a few moments of laughter in there. Because *anything* is a *bit* fun when you get to do it with friends beside you.

'Right,' she said, turning to the rest of them. 'I need to get out of these wet clothes before I freeze.'

'Um, Alison?' Frankie said, wrinkling up her nose. 'I don't suppose you've got a spare towel, have you?'

She smiled. 'Silly question.'

CHAPTER FORTY-FIVE

Frankie's teeth began to chatter as they walked up the hill to where Alison's car was parked.

'Are you sure Simon's okay with all the children?' Kate asked, looking worried as she followed behind her mud-covered friends, carrying their bags.

'No,' said Alison. 'But don't worry, I don't think he'll lose any of them, given that he's promised to buy them all Fruit Shoots and Kinder Eggs.'

'Gotta love bribery,' Frankie said, folding her arms over her chest and hugging herself, feeling her goose-pimpled skin beneath her fingers. She was sure she hadn't felt this cold out on the course, although she had been running then.

'Here we are,' Alison said, pointing the key at the car and pressing to unlock. Frankie followed her as she went round to the boot and rummaged in an IKEA bag before passing across a couple of towels. 'Do you need any clothes?'

'Umm…' The reality of being so far from a warm shower and spare clothes was only just beginning to hit her. 'I've got my hoodie…'

'I've got a long-sleeved top you can have and these leggings I was going to wear under my jeans if that helps… And spare socks… hmm, but no shoes, I'm afraid.'

Frankie waited while Alison folded the clothes into a plastic bag, with a bin liner on top. 'Thank you,' she said. 'Please don't ever be less organised.'

Alison smiled. 'You might want a wet wipe to sort out your mascara, too.'

'Do you think there's a changing area?' Frankie asked, accepting the packet of wipes.

'There is, but it's just one big tent,' Kate said with a frown. 'There's loads of people just getting changed next to their cars.'

Frankie looked around and saw she was right. 'Good thing I have no shame, then!'

Kate looked horrified.

'Let's open the doors for a little privacy, shall we?' Alison said.

Frankie laughed as Kate opened the passenger and back doors to create a cubicle. 'Oh, do you still have my phone, Kate?' she asked, pulling off her wet layers and rubbing herself furiously with the towel to get some of the damp mud off.

'Yes… somewhere in here. Got it! You have a message from Ben, by the way.'

'What does it say?' Frankie pulled up the leggings, enjoying their lack of clinging dampness, and reached for the top.

'It says: *Did you know Jo is doing that run too? Be careful.*'

'Ha!' she replied. 'Can you send him a message saying, "I know – I just pulled her out of the mud"?'

Alison's top was a bit tight on Frankie, but definitely warmer than her wet T-shirt. Towelling her hair dry, she gathered up her mud-soaked clothes, dropping them in the bin bag with the now-brown towel she'd used on her body. She sat in the passenger seat and angled the rear-view mirror to check the state of her face, swearing when she saw the absurd panda eyes. Alison was right: she did need those wet wipes.

'How do I look?' Frankie said, getting out of the car and closing the door to the back seats to reveal herself.

'Like someone who needs a hot chocolate?' Alison said, handing her the lid of the thermos to use as a cup and filling it with steaming hot liquid.

'Oh, you beauty,' she said, taking it and wrapping her hands around it. Kate held a travel mug, while Alison drank straight from the thermos.

'You've got nothing on your feet!' Kate said, with a slight note of hysteria. 'You'll catch your death.'

'Better nothing than those ice blocks,' Frankie said, motioning to the bin bag where the shoes now lay, the laces clogged with mud.

'What are we drinking to, anyway?' she said, raising her cup.

'Oh, I don't know…' Alison looked at Kate.

Kate smiled. 'I think you two deserve a medal for getting all the way round that course. We should definitely be drinking to *that*.'

'And especially, to Frankie, who didn't know she was going to be doing that today,' Alison added.

'I'd never have come if I'd known,' Frankie replied.

'Oh, wait,' said Alison. 'I think I've just achieved my New Year's resolution.'

Which one? Frankie thought, but was careful not to say. 'And I've still got my job – so I've achieved mine. Kate?'

'I think I'm doing alright… I mean, I lost my Zen a little last month, but I think I might have found it again.'

'Definitely,' Alison agreed. 'It's not easy staying calm in the face of someone getting all judgy on you.'

'Still think you should have punched her,' Frankie muttered and was rewarded by a look from Alison.

'I think our little Happiness Project has been a success,' Alison said.

'So,' Kate said, holding a hand up, 'I think we should toast all our achievements. Here's to doing difficult things, whether we knew we'd have to or not.' They lifted their cups of hot chocolate towards one another.

'And for having friends to help us do it,' Alison said.

'And for generally just being badass mothers,' Frankie added.

A LETTER FROM PIPPA

I want to say a huge thank you for choosing to read *The Happiness Project*. If you did enjoy it, and want to keep up-to-date with all my latest releases, just sign up at the following link. Your email address will never be shared and you can unsubscribe at any time.

www.bookouture.com/pippa-james

I hope you loved *The Happiness Project* and if you did I would be very grateful if you could write a review. I'd love to hear what you think, and it makes such a difference helping new readers to discover one of my books for the first time.

I love hearing from my readers – you can get in touch on my Facebook page, through Twitter or Goodreads.

Thanks,
Pippa James

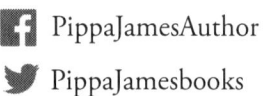

PippaJamesAuthor

PippaJamesbooks

ACKNOWLEDGEMENTS

I have to start with a huge thank you to all the team at Bookouture, especially my editor Natasha Harding and publicity superhero Kim Nash, who are wonderfully supportive even when I'm being stupid, and also the whole of the Author Lounge, who do great hand-holding and cheerleading and make me laugh a lot.

I'm immensely grateful for the support from my fellow members of the Romantic Novelists' Association, both in person, when I get to see them at the annual conference, and online via Twitter and Facebook. This book also owes much to the wisdom of writing tutors Alison May and Janet Gover, who have always championed my writing while, very kindly, pointing out ways to improve it further. It takes a special skill to make someone feel good about being wrong, but these guys have it!

I also feel the need to do a shout-out to my fellow authors (across many publishers and genres) and book bloggers who have supported me on Twitter with retweets, sharing good advice along with the highs and lows of writing life. The writing community is a lovely one and their corner of Twitter is probably the nicest (and wittiest) corner of the internet!

I have written quite a lot about things I haven't experienced in this book and I am indebted to midwife Kate Bedford for talking me through the pitfalls of missing midwife appointments and the many perils of pregnancy and childbirth. Any mistakes here are entirely my own. Thanks must also go to my friend and Alpha Wolf, Lauren Lawrenson, for not only answering all my questions about mud runs, but also inviting me down to Leicestershire to witness first-hand the atmosphere and camaraderie of the event. Both she and her team (the Crack Smoking Monkeys) were very patient in explaining the mechanics of the course and their love of obstacle course races and by the time I left them, there was a part of me thinking maybe I'd like to do it one day (when I've managed to run more than a 2K Junior Parkrun!). I hope I've done it justice in the final few chapters here.

Although this book is entirely fictional, many of the events in it were inspired by the stories of my many mum friends, both local and further afield, which made me feel that writing about women who are mums, rather than about mums *being* mums, was both interesting and important. Thank you to those who have shared their experiences.

My beta readers, Lizzy, Michelle and Sarah, have once again done a fantastic job in highlighting inconsistencies, pointing out confusing parts and drawing smiley faces at the funny bits. It really helps to have another perspective (or three!) and I really appreciate the time you spend reading my work and the tact you employ when you talk to me about it.

As ever, I need to say a huge thanks to my family for their practical help with childcare as well as their enthusiasm for my writing and insistence on mentioning that their daughter/daughter-in-law/mum is an author to everyone they meet. I must single out my husband, Pete, for special thanks, for giving me the time to write, allowing and encouraging me even though he doesn't understand my compulsion to do *this* when I could be doing something much better, like being his pit crew at cyclocross races. Also, he has excellent taste in chocolates.

Printed in Poland
by Amazon Fulfillment
Poland Sp. z o.o., Wrocław